ECLIPSED

"Dawn…" I start, trailing off, not even sure how to begin. I mean, how do I get him to understand? Deep inside, with every fiber in my body, I want nothing more than to leap back on that futon couch and throw myself at him with wild abandon. To kiss him senseless, claim his mouth as mine, and never let him go. But it's wrong, wrong, wrong, wrong, wrong.

"Dawn," I start again, swallowing back the lump the size of a basketball that's formed in my throat. "I'm so sorry, but this isn't right. You know it's not, deep down. After all, you don't want me. You want Mariah. And even if in some crazy way I was once her, I'm not right now. I'm Skye Brown and we…well, we barely know each other."

I know that I'm protesting too much. After all, even though I barely know anything about Dawn, the connection between us is undeniable. There's a bond so strong it feels dangerous. Which is why, I remind myself, it's best to stay aloof. At least until we figure out what's going on.

Because, if I'm not Mariah—which, of course, I know I'm not—that means someone else is. And if I let myself succumb to Dawn's advances, fall for him and allow myself to care, then the real Mariah could someday come back to reclaim Dawn as her own. And then where will that leave me?

MOONGAZER

Marianne Mancusi

LOVE SPELL

NEW YORK CITY

To my World of Warcraft guildies of Meiyo Seraph:
Yz, Bump, Set, Zel, Kel, and Rukku. Thanks for all the
pyro-blasting, mind-controlling, tanking, healing,
sapping, and hmm, what is it you do again, Ruk? ;-)
And to my GONG and GAG cyber buds as well.
You all are teh 1337 rox0r, FTW!

Love Allora (who once tanked Ony...)

LOVE SPELL®

August 2007

Published by

Dorchester Publishing Co., Inc.
200 Madison Avenue
New York, NY 10016

ISBN-10: 0-505-52725-1
ISBN-13: 978-0-505-52725-7

The name "Love Spell" and its logo are trademarks of Dorchester Publishing Co., Inc.

Printed in the United States of America.

Visit us on the web at www.dorchesterpub.com.

ACKNOWLEDGMENTS

Much thanks…

To editor extraordinaire Chris Keeslar for developing the Shomi line and inviting me to be a part of it. Your willingness to let authors flex their creative muscle is more appreciated than you can ever know.

To my partner in crime, fellow Rebel of Romance (www.rebelsofromance.com) author Liz Maverick. World domination would be no fun without you. To Alesia Holliday, Cindy Holby, Serena Robar, and Barb Ferrer who cheer me when I'm up, comfort me when I'm down, and let me steal their conference costume weapons for photo ops at RT.

To my Boston University screenplay class professor Stephen Geller, for whom I originally wrote *Moongazer* (then called *Mariah's Web*). Thanks for all your encouragement—and the A grade! And to my critique partner and fellow author Hank Phillippi Ryan who now has fabulous books of her own—your edits and insight are invaluable to me.

To my family for all their encouragement over the years and my friends for allowing me to babble on and on about my books. To Bobby, for his plot and character analysis even though I will deny, deny, deny, and to Mary for giving me much book fodder through our real life adventures. I miss you both!

And lastly, to all you readers out there for picking up this book! I hope you enjoy reading it as much as I enjoyed writing it!! Find me online at www.mariannemancusi.com.

MOONGAZER

PROLOGUE

Running. I am running for my life. That much I know as
my silver stiletto boots clink a rapid, repeating staccato
beat against the metal floor. But where am I? Who's
chasing me? And, most importantly, why?

I have no idea.

Run faster. Run harder. Run from the moon.

A strange voice echoing through my brain seems to
mock me as it begs for speed with an urgency I can't
comprehend. Endless demands competing with my
own frantic thoughts skitter across my brain like a
dog's claws on slick linoleum.

Where am I? *Run faster.* Who's chasing me? *Run
harder.* And why? *Run from the moon.*

But there is no moon. The corridor is black, skyless,
deep underground. And I'm already running as fast
and as hard as I can.

I suck in a breath and take in my surroundings—
trying to think, to process, to find a shred of familiarity
in the dark steel beams crisscrossing the black ceiling,

the mammoth fans cut into the walls every few feet, expelling hot, sour air that my already burning lungs struggle to accept. It all seems so familiar and yet at the same time completely foreign. Like a déjà vu pricking at the dark recesses of your brain, or a name on the tip of your tongue—the one you always remember at 3:00 a.m., when it no longer matters.

Except, this time I think it might still matter. And 3:00 a.m. may be too late.

"Don't let her reach the hatch!"

My heart slams against my chest as I realize my pursuers—whoever they might be—aren't far behind. Sweat pools in the hollow of my throat, then drips down, soaking my breasts. My muscles burn, my lungs refuse to take in air, I can barely swallow, and my vision has gone spotty. Soon I'll have to stop. To take a break.

But to stop is to die. That much I know. And so I keep running.

I turn a corner and my bleary eyes catch sight of a ladder in front of me, embedded firmly into the wall, a potential salvation ascending into the darkness. Where does it go? Could it lead to the hatch my enemies seek to keep me from? To stop and check it out will eat up valuable time—time I don't have. But I have to take a chance. I can't run forever.

I throw myself against the ladder, wrapping my hands around each rung as I climb, step after step. The ground falls away, and with it the dim tunnel lighting, and soon I am engulfed in blackness.

A few seconds later I bang my head against something, almost falling off the ladder from the impact. I steady myself, then reach up with one hand, fingers exploring the ceiling until they come upon a latch. More frantic exploration reveals a handle. There's definitely some kind of trapdoor.

"Up here! Get her!"

I hear feet clanging against the metal rungs as my pursuers start up after me. I don't have much time left. Wrapping my hand around the trapdoor handle, I yank on it with all my might. This is my one chance to escape.

It doesn't budge.

I pound on the door, my heart exploding in my chest as I realize that I likely have precious seconds to live. Surprisingly, my life does not flash before my eyes; in fact, I'm still having difficulty remembering any life at all. Who I am. What I do. How I got into this mess.

Run from the moon, the mysterious voice in my head demands.

"Shut up," I mutter, tired of its useless advice.

The first man reaches me, paws at my feet through the darkness. "We've got her!" he cries. And indeed, it seems he has.

Not willing to give up without a fight, I slam my foot down on his hand, the stiletto heel driving into his palm. A crunch of bone. A yelp of pain. I repeat the blow, then follow up with a wild kick to where I estimate his head to be, all the while clinging to the ladder for dear life. I don't miss. Knocked off balance he loses his grip, falls backward, and hurtles screaming down into the blackness. A sickening thud, followed by silence, tells me he's likely met his maker below.

But his death is not enough to save me. The second guy is right behind him and much more prepared for my alley cat tactics. There's a flash of light—a crimson beam cutting through the darkness—then a sharp, icy pain spreading through my ankle, shooting through my veins at a lightning pace, reaching my toes, my fingers, my brain simultaneously. My grip loosens, my head swims, my muscles fail. At first I fear he'll just let me fall, hurtle down to my death. But my attacker grabs on and starts dragging me down the ladder.

Not good.

At the bottom, the men flip me over so I'm lying on my stomach, spread-eagle on the ground. I can't move at all, my body is Jell-O, my muscles completely useless.

But I can see. I can hear. I can feel.

Three men kneel above me, armed with some pretty scary-looking tools, including something that looks like a high-tech electric syringe, complete with gauges and lights and a really long needle. I'm not sure what it does, but I know for a fact that I don't want it done to me.

The first man reaches into his bag and pulls out a small silver box. He presses his thumb against the top. The box beeps and flashes a green light, then pops open, revealing a vial of some sort. He presents the vial to the man with the syringe, who takes it and sticks the long needle inside, sucking up the unidentified contents. The syringe beeps in approval and a few green lights flash in sync.

"Are you ready, my dear?" the man with the gun asks, his lips curled in a sneer. He's big, built like a soldier and sporting a trim gray beard. He's wearing a shiny metallic belted uniform reminiscent of Michael Jackson's costume in *Captain Eo*.

"Please!" I beg, not thinking for one second that anything I say will make a difference, but at the same time desperate to try. "Just let me go!"

The men laugh, shaking their heads in mirth. "Oh,

you'll go all right," replies the second guy. He's smaller than the first, but no less menacing. "Pow!" he quips. "Straight to the moon."

They grab my arm and flip it over. I watch helplessly as they stab me with the syringe, injecting silver liquid into my unwilling veins. I scream and scream and scream, knowing it will do no good. Knowing that there's no escape.

Like it or not, I'm going to the moon.

ONE

"Skye, Skye! Wake up!"

The voice seemed a thousand miles away as I clawed through the blackness, struggling to regain consciousness. After a few futile attempts, I managed to pry open my eyes and shake off the nightmare's iron grip.

"Ah, she rejoins the living. Welcome back," Craig teased, having no idea of the hell I'd just been through. He lay back down on his side of the bed, evidently satisfied he'd sufficiently fulfilled his duty as a boyfriend by waking me, and now felt justified to go back to his own much more peaceful dreams.

I rubbed my eyes and sat up in bed, taking in my surroundings, still trying to catch my breath. My eyes sought and focused on the familiar: The slightly battered four-poster bed, draped with my aunt's home-made quilt. My ragged teddy bear Melvin, strewn to one side. My antique bookcase against one wall, crammed with well-worn fantasy epics I couldn't bear to throw away. My prized Alienware computer, souped up to run the latest and greatest video games. And, of course, my framed movie posters on the wall—*Star Wars*, *The Matrix*, *Phaze Runner*. I smiled a little as Luke, Neo, and Deckard all glowered down at me, as if daring me to claim my nighttime adventure was more hellish than their everyday realities.

I took a breath and plopped my head back down on my pillow. My closet of a New York apartment, the one the Realtor called "cozy" in the way only Realtors can get away with while keeping a straight face, for once actually did evoke a feeling of comfort and warmth.

I was home. I was safe. I was me again.

"Wow, that was the worst one yet," I remarked to Craig, in the rare hope that he was still conscious. There was no way I was going back to sleep now, and it would help to have someone to talk to. Not that Craig was the greatest of listeners, but he did have a knack for responding with a grunted "mm-hmm" at appropriate pauses in the conversation.

"Yeah?" he asked, for once going above and beyond.

"Yeah. I can't remember all the details. I mean, you know how dreams are. But it's like I'm running down this underground corridor, fleeing for my life. Someone's chasing me, but I don't know who—or why, for that matter. And then they inject me with some kind of drug. But the weird thing is it's, like, not exactly me. It's almost as if I'm someone else. . . ."

"Were you naked?" Craig queried, rolling over on his side to face me, his green eyes dancing mischievously.

I swatted him. "No!"

He laughed. "Too bad. Here I thought this was going to turn out to be some really great sex dream. Like the one I was having with Scarlett Johansson before your screams woke me up."

I grimaced. "Uh, thanks for sharing your nocturnal infidelity."

"No, no," he corrected with a smile. "You were there, too. And amazingly enough, you'd just agreed to a three-some. Damn shame I woke up when I did, actually."

I forced a chuckle, but it sounded more like a sigh. I knew he was just trying to cheer me up. To make me feel better. Normally it would probably work. But after night upon night of horrible nightmares and little actual rest I was at my breaking point. Irritated, frustrated, and oh so tired. It was no wonder his lighthearted manner only succeeded in annoying me.

"Look," I said, "I know it sounds funny, but when I'm dreaming it all seems so real. And when I wake up, I'm . . . terrified." I choked on the word. Great. The last thing I needed was for him to see me cry. I was supposed to be tough. The cool chick. In control of every situation thrown my way. And here I was, crying like a baby over a stupid dream.

Can we say, loser?

Craig's face softened, the way some guys' faces do when the girls they're sleeping with turn on the water-works. Maybe he figured he could soothe my vulnerability and get some action at the same time. But lovemaking was the last thing on my mind. In fact, since I'd started having the dreams, I'd pretty much lost my sex drive altogether. Poor Craig. He'd selflessly gone without for nearly a month now. Who could blame him for trying to take advantage?

I allowed him to grab my hand and pull me into a hug. But just as I'd resigned myself to settle into his arms, he shoved me away again. "Ew, you're all sweaty," he complained, wiping his hand on his boxer shorts. So much for the comfort of a lover's embrace.

"Fine. I'm going to take a shower," I muttered, accidentally on purpose kicking him as I crawled out of bed. I headed to the kitchenette to pour myself a cup of yesterday's leftover coffee. I didn't care that it was ice cold or tasted like tar. It had caffeine; that was all that mattered. "And then maybe play some *RealLife*."

Craig groaned, grabbing a pillow and throwing it in my general direction. It fell short, landing on my unswept floor with a soft plop. I made no move to pick it up.

"You know, staying up all night with your little games can't be healthy," he lectured.

I narrowed my eyes. Little games? That was my livelihood he was talking about. At age twenty-four, I was the youngest game designer at ChixOr, the world's first all-girl-run computer gaming company. The launch of our massive multiplayer online game *RealLife: Medieval Times* was scheduled to happen in two weeks, and it'd been hyped by *Wired* magazine as the biggest thing since *World of Warcraft*.

Little games, indeed.

"How about you take your shower and then play some *real* real life instead of your virtual version?" Craig continued. "You know, maybe do your 'sleeping quest' tonight so that tomorrow you can be awake enough for your 'work quest' chain?"

"Hardy-har-har. You're so funny." He was always teasing me about that—implying that I considered my real life a series of quests, just like a character would in a video game. Accomplish one goal, get your reward, move on to the next. Level up day by day in the game of life. In a way, he wasn't far off the mark.

"Look, I can't go back to sleep," I said, forcing back my annoyance and focusing on his suggestion. I mean, what good did it do to justify my career to him? He was a techno DJ, for chrissakes. "I'm afraid I'll have another dream."

Even from across the room, I could see him rolling his eyes. "They're just dreams, Skye," he said slowly, as if addressing a child. "They're not real."

"They might as well be."

"Look." He sat up in bed. "I wouldn't worry about them. Unless you start seeing Freddie Kruger wielding some terribly creative weapon of dream destruction, then you're *not* living *Nightmare on Seventy-second Street*, and you *will* be fine." He chortled to himself, evidently pleased by his wit.

"Whatever," I replied wearily. "I'm going to take that shower."

In the bathroom I switched on the light. The Realtor had described my apartment as having a marble bath and Jacuzzi tub. I assumed the marble was the cat's eye a past tenant had stuck in the window to plug an old bullet hole, and the tub did bubble when the plumbing failed and spurted out used bathwater from the neighbor downstairs. You had to love New York.

I turned on the shower and crossed my fingers. I had about a fifty-fifty chance of hot water at this time of night. In the morning, those odds would go down to about twenty-eighty. But hell, I only paid twenty-one hundred a month for the place. What did I expect?

I caught my reflection in the mirror. This no-sleep thing was definitely affecting my looks. Dark, puffy splotches circled my eyes. An unsightly zit had made itself at home on the tip of my nose. My once-stylish shag cut stuck out in all directions like straw from a scarecrow. In short, I was a mess.

Suddenly, my breath caught in my throat, which was constricting and making it nearly impossible to breathe. Argh. This was the last thing I needed tonight. I'd had asthma since I was a kid and sometimes it got pretty bad. Especially in stressful situations. I reached into the drawer under the sink and pulled out my inhaler. Putting the device in my mouth, I released a dose of Lunatropium into my lungs. Recently I'd been trying to cut back on the amount of times I used the inhaler each day and had been learning to control my breathing through yoga instead. But tonight seemed like a good time to give myself a break and let modern medicine lend a hand.

After my shower—there was hot water, thank God—I toweled off and headed back to the main room of my apartment. Changing into clean pajamas, I sat down at my computer desk. I glanced over at Craig. He'd fallen back asleep and was sure to be out of it until at least noon. As a DJ, spinning nights at a Lower East Side club, he was entitled to spend his mornings dead to the world while the rest of us sorry humans put in our Starbucks orders and jockeyed for positions on the subway.

Not that I didn't like my job. It was just with the lack of sleep I'd had, these days it was harder and harder to stay awake for it. I was pretty sure my boss had begun to notice my sudden drop in performance, too. Not good. Because Foosball table, creative dress code, and free Diet Cokes aside, twenty-first-century dot-coms like mine were downright traditional when it came to clocking in and working hard.

I logged in to the server and selected my game character. I was doing beta testing for the soon-to-be-launched *RealLife*, checking for bugs and other errors before it was distributed to the general public. The medieval virtual earth I'd created was practically empty now, inhabited only by computer-generated characters and myself. But soon it'd be alive with avatars from all over the world; players logging in to live a virtual existence, creating characters to fight digital monsters, competing for epic weapons and armor, and forming lifelong friendships with fellow gamers.

For now, though, it was empty and mine to explore. An escape from all that plagued my reality. I loved it in there. It was a haven, a solace.

From my twenty-one-inch monitor, my game character "Allora" looked back at me impatiently, probably wondering why I wasn't moving her. As an all-girl company, Chix0r had gone one step further than the traditional guy-centric games like *World of Warcraft* or *Everquest*, where the player characters were flat and static and did exactly what you told them. Our characters had their own personalities, their own artificial intelligence built into their code. Sort of like if you could put *The Sims* in chain mail and give them swords. So while you could control your character's movements and direct his or her career path, you couldn't make them do things they didn't want to do. They wouldn't fight if you didn't feed them first. They'd refuse to accept a quest if they were tired. They got lonely if you didn't socialize them, and angry if someone did them wrong. Sometimes they were scarily like real people.

"Okay, fine, Allora. Let's go to the pub," I whispered, moving the mouse to direct her to the local tavern. "We'll get you a beer." For beta-testing purposes we'd temporarily sectioned this virtual town off from the rest of the game. Allora had no idea there was a world outside her city. To her, the outskirts of *Mare Tranquilitatis* were the ends of the earth. She was fortunate that way.

I sat her down at a table and bought her a beer. She raised her glass and drank, blissfully unaware of her own plight or her operator's exhaustion. So innocent. So happy. So content. If only I could join her there—crawl into my computer, immerse myself in my virtual world, and block out my reality. How wonderful would that be?

But that was just another dream. I took a big slug of coffee and started testing settings.

I entered Chix0r's SoHo headquarters at exactly 9:30 a.m., aka one hour later than I was meant to arrive. At some point I'd passed out at my computer (no dreams, thank God) and had fallen into such a deep coma that I completely missed my alarm clock. In fact, it beeped for about forty minutes before Craig got fed up and proceeded to knock it off the nightstand. The destruction of the third alarm clock I'd gone through that month finally succeeded in rousing me. Then there was the forty-five minute wait for the subway. Sigh.

I stepped off the elevator, greeted the receptionist, and walked through Cubicle Land until I got to my office. I loved it there. Getting out of Cube Hell had been the best thing about my promotion to senior game designer. Sure, it was small as anything, but the room had a floor-to-ceiling window, complete with an amazing view of a Chinese laundry and pizza stand. The only thing that slightly unnerved me was the smoked-glass inner walls. As people walked by, they inevitably peeked in—either to spy on whether I was actually working (my boss) or for the sheer pleasure of voyeurism (everyone else). After the first week of this, I went home and designed curtains for the bowl of my poor fish Omi. Unfortunately, I wasn't permitted to do the same for myself.

I walked over to my desk, sighing at the mess. Had I really left all these papers strewn about when I left last night? I used to be so conscious of organization, but now I barely had enough hours in the day to finish work, never mind scheduling time to clean up after myself. I needed an assistant, badly. Or a clone. That would be nice.

I settled into my chair and logged in to my computer. As I waited for Windows to start up, I heard a rap on my door. Great. Interruption number one, right on schedule. "Yes, what is it?" I snapped, trying not to sound cross even though I was. After all, it wasn't my visitor's fault I hadn't had a good night's sleep in weeks.

"It's Suzy. Can I come in?"

I groaned, suddenly shifting from merely tired to downright irate. I'd told security time and again not to let my cousin into the office during work hours. But they couldn't seem to resist her sweet talk, low-cut dresses, and chocolate chip cookies, which she bragged were homemade. Yeah, they were homemade all right— homemade by Jackie, Suzy's family housekeeper. Suzy wouldn't know the way to the kitchen if it wasn't where her stepfather stored the gin.

Since it would be easier to stop the running of the bulls than deny the vivacious eighteen-year-old entrance, I wearily instructed her to come in. She pranced into the room, enveloped in a cloud of Dior's Poison and dripping in diamonds, and approached my desk. She'd changed her hair color since the last time I saw her—surprise, surprise—and was now sporting a spiky, fire-engine red. It was a look few could pull off without channeling Bozo the Clown, but somehow Suzy managed to do it with style.

"Darling!" she cried in her slightly English-accented voice, throwing out her arms to hug me. Suzy was born on Long Island, but was constantly pulling a Madonna. She waltzed behind my desk, invading my space, and leaned over to plant air kisses on each cheek. Ugh. The girl was a walking, talking society-girl stereotype, and I always found myself biting my tongue not to tell her to get a real personality. "Where have you been all my life?"

"Suzy," I acknowledged, keeping my voice level and calm. "What can I do for you today?"

She threw on a wounded face. "Does a girl need a reason to come visit her favorite cousin in the whole wide world?"

"We've discussed this. Seventeen times at last count. I'm very busy when I'm at work. I don't have time for visits." Out of the corner of my eye I watched my boss walking past my office, staring in. Her displeasure would be readable a mile away. Damn these glass walls. Now, if the game had one tiny little mistake, she was going to blame me for socializing on the job. As if I had a choice.

"Oh yes," my cousin sniffed, taking a seat instead of

my not-so-subtle hint to leave. "You and your important job. The free world as we know it would just collapse if gamer girls couldn't get their geek on."

"Did you come here solely to disturb me and insult my livelihood, or did you have some other purpose?"

"I wanted to see if you were going to Luna tonight. Craig's spinning, right?"

Luna was a nightclub on the Lower East Side where Craig occasionally DJ'd. Once a decrepit hole in the wall, it had gotten a write-up in the *Village Voice* and had recently become the trendiest place in town. Suzy's boyfriend managed the joint and she was always trying to get me to go.

"No way." I shook my head. "I haven't slept well in two weeks. The last thing I need is to go clubbing."

She puffed out her lower lip in a pout. "Aw, come on, Skye," she begged. "You haven't been out in forever. We miss you."

Yeah, they missed me. The *old* me, that is. The carefree, happy-go-lucky club kid who loved to dance and drink and party. The new Skye, the one haunted by nightmares, the one who hadn't had a decent night's sleep in eons, would prove to be a dud who rained on their Ecstasy parade.

"Besides, rumor has it Paris Milton and her entourage are supposed to be showing up. Haven't you always wanted to meet her? Maybe she'll start dancing on tables like she always does in Vegas. How cool would that be?"

"Sorry, Suze. I'm just not feeling well. I've been having these horrible nightmares and—"

"Ooh, that reminds me, I had this crazy dream last night," Suzy butted in. "Jude Law and I were getting it on, and then in walks Ewan McGregor, right?"

I sighed. Was everyone beside me just ménage-à-trois-ing away nightly while I was stuck being chased and tormented?

"Sounds great," I interrupted. "A bit TMI for this early in the morning, though, don't you think? I haven't even drunk my coffee yet." I gestured to the triple Venti caffeine blast sitting on my desk. It was actually my third cup that morning, but she didn't need to know that.

Suzy stopped, the smile fading from her face. I watched, a bit confused. What had come over her all of a sudden? The change in expression was so abrupt. Almost as if someone had flipped a switch.

"What's wrong?" I asked.

"Skye, I *need* you to go to Luna tonight," she said in a detached, almost mechanical tone. "I think Trent is cheating on me and I need you to find out if I'm right."

Without even going to the club I could make a pretty educated guess that she was, but I felt bad admitting it. I knew that under her carefree, party-girl exterior Suzy was vulnerable and innocent and really loved her cokehead club manager of a boyfriend.

"Why me? Why don't you hire a private detective or something?" I asked. Certainly the girl could afford it. "Have him follow the guy around for a few days."

Suzy frowned. "Duh," she replied, seeming to gain a bit of her personality back. "A private detective can't get into the VIP room at Luna. Only you can."

"What makes you think he's bringing the girl there, anyway? He knows he might run into you. And it's not like you can't get into the back rooms."

"I told him I wasn't going tonight. That I was visiting my mom on Long Island," Suzy explained. Evidently she'd been working out this plan for a while. "And he's asked me like a thousand times whether I'm still going. I know he's planning something."

I sighed. It did sound likely.

"Please?" Suzy's eyes filled with tears. "I need to know, Skye. I mean, this is the guy I've been planning on marrying. If he's cheating on me"—her voice cracked—"I need to make some hard decisions."

Argh. It was the last thing I wanted to do tonight. I had a ton of work to get done on the game before release day. Not to mention I was existing solely on coffee fumes. But Suzy was my cousin. And I'd always prided myself on being there for people when they needed me.

Against my better judgment, I walked around my desk and put my arms around her. She buried her face in my shoulder and sobbed. I stroked her spiky hair. "Shhh," I hushed. "It's going to be okay. No matter what I find, we'll get through this, all right?" From this angle I noticed a small moon-shaped tattoo just below her neck. For some reason it reminded me of my crazy dreams.

She pulled her head away and met my eyes. "So, you'll do it?" she asked, her face hopeful. "You'll go to the club tonight? See if he's got a girl on the side?"

"Yes," I assured her. "I'll go."

"Oh, thank you, Skye! You're the best cousin in the history of cousins!"

I laughed. "I don't know about that, but thank you anyway. Now go away. I've got a busy day ahead of me. Especially now that I can't work tonight."

Suzy thanked me about four more times and then exited my office. I sighed and walked back to my desk, slumping down onto it. This was *so* not how I wanted to spend my evening: going to a club. Ugh. But what could I do? I'd promised.

My lungs constricted. Great. All this drama was inducing my asthma. I started to reach for my inhaler, then changed my mind and started my exercises.

Breathe in. Hold it. One, two, three. Breathe out.

Breathe in. Hold it. One, two, three. Breathe—

God, I was so tired. My eyelids weighed a ton. If only I could close them for two seconds. Just lay my head on my desk and . . .

I'm walking across a long suspension bridge made of rope and anchored by cracked stone pillars, spanning a chasm of undeterminable depth. Underground again: an inky blackness stretches high above. The surrounding cavern walls emit a dim glow, like there's phosphorus embedded deep inside. The air smells acrid. Of sulfur, or really cheap cologne.

I step gingerly, placing my foot down on one of the small wooden planks. A slight wind catches the bridge, swinging it back and forth, and I grip the rope handrails tightly, my heart beating fast.

I look to the other side, my apparent destination, and to my surprise I see Glenda standing at the bridge's end. Glenda's my yoga teacher, the one who's been giving me breathing lessons to lessen my dependence on asthma medication. She waves, offering me one of her trademark smiles. I try to smile back, but my mouth seems frozen in place. Why is she here? What does she want from me? And why are her eyes glowing an iridescent green?

There's only one way to find out, so I draw in a deep breath and take another step. I can hear the bridge groan under my weight. It must be ancient, and the rope looks brittle. I look behind me. I'm too far to run back. I have to keep going. I have to hope it will stay to-gether for one more crossing.

"Keep walking," Glenda encourages. "You're almost there."

I step again. And again. Step after step after step. The bridge seems endless, but still I persevere. What choice do I have?

Finally, I'm close to the end. Near Glenda. Near the solid ground of the rocky bank beyond the bridge. But just as I'm about to make that final leap to safety, I hear a loud cracking. I whirl around just in time to see the stone pillars on the other bank disintegrate before my eyes. The rope suspension splits. The bridge shudders and cracks, the far side swinging down into the cav-ern. A split second later I'm vertical, hanging on to the handrails for dear life.

"Help!" I scream to Glenda, who is standing above me, arms crossed and a serene smile on her seamless face. She's wearing a long white robe, the costume of a Greek goddess. A white crescent moon seems to glow from her forehead.

"You've got to help me!"

"Pull yourself out, Mariah," she commands in a calm voice. "You have the power to do so. You always have."

Terrified, I try to pull myself up, my feet dangling uselessly, clawing for some kind of purchase. I'm not making much progress. My heart pounds in my chest. My arm muscles burn. I won't be able to hold on much longer. "Please!" I beg, tears streaming down my cheeks, blurring my already spotty vision. I can't be-lieve she's just standing there when I'm about to fall to my death. "Just help me. Give me your hand."

"You don't need my help anymore, Mariah," Glenda

says with a gentle smile. "Look within yourself. You have the power."

I have no idea what she's talking about, but now is not the time to try to puzzle it out. Summoning all the willpower and adrenaline I can muster, I give one last heave and hoist myself onto the bank. My chest slams into the solid rock floor, knocking the wind out of me. Automatically I search my pockets for my inhaler, but Glenda steps lightly on my hand with a ballet-slippered foot.

"No," she says, shaking her hand. " 'Gazers enhance the pull of the moon. For successful reentry you must stop inhaling."

Is she crazy? I have asthma. Of course I need my inhaler. But then I realize she's right. I can breathe. Large lungfuls with little effort. I gulp them like a fish that's been out of water almost to the point of death.

When I've finally caught my breath, I scramble to my feet. "Why didn't you help me?" I demand, crossing my arms on my chest.

Glenda just smiles her strange serene smile. I don't know if I want to punch her or hug her. "Because you didn't need me to," she says, placing a white hand on my arm. "You are almost ready."

I cock my head. "Ready? Ready for what?"

"For reentry. The Eclipsers have been working to get you out for a long time now. Myself included. Our doctors think you're almost there."

"Reentry?" What the hell is she talking about?

"You're starting to remember. These dreams are a good sign of that. Pretty soon you will awaken back home. But you've been gone a long time, Mariah, and your mind has been through a lot. Moongazing can cause serious brain damage. Our doctors believe your brain is still intact—all the vital functions. But we're not sure about your memories."

My head hurts, my body hurts, and now I'm baffled on top of it. "Why do you keep calling me Mariah?"

"Because that is who you are." Glenda reaches over to pull a strand of hair out of my face and gazes at me with tender green eyes. "Do not worry, little one. All will be clear in time. First we must get you out. Then we can start work on your recovery."

"Recovery? Out?"

"Sadly, there's no time to explain." Glenda glances at the watch on her wrist. "But listen carefully. When you finally go through reentry, you won't know where you are. Maybe not even who you are. You'll be vulnerable. Alone. If Duske finds you, he may try to suck you back in—get you back on the 'Gazers. Don't trust him. We may not be able to rescue you a second time."

I feel like I've walked into a movie late, and the rest of the audience knows way more than me. I don't even know what questions to ask.

"When you get home, call Dawn. He will be able to help you." Glenda reaches into a small reticule tied to her belt and pulls out a feather pen. She takes my hand in hers and scribbles something on the back.

Don't trust Duske. Find Dawn.

-.. .- ..- -.

"What does that mean? What are these symbols?"

"I'm sorry, child. We're out of time. It's pulling you back now." Suddenly her voice sounds a million miles away. "Just remember—seek Dawn. Avoid Duske."

"Seek Dawn, avoid Duske," I repeat helplessly. I can feel the darkness creep around me, yanking at the edges of my sanity. "Anything else?"

"Yes. One other thing," Glenda says, her voice taking on an ultraserious tone. "Whatever happens, whatever you do, promise me you'll never, ever look into the moon."

TWO

I ignored the seemingly never-ending line, which wrapped almost all the way around an entire city block. Luna. The once hole-in-the-wall nightclub had become such a must-go destination for Manhattan's rich and bored, the designer bags alone in this line could be the down payment on a Park Avenue penthouse. Disgusting.

The jealous stares of the line-waiters burned my backside as I waltzed up to the velvet ropes and gave the burly bouncer a hug. Bruno had been working the door since the days Luna paid actors to line up and attract a crowd. He looked like a thug but was actually a teddy bear.

"Hey, doll-face," he greeted me. "Haven't seen you in a while. Slumming it tonight?"

"Yeah," I said with a shrug. "I've sort of given up the club scene now that I have a real job and all. Going to bed at three a.m. just doesn't work for me anymore."

Technically I'd gotten more sleep back in my club kid days than recently, but I didn't want to explain my nightmares to anyone else.

He laughed. "Good for you, kid. Good for you." He unclipped the velvet rope and I noticed a small moon tattooed between his thumb and forefinger. It looked just like Suzy's. Was this some kind of new trend I hadn't heard about? I supposed I'd learn about it soon enough.

Bruno ushered me in. "Have a good time," he said, flashing me a toothy grin.

I walked over the threshold, down a dark corridor, and into the main room. The club was packed with hot, blinged-out dancers, gyrating to a fast-paced techno beat. In the old days we used to have real raver kids at Luna, complete with baggy pants, glow sticks, and whistles; a fun-loving crowd without the attitude. These days the club was packed with insecure socialites and the Wall Streeters who fucked them. Nope. Not really my scene.

But it didn't matter; tonight I wasn't there to play. I had a mission: Get to the VIP room, find Suzy's stupid boyfriend, see if he's sucking face with another chick, then head back uptown for another sleepless night.

I pushed my way through the crowd and made my way to the VIP section. The bouncer, a new guy I didn't know, checked his list, then unclipped the rope. I climbed the stairs to the elite lounge where only Manhattan's finest were deemed worthy to hang. I felt a bit like an intruder, being far from Manhattan's "finest," but seeing as my boyfriend had spun here for the last four years, I probably had more right to hang than any of them.

It was still early and there were only a few inhabitants: women in low-cut sparkly dresses and killer heels, a group of Armani-clad businessmen eyeing them. They all lounged on designer couches, sipping champagne and blatantly ignoring the NYC smoking ban. Trent was nowhere to be seen. I sank down into a nearby chair and allowed a cocktail waitress to take my drink order. Trent would show up eventually, especially if he had a new girl he wanted to impress. In the meantime, I might as well relax and enjoy the music. I waved at Craig over in the DJ booth. He grinned, probably thrilled to see I'd left my apartment, and blew me a kiss. For the first time in a while I felt kind of good. Even with its newfound cheesy club-goers, Luna was a place where I felt somewhat at home. It was safe. It was familiar. And it was loud enough to ensure that I wouldn't fall asleep.

The last dream, the one I'd had at work that afternoon, had been especially bizarre. My yoga teacher's words echoed through my brain.

"*You can resist the pull all by yourself.*"

I laughed. Had to give my brain credit; it sure could be creative when it wanted. Wait till Glenda heard about her starring role.

I glanced down, my laughter dying in my throat as my eyes fell on the spidery handwriting scrawled across the back of my hand. The marks Glenda had made were there clear as day.

Don't trust Duske. Find Dawn.

-.. .- .-- -.

I jumped up from my seat, pulse racing as I stared at the message, hardly believing what I saw with my own eyes. How could words, written in a dream, still be written on my hand? Had I somehow written them myself? Done some sleep-scribbling or something?

You will be back with us very soon, Mariah . . .

I shook my head, trying to clear my thoughts. This was stupid. So I'd fallen asleep at my desk. So I'd had another nightmare. I'd been having them for weeks; it didn't make them real. And the writing on my hand? There had to be some logical explanation for that—

A flash of hot white light suddenly blinded me, hurling me back into my chair. The floor buckled, as if jarred loose by an earthquake. I grabbed the armrests for support, frantically scanning the room—expecting screams, stampedes, club-goers tripping over their stilettos as they fled the premises.

Horrifyingly enough, no one else in the club seemed the least bit disturbed. They talked, they laughed, they had no idea. I was evidently the only one seeing the streaks of lightning arcing down the center of the room. The only one feeling the jarring aftershocks.

My heart banged against my rib cage, a fight-or-flight mechanism kicking in. Something was wrong here. Really, really wrong. Was this it: Was I finally losing my mind?

"I'd like a Jack and Coke, please," a man said. I turned to watch him order his drink, hoping to regain some semblance of control by doing so. *Just watch the encounter. Focus on something normal. Something real. Something not ripped from my evidently psycho delusional brain.*

My heart stopped. Literally.

The man was the same as the one who'd chased me

in my dream. The one who'd caught me on the ladder, dragged me down, stuck me with the syringe. The gray-bearded man from my nightmare, the one in the Captain Eo suit who shouldn't really exist, was now sitting next to me. Real. Alive. Here.

He caught my eye and gave a friendly wave. I started to scream. The world spun off its axis like a bum needle skimming across a record, and I was suddenly spiraling into a strange white light. Then I blacked out and saw no more.

I open my eyes. I'm no longer in Luna, no longer safe and sound in the VIP section of Manhattan's trendiest club. Instead I'm standing in some kind of small, box-like room. It's the size of a telephone booth, but with opaque movie screen panels on all four sides, swirling with kaleidoscopic color. The air is thick, with a sickly sweet odor that's nearly overwhelming.

I realize I'm wearing some sort of dark glasses, and I reach up to pull them off. Blinking a few times, my naked eyes struggle to become accustomed to the brightly lit walls. I glance around. The ceiling is a mess of wires and tubes and the floor is made out of a metal grate. The glasses are attached to some kind of retractable cable so that, when I release them, they are sucked up into the ceiling, completely disappearing from view. I swallow hard. I hope I didn't need them for anything.

Swallowing my rising claustrophobia, I feel around for an escape route. I find a lever and push down on it, breathing a sigh of relief as the wall in front of me collapses, revealing an exit. Stepping outside the box, I enter a long hallway, carpeted with crimson-colored shag. Every few feet there's an identical door to the one I just exited. Each is painted black and emblazoned with a gold crescent moon. My heart stutters in my chest as I remember Glenda's warning.

Don't look into the moon.

Could this be what she meant?

Just in case, I avert my eyes, feeling a bit silly for doing so. I mean, how can a door decoration hurt me?

It's then that I notice the small gray pads next to each door, each with two tiny red and green lights. All the red lights flash in sync, except for the door closest to me. The lights there glow a solid green.

I shake my head. Am I having another dream? No, this seems different. Solid. More real. And I know I didn't fall asleep in the club. Impossible, with all that shaking and bright light. Unless that had been a dream, too.

You won't know where you are. Maybe even who you are.

I frown. But I do know. I'm still Skye Brown. Manhattan resident. Game designer. A girl currently awaiting men in white coats to take her away.

I look down one end of the hallway and then the other. Each seems to stretch off into infinity. Which way to go? I haven't a clue. Swallowing down my rising fear, I choose a direction and start walking. Soon I discover a cleverly angled and mirrored door. The endless hallway is only an illusion.

Could this be the way out, or will I be stepping into more danger? I look back down the hallway, realizing I don't have much of a choice. I push a button and the door slides open. I step over the threshold, terrified as to what I'll find on the other side. Judging from past dreams, it could be anything. It could even be my death.

"Ah, you awake. You enjoy trip?" asks a small, wizened Asian man, bowing low. He stands behind a counter, dressed in an old-fashioned suit, like a character out of a Charlie Chan movie. His name tag simply states PROPRIETOR. I stare at him, not sure how to respond.

"What trip? Where am I?" I ask at last, completely bewildered.

The man only laughs.

I look around, trying to take stock of my surroundings. The place is over-the-top gaudy. Red velvet sofas, shiny mirrored coffee tables. Elaborate decorative lamps. Totally Las Vegas brothel chic. I notice a few twenty-somethings lounging on the couches, chattering and laughing amongst themselves. The girls wear cute little tank tops, flouncy miniskirts, and thigh-high stiletto boots: manga characters come to life. The guys are in long belted tunics over tight black leather pants. I surreptitiously check out my own reflection in a nearby mirror. I'm still wearing my club clothes from Luna. Black corset top, short plaid skirt, platform boots. That's good. At least I somewhat fit in.

I look back at the group. One of the girls has pulled out an inhaler that looks just like mine. She takes a quick puff, then waves good-bye to her friends as she heads toward the hallway I just exited.

Curiouser and curiouser . . .

"Man come look for you," the proprietor informs me, drawing my attention away from the other guests. "You gone long time, I tell him you may not come out. People in as long as you seldom do. But he insist on leaving card." He takes my hand in his own wrinkled grip and presses a piece of paper into it.

Someone was looking for me? Here? I stare down at the card, confused. It's then I notice the name.

Reginald Duske, Senator.

A chill trips down my spine. The guy Glenda was talking about, the one I'm supposed to avoid, has been here. Looking for me. That doesn't seem very good. Underneath the name there's another of those long strings of dashes and dots. "What does this code mean?" I ask, my voice trembling.

The man looks at me like I'm insane. "Phone number, of course," he says in a total "duh" voice. "You need to use phone?" He picks up a silver, crescent-shaped object that looks like no phone I've ever seen and offers it to me.

"Um, no. I mean, yes?" I decide, having no other idea what to do. I glance down at my hand. Sure enough, Glenda's warning is still inscribed on my palm.

I glance at the card again. Duske. Who is this guy? A senator? What makes Glenda say not to trust him? Can I trust Glenda? And what about this Dawn?

The proprietor frowns and taps his foot impatiently. "You make call," he demands, and suddenly the whole situation seems even more sinister. Could this guy be in cahoots with Duske?

"Can I . . . have some privacy?" I ask, stalling for time.

For a moment, I see a sheen of annoyance flit over the man's face, but he forces it back and smiles at me. He's got perfectly white and shiny teeth. "Of course," he says, bowing again. He steps back from behind the counter and heads to one of the unoccupied couches.

I stare at Duske's card, then the name on my palm, wondering what I should do. Who I should call. If I should call anyone. Then something deep inside me stirs and Dawn's name drifts through my conscious-ness, a shard of glass washing up on shore, dulled by the sea. Dawn can help me, I realize, having no idea why I believe this to be so.

Deciding to trust my subconscious, I set down the card and use the code written on my hand instead, then bring the phone to my ear. It rings twice before a man answers. "Yes, what is it?" he asks impatiently.

"Um, I'm l-looking for Dawn," I stammer, not quite sure what to say now that I've made the call. *I'm having this weird dream and my yoga instructor thought you could help me with it?* He'd probably hang up then and there.

"This is Dawn."

"Oh." I pause, taken aback. "I'm sorry. I thought, well . . . I figured Dawn would be a girl."

Silence on the other end. Then, "Mariah?" the voice asks. "Is that really you?"

I frown. What is it with this girl Mariah? Why does everyone think I'm her? "Uh, no. This is Skye," I correct him. "And, well, I'm not actually sure why I'm calling. It's just I woke up in this weird place and had your phone number written on my hand." Jeez, he's going to think I'm some drunk chick he met at a bar last night. "I know that sounds really bizarre, but—"

"You've got a hell of a nerve calling here, Mariah," Dawn interrupts.

I frown. "I told you. I'm not Mariah. I'm Skye. I don't know who Mariah is."

I can hear the heavy sigh on the other end of the line. Silence, and then: "Where are you?"

Good question. I glance around. "Uh, I don't know. I woke up in some small room with movie screens or something, and walked down a hallway into some weird brothel-looking place and—"

"A Moongazer station. Of course," Dawn concludes, not sounding too happy about it. "Which one?"

I glance around, looking for some sort of locator. "Um . . ." My eyes fall upon some sort of bill, lying on the counter. "Area 52?" I read.

"Ah," Dawn says, seeming to recognize the place. "Slumming it, are you? The senate wouldn't pay for a trip from one of the high-class joints? What a shame." His voice is thick with sarcasm.

"What? I don't—" I couldn't be more seriously lost in a conversation if I tried. Maybe I should have called the Duske guy instead.

"Well, at least you're close. There's a Rabbit Hole on Fifty-third. I'll meet you there in five."

"Uh, I'm not sure . . ." I realize I'm talking to no one. Dawn, whoever he is, has already hung up and is on his way to collect me. I really hope I didn't make some huge mistake calling him. . . .

I notice the proprietor is staring at me suspiciously from the couch. I pretend to continue my conversation. "Oh yes, Duske. It's great to talk to you, too," I say loudly, forcing a laugh. "I'm sure I'll see you soon. Goodbye, now!"

I click END on the phone and set it down on the counter. "That Duske," I say, shaking my head and smiling as the Asian gentleman rises from the couch and walks back to the counter. Luckily, he seems to be buying my act. "He's coming to pick me up. I'm going to wait outside for him." I start heading to the doors.

"Wait!"

I freeze in my tracks at the proprietor's words. Now what? Did he not buy my act? He shuffles over to me and, to my surprise, reaches up to wrap his fingers around the moon necklace I wear around my neck.

"You must return charm before you leave," he says firmly. "No keeping."

"Wait!" I grab for the necklace but he's too quick, yanking it away. The delicate clasp gives way and the chain pools into his hands. "That's mine! My mother gave it to me for graduation."

He rolls his eyes. "You no play game," he scolds. "That my necklace." He palms it and heads back behind the counter, opening a cabinet. I gasp as my eyes fall upon the contents—hundreds of silver necklaces, identical to mine. The Asian man slips my chain beside the others and then proceeds to close the cabinet door. "Now you go," he says, turning back to me and giving a toothy grin. "Maybe I see you later."

In a daze, I head toward the exit. Every time I think this experience couldn't get weirder, it does. My eyes widen as I step outside. I'm not sure how I was expecting the exterior to look, but it definitely wasn't this.

Moongazer Palace, in all its neon, Vegasian glory, sits plopped in the middle of a dark, post-apocalyptic-looking nightmare world. Dim streetlights cast a sickly orange glow on narrow dirt alleys framed by crumbling, decrepit buildings. Barred windows, battered doors, chipped paint. Dawn wasn't kidding when he'd called the place a slum.

The breeze, man-made from a gigantic fan down one end of the road, whips through the street, swirling up small whirlwinds of debris. I cough to clear my lungs. The smell of decay and garbage is overwhelming, inescapable, nauseating.

I look up and see a high rock ceiling. Like in my dreams, this place appears to be completely underground. A bubble world, a large stone cave.

I glance back at the building I just exited. Its neon light, advertising something called "Moongazing," buzzes and flickers. Its tagline, "Are you ready to look into the moon?" is slightly unnerving. The gaudy exterior clashes with the rest of the nondescript gray buildings in the neighborhood, making me wonder the story behind how it came to sit there.

I look down the alleyway and notice a bright crimson stain splattered against a brick wall. Red liquid drips down, soaking into a dirt puddle. Is that blood? Human blood? I glance around nervously. I'm in danger. Maybe. Or maybe someone else needs help.

I step into the alleyway to take a closer look. It's then that I feel the presence. Someone has stepped in behind me. I search for an escape. It's a dead end. I tense as I hear the heavy footsteps approaching. Is it friend or foe? I take another look at the blood. I've got to assume foe.

Strong hands clamp down on my shoulders, nails cutting into bare flesh. But I am not a victim. I let out a yell and then kick my foot behind me, going for the groin. The solid contact, followed by a cry of agony, tells me I didn't miss. I whirl around, raising my hands in a defensive stance, ready for round two. It's then that I get my first real glimpse of my attacker.

Wow.

Broad shoulders narrow to a lean, trim waist; that muscular chest is encased in black leather. He's got chiseled, high, delicate cheekbones and a full, luscious mouth. His eyes are hidden behind mirrored sunglasses and long layers of almost translucent platinum-colored hair fall into his face, giving him an unearthly look. But the weirdest thing is, though I know I've never seen this man before in my life, he somehow looks familiar. The déjà vu is once again pricking at my brain.

He stares at me for a moment, crouched in agony, then straightens and steps forward. "Nice to see you again, too, Mariah," he snarls, not looking at all pleased.

"Don't come any closer!" I command, praying he'll obey. I know some self-defense, but it's not like I'm very practiced on a real opponent. Besides, I've used my one trick. "I've . . . got a gun and I'm not afraid to use it." *Yeah, right, Skye. And a bridge to Brooklyn, too.*

The man ignores my threat, leaping forward too fast for my eyes to follow. He reaches me in an instant, slamming me against the brick wall, bruising my back. He grabs my arms and wrenches them above my head, pinning me by my wrists. I'm his prisoner. Flush against him, breasts squashed against chest.

"Is this what you want?" he asks in a husky voice. "You want to fight?"

His muscled thigh presses between my legs and a sensual tingle competes with my fear. He smells of the earth—rich, dark, musky. Face inches from mine, his luscious mouth set in a scowl, his eyes are unreadable behind his glasses.

"Let me go!" I demand, squirming against him, a movement that only succeeds in heightening my arousal. What is wrong with me? I should be screaming for help, not getting turned on. Yet there's something about this experience, some weird glimmer of familiarity.

He stops and stares at me for a moment, and I catch my flushed reflection in his mirrored shades. Then he leans into me, crushing my mouth against his, taking possession, wresting from me my submission. My traitorous body burns as his fingers claw at my trapped wrists, his mouth bruises my lips, his thigh grinds between my parted legs.

A moment later he jerks back and shoves me into the brick wall, turning. Head bowed, he glowers at the ground, hands balled into tight fists.

"What the hell did you do that for?" I cry, rubbing my back. I should be relieved at being let go, but instead, for some reason, I feel the sting of rejection.

He turns to me, ripping off his sunglasses. I gasp. His eyes are the most brilliant blue I've ever seen. They're so intense they practically glow. I'm mesmerized, and for a moment I can't look away. This is, without a doubt, the most beautiful man I've ever laid eyes on.

Also, perhaps, the angriest.

"You think you can just waltz back into my life after what you did?" he demands, pacing the width of the alley like a caged tiger. "That I'll take you back with open arms? Well, you're wrong, Mariah. I'm done. This time, I'm really done."

What is he talking about? He obviously recognizes me. Does he, too, think I'm Mariah? Then that must mean . . .

"Are . . . are you . . . Dawn?" I venture, though I'm pretty sure I know the answer.

He rolls his eyes. "I can't believe you have to ask me that! Of course I'm Dawn. God, Mariah. Why are you fucking with my head. I can't take it."

This is Dawn? The guy Glenda says I'm supposed to trust?

I glare at him. "Look. I only called you 'cause my yoga instructor said you could help." God, that sounded so stupid when I said it out loud. "But obviously she was wrong. Just forget it." I push past him and head down the alley, as fast as my platform boots can take me. Screw him. I'll put in a call to Duske instead. Or maybe I'll just head back to Moongazer Station, chill out on one of the couches while I'm waiting to wake up. Doesn't matter, really. As long as I'm as far away from this asshole as I can—

"I should have known they'd try to bring you back."

I stop walking. "Who?" I ask, not turning around.

"The Eclipsers," Dawn replies, his voice sounding tired and drained. "Glenda and her gang. I told them not to. Said you'd made your choice and were gone forever. But they couldn't accept that. They never could."

I turn around slowly, curiosity eroding my anger. "Why did Glenda tell me to call you, then? If you're all anti me being here and all."

Dawn shrugs. "She probably figured if I saw you again I'd take pity on you. Forgive you. Hop back on the Eclipser bandwagon." He scowls again, and I notice his beautiful, angry eyes are shining, wet. "But I don't forgive you. And I never will. To me, you'll always be a traitor." His voice cracks. "I *hate* you, Mariah Quinn."

He turns away, but not before I can see his face start to crumble. Pain radiates from his body as he leans against the brick wall, stone cold but ashen-faced. I have to fight the nearly overwhelming urge to walk over and hug him. To pull him into a warm embrace and tell him everything will be okay. Not that I have any idea of whether or not that's true.

"I'm sorry," I say in my gentlest voice, placing a hand on his back. I don't have a clue as to what I'm apologizing for, but I feel the need to say something. Of course, I should be insisting I'm not Mariah, but I don't want to set him off all over again.

He turns around slowly, looking down at me with his glorious eyes, and for a moment I think he's going to kiss me again. Instead, he reaches up and strokes my face with the back of his hand. So soft, so tender. The wisp of a butterfly's wing against my cheek.

"Look 'Ri, we can't stay here," he murmurs. "It's too dangerous for a Dark Sider to be so close to Luna Park. We must go under."

I cock my head in confusion. "Under?"

"We can hide out at my house until I inform the Eclipsers you're back. I'm sure they're waiting for you." He offers his hand. "Come on."

"I don't know if that's a good idea. . . ."

Dawn frowns and drops his hand. Then he reaches

behind him and pulls out a small, sleek silver knife, pointing it directly at my heart. I jump back, shocked.

"I'm sorry to do this," he says in a terse but even voice. "But if you value your life—what's left of it, anyway—you'll come with me."

THREE

I take a step back, surprised, shocked, stunned. Isn't Dawn supposed to be one of the good guys? The one Glenda told me I should seek out? So how come he's got a knife pulled on me? On the Good Guy scale of one to ten, slicing and dicing the heroine hovers a bit below negative two in my book. Of course, that's assuming I *am* the heroine in this story. At the moment, I'm not a hundred percent on that.

Dawn seems to share my confusion. He's white-knuckling the blade, hands trembling. Could a precisely placed kick knock it out of his grasp, or will that impulsive trick only leave me with a bloodied foot? My life may depend on the answer. And right now, my only friend is surprise.

Do it!

Suddenly, a strange confidence wells up inside me. For no logical reason at all, I know—beyond the shadow of a doubt—that I can take this man in a fight. Steal the blade and turn the tables, draw all the power into my own two hands.

And so, as if compelled by ancient training I never had, I hold up my hands in fake surrender and take a step forward, waiting for the moment I see him relaxing his grip, thinking I'll give in sweetly and come along like a good little girl. At that instant, I launch into a roundhouse kick, my heel slamming into his palm. With a shocked grunt, he loses his grasp on the weapon, sending it skittering across the ground. I lunge forward, head-butting him with all my might. Our skulls collide with a sick clunking sound. He flails, stumbling backward. Seeing stars myself, I lose my balance, falling into him, and soon we're both entangled on the floor.

Now I need that knife. I roll off my would-be kidnapper, scrambling to my feet, ready to make a mad dash for it. But Dawn reacts, grabbing my boot heel, and I trip, falling flat on my face, hands and chest slamming into the hard cold street. For a moment I can't breathe. The wind is literally stolen from my lungs. Dawn takes advantage with lightning speed, dragging me by my heel, then my ankle. I kick backward, using my free foot to slam my boot into his face. He bellows in rage but can't hold on. I wiggle forward along the ground like a worm, fingers outstretched, reaching, straining—only millimeters away from the weapon. Finally I feel its cold metal connect with my hand. Got it! Wrapping my fingers around the knife hilt, I flip over, grasping it in both hands, waving it unsteadily in his direction. Advantage: me.

"Freeze!" I command. "Don't fucking move a muscle."

Dawn starts laughing.

I squint at him, confused and angered by his reaction. I just bested him in a fight. I've got a knife and I'm poised to strike. He's lying there, helpless, bloody, and bruised. Left eye swollen, his lip's split, and his nose is gushing. What the hell does he find so funny?

"That was great. You're a much better fighter than you used to be," he remarks, shaking his head with apparent amusement. "Get a lot of practice on Earth?"

"Shut up. I'll gut you," I growl, struggling to maintain some semblance of control of the situation. Kind of hard to do when the man you're threatening to kill is too busy laughing at you to care.

"Go ahead and try," he says, brushing himself off and climbing to his feet.

"Hey! I said freeze!"

He grins cockily, his bloody face both arrogant and disturbingly sexy. He holds up his hands, but the gesture is one of amusement instead of surrender. "Oh, go ahead, Sister Mariah," he snorts. "I dare you. And then, when you're done fooling around, get down the damn Rabbit Hole before the patrol comes for us."

My fingers caress the hilt, my pulse beating a mile a minute, knowing he's called my bluff. There's no way I can bring myself to drive a blade through an actual person, extinguish their spark of life with my own two hands. Dawn, somehow, seems to know this. And he's using this knowledge to turn the tables once again, effortlessly taking back control of the situation.

I lower the knife, defeated. Dawn smirks, as if he knew all along I didn't have it in me. I want to smack the self-satisfied grin right off his face. But suddenly I feel too weary to fight.

"Earth make you weak? Cause you to lose your

nerve? Don't worry, 'Ri," he says, walking over and holding out a hand, inviting me to get up off the ground. "It's all good."

His patronizing attitude burns in my gut. I ignore his hand and scramble up by myself. "Watch it. I can always change my mind," I remind him, shoving the knife into my boot.

"Of course, princess. I'll be on my best behavior. Dark Sider's honor."

We stare at each other for a moment, me angry, his face cocky with a trace of underlying sadness. Neither of us seems willing to look away first. To submit to the other. That is, until a siren's mournful wail shatters the silence. Dawn's arrogant expression fades, and concern takes its place.

"Enough games," he says. "That's the Park Patrol. Underground. Now." He turns tail and strides out of the alley and onto the street. He pauses, pivoting back to me, his face beseeching. "Seriously, 'Ri. You don't want to be caught out here alone."

I want to tell him to go to hell, but something in his voice gives me pause: serious concern, laced with fear. Could we really be in danger? I remember Glenda's words. *Trust Dawn.* At the end of the day, that's all I have to go on in this crazy world. I'm a stranger in a strange land, and Dawn's the only one I've met so far who seems to know why I'm here. Even if his comments don't make any sense.

"Okay," I agree, firming my resolve. After all, I still have the knife. I can always escape later. "Lead the way."

He nods and I follow him out of the alley and onto the street. We make a left, walking briskly past Moongazer

Station, and then another left turn at an abandoned building. Dawn stops in front of a small manhole cover in the center of the street, silhouetted in sickly orange by one halfheartedly flickering streetlight above. He gets down on his knees and starts twisting it in his hands.

The siren wails again. This time louder. Closer.

Dawn looks up. "Give me a hand with this," he orders. "We don't have much time."

I drop to my knees, still sore from our fight, and help him wrench the cover off. We toss it to one side, revealing a metal ladder leading down into the blackness. Just like in my dream. The one where I was on the other side, in the pit, banging on the manhole cover above me, unable to get back up. I shiver, praying this will not be some one-way trip as well.

"Go ahead, I'll be right behind you," Dawn instructs.

I stare down into the hole, trying to work up my nerve. I've always been a bit claustrophobic, even when I'm not running around in some kind of weird postapocalyptic underground dreamworld. Climbing down into a black pit with no idea of what awaits me below? That's a bit much to swallow.

The siren wails again. Piercing. Right around the corner now from the sound of it.

"They're at Moongazer Station," Dawn says in a hoarse whisper. "They'll be here any second. Please, Mariah. Just go down the damn Rabbit Hole."

The panic in his voice compels me to obey. I suck in a breath, wipe my sweaty palms on my skirt, then stick my legs down the hole. Carefully I find each foothold, securing my step before lowering myself to the next rung. The blackness quickly swallows me with only a dim circle of light from the opening above to guide my way. Down, down, down. How deep is this "rabbit hole" anyway? And what if there are multisized doors and cupcakes reading EAT ME at the bottom?

I glance up to see Dawn's silhouette far above as he starts his own descent. He's still way up high. If I wanted, I imagine I could jump off the ladder now and make a run for it. But where would I go? I'm completely at his mercy. Better to just bide my time, figure out what's going on, and then make my escape.

Or, better yet, wake up. Realize this is all just another one of my psychotic dreams. That's still a possibility, right? But something inside me, some niggling know-it-all voice, tells me that this isn't like the other times. Those dreams were ethereal, mystical, ungrounded in any kind of reality. This seems different. Solid. Like I'm . . . actually here. In the present. Now.

Dawn drags the cover over the manhole and the dim light above me fades until it is gone altogether. The metal has clanked into place, leaving us smothered in blackness. I hold out my hand; it's so dark I can't even see it. Cave darkness. Panic bubbles into my throat, but I swallow and force myself to begin my breathing exercises as I keep climbing farther down. No time to freak out. I need to keep my wits about me now more than ever.

The ladder ends and my boots struggle to find purchase on a surprisingly slick metal-surfaced road. My kingdom for a pair of sneakers. It seems a bit lighter down here and I notice there's dim crimson-colored track lighting running along a small underground road. I use the illumination to take stock of my surroundings. It appears I'm in some kind of wide circular aqueduct, a smooth stone tube, like a sewer (and it certainly smells like one), but with a metal highway running its length. Every few feet, mammoth fans, cut into the stone, blast hot, stale air through the tunnel, whirring loudly, drowning out most other sounds. I gasp, recognizing the scene. The tunnel from my dream. It has to be.

What if the dream was a premonition of some sort? What if there are uniformed men just around the corner, ready to chase me, to pin me down, to "send me to the moon"? Should I be ready to run?

My panicked thoughts are interrupted as Dawn jumps down off the ladder, landing with a thud by my side. He pulls an industrial-strength flashlight from a utility belt and switches it on. I relax a bit. In my dream I was alone. Here, at the very least, I have my reluctant hero/kidnapper by my side. Can I trust him? I have no idea. But what choice do I have?

"Ready?" he asks. "My bike's stashed in a side tunnel nearby. I don't think they saw us and I did lock the hole, but I don't want to take any chances."

"Where are you taking me?"

"I told you. To my house. I'll contact Glenda and the Eclipsers and let them know you're here." He grunts. "They can come get you and then you won't have to deal with me anymore."

"Uh, okay." At least Glenda will be a familiar face. Maybe she can tell me what the hell is going on.

Dawn leads me down the corridor, his flashlight casting sharp silhouettes against the smooth cave walls. I resist the urge of grabbing his arm like a girly girl frightened by her own shadow. I square my shoulders and force myself to keep a brave face. Can't let him know how freaked out I am; he might try to take advantage.

The tunnel breaks ahead, forking one way into an unlit side passage. Dawn motions for me to wait and then disappears into the darkness, returning a moment later leading a small motorcycle. He straddles it and then instructs me to hop on the back, after handing me a helmet. I hesitate at first, weigh my options, then reluctantly pull the helmet over my head and climb on.

"No handholds," I remark, looking from side to side on the bike.

"Sorry, princess," Dawn says mildly, "you're just going to have to hold on to me."

I want to be annoyed at that, but my body betrays me with a shiver of involuntary excitement. The idea of wrapping my arms around this stunning specimen of a man, pressing my chest against his taut back and holding on for dear life . . .

God, Skye. I shake my head. *Sexually frustrated much?*

"Come on. We've got to go," Dawn prompts, tapping his fingers against the handlebars.

Seeing no alternative, I tentatively guide my arms around him, clasping my hands together in front. His chest is as built as I had imagined it. Solid, toned. Not an ounce of fat encasing his well-defined ribs. With me crushed against him, the tingling feeling returns and I find myself resting my head against his back, even though it's not necessary for my safety. I can feel his heartbeat through his leather jacket, thudding too fast. Matching the beats of my own. Am I having a strange effect on him as well? Is all the bitter sarcasm just a cover for his underlying attraction?

He starts the engine and the bike roars to life. It's then that I realize this is not a regular motorcycle.

Namely because regular motorcycles do not hover six inches off the ground.

I open my mouth to remark on the unusual mode of transportation, but my words are drowned out as Dawn releases the brake and we begin to fly down the corridor. Yes, literally *fly*.

The wind whips through my hair as we soar down the road. The ride is smooth; by hovering we avoid any potholes or rocks. Dawn seems to steer the bike effortlessly, tipping to one side and then the other as he maneuvers down the sharp tunnel turns. I tighten my grip around him—we have to be going nearly a hundred miles an hour—and I wonder what would happen if someone comes around the corner in the other direction. A high-speed flying collision? No, thanks.

It doesn't happen. About ten minutes later Dawn slows the bike. I tilt my head to the side to get a better glimpse as to why we've stopped. We've come to a large, rusty gate that extends from the ground to the cave ceiling. Two identical spotlights cast shards of illumination against its closed metal mouth.

"Welcome back to the Dark Side," Dawn says grimly. He presses a button and the bike sinks back to the earth. He dismounts and walks over to the gate.

"The dark side?" I can't help but laugh. "As in, 'Use the force, Luke'?"

"Hardy-har-har," Dawn mutters, not sounding the least bit amused. But he does seem to recognize the *Star Wars* reference. Weird, for such an Un-Earthlike place. "Dark Side. Like, the place where the Dark Siders live," he clarifies with more than a tinge of sarcasm in his tone. "You know, those of us deemed unworthy to mingle with the Indys of Luna Park?"

"Indys?"

He sighs. "You really have forgotten everything, haven't you? Indys. Short for Independents. The free citizens of Terra. The bankers and lawyers and teachers and other white-collar types. They live on Level One of the underground strata in their luxurious condos with sparkling swimming pools, tennis courts, and expensive restaurants. While we, the working class, the ones who keep Terra running, are trapped down here in Stratum Two. Doomed to live in the dirt and squalor and work like slaves our entire lives."

"You're really forced to live down here? That's terrible."

Dawn chokes out a laugh. "Funny you should say that." He presses his thumb against a small screen embedded into the gate. The device beeps twice and the gate creaks open. "I mean, seeing how you betrayed us and all."

I cock my head in confusion. Betrayed them? Is that what he thinks? That this Mariah girl did some kind of double cross? I guess that must be why he seems to hate her so much.

Dawn joins me back on the bike and turns over the engine, drowning out my billion questions, so I put them temporarily away and content myself to just wait and see. After all, what choice do I have?

We head through the gates and into the tunnel beyond. The Dark Side is very unlike the town I found one stratum above, where buildings, while decrepit, still seemed seminormal and recognizable. This place is more like an ant farm, an intricate set of tunnels with twisty, low-ceilinged passageways and doors embedded in the rocks every few feet.

Dawn banks a sharp left, we glide down a corridor, and suddenly the world opens up into what appears to be a town square: rusty trailers haphazardly plopped down in random spots, tattered canopies, and multicolored Christmas lights serving as gaudy decoration. We pass junk stores selling indecipherable odds and ends, and tiny grocers doling out moldy vegetables and crusty breads. Scantily clad women hang out of rusty metal buildings that presumably serve as brothels.

Steam rises from the grated floor, and condensation drips from the high ceiling, giving the impression of a drizzly rain. The place is packed, too many people for such a small area, all milling about, many waiting in ridiculously long lines for the aforementioned groceries and junk. Most are dressed in gray rags and appear scrawny, impoverished, and blindingly pale.

Dawn parks his bike and we disembark. He gestures to the scene. "Spark any memories?" he asks, a hopeful note in his voice.

I shake my head. I've never seen anything so foreign in my whole life. I try to imagine what living down here would be like. Trapped in an underground ant world with no hope of ever going up to the surface. Living your whole life as a blind mole without ever catching the merest glimpse of the sun. Sad. So sad.

We pass an old man, hobbling down the street on a bent metal cane. I can't help but stare as I realize he's got an extra eye growing out of his forehead. He looks up, his trifold gaze meeting mine. His forlorn face lights up like a child's on Christmas morning.

"Mariah?" he cries, his voice full of wonder. "Is that really you?"

"Oh, great. I was afraid of this," Dawn mutters. "Look, Brother—we're trying to keep a low profile—"

"Hey, everyone, it's Mariah Quinn!" the man calls out loudly before Dawn can silence him. A moment later I find myself rushed by what appears to be the entire town, encircled, entrapped, and completely engulfed by eager Dark Siders, their eyes shining, their voices animated as they demand to know where I've been. I'm smothered in hugs and questions and requests for help. I look around wildly for Dawn, pleading for his assistance.

"Hey, hey!" he yells over the roar of the crowd, shooing them away. He manages to carve out a small space between me and the Dark Siders. "I know you're excited to see her, but Mariah's been through a lot. She needs some time to recover before you bombard her with requests. I'm sure she'll be setting up visiting hours soon. So just hang on until then, okay?"

"Sorry, Mariah," several townspeople say, looking appropriately abashed. "We're so glad to see you again." They step away slowly, retreating, respectful. Some touch their caps; others bow their heads.

I look over the crowd, realizing that the man with three eyes is not alone in his deformities. A young woman has an extra, useless arm hanging to one side. A small boy has a tooth growing out of his chin. A middle-aged guy has an extra set of ears. They're all mutants. Every last one of them. I glance over at Dawn. Is he deformed somehow as well? But no, he seems normal. Flawless, even. A perfect specimen.

Before I can question this, Dawn grabs my hand and leads me through the crowd. It parts like the Red Sea, heads bowing reverently as we pass. Whoever this

Mariah is, she certainly has the respect of the people. Almost as if she's some kind of demigod to them. Did she really betray them all as Dawn says? If so, what happened to her in the end? And most importantly, why does everyone think I'm her? It's unnerving to say the least.

Dawn leads me out of the town square and down another tunnel. We come to a metal door, embedded in a stone wall. "Home sweet home," he says as he presses his thumb against the sensor. The door slides open and we step inside.

The apartment is no more than a small cave; it's windowless and literally carved out of rock. The walls are smooth, as if they've been sanded or something. The décor and furnishings are beyond sparse, with only a small metal futon couch, coffee table, and bookcase. There's a kitchenette with a half fridge and stove top burners at the far end. Two doors lead off to the side. Bedroom? Bathroom?

The front door slides silently shut behind me. Dawn walks over to the futon and collapses on it, head in his hands. He scrubs his face, staring down at the rock floor, silent.

"Um," I say, still hovering by the door. "So now what?" God, I just want to go home. I want this nightmare to end. I'm tired. Sick. Scared. Confused.

Dawn grabs a small silver phone off the coffee table and presses in a code. He puts the receiver to his ear. "Yeah," he says, after a pause. "I got her. Yeah, she's at my place. No. No, she has no idea who she is."

"Is that Glenda?" I ask, reaching for the phone. Dawn dodges my hand and stands up, walking to the other side of the room.

"No, *you* come get her. I told you I wanted nothing

to do with this. . . . Nice trick, telling her to contact me when she reentered. . . . Yeah, whatever. . . . As far as I'm concerned she could have rotted in Moongazer Station" He grips the phone tightly, his knuckles white. "Yes, I really do mean that. Look, you guys have your own agenda and that's fine by me. But I want no part of it. I told you. I'm done. Ready to lie low. I've no interest in fighting the good fight anymore. And you know what? I don't think your fearless leader even knows there *is* a fight." He pauses again. "Whatever. Just come get her so I don't have to look at her pointy little nose anymore."

I frown, resisting the urge to check my nose. Pointy, indeed! Where does this guy get off? Whatever this Mariah chick did to him must have been pretty bad. So, how come everyone else sees her as some kind of hero? And how do I convince them all that they've got the wrong girl?

Dawn presses a button on his phone and looks over at me. "The Eclipsers are on their way," he says. "So you can relax. You'll be rid of me soon enough."

"Look," I say, figuring now that we're relatively safe I should put all my cards on the table. "No matter what you and the people out there think, I'm not Mariah. I'm Skye Brown—a video game designer from Manhattan. I don't know what's going on or how I got here or where here even is, but I'd really like to go home now." My voice breaks, the strain and stress and horror of everything I've gone through finally overwhelming. Tears well up in my eyes. Tears of frustration, helplessness, and rage.

There's a pause, then a crash, as Dawn slams his phone against the stone wall; smashing it into a thousand pieces. "Goddamn you, Duske!" he roars, so loud I think I feel the apartment shake. "Goddamn you and your fucking 'Gazers!"

I jump back, afraid of his violent outburst. "What are you talking about?" I ask, trying desperately to keep my voice steady. "Who's this Duske? And what the hell is a 'Gazer?"

He turns to me. "You, my dear," he says, "are not who you think you are. You think you're this Skye girl from another world? Skye doesn't exist. You're really Mariah Quinn. You're from here. Terra. In fact, you've lived your whole life on Terra, up until a couple months ago."

"Terra?" I screw up my face. "What the hell is Terra? This crazy world?" I shake my head. "Ridiculous. I'm telling you the truth. I'm Skye. I'm from New York."

"No. You only think you're from New York because of the drugs you've been taking."

"Drugs? I don't take drugs!" I retort. Well, not since college anyway.

"Yes, you do. And they've made you forget who you really are."

"I haven't forgotten *shit*," I say, gritting my teeth. "I have a whole lifetime of memories up here in my head," I add, tapping my noggin with my index finger.

"Likely implanted."

Sigh. Of course he would say that. "Fine. What about my family and friends, then? My coworkers?"

"Strangers introduced into your new life. I guess they were similarly wiped and implanted when you started Moongazing."

I squeeze my hands into fists and stare him down. "What . . . the hell . . . is Moongazing?"

"I . . . well, I'm not entirely sure how it works." Dawn

sinks down to the futon, his anger dissipating into a sort of sadness. "The government discovered a . . . well, I guess it's another plane of existence. They found it during some astrophysics experiments they conducted about a decade ago. They perfected a way to send people there. To offer them a 'new and improved life'—a better world where the moon still shines at night and the air's still sweet enough to breathe above-ground. They call the program Moongazing. And the alternate reality is Earth as it once was."

"As it once was? What? This is crazy. Impossible," I say, fear pounding through me. "Though . . ."

I trail off, realizing that if I suspend disbelief for a second, what he's saying does make a weird sort of sense. Not the Mariah thing—that's obviously ridiculous. But what if this world is somehow linked to Earth? That would explain how he recognizes my pop culture references, right? Sort of? What if I somehow really did slip through a tear between worlds and accidentally wandered into this underground alternate hell? It seems ridiculous, but here I am. And if I'm not having the longest dream of my life, I'm running out of rational explanations.

The good thing is, if his explanation is true—if the government is sending people from here to Earth—they can send me back. I'll be able to go home.

"Look, as I said, I don't know exactly how the whole thing works," Dawn says. "It's not like the government clues me in to their schemes. Hell, most of the stuff I know is from what you told me when you started investigating the program in the first place. In the beginning you kept insisting it was a one-way trip to insanity. That it was deadly and dangerous and, even though the government knew it, they were letting people 'Gaze anyway."

Okay, something in this isn't exactly adding up. "Uh, if *Mariah* was so against Moongazing, then why would she do it?" I ask.

"Well, no one knew whether it was dangerous or not when it was first introduced. And you were all gung ho to check it out for yourself, find out for sure if it really was the be-all and end-all that our great and glorious Senate was advertising."

"And if it was?"

Dawn rakes a hand through his platinum hair. "I guess you figured that if they really found a new above-ground Garden of Eden world, then it should be for everyone to enjoy. After all, it didn't seem fair that only those with disposable income could pack up and move to paradise while the poor bastards down below were stuck in hell."

"Well, that sounds like a pretty noble cause," I venture, wondering where everything went wrong.

"Sure, I guess," Dawn says. "Until you started getting addicted to the drugs."

I frown. "I still don't get what drugs have to do with all of this."

"You need 'em to 'Gaze, I guess. I don't really understand the whole reason," Dawn says. "Something to do with the brain needing a cushion for the travel. After all, at the end of the day, Moongazing is a pretty big mind fuck." He snorts. "Anyway, you started 'Gazing back and forth on a regular basis and using more and more of the drugs. It was like you became hooked or something. And after a while you starting letting things in your real life here on Terra drop. Important things, like your plans for revolution. And on the night we planned our biggest victory, you disappeared. Abandoned the Dark Siders just as you once accused the Indys of doing."

I cringe, wishing he'd stop saying "you" when referring to this Mariah girl.

"That night, the government swept in and took out half the resistance. Whatever information you gave them in exchange for that last trip was enough to allow them to destroy much of our infrastructure and vital programs—ones we spent years implanting. We nearly lost everything we'd worked to build, all because you chose Earth."

"But—"

"Whatever. I look at you now and I see nothing but an empty shell. A shadow girl with false memories to lull her into a peaceful sleep while her people suffer and die—lost without their leader." He stares at the wall so hard I half wonder if he'll burn a hole in the rock. "You make me sick, Mariah Quinn."

"I'm not Mariah," I protest again, weakly this time, most of the fight gone out of me. I wish he could just accept the fact that I'm not who he thinks I am. I'm not a revolutionary. I'm not a traitor. I've never been here before. I've never laid eyes on Dawn. I've never laid eyes on *any* of these people.

Have I?

Oh my God, I can't handle this. I want to go home. I want to curl up in my bed and be surrounded by my real life. My real friends. My real family. My real reality.

My throat constricts, asthma kicking in with a vengeance. Do I have my inhaler? I pat my skirt anxiously, praying it's still in my possession. I feel a lump and reach into my pocket, hands curling around my salvation. Forget breathing exercises; in a time like this I'm ready to let modern medicine lend a hand. I pull out the device and put it to my mouth—

Dawn's hand knocks the inhaler from my lips milliseconds before I can take a puff. It skitters across the floor, banging against the rock wall and coming to rest a few feet away.

I stare at him. "What the hell did you do that for?" I demand. I dive for my medication. He's too quick, jumping in front of me and grabbing it in his hand.

"Give that back!" I cry, my voice cracking as I struggle to take in air. I double over, wheezing and choking, my hand out, uselessly begging.

"Look at you," Dawn says, his voice cold. "You're so addicted you can't even breathe without the 'Gazer drugs. Pathetic."

"That's not . . .'Gazer drugs." I wheeze. "It's my . . . asthma medication."

"You really think I'm stupid, don't you?"

My heart pounds in my chest. My skin's clammy and cold. If I don't get my breath under control soon, I'm going to die. Here, in this horrible place. Where no one knows where I am. Or even *who* I am.

I lunge at Dawn, but he's ready for me, shoving me backward. It's no use. I can't fight without being able to breathe.

Dawn drops the inhaler on the floor and crushes it under his boot.

"No!" I scream, my world flying out from under me. I fall back onto the futon, struggling to fill my lungs. My vision's gone spotty and I'm close to passing out and probably dying from asphyxiation.

Breathe in, hold, one, two, three. Breathe out, hold, one, two, three.

Please don't let me die. Not like this.

Suddenly I feel a presence inches from my face. My eyes flutter open, to find Dawn, kneeling in front of me, holding a paper bag to my lips. Desperate, I breathe into it, then suck out the air. *Breathe in, suck out, breathe in.*

"Come on," he urges. "Breathe, Mariah. Just breathe."

After what seems an eternity, I manage to wrestle my lungs back into submission. Dawn removes the bag from my face and rises to his feet.

"Thank you," I murmur weakly, though I should be yelling at him. Sure, he helped me. But if he hadn't broken my inhaler I wouldn't have needed his help to begin with.

"God, you're in worse shape than I thought," Dawn mutters, grabbing a burlap bag off the floor and swinging it over his shoulder. "But you're back now. Time to stop taking that shit. It'll do you no good here anyway."

"You don't understand," I argue weakly. "My medicine—I could die without it."

"That's what they've taught you to believe," he says gently. "But you didn't die, did you?"

"Um, well, no. But that doesn't mean . . ."

He shrugs. "Anyway, I've got to go stand in line for rations. The Eclipsers are on their way to get you. They'll explain the rest."

And with that, he stalks out the door, shutting it behind him before I have a chance to follow. I'm trapped. And at the moment I'm also too weak and dizzy to do much about it. I pull myself off the couch and examine the inhaler. The glossy purple case is shattered, the vial cracked. Not good. I need to find more medication or next time I really could die, no matter what Dawn believes.

I spot an ID card of sorts, lying on the coffee table. Dawn's picture smiles back at me. Despite being a complete psycho, he really is a beautiful man. I notice the ID lists him as *Dawn Gray—Surface Medic, nT Alpha*. Surface medic? Is that like some kind of doctor? My mom would be so impressed if I told her I just made out with a doctor. Less impressed that I kicked his ass a few minutes later, however. Of course, if he really is in the medical profession, he should know better than to withhold someone's medication.

I discard the ID on the coffee table, deciding to explore the rest of the apartment. I walk over to the bookcase. There's only one book, lying on a top shelf that I can't reach. Besides that, there are just a couple of photos, framed with crude glass and metal. The first is a group shot of a bunch of boys, all in cranberry-colored school uniforms. All are smiling as if none of them has a care in the world. The caption below reads ACADEMY ALPHA. Was that Dawn's elementary school? I set the picture back on the mantel and pick up the other. It's a black-and-white portrait of a girl weilding some sort of Japanese sword. Underneath it says *Mariah Quinn: Champion Swordswoman—Lunar Park Pro Division*.

I take another look, my eyes widening in disbelief.

What the hell? No! It can't be.

I grab the picture and stare hard, my fingers trembling so badly it's hard to get the image to focus. But suddenly it all becomes crystal clear.

The girl in the photo—the one with the sword—it is me.

FOUR

My fingers fumble; I drop the picture onto the stone floor. The glass frame shatters into a million pieces, cutting into the face of the dancer. Into *my* face.

I sink down onto the sofa, trying to get a grip, not wanting to lose my breath again. I've never posed for a photo with a sword. And yet, there's no mistaking it. This is a picture of me. My face. My body. It's absolutely identical, down to the exact heart-shaped beauty mark on my left shoulder—the one Craig used to like to nibble on when we'd make love—and the same winding daisy chain I'd regrettably had tattooed around my ankle back in college.

The girl in the photo—she wasn't just a look-alike, someone who could easily be mistaken as me; she was an exact replica. She was, in all respects, me.

What the hell is going on here?

It's almost like I was back in my club kid days, when I'd bring a camera out with me. I'd get really wasted, maybe not even remember how I got home. The next morning (after downing seven or eight Advil) I'd upload the photos that had been taken the night before. There would always be the strangest pictures of me— ones I never remembered posing for. I used to love it, considering them some kind of surreal art form, photographic evidence of the human body on autopilot. A digital reminder of what alcohol purged from my brain.

This whole experience reminds me of that: the barest glimmer of familiarity drowning in sea of black holes. But how could any of it be true? Unlike the nightclub adventures, I don't have gaps in my memory. I remember exactly what I did the day before and the month before and the year before that. And I think leading a revolution against an underground regime would stick in one's head a bit more solidly than a drunken pub crawl.

But what other explanation is there? It's not like Mariah is just a figment of Dawn's imagination. The whole town recognized me. And then there's the picture. . . .

A loud knock on the apartment door causes me to nearly jump out of my skin. I glance over, nervous. Who could it be? Then I remember. The Eclipsers. Glenda and her friends. Dawn says they can help me. And Glenda can obviously travel between worlds. If anyone has answers, she will.

"Glenda?" I venture. "Is that you?"

The door swings open and a tall, broad-shouldered man steps through, surrounded by a group of six soldiers, all dressed in silver uniforms. I relax a bit. These must be Eclipsers. Sent to retrieve me and bring me back to Glenda. She'll explain everything. I hope.

"Hello, darling," the man coos in a sexy English accent. I give him a once-over, quickly cataloging him. Blond. Handsome. Strong Roman nose, piercing green eyes. Well built, too. As if he's clocked in quite a few hours at the local underground gym. He's dressed much differently than Dawn, wearing an old-fashioned black suit, much like the proprietor at Moongazer Palace, though his is tailored to fit and the fabric looks expensive.

"Thank goodness we found you," the man says, stepping across the room and taking my hand in his. He pulls me up off the couch and kisses the back of my hand.

I frown in confusion. Something's wrong. This isn't right. I don't know why, exactly. Just, these guys don't seem anything like how I'd imagine Eclipsers. Not that I had a clear picture, mind you, but still . . .

"I, um—"

The blond man waves a hand. "No, no, dear," he interrupts. "No thanks necessary. It was my pleasure to rescue you. After all, you wouldn't be in this horrid mess if it weren't for me. I tried to take all the precautions, but they stole you away seconds before I could arrive. I do apologize for the inconvenience. For making you have to spend time in this"—he looks around the room, disdain written on his face—"squalor." He smiles. "Now, come along. We've got reservations at Luna Park Terrace and the maitre d' simply deplores tardiness."

He gestures to the open door, and his guards step aside to allow me exit. I rise from the couch, confused and indecisive. Should I go with them? Where will they take me? Are they Eclipsers, or some other group entirely? How am I supposed to know whom to trust?

"I don't . . ." I hedge, trailing off, not even sure what questions I should be asking.

I catch the man's glance at my shattered inhaler, still lying where Dawn left it. He looks up at me. "Your asthma medicine," he says. "What happened?"

"Uh, it . . . well, there was an accident." I feel like I'm telling a spousal abuse counselor that I fell down the stairs.

"I see," he says, raising an eyebrow, evidently not believing me any more than the social worker would. "Well, we'll get you set up with a new one." He pauses, then adds, "Skye."

My jaw drops open. "You know who I am?" I ask. "You don't think I'm . . . Mariah?"

The man chuckles. "Mariah. What rubbish. Don't tell me you're starting to believe the Dark Siders' wild tales. You're Skye Brown, resident of the city of New York on the planet Earth. You're only a guest here in our humble land of Terra. But surely, my dear, you know that already."

Finally, someone who knows who I am. He recognizes the real me. And here I was starting to believe Dawn's crazy stories. What an idiot. A million questions bubble inside me, each warring to be first asked. "Why am I here? How did I get here? What's Terra, anyway? Why does everyone seem to think I'm Mariah? How do I get back home?" The questions come fast and furious, not waiting for answers.

The man chuckles again. "All in good time, Skye, all in good time. But first, I think you need your medicine. You're looking quite pale. Come with me and we'll arrange for a new inhaler."

I'm torn. On one hand, finally I have someone who

recognizes me as me. Who is promising a sensible explanation that doesn't involve revolutions and me being someone I've never heard of. On the other hand, shouldn't I wait for the Eclipsers? After all, Dawn said they could help.

Why trust Dawn? asks a voice in my head. *He kidnapped you and tried to delude you into thinking you're someone else. He's threatened you with weapons, dragged you underground, and locked you in his house after almost killing you by destroying your medication. Not really a guy who inspires much confidence.*

I make my decision: I'm going with the stranger who at least seems to know who I really am. Who accepts the fact that I'm from Earth, and isn't going to give me a lot of disturbing bullshit. I tell him I'm ready and follow him outside Dawn's cave and down the twisty passageways. We walk through the town square, which is now strangely empty. Where did the throng of people go? At the moment I almost expect tumbleweed to float across the vacant space.

Then I see the eyes peeking from every window. From around every corner. The people are all hiding. Are they afraid of this man and his guards? And if so, have I just made a horrible mistake? I suppress a shiver, trying to convince myself it's just from drafty caves.

Seeing no other option, I follow my entourage to a shiny black limo parked just outside the Dark Side's gates. My host presses a button on a remote and the car doors rise open like those of the DeLorean in *Back to the Future*. Still not quite sure I'm doing the right thing, I crawl inside. The interior is luxurious, made of some rich, soft, leatherlike material. The blond man takes a seat across from me and his guards file in, two up front and four at our sides. The driver fires up the engine and the doors swing silently shut. Like Dawn's bike, the limo rises a few inches off the ground and takes off down the tunnel.

"So, what's your name?" I ask my host. "I mean, since you seem to know mine."

He smiles. "They call me Brother Duske. I'm a senator. A member of the Circle of Eight."

I stare at him, cold seeping through my insides, even though the car is well heated. This is Duske? The man I was warned about by Dawn and Glenda? The one I was told to avoid at all costs? And here I am, in a hover car with him and his soldiers, flying through the tunnels at top speed. *Oh, Skye, what have you gotten yourself into?*

"Judging from your face I gather you've heard terrible rumors about me from the Eclipsers," Duske says, raising an eyebrow. "How embrassing."

I blush. "It's just that . . . well . . ."

Well, what, Skye? You think he's evil because some random strangers told you he was? The same people who also told you that you are a revolutionary leader for their downtrodden world? Maybe not the most reliable source, just FYI. In fact, maybe they wanted you to avoid senator Duske because he would tell you the real truth—that you're not this rebel leader they want you to be. Ever think of that?

"Sorry. It's just . . . well, I'm feeling a bit like Alice in Wonderland today. You know . . . I knew who I was this morning, but I've changed several times since then?"

Duske laughs appreciatively. "I promise, Skye," he says. "All will be made clear to you very, very soon."

We zoom down the underground highway and I lose

track of the twists and turns. Finally, we stop in front of a long glass tube shooting up into the darkness. The driver presses a button on the car console and the tube door slides open. He backs the car into the tube and then presses another button. I realize that we must be in some kind of glass elevator. Very Willy Wonka. The door slides closed and I feel us shoot upward.

A few moments later, the elevator shudders to a stop and the doors slide open. The driver steps on the gas and we float out into the open road. I gasp as I take in the stunning landscape we enter. It's entirely the opposite of the bleak reality we just left.

We're in the center of a city, a hustling, bustling area that looks remarkably like Times Square if Times Square were set deep underground. High above the city, stadium-strength lighting offers the illusion of daytime drowning out the cave darkness of below. Neon signs and billboards advertise fake tanning, cosmetic surgery, and the latest and greatest in hover cars. Tall buildings crowd the streets, shooting up into the high ceiling of the cave. Corner boutiques spill out onto sidewalk sales. Waiters serve heaping plates of food to café patrons. There's even (get this!) a Starbucks on one corner! I look more carefully at the electronic billboards covering almost every possible surface in a garish Tokyo-esque style. "Are you ready to look into the moon?" one asks. "Try it for a day—or a lifetime!" suggests another. And one tongue in cheek recommends: "One of these days, POW! Straight to the moon!"

Whatever this Moongazing is, there's certainly a big promotional push for it. Could it really have been responsible for Mariah's ultimate demise?

Everywhere I look there are bustling people going

about their days. Girls in short skirts and high boots. Guys in black trench coats. Fashionable, well fed, happy-looking everyday people of seemingly every race. No mutants in sight, either. In fact, most of them are Barbie and Ken dolls incarnate.

"Is this . . . is this where the Indys live?" I ask.

Duske nods. "We call it Luna Park. Pretty, isn't it?"

It is. If one discounts the neon billboards above. The stone walkways are elegant and well designed. The buildings are sleek and some made entirely of glass. And the centerpiece of the city, a spiky post-modern fountain, glitters as water droplets capture the lights and fragment them into a shower of kaleidoscopic color.

"Such a difference from down below," I remark, my mind flashing back to the dirty mutant children of the Dark Side, playing in the glass-strewn streets with deflated balls. Are they doomed to live in the gutters their whole lives, or is there a way for them to escape their destinies and become one of these shiny, happy people in the end?

"Yes. It's unfortunate," Duske agrees, his face earnest. "But we're working on that. You'll see."

We leave the town, turning left and driving down a long road until we pull up to a mammoth Tudor-style mansion. It's set high on a hill, is at least four stories tall and made of white stone—a single candle illuminating every window. It's elegant, but at the same time a bit foreboding. The driver pulls up and around the circular driveway, stopping in front of the house.

A few moments later I'm inside a majestic foyer. The walls and floor are made entirely of marble. Cold. Glittering. Unreadable. A crystal chandelier hangs from a vaulted cathedral-like ceiling. In the center of the room is a mammoth staircase—like something out of *Gone With the Wind*—sweeping upward.

But I'm not here to be impressed by architecture. I turn to Duske. "Can I have my asthma meds now?" I don't mean to sound ungracious and hasty, but before I get completely blown away by the opulence, I want to make sure he can deliver on his promises. After all, I'm still not sure who to trust in this foreign world.

Duske nods and claps his hands twice. An old, gray butler wearing a tuxedo enters the room, bowing his head as he approaches my host.

"Brother Thom, could you get Sister Skye her medication?" Duske asks. "And," he says, after scratching his chin, "a dress suitable for dinner."

The butler nods and disappears into the house.

"No offense to your current clothing," Duske says, giving me a somewhat disdainful glance. "But the Park Terrace has been picky about dress codes lately. Forgive me."

I'm about to remind Duske he didn't tell Thom what kind of medication I needed, but the butler's already returned. Almost as if he had exactly what his master would ask for just waiting in the next room. Of course that's impossible, but . . . He presents me with the inhaler and then a hanger covered in plastic. Inside, almost glowing with its own brilliance, is what may be the most beautiful dress I've ever seen.

"I suggest you save your medication for when you really need it," Duske says. "There's not a full bottle worth left. Asthma medication can be so hard to acquire here."

I take the inhaler and tuck it protectively in my

pocket. Then I accept the dress, holding it up in front of me to get a better look. It's breathtaking. A halter-top, floor-length gown with a slit that cuts to midthigh. It's red, with sparkling multicolored gems seeded into the fabric.

Thom bows stiffly. "One flight up," he instructs. "Two doors to the left. A private bathroom where you can bathe and change."

"Dinner's in an hour," Duske adds. "I trust that's enough time to get ready?"

I nod, unable to speak, not taking my eyes off the gown. Sure, I've never been into high fashion and material possessions, but this is just so extraordinary. A piece of fabric art.

"One more thing," Duske says, reaching into his pocket. He pulls out a long silver chain with a sparkling moon charm attached. He drapes it over my head and it falls just between my breasts. "Beautiful," he proclaims. "Just the piece to accentuate that dress."

I finger the charm, too taken aback to speak. It's identical to the one I got from my mother on graduation day. The one the proprietor took from me. Identical to the hundreds of others hanging in the Moongazer Station cabinet. What does it mean?

"Um, thanks," I murmur, not knowing what else to say.

"It is my pleasure," Duske replies. "After all, it's so rare we in Terra are able to entertain guests from Earth. So few make the trip *this* way, or even learn about us."

I'm about to ask questions when he excuses himself, citing important business. I head upstairs, trying not to drag the dress on the ground. I find the bathroom and draw in a breath as I step inside. The entire room is constructed of etched glass and marble. A hundred tiny teacup candles flicker from various nooks and crannies. Some are encapsulated in glass, others float in small vases of water. The Jacuzzi tub is big enough for three and filled to the brim with steaming bubbles. The vanity is covered with brightly colored soaps, glass bottles of flowery perfumes, and earthen jars of creams. There's a video-screen embedded in a wall, playing back some sort of soap opera. I watch as it goes into commercial.

"Are you looking for a new adventure?" the voiceover asks, showing film of a large full moon. *"A new world where all your dreams can come true?"* The video switches to a scene of a sunny beach with bathers frolicking and tanning and downing fruity cocktails. *"Imagine a world where you can lie out in the sun and won't get sick."* The picture switches to a swinging nightclub. *"Where you can dance the night away under the waxing moon."* I stare, my eyes widening as I realize the club is Luna. Is that Craig in the DJ booth? *"Well, look no further than Earth—a new world that mirrors the Terra of old in all the best ways. Try it for a day—or take the journey of a lifetime."* The scene closes with two people cuddling up to one another on the hood of a car under a star-filled sky. *"Are you ready to look into the moon?"* the voiceover asks alluringly.

The commercial ends and we go back to our regularly scheduled soap opera. I shake my head. This Moongazing thing, whatever it is, is everywhere. And they make it look so great. No wonder people want to take the trip. Heck, the commercial made me excited about Earth and I've lived there all my life. I wonder how many Terrans have journeyed there and are currently living among us. More importantly, I wonder how easy it will be for Duske to send me home.

I hold the dress up in front of me and stare into the mirror. If only Craig could see me in this! He'd go crazy. Or what about Dawn? Would he like his Mariah dressed in something so elegant?

I shake my head. What am I doing thinking of Dawn? I'm finally free of that psycho. The last thing I need to be wondering is what he'd think of me in a dress. Knowing him, he'd probably moan that I was betraying the cause or something. No wonder Mariah took off on him in the end.

I hang the dress on a hook and pull off my dirty, bloody clothes, thankful to finally be out of them. I test the water with a big toe. Perfect. Of course. Everything in this part of the world seems to be flawless—the polar opposite of the world beneath. I feel an odd pang of guilt. Should I be enjoying this luxury while so many below are going without?

I shake my head. All will be answered in good time, and my refusing a warm bath will not feed a hungry child. I lower my body into the tub and force my brain to stop whirring.

This is better, I tell myself as I relax in the bubble bath's embrace. I'm in a safe place, here by my own free will. My host knows exactly who I am and he's not playing games with my head. He rescued me from my kidnapper and gave me my lifesaving medication. And now at dinner I'll get to ask him all my questions: What is this place? How did I get here? Who are the Eclipsers? What do they want with me?

And most importantly . . .

Who the hell is Mariah Quinn and why does she look exactly like me?

FIVE

"This place is gorgeous. I've never seen anything like it," I exclaim about an hour later, seated in a plush booth at the back corner of Luna Park Terrace restaurant. The entire room is carved out of a sort of polished smoky blue glass—the tables, the floors, even the walls—allowing for a tremendous view of a nearby lava-filled crater. The lava bubbles and boils beside us, but we're cool and comfortable. This place is beyond breathtaking; it's a study in fire and ice.

"Haven't you?" Duske asks. "What a shame. But you have so many other lovely things where you come from. I hardly think you should complain."

"Oh," I say, taken aback. "I'm not complaining. I'm just impressed."

Before Duske can respond, a wrinkly man dressed in a tux and with a name tag that simply reads WAITER approaches our table. He bows at the waist.

"How do you do this fine evening, Brother Duske?"

he asks with an impeccable English accent. "It is an honor to have you patronize our humble restaurant."

"It is an honor to be here, Brother Claude," Duske says with the same respect.

The waiter turns to me. "And you, Sister. It is an honor to—"

"A bottle of your finest vodka," Duske interrupts.

The waiter nods, seeming a bit taken aback by the interruption. "Of course," he says, bowing low again. "So sorry, Brother Duske." He stands, hesitates for a moment, as if daring to speak again. "And would you like your usual entrees?" he asks at last.

Duske glares at him. "I would like my usual," he says. "But this young lady has never dined in your establishment. So I am sure she would like to hear the specials."

"Right. Right. Of course," the waiter says. I raise an eyebrow. Does he also think I'm Mariah? This is just too weird.

The waiter reaches into his pocket and pulls out a handkerchief, patting his brow. "Today we have a lovely butternut squash ravioli, dusted with sage and swaddled in a lovely soy cream sauce. We also have a black bean and tortilla pie, glazed with a faux honey chipotle."

"I'll take the ravioli," I say, relieved the options aren't cow brains or monkey livers. I glance over at Duske, who nods his approval. The waiter bows once again before retreating to presumably fill our orders. Duske watches him go. "Don't mind him," he says. "Brother Claude spent too much time on the surface during the early years. It's a shame to see a mind go to mush like that." He shakes his head. "In any case, what was I saying? Oh yes, how lovely it must be to live on Earth."

I shrug, not sure how to respond. "Yeah, I mean . . . I like it, of course. Not that I have much to compare it to, obviously."

"We on Terra are quite envious of all the opportunities your world affords. There are people here who would give their right arms to live on Earth." He strokes his chin with his forefinger and thumb. "Come to think of it," he adds, "I believe some have."

I start to laugh until I catch his expression. Is he for real?

"Perhaps, Skye, you would like a little history lesson of our humble world?" Duske asks.

I lean forward eagerly. "I'd like that." Good. Now maybe I'll get some answers.

"Once upon a time," Duske says with a grin. "Isn't that how you Earth people like to begin your stories? Once upon a time there was a great land and a great people who lived like normal human beings on the surface of their planet. But they did not take care of their world. Nor did they take care of each other. Instead, they fought over petty lands until the world was split in two. There was a great war and a great bomb that poisoned the land and sent everyone underground. At first it was total anarchy. Governments were ripped apart, people scrambling just to survive."

I stare at him, digesting the information. Hard to believe, even with the close calls we've had on Earth, that it could actually happen. That two warring countries could really go that far—pressing the red buttons and sparking a raging apocalypse.

"How long ago was this?" I ask.

"Nearly a hundred years," Duske replies solemnly. "And still the world is uninhabitable above. Of course, now we have elaborate cities below the surface and there's no one left who even remembers living under the open sky."

"That's so sad," I say, trying to imagine a life completely underground. No wonder everyone wants to go Moongazing. The finest shops and restaurants in the world can't replace a day at the beach or a walk in the park.

"Indeed. But the alternative is far worse. The total annihilation of the human race."

"Good point," I agree. "So, how did you all end up here underground?"

"It's all thanks to the Circle of Eight," Duske explains, "the forefathers of our current Senate Circle, of which I am lucky enough to have been born a member. The original group was founded about a hundred years before the Great War. At the time, our country's government was corrupt and chaotic. A democracy in name, it was really a totalitarian regime, controlled and manipulated by the rich, powerful, and greedy. This government felt it was perfectly within its rights to invade other countries and force their sham of democracy on them in order to covertly steal their resources. The Circle of Eight formed secretly during that time, knowing that the end result of this behavior could only lead to apocalypse once the smaller countries upgraded their nuclear technology and decided to fight back."

I suppress a shudder. This all sounds scarily parallel to my own world.

"So, using their foresight, they bought up large quantities of useless desert and constructed secret underground cities like Luna Park, cave by cave. By the time the war inevitably hit, they were ready and able to welcome the refugees below. They took in people from around the world to try to preserve as many ethnicities as possible."

I think back to the Asian proprietor at Moongazer Station, and the wide variety of people wandering around Luna Park. They'd definitely done a good job preserving diversity. Pretty cool.

A scantily clad waitress chooses that moment to interrupt Duske's tale, approaching the table with an open bottle of vodka. She giggles, batting her eyelashes at Duske as she pours. He winks at her and reaches over to grab her ass under her short skirt. Her face falls and she scrambles away, red-faced. Duske watches her go, a smarmy grin on his face, his eyes glued to her bottom. Yuck. Great and glorious government leader or not, he's still a perv.

"Go on," I say, wanting to get back to the story.

"So, the Circle of Eight saved the people. You'd think the people would be grateful. Sadly, this has not proved to be the case. While some of the people acclimated quickly to their new world—finding jobs, buying homes, raising families—others became depressed and angry, refusing to work to better their society. They began preaching that it was the government's fault that they were poor and helpless. They wanted handouts—and didn't think they should have to work for their bread. They began to convince people that the great and glorious government who'd saved them was actually brutally exploiting and controlling them." Duske shakes his head, a disgusted scowl on his face. "In reality, of course, nothing could be further from the truth."

I'm so fascinated by his tale I scarcely notice that

the waiter has returned with our food. He pulls the silver cover off my plate, revealing multicolored ravioli that smells of cinnamon. He places a similar plate in front of Duske, then passes him a small black handheld machine. Duske presses his thumb against the sensor and the machine beeps and flashes green. Evidently it's some high tech payment option, just like the locks on the doors. Thumbs sure are useful in Terra. I wonder if I have any credit on mine. . . .

"My apologies for the dinner," Duske says, picking up a pair of chopsticks. "I know on Earth you dine mostly on meat and fowl. Here in Terra we have very limited access to animals. The war eliminated most species altogether, and the ones that were saved and brought underground proved sterile. We've been working in labs to clone what we have to increase the population, but the clones are not able to reproduce either. So, every animal is precious and protected."

I try to imagine a world without animals. No dogs to greet you with snouty noses and slobbery tongues. No cats to rub up against your leg with a purr.

"Well, don't worry about the meat thing," I say. "I'm a vegetarian anyway."

"Of course you are, my dear," Duske says with an odd smile. "And I trust you will enjoy this meal."

I take a bite, savoring the smooth creamy taste and herb kick. "It's delicious," I say, surprised and delighted. "In fact, it tastes just like the kind they serve up at ArtePasta in the Village." I laugh. "Like, exactly. So strange." I take another bite.

"Perhaps Earth and Terra aren't so different after all." Duske comments, taking his own bite.

"Well, I definitely agree with you there. In fact, it's

crazy," I remark, wondering what answers he is going to provide me. "I mean, we speak the same language. Share the same pop culture. You even have a Starbucks, for goodness' sake."

"Indeed," Duske says. He refills his tumbler and downs the shot. "Which is why we felt your Earth is such a good fit for our people."

"A good fit? What do you mean?"

Duske takes another bite, chews, then swallows. "Terra, as much as we've tried to make it a self-sustaining, viable world, is overcrowded. It has huge shortcomings. We can't make enough food. We can't breed animals. We're lost a great deal of aesthetic beauty because of limited access to trees. There are some surface logging companies that risk the radiation to supply us with wood, but there's never enough."

"Okay . . ."

"So, a few years ago, the government came up with a plan to export our people to a more inhabitable world—a world that can support them and give them a comfortable and familiar lifestyle. Even better, it's a life aboveground, where they can dance under the moonlight each and every night without worrying about becoming sick."

He sounds like one of the advertisements. "You mean Moongazing," I conclude.

Duske nods. "Well, the technical term is interdimensional relocation. We decided to brand it 'Moongazing.' More commercially appealing, we feel. Gives it an aesthetic beauty, don't you agree?"

"I see," I say. "And you're able to do it? You can send people from here to Earth? It's technically possible?"

Should I just come right out and ask him if he'll send me back? Or do I need to schmooze a bit more first?

"Of course," Duske replies.

"Is it . . ." I remember Dawn's story about Mariah. "Is it . . . addictive?"

He laughs. "Not at all," he says. "It's quite safe. We did a great deal of research and testing before we introduced it to the public." He pauses, then asks, "What did the Eclipsers say about it?"

"Oh God." I lean back in my chair and sigh. "They think I'm some girl named Mariah who's been Moongazing and doing drugs or something. This guy Dawn told me that my 'Gazing has destroyed all my memories and that's why I think I'm Skye and not Mariah."

Dawn laughs, long and hard, shaking his head and patting his belly. "They are just too much," he says. "How did you ever keep a straight face when he was spouting off this nonsense?"

I shrug. "I was more freaked out than amused, honestly. I mean, I don't even know where the hell I am or how I got here, never mind who this Mariah chick is. I just know she's not me."

"Mariah Quinn's the daughter of Sister Estelle, a retired member of our Senate and Circle of Eight. She was in training to join our ranks and become a member of the Senate until she got . . . distracted."

"Distracted?"

Duske rolls his eyes. "She started socializing with the wrong crowd, a group of rebellious and bored Indys who like to cause trouble. They brainwashed her into thinking that The Circle was somehow the enemy, and so she abandoned her training and moved down to

Stratum Two to start up some silly group she called The Eclipsers with her little Indy rebel friends."

I lean forward, fascinated. And here I had assumed Mariah was just another one of the Dark Siders, unhappy with her lot in life. But she was of royal blood, in a sense. One of the ol' Illustrious Eight. I wonder what led her to make that choice—to give up all she'd been born to inherit, trade her life of luxury for the poverty down below. You gotta kind of admire a girl for that.

"So, what happened to her?"

Dawn shrugs. "She played her little revolution thing for a time, but then got bored with it all. She started Moongazing and realized that making a new life on Earth was a lot more fun than fighting some silly and unhelpful rebellion here on Terra. And so, in the end, she decided to purchase a permanent migration package. Last I heard she's living quite happily on Earth."

"But the Eclipsers couldn't accept her disappearance," I conclude, wondering how much of Duske's story is true. Had she really just got bored? Or, like Dawn suggested, did she become an addict, unable to help herself?

"Right," Duske says. "Poor bastards. They've been searching for her on Earth ever since, trying to get her to come home and continue leading their impotent revolution. It was damn lucky I rescued you before they could poison your mind."

"Yeah, definitely," I say, absently. Something about this whole explanation still troubles me, though I can't put my finger on what it is.

"You look a hell of a lot like Mariah," Duske explains. "Which is probably why they think you're her. I can actually see similar mannerisms in you, too. But trust me, Skye Brown. You are from Earth."

I nod. Right; of course, he's right. It only makes sense. Dawn, Glenda, the Eclipsers. They made a mistake. A simple mistake. Dawn even admitted he didn't know exactly what was going on.

"So now what?" I ask. "How do I get back to Earth?" Under the table I cross my fingers, my mind begging any higher power who might be listening to offer up a simple way for me to return home.

"Easy," Duske says. "You use one of my private 'Gazing booths at the house. A whiff of your asthma medication and the press of a button and poof! You're back on Earth."

I scrunch my face up in suspicion. "Why my asthma medication?" I ask, remembering Dawn denouncing the stuff. What was the correction?

Duske shrugs. "Sometimes the journey can be rough. I'd want to make sure you don't have an attack en route."

Something feels odd about his manner, but I'm afraid questioning him too much might cause him to revoke his invitation. "Okay. Whatever it takes," I say, setting down my chopsticks. "I just want to get home as soon as possible."

Duske smiles indulgently. "Of course," he says. "And you will go back soon enough. But first, I wonder if I might ask you a favor."

"Uh, sure. I think," I say, trying to ignore a gnawing worry at what that request could possibly be.

"You think of Terra much the way Terrans think of Earth. You're here, living, breathing, and experiencing, but I can tell that you don't quite believe this is all real," he says. "Well, imagine the Terrans. They've never seen Earth, and so many are afraid. Afraid of the unknown. Afraid of what might happen if they Moongaze. Their fear is holding them back, trapping them here on our dead world when they could be living real lives on Earth."

"Oh-kay. So what does that have to do with me?" I ask.

"In a way, the Eclipsers did me a tremendous favor by bringing you here. You're the first Earth person to ever set foot in Terra. It's almost like you're an ambassador of your world. What I humbly ask of you is that you continue in that role awhile longer. I'm holding a Moongazing seminar this weekend. In the meantime, I'd like you to go back to Earth and take photos of your world. Anything you think will make it seem more real to the Terrans. Animals, sunshine, grass, trees. All the things you take for granted. Photograph them and return to Terra and speak to my people at the convention. Tell them what Earth is really like."

"You want me to take photos? And then come back?" I stare at him, incredulous.

"Yes." He nods. "Together you and I can prove to the people of my world that Moongazing is not just some field trip from reality, but a doorway to a new and better existence." He says the last part so grandly that I assume it's part of his sales pitch. Is he profiting off this? Is he an alternate-reality travel agent, if you will?

"Why can't you just get the photos yourself?" I ask. "I've seen the tv commercials. Obviously you have stock footage of the place. Why would you need me?"

He sighs. "I could take pictures, yes, but the people

need to see them from an objective source. I need someone who's actually from Earth. You can go beyond the facts. Explain what it's really like to live there. Not as a tour guide, as I would be, but as a citizen of that brave new world. You would be Earth's first ambassador to Terra."

"I do see what you're saying," I begin cautiously. "But to tell you the truth, I'm really swamped these days. My video game is launching soon and we've still got a lot of bugs to work out. I mean, don't get me wrong—I'd love to help you out. But I really think you'd do much better finding another girl." I cross my fingers, hoping he'll buy my admittedly lame excuse. But what else can I say—once I get back to Earth, no way in hell I'm coming back to this godforsaken place?

Duske's handsome face darkens, his mouth twisting into an unpleasant scowl. "Listen to me carefully," he says in a slow, tight voice. Gone is the honey-sweet sales pitch. "I need those photos. And I need you to get them for me. There is no one else."

"But—"

"If you do not get me my photos within two days, though I am a very busy man I will make the time to yank you back to Terra myself. And trust me, it will not be to take you to dinner."

My pulse kicks up a few notches. A moment ago he seemed so debonair. I can't believe he's threatening me. But what can I do? I'm totally under his power here. If I refuse, he might not send me back to Earth. I'll be stuck here forever. And if I try to trick him, get back to Earth and hope we don't cross paths—well, that seems a risky move as well.

My throat closes up and I wheeze, trying to take a

breath. I reach into my pocket for my inhaler. I can feel Duske's pleased eyes on me as I put it to my mouth and take a puff. I pull the inhaler away, disturbed by his reaction, remembering Glenda's warning, Dawn's warning.

"Are you ready to go back to Earth?" Duske asks, his voice back to its pleasant self.

I should be. I should be more than ready. So why am I suddenly hesitant? Worried?

"Um, yes, I guess I am," I say, shaking the doubt away. Do I really want to be here another moment? No, of course not. I want to go home and forget all of this ever happened.

Duske rises from his seat and I follow him out of the restaurant. As we walk down the dimly lit path and to the awaiting car, a man suddenly jumps out from behind a rock sculpture, blocking our path. His eyes are rimmed in black bruises and his mouth's hanging open sideways. He looks utterly insane.

"Don't look into the moon!" he cries, waving a placard on a stick. "It'll destroy your life—your very soul!"

Startled, I take a step back, not sure what he's going to do next. My eyes lift to the placard. MOONGAZING FTL! it reads. I know that in geek speak (at least back on Earth) that acronym stands for "For the Loss"—a videogame term that stood for something bad, terrible, and shouldn't be touched with a ten foot pole.

Nervous, I glance over at Duske. He's talking into some kind of communization device strapped to his wrist. Obviously he's summoning the cavalry.

"I'm not crazy," the man continues, grabbing my hand and staring at me beseechingly. "I'm an Indy, just like you. I had a job, a family, a life. Moongazing stole it all from me. Put me in a game I could not win. I barely made it out alive. Whatever you do, don't look into the moon!"

Before I can react, three silver-clad soldiers appear, dragging the man backwards. He screams in rage, trying to fight, but they quickly overpower him, stunning him with some kind of crimson-beamed taser.

Like the one in your dream, an inner voice reminds me. I shudder.

"Sorry about that," Duske says, putting an arm around my waist and leading me down the path. "As you can see, like any new program, we have our detractors."

I realize I'm still trembling from the encounter. I glance back at the man. He's now spread-eagle on the ground, sobbing hysterically. Could what he said have any truth to it? Was he a victim of Moongazing just like Mariah was?

And if so, was what I was about to do—go Moongazing myself? Was that a good idea?

I shake my head. Dangerous or not, it's my only ticket home. What, do I want to hang out here for the rest of my life? I need to get back to my world as soon as possible and put all this behind me.

We enter the awaiting hover-car and zoom back to Duske's mansions. He leads me up the stairs, down a hall, and into a long passageway similar to the one at Moongazer Station. He stops in front of a red door with a crescent moon carved into the metal.

"Here we are," he says. "Are you ready to look into the moon, Skye?" he sneers, quoting the Moongazer promos. What once seemed an innocent slogan now fills me with dread.

I draw in a breath, remember this is the only way home. "I am."

He hands me a small piece of paper with a Web site url scribbled on it. "When you have your photos, upload them to this site. That way I'll know you're ready to journey back to Terra, and I will activate the retrieval program."

"Are you sure you really need me to do this?" I ask. "I mean, there's no one else?"

Duske puts his hands on my shoulders and leans forward, kissing me once on each cheek. "You are my chosen one, Skye," he says reverently. "You will be a great symbol of Earth to all the people of Terra. You'll be a symbol of a better life."

I stifle a sigh, trying to push down the worry gnawing at my stomach. But I'm going back home, I remind myself. That's what's important. I'll worry about the photo thing later.

Duske presses his thumb against a sensor. It beeps once, and then the door swings open. It's time to look into the moon.

My cell phone was ringing. I opened my eyes, blinking the sleep away. I'd never been so happy to hear to hear the silly *Star Wars*–themed ring tone in all my life. I sat up in bed and looked around, gratefully taking in the cozy familiarity of my bedroom.

I let out a breath. It was all a dream. All one crazy, messed-up, freakish, ridiculously long dream.

Hallelujah.

Though . . . how did I get here? Last thing I remember was being in the VIP section of Luna. Had I had some sort of blackout? I wasn't even drinking. I'd better go see a doctor tomorrow. What if I had a brain tumor or something?

Still, nothing could eclipse my joy of escaping the crazy, messed-up nightmare world I'd been trapped in. I felt like singing. Shouting. Jumping up and down. My bed. My books. My computer. My teddy bear Melvin. All here. I was back. I was free.

The answering machine clicked on.

"Skye? It's Craig. Guess you're asleep. I just wanted to check in on you since you left Luna so suddenly. Where are you?" He paused and I searched for the phone, unable to find the cordless receiver in the dark bedroom. "Please, call me the second you get this. I'm worried about you."

The machine clicked again, indicating the end of the message. I crawled out of bed and fumbled for the light switch. I'd better call him back before he sends out the National Guard. So, I left Luna suddenly? That was odd. And why didn't the phone wake me up before? Was I in that much of a deep sleep? Did I get dosed with something?

I found the switch and flicked it, flooding the room with warm light. Momentarily blinded, I rubbed my eyes. I was going to look great tomorrow at work. All bloodshot and black circles for sure. I glanced in the mirror for confirmation, dreading to see the state of my face.

My heart stopped.

Mirror girl stared back at me, her expression reflecting my horror.

Because instead of the typical boxer shorts and t-shirt ensemble I usually wore, I was wearing a gown. A gown that in reality shouldn't exist.

SIX

Half a box of No-Doz, a full carafe of coffee, and three Diet Pepsis later, I found myself buzzed and bleary as I dressed for work. It was eight a.m. I'd thought I'd been exhausted yesterday, but there was no way in hell I was going to risk shutting my eyes and returning to the crazy world of my dreams. The one where I was able to somehow bring dresses back with me.

I jumped into a cold shower—of course no hot water today of all days—and tried to ignore my pounding heart and shaking hands as I went through the routine of washing my hair. Hopefully work would be a better distraction. I had a lot going on. I'd been given a list of bugs to work out before our launch, and I had to get them done today. That promised to be real fun on no sleep. And how was I supposed to concentrate on reality? All I could think of was my nightmare come to life.

I got out of the shower and towel-dried myself, then headed into the bedroom to change. My eyes fell to the dress, which I'd hung in my closet. There had to be some logical explanation. Maybe I'd bought it on my way home. Or I'd drunkenly switched clothes with someone at the club. Because what other explanation could there be besides the obvious—and unbelievable—one: that I had somehow traveled to an alternate reality and brought the dress back myself?

I was cracking up. Had to be. Maybe instead of heading to work I should check myself into some psych ward. Don a straitjacket, swallow some hardcore antipsychotics. Drool in a padded corner for the next six years. Didn't sound like a terrible plan at the moment.

I arrived at work fifteen minutes late and headed straight to my office and closed the door behind me. Sitting down behind my desk I dialed my voice mail, praying for additional distractions. Judging from the typical voice mails I usually got, I was betting this would do the trick.

Beep!

"Hey, Skye, it's Suzy! Did you have any luck at Luna last night? I'm still on the island, so, like, call my cell, okay?"

Beep!

Ugh. Erase.

Beep!

"Two days, Skye. Two days."

Beep!

Wait! What was that? My heart thudded against my chest as I pressed 2 to repeat the last message. Except, in my fright, my finger slipped and I hit 3 instead. Which wouldn't be a big deal except that 3 was the erase button.

Shit, shit! How could I undo? I frantically began

pressing random buttons. Why oh why didn't I pay attention when the receptionist was giving me the new voice mail system demo last week?

"Good-bye," the cheerful computerized female voice chirped before disconnecting.

"No! No good-bye!" I cried, banging a fist against the phone keypad. I must have hit '9'—the disconnect button—by accident. Damn it! What was that message? Was it from him? It had said "two days." It sounded just like his voice. It had to be from him. But he was in the other world. Wasn't he? How could he access my voice mail?

I fought the urge to crawl under my desk and hide as I glanced around the office. Was Duske here? Did he know where I worked? Would he really come after me if I didn't provide him with photos?

Everyone was going about their business seemingly without a care in the world. It was only me with my heart in my throat, ready to jump out my office window in an inane chance at escape. I took a deep breath. What was I going to do?

Take the photos.

I froze. The command seemed to be coming from inside my head.

Take the photos.

Again, more insistent.

"Fine. I'll take the stupid photos," I muttered. "I'll do everything I'm supposed to. And in two days, when I don't get magically flown back to Terra, I'll know for sure, once and for all, that this was just one big, bad, crazy dream."

"What's a dream?"

I looked up from my desk to see that my boss, Madeline, had entered my office just in time to catch the end of my crazy rambling.

"The idea of getting all these bugs worked out of the game before release date," I answered, lacing my voice with the appropriate level of sarcasm.

Madeline sat down in the armchair across from my desk, folding her hands in her lap. She'd founded Chix0r five years ago, after becoming disenchanted by all the sex-laced trash-talk commonly heard on androcentric online role-playing games. She'd imagined a virtual world where girls could feel safe strapping on a sword and contributing to the community with no fear of being smacked down by an arrogant metal-mouthed fourteen-year-old boy who, in real life, would never be able to get a real girl to acknowledge his existence.

"Are you okay, Skye?" she asked, peering at me through her black-rimmed glasses. "I don't mean to sound critical, but the last instance you created had more bugs than a New Orleans motel room."

I hung my head. Madeline was the coolest boss in the universe and I hated letting her down more than anything. After all, as she'd said so many times, we weren't just coworkers here at Chix0r. We were family.

"I'm sorry," I said. "It's just . . . I've been having this horrible insomnia lately. And when I do fall asleep I have these crazy dreams. I wake up feeling like I've been run over by a truck."

Madeline nodded sympathetically. "Prerelease jitters," she concluded. "Don't worry, kiddo, your work is great. It's gonna win every design award in the book this year. And we're in the home stretch. Just got to buckle down now and get through the next two weeks. Then we'll be able to relax a bit."

I threw her a halfhearted smile. Prerelease jitters? If only it were that simple.

"Yeah, you're probably right," I said, not wanting to go into it any further. "I'll get through somehow."

"I know you will." Madeline smiled. "Now, I wanted to talk to you about your redesign of the knight class's talent tree. Can you pull up a character for a second?"

I logged into *RealLife* and repositioned my monitor so she could see the screen. I selected Allora, my character. She was right where I'd left her the last time I played: in the bar. She turned and looked out from the game, as if she could see us watching her, then broke out into a big smile and waved a greeting.

"She likes you," Madeline commented. "You must treat her well."

I smiled. It was so cool how lifelike the characters were. "I like her, too. She's very kick-ass."

"Okay, now take her outside and have her attack something."

"Oh, you've opened up new terrain?"

Madeline nodded. Evidently the other designers had been hard at work during my mental collapse.

I obeyed my boss's directive, using the keyboard and mouse to run Allora outside the limits of the city of Mare Tranquilitatis and into the frozen tundra of Serenitatis. The other designers had been working hard, adding weather effects, so the scene looked like it was really snowing out. Very cool. I led Allora down the hill, off the safe road, and into the wild. A moment later, a bandit troll jumped on her, initiating the game's fight mode. On my command, Allora whipped out her sword and started swinging.

"This is all good," Madeline commented, leaning forward to get a better view of the screen. "But now, show me her finishing move."

I clicked the hot key to have her execute her special move. Each class had one built in: a deadly last strike designed to finish off one's opponent. I'd programmed Allora to fall to the ground and slash out to cut off the monster's feet, leaving him incapacitated and unable to run away. It was a very dramatic, visual finishing move, and I was pretty proud of it.

"Hmm."

I glanced at Madeline. She didn't look quite as impressed. She sat back in her chair and rubbed her chin with one hand. I noticed she had a moon tattoo between her thumb and forefinger. Was *everyone* in on this new trend? And why did it have to be a moon? "Yeah, we're going to have to fix that."

I scrunched my eyebrows. "But why? It's so cool-looking!"

"Sure, it's cool-looking. But it doesn't make any sense in the rules of chivalry. True knights fight within a strict set of protocols. They have an inborn sense of honor. They would not suddenly turn rogue and slash out with such a cheap move."

"Well, they should consider it," I argued. "If it helps them defeat their opponent."

"But then it would be a battle fought with no honor," Madeline explained. "I'd have no problem with you giving that move to a rogue character. They're supposed to be sneaky and underhanded. But I won't have knights fighting dishonorably. You need to stick with the world-building."

I sighed, knowing there was no use arguing. Once Madeline had something in her head, she'd never be persuaded otherwise.

"Okay, I'll come up with something else," I said, running Allora back into the city. "Something more honorable."

"I know you will." My boss rose to her feet. She stared at me for a moment, then said, "But why don't you take the rest of the day off? You look like shit."

"Are you sure?" I asked.

"Definitely. Even I know that *RealLife* has to take a backseat to real life once in a while," she quipped. "But get your ass in tomorrow and be prepared to dive back into this."

"I will," I promised, grateful for the reprieve. "Thank you. I really appreciate it."

"No problem, kiddo. Now get some rest." And with that, Madeline turned and headed out of my office, closing the door behind her.

I sent Allora back into the bar and got her some cake to eat. She gratefully shoveled it into her mouth, glancing up at me from time to time with gratitude.

"Okay, I'm going to log you out now," I told her. "I've got to go take some photos."

The hot dog man. The Statue of Liberty. The camels at the Bronx Zoo. The maple trees in Central Park. The carousel on Coney Island. I shot them all. Close-up, panoramic, artsy, straight. Duske wanted photos? He'd get his photos. And then maybe he could leave me the hell alone so I could get back to my life.

I arrived back at my apartment around five and headed straight to my computer to start uploading. Maybe I'd get bonus points for turning in the photos a day early. At the very least I could get this assignment off my plate.

My cell phone rang just as I began the upload—the sudden burst of the *Star Wars* ring tone caused me to nearly jump out of my skin, my heart skipping like a broken record. Was it him?

With trembling fingers I reached into my bag and pulled out the phone. Relief washed over me as I recognized the name on the caller ID. Just Craig. Thank God.

"Hey, Craig," I said, selecting the photos out of my My Pictures folder. If only he knew what I was trying to do. He'd be sending the men in white coats over as we spoke.

"Hey, Skye, where have you been?" he asked, sounding concerned. "I thought I saw you at Luna last night, but then you disappeared."

I swallowed a bitter laugh. Disappeared? He was more right than he knew.

"And then I tried your cell a dozen times, but you didn't pick up."

"Yeah, sorry about that. I wasn't feeling well and decided to go home about five minutes after I got there. I, um, came home and crashed hard-core."

There was a beat of silence on the other end of the line and then: "But I came by your place after my shift."

Uh-oh. Thank God I'd never given him a key.

"Like I said, I really crashed. You know, not having

had a good night's sleep in ages. I don't think stamped-ing elephants could have woken me last night."

"You sure you just didn't have another guy over or something?" Craig asked. His voice was only half teasing.

I forced myself to laugh, trying to push a sudden im-age of Dawn out of my mind. After all, being brutally kissed by dream guys in postapocalyptic alleyways didn't count as cheating, did it?

"No, no. Nothing as exciting as all that," I lied. "Just lots of drooling on my pillow."

Craig's laugh sounded more genuine this time. "Okay, okay," he relented. "So, what are you up to now?"

Oh, not much. Just playing alternate reality travel agent to the postapocalyptic crowd. . . .

"Oh, not much, just doing some work on the old computer."

"Want me to come over?"

"Um . . ." I glanced at the clock. Did I want him to come over? Not really. I'd have much preferred to curl up in a ball and sleep for the next forty-eight hours. But that wasn't really an option. Duske told me after the photo upload, he'd be calling me back to Terra. And when/if that happened, I wanted a witness this time. Someone to let me know exactly what happened after I blacked out and woke up in Terra. Did my body literally disappear with my mind, sucked into some kind of alternate reality wormhole? Or did I fall into a comalike sleep and only travel in my dreams?

"Skye? Are you still there?"

"Yeah," I replied, making my decision. "And sure. Come on over whenever you can."

"Great." I could hear his relief. Poor guy. My mental

collapse had to be hard on him as well. "I'm not far from your place, actually. I'll be there in, like, ten minutes. Want me to pick up something from Mana for dinner?" he asked, naming my favorite Japanese vegetarian take-out spot.

"Oh, yum. Yes. I'm totally in the mood for their yakisoba," I told him. "And add in an order of edamame as well, okay? See you soon." I hung up the phone and set it down next to my computer in case he called back for clarification of my food order. Poor guy. All things considered, he'd been pretty patient through my ongoing mental collapse. Cheerful, loyal, supportive. Even when I'd been nothing but a pain in the ass.

I decided to make a resolution. Once I proved this dream-Terra thing was all fake, all a delusion of my overworked brain, then I would move on with my life and take my relationship with Craig to the next level. He was a good, decent guy, and he loved me. I was lucky to have him. Sure, there weren't a lot of fireworks when we came together these days, but that was bound to happen eventually in any long-term relationship. The stupid hormones faded and you learned to simply cohabit with your best friend. Those people who always sought out new excitements and new relationships were just setting themselves up for a lifetime of heartache and pain. Yes, in the end it was much better to find a solid guy who paid his share of the bills on time and would never think of cheating on you.

Of course at that moment my brain decided to betray my best intentions with a flash-bake memory of Dawn's lips crushing mine, claiming my mouth as his own. I shivered as I couldn't help but relive the all-consuming fire sparked by his possessive touch—

those aforementioned "stupid hormones" instantly raging in an all-out conflagration of lust.

Okay, fine, there was *something* to be said about passion. But it never lasted. And it wasn't the be all and end all in a relationship. . . .

I forced my brain back on task and pressed upload, launching the final photo into cyberspace, wondering, not for the first time, where these pictures were actually being zapped. Perhaps the URL was linked to a sort of interdimensional Photo-Mart where Duske could pick them up in an hour? It seemed insane, of course, but hell, if they could send *people* to other worlds, I guess photos would be nothing.

The on-screen message confirmed my pictures had been sent. I leaned back in my computer chair, wondering what would happen next. Would Duske e-mail me back? Would he give me a call? Or would I never hear from him again and live out my whole life wondering at the validity of my memory of this adventure? If I had to pick, I'd go for door number three every time.

But life was no game of "Deal or No Deal," and I didn't get to choose my destiny. A moment later the whole apartment building started to shake, just as Luna had the night before. Flashes of lightning sliced through the air and my stomach rolled as I swam in and out of a blurry, dizzy consciousness.

Finally, just as before, the darkness came and oblivion gripped me with invisible hands.

Oh God, here we go again.

SEVEN

I open my eyes. At least this time I know what to expect, though that doesn't really make the experience any more comforting. A tiny room. Video screens on the four walls, ceiling and floor, all still swirling in a nauseating kaleidoscope of color. Dark glasses on my eyes. Yup, I'm back.

I smack the wall with the palm of my hand, annoyed beyond belief. I can't believe they dragged me back to this hellhole yet again. At least they could have waited till Craig showed up with dinner. Not that I care about the calories; I'm more concerned with the fact that he's going to think I took off on him again. I imagine him showing up at my door, vegetarian goodies in hand, only to have no one answer the intercom. How long will he wait before giving up? He'll probably end by breaking up with me. I wouldn't blame him if he did, either. I mean, how can I even explain what's happened in a manner that he could possibly begin to believe?

I shake my head, ripping off my glasses. I've got bigger things to worry about than a boyfriend's disappointment, and I need to concentrate on those. Say, for example, the interdimensional travel I just experienced a moment ago. There's no way I can pretend this is all some kind of weird dream anymore. Whatever's happening to me, it's all real, and I need to deal with it and figure out a way back home. I do not want to be stuck here in Terra for any reason, and I don't want to be dragged back and forth at someone else's whim.

I push the button in front of me and the booth's front panel slides open with a high-pitched beep. Stepping out into the hallway, I find Duske standing there, right where I left him. How long have I been gone, Terra-time-wise? Is it like Narnia in reverse, where twenty-four hours on Earth pass in just a few minutes here? I glance down at myself. I'm still wearing the same dress I wore when I entered the booth. The necklace is back around my neck. And a surreptitious sniff at my armpits tells me I can't have been inside that sweatbox for twenty-four hours. There's definitely something slippery with the way time's working here.

Duske bows low. "Welcome back, Skye," he says with a flourish of his hand. "It's lovely to see you again, my dear."

I scowl. I'm not buying his pleasantries this time around. "I'd love to say the same," I counter. "But really, I've got to tell you, I'm not very happy about being dragged back. I was just about to have dinner with my boyfriend and I've got a ton on my plate at work tomorrow. I simply don't have time to take any more field trips." I cross my arms under my breasts and throw him an annoyed look. "I mean, I took your photos like you asked. I uploaded them into the system. So, how about you fulfill your end of the bargain and let me go back to my real life?" I can't believe how confident and cool I sound, considering on the inside I'm totally freaking out.

Duske smiles patronizingly. "My dear, dear Skye," he coos. "I'm so sorry if I've upset your dinner plans. But I did warn you. Your services are needed at my Moongazing seminar two nights from now. There will be Indys from all over Terra gathered in the Luna Park Auditorium and waiting to hear all about Earth. It will be our biggest, best presentation to date, and I need you there."

"But why?" I demand. "Why do you need *me?*"

"Didn't we already go over all of this?" Duske asks. "You are Terra's first ever ambassador from Earth. You're the only Earthling to ever pass through the interdimensional curtain and visit our little world. Who better to explain the wonders of Earth than a girl who has spent her whole life there?"

"I see your point," I say, trying to be reasonable. "But I don't think you see mine. I didn't ask for this gig, and I don't have time to take it. I'm sure there are a billion alien-abducted, *X-Files* freaks on Earth that would simply love an opportunity to travel between worlds and give motivational speeches. I'm simply too busy. I've got a huge deadline at work and my boss is ready to kill me if I don't make it."

"Yes, yes, you and your important job," Duske says. He's wearing a slight sneer. "Aren't you a video game designer or something?"

I can feel my face heat, which only serves to annoy me further. I can't stand when people make light of my career. Just because I create fun and games full time doesn't mean my responsibilities and deadlines are frivolous, too. I take my design work as seriously as any doctor would take his patients, and yet everyone I know believes I simply fiddle around with a joystick for a living and that it's fair game to tease me about or simply deem unimportant in the grand scheme of life. Sure, I'm not literally saving lives on the operating table, but consumers will find relaxation, joy, and stress relief when they log in to any game. That will cut down on their ulcers and high blood pressure and perhaps save them from that surgeon's knife in the future. But try to tell anyone that and they'll just start laughing. Whatever.

"Look, whether you respect my career or not is moot," I retort. "We're talking about my life here, not some game played for your amusement."

Duske's lips twist, as if he's trying to suppress a smile. I glower at him. What the hell does he find so funny? Then he shakes his head and clears his throat. "I know, I know," he says, placing a hand on my shoulder. I shrug it away, not wanting him to touch me. "It's a great inconvenience for you to be here. I understand."

"Yes. It is. And I'd like to be sent home." I look back to the Moongazing booth. "So, tell me how this thing can zap me to Earth and I'll be on my way."

"Look. I understand your time is valuable. I do. So, what if I agreed to compensate you for it? Would that make things better?"

"Compensate?" I look at him skeptically. "What would I do with Terran money?"

"Play Monopoly?" he suggests. Then he laughs. "Just

kidding. I'd give you Earth dollars, of course. American currency. We've been farming Earth for quite some time now. Made some investments, started a few corporations even. We've even started introducing Terran technology to your world. You lot are so far behind us it's like introducing the abacus to apes. No offense."

"None taken. So, you want to pay me to speak at your seminar? How much are we talking about here?" Not that I can really afford to take the time off work for mercenary reasons, but I have to admit, a freelance project will really help out with this month's rent. And this guy seems pretty well off.

Duske rubs his chin with his forefinger and thumb. "Hm," he says thoughtfully. I narrow my eyes. He's going to try to lowball me, isn't he? Probably offer me like a hundred bucks or something. Well, no, thank you. I'm not about to get in trouble at work, not to mention screw up my relationship with my boyfriend for a mere—

"One million dollars."

I stare at him, eyes wide, doubting my ears, working to stop my jaw from dropping to the floor. Did he just say what I thought? No, that was impossible. And yet . . .

"Does that seem too low?" Duske asks, cocking his head. "Hm. How about a million five, then?"

"One and a half million," I repeat slowly. "In U.S. dollars?" I had to make sure he wasn't confusing our currency with Japanese Yen or anything.

"Yes. American money. We could deposit it directly into your account so that when you return to Earth it will be waiting for you."

I give up on the jaw, let it drop. A million dollars? A

fucking million dollars? Are you serious?" I have to ask. "You'd really give me over a million dollars just for speaking at your convention?" My mind greedily races with the possibilities a million dollars could afford me. Finally buying that condo. In a doorman building. With an elevator. And a balcony. Laundry in the unit itself. Well, New York . . . perhaps the laundry is out of reach.

Duske shrugs. "Sure, why not? It's a good investment for me. Spending Earth dollars, of which I have many, to earn real money here on Terra. You convince a few families to purchase Earth-relocation packages and I'll be a rich man here on my own world. You scratch my back, I'll scratch yours."

My mind whirs as I try to make my decision. A million and a half dollars! And all he's asking for is two days of my life. Sure, I'm supposed to get back to work to finish up the game, but what's two more days when I'm already so behind? I can just go back and work twenty-four-seven for the next couple of weeks. Drink a ton of coffee and Diet Coke and skip sleep. I'll have plenty of time to finish things before our official launch, and I can go buy a killer dress for the launch party. . . .

If he's telling the truth about the payoff that is. It's very possible, I suppose, that he's making this offer up to appease me and doesn't plan to follow through. How do I know I can trust him? How can I be sure that the money will be waiting for me?

But, a million dollars! Maybe it's worth gambling for.

Duske gestures for me to follow him down the hall. "I'll take you to your suite," he says. "I'm sure you'd like to shower and change."

It's then that I realize I have very little choice in the

matter. Whether I accept his money or not, it seems there's no way he's going to send me back to Earth until I give my little speech at his seminar. And arguing with him about it may only cause the monetary offer to be rescinded. All in all, it seems best to play along—at least for now. After all, what alternative do I have? It's not like I can just click my heels three times. (Though, how cool would that be if I could?)

I tune back in, resigned to accept my fate. At least temporarily.

"And I do apologize," Duske is saying, "but I must insist you remain in your assigned room until after the convention. It's too dangerous for you to be wandering out and about in Luna Park. Those vile Eclipsers may try to kidnap you again to further their pathetic rebellion." He snorts, making it clear what he thinks of them.

The Eclipsers. In all of this craziness I'd nearly forgotten them. Glenda and her gang claim they are the ones who dragged me to this godforsaken world in the first place. What did they think when they arrived at Dawn's house and found it empty? Discovered the framed photo of Mariah lying shattered on the ground? Did they think I'd been kidnapped? Or did they conclude I'd taken off willingly? Do they know I'm with Duske now? Or do they assume I jumped back to my own world, unwilling to play their reindeer games?

My mind flashes to Dawn's scowling face. At least now he can go around telling the Eclipsers that he was right and they were wrong. Especially once they hear that I'll be speaking at an actual pro-Moongazing seminar in two days. He'll believe that his precious Mariah betrayed the revolution a second time.

I frown and hasten my step to match Duske's long

strides. Well, there is nothing I can do about that. Had I really been Mariah, I'm sure things would have been different. But they dragged out the wrong girl. Not my fault. I'm not a revolutionary. Not a rebel leader. So really, what good can I do if I stay down below in their cave world and join their rebellion?

Still, my guilty brain lectures, you didn't have to go as far as to start helping the other side. I mean, what if the crazy guy with the placard is right? What if traveling between worlds—Moongazing—is a dangerous, even deadly, pastime that will ultimately destroy those who practice it? What if my promoting Earth travel to the masses ends up the equivalent of leading sheep to the slaughter? Am I selling out the people of Terra for a million dollars?

That's stupid, I tell myself. Why would the government fund and promote a program that would lead to the deaths of their citizens? Totally counterproductive. Besides, I've 'Gazed twice now. I feel completely fine. And the great Mariah herself, the one they're all in love with, is a 'Gazer. They're probably just annoyed that she left them high and dry to go live a better life. Sure, that was pretty shitty of her, but it doesn't make the program deadly and dangerous.

Swallowing my doubts, I follow my host down the hall and up another flight of red carpeted stairs, gripping the golden banister. At top of the stairs, we come to a door. Duske presses the sensor with his thumb and it slides open. I step over the threshold into an elegant, well-lit room. It's done up in gold and mauve, a canopy bed draped with gauzy curtains serving as its centerpiece. There's a flat-panel TV hanging on the far wall of the room, several armchairs and coffee tables, and a sliding glass door leads out to a balcony. The room smells of rose petals, and dozens of flickering candles on every surface give it a sparkly glow.

"I trust this will suit your needs?" Duske asks.

I nod. It's tempting to be swept away by the luxury, but at the same time I can't get the Dark Siders out of my head. Those sick, mutated people. Their stores of moldy bread and tiny cavelike dwellings. Their desperate poverty and helplessness makes this opulence seem obscene. How can people be content to live like this when they know others are suffering one level down?

"Yeah, I guess it'll do," I reply, glancing over at my host. I catch him staring at me, his eyes fixated on my chest. I squirm, suddenly uncomfortable. The guy really is quite the perv. I need to get him out of here before he gets the wrong idea or something. "Um, did you need anything else from me?" I ask, lamely.

He smiles. "Only if you want it, my dear."

Gross. As If I'd touch this guy with a ten foot pole. I mean, sure he's good-looking, but he's so slimy. And he's dragged me here against my will. Does he really think that will win my affections or turn me on? No freaking way.

"I, um, think I'm all set," I say, bobbing my head enthusiastically, hoping he'll get the hint. "In fact, I think I'll take a nap before dinner. I'm pretty beat." I fake a yawn to make my excuses more realistic. "So I'll, uh, talk to you later, okay?"

I watch as annoyance shadows Duske's face for half a second; then he shakes it away and offers me a large smile. "Very well, Sister Skye," he says, bowing at the waist. "I will leave you then. If you get hungry, just activate the intercom and Brother Thom will bring up some supper." He backs out of the room and the door slides closed behind him, clicking shut with a high-pitched beep. Instinctively, I try to reopen it. Locked, of course.

I wander around the room, examining everything, but find nothing out of the ordinary. It looks just like any other luxury bedroom you might find on Earth. I switch on the television and am surprised to see *Casablanca* pop onto the screen. Bogart's telling Bergman they'll always have Paris. I watch, fascinated. It's kind of creepy how alike Earth and Terra are. Pop culture, movies, coffeehouse chains. Were the two worlds once exactly the same until one day there was a decision to make—a red button to press or not? Could one fateful action have caused Terra to spin off its projected course and onto a skewed path of apocalyptic destruction? But then how did my Earth manage to avoid it? Or is Terra's underground wasteland something we have to look forward to in our future? And if Terra is a future Earth, why are they still reliving our past culture hundreds of years later?

I wonder what Terrans think of Earth when they arrive. When they first open their eyes and see sunshine, grass, flowers, dogs, cats—everything that makes Earth's present reality superior to their own. When they first see the mighty ocean waves crashing to shore. When they watch their first bald eagle soaring majestically through the sky. When they climb up the Empire State Building and gaze down at their vast new world. When they realize they can now live aboveground without getting sick. It must be thrilling, but at the same time incredibly frightening. Are they forming their own close-knit Terran societies as American immigrants have done for centuries, carving out small neighborhoods to inhabit and keeping with their own traditions? Or are they adapting, blending in with the rest of us, making Earth friends, marrying Earth people?

I find myself laughing. Homeland Security is so worried about closing the Mexican borders. Imagine if they knew there were interdimensional illegal aliens living among us!

In a way, Moongazing makes a lot of sense. Especially if the Terran world really is as overcrowded as Duske claims. If you have the option, why not emigrate to a better world? And if they bring all their superior technology with them, we'll benefit from the relocation as well.

So then, why are the Eclipsers against it? Are they just jealous because they're not on the guest list? Or could there be something more sinister lying beneath the surface of this alternative reality trip?

It's all too much to think of now, so I continue my exploration of my room, opening the wardrobe door and revealing a closet full of clothes. Anxious to get out of my beautiful but scratchy evening gown, I select a black cotton tunic and a pair of leggings and change clothes. Much more comfortable. I'm just slipping on a pair of black boots when a knock sounds at the door.

"Come in," I call, wondering who it could be.

Brother Thom steps in, a silver tray of covered dishes in his hands. He sets the tray down on the dresser and pulls off several covers to reveal a meal of a burger and french fries, with a piece of chocolate cake for dessert. At first I'm about to protest the nonvegetarian selection, but then remember there's no meat here on Terra.

Must be soy or something. My mouth waters as the rich smell fills the room. I got pulled back to Terra before dinner and now I'm starving.

"Thanks," I say gratefully, walking over to the table and selecting a long fry. I pop it in my mouth. Salty and delicious.

"You are most welcome, Sister," Thom says in an overloud voice. "I hope you enjoy it." Then he throws a furtive glance around the room and lowers his tone to a barely audible whisper. "Don't worry," he hisses. "We've got a plan in place. They'll come for you soon. Get you out."

Uh, what? I squint at him, swallowing my fry, my mouth suddenly dry as cotton. "What? Who?"

"Brother Dawn should never have left you unattended like he did. They must have injected you with some kind of nanotracker to have found you so quickly. Most unfortunate. But do not fret, Sister. We will free you soon."

I stare at him, my mind racing. This does not make any sense. Unless the butler is secretly playing for the other team. "Wait. Are you . . . an Eclipser?" I whisper back.

Thom releases a frustrated sigh. "You have not regained your memories, I see," he says, sounding vastly disappointed.

Great. Here we go again. "You think I'm Mariah," I conclude.

"You *are* Mariah," the butler corrects. "Whether you know it or not."

"But Duske said—"

"Don't you get it? Duske is trying to trick you. He's

taking advantage of your amnesia to further his vile agenda."

I close my eyes, wishing I could just somehow zap myself home. Now I'm back at square one. How the hell can I know who to trust—the guy who calls me by my real name and has offered me over a million Earth dollars to speak at his seminar? Or the determined, passionate rebels who swear that I'm someone I'm not and insist that Duske's up to no good?

"You're going to have to try to trust us for a bit," Thom says. "Your life will depend on it." He turns and heads to the exit. At the door he turns back to me. "It might be better if you cut up your burger before taking a bite," he suggests cryptically. He leaves before I can ask why, the door sliding closed and locking behind him.

Alone again, I stare down at the plate of food, wondering what he meant. The way he said it, it has to be a hint or code of some sort. Curious, I grab the butter knife on my plate and slice into the patty. The knife strikes something hard and I pull apart the burger, discovering a tiny, plastic, thimblelike device.

As I slip it on my thumb the thimble constricts, wrapping tightly around the digit like a second skin. It's then I notice it has its own fingerprint. I look over at the sensor on the wall, the one I need a magic thumb to operate. Could this thimble be what I think?

Hunger forgotten, I walk to the door and press the thumb against the sensor, praying it won't set off an alarm or something. This wouldn't be easy to explain if someone comes to investigate.

Nothing happens.

I try again, rubbing the thimble over the sensor. Still

nothing. Just as I'm about to give up, the door suddenly beeps and the LCD indicator by the sensor goes from red to green. My eyes widen.

I'm free.

The door slides open, revealing my exit. I slip outside, peering up and down the corridor to make sure the coast is clear. There's no one in sight.

I tiptoe down the hall, not sure exactly where I'm going or what I'll do when I get there. Maybe I can find the Moongazing rooms and figure out how to make them work so I can go home. Leave this nightmare world forever. Of course, Duske might try to come after me. He obviously knows where to find me on Earth, and he'd probably be very angry I slipped away before speaking at his seminar. But maybe there'd be a way to hide. Head out to California or someplace even more obscure. Change my name, become someone else. Find a village in Nepal, a shack on a Costa Rican beach. Somewhere, anywhere that he couldn't track me down and drag me back to Terra.

I freeze as I suddenly hear Duske's voice. I flatten my body against the wall and peer into the room next to me. It's some sort of library, stacked floor to ceiling with dusty tomes. Duske's sitting at a large desk, speaking into something that appears to be some kind of videophone. Luckily, he doesn't seem to be aware of my presence.

I prepare to slink away in the other direction, but his words make me pause.

"Yes, she's here," he is saying. "Oh, indeed, it worked brilliantly, Brother. Kudos to you and your crew. The new memories have bonded completely with her psyche. She's utterly convinced she's from Earth. . . . Yes!

Even after those pathetic rebels tried their damnedest to tell her otherwise. . . . I know! I would have loved to see the look on their faces when their precious Mariah insisted she's some random girl from Earth." He chuckles, a low guttural sound that makes me suddenly feel sick.

My heart slams against my chest as my whole world skids off its axis. My stomach twists and for a moment I'm sure I'll throw up. I can't believe this. The one person who said he believed me—who swore up and down that he knew me as Skye—has just admitted to his crony that he, like everyone else, thinks I'm her. Mariah.

Oh my God.

"She even logged in willingly!" I hear him continue. "Thought she was going home! . . . I know, I know. It's priceless. . . . Oh yes, of course I recorded it. I plan to play it at the seminar. Wait till the Indys see a video of the great Mariah Quinn entering a Moongazer booth. They'll be begging us for the opportunity to hand over all their possessions for a chance to play. Your plan was brilliant. Utterly brilliant. I couldn't be more pleased."

He pauses as the other voice on the video screen speaks. I strain to hear. "So, what are you going to do with her after the seminar?" it asks. "Send her back? Let her burn out on her own?"

"No way," Duske says. "It's too dangerous. As we've learned from this experiment, as long as the people believe Mariah Quinn is alive, they'll continue with their silly little revolution. Natural burnout will take too long, and I don't want to have to deal with the possibility of those pesky Eclipsers pulling her out over and over again, convinced they'll eventually get her to join them. It's expensive and irritating."

"So, what are you going to do?"

"Early retirement," Duske says. He makes a throat-slitting gesture, and I suddenly realize this particular package probably doesn't come with a pension plan.

I cringe. I've got to get the hell out of here.

I sprint back down the hall, fast as my legs can carry me, no idea where I'm going. I bank a left, then a right. I scurry down stairs and around corners. But no matter where I turn, I can't seem to locate an exit. The place is a maze and I have no idea how to get out.

"Psst."

I whirl around at the whisper, praying it's friend and not foe. A lone figure, encased entirely in black and wearing a black mask and hood, stands in the middle of the hallway. I can tell from her curvy silhouette she's a woman, but all that's exposed are radiant green eyes. She puts a finger to her lips, stilling the questions on my tongue. Then she motions for me to follow.

Should I? What if it's just another trap? But what choice do I have? To stay here is to die. At least if I leave now I'll be able to come up with a plan B. Find Moongazer Station and get back to Earth.

Duske's words flash through my mind.

She's utterly convinced she's from Earth.

Could it be true? Could my whole life be some kind of lie? Implanted memories, he said. Is that even possible? Could everything I know and love be just an illusion? Impossible. And yet . . .

I nod to the figure, realizing I have little choice but to trust her. Maybe she can lead me to Glenda and the rest of the Eclipsers. Maybe they can give me a better idea of what's going on.

The woman bows her head, then turns and starts slinking down the hallway, her steps light and silent like a cat stalking its prey. She pauses at every turn, peering around each corner before motioning me to move forward. She has a Japanese-style sword—a katana of some sort—slung from a utility belt low on her waist. I hope we don't need to use it.

We scramble up a flight of stairs, then another and another. Are we running to the roof? Finally the figure stops climbing, pulls off a glove, and studies her hand. I realize she's got some kind of map scribbled onto her palm. Thank God for that.

She reaches into her pocket and pulls out a plastic thimble identical to the one Thom hid in my soy burger, and slips it onto her thumb. She presses it against the sensor and, after a moment's pause, the LCD flashes green and the door slides open. She motions for me to follow her inside.

It's a bedroom similar to the one I'd been kept prisoner in, and there the figure reaches under the bed and pulls out a length of rope and a few metal clips. She heads over to glass sliding doors leading out to a balcony. I watch, unsure, as she detaches a small black box from her utility belt and presses it against the door. She pushes a button and without warning the glass explodes. I duck, hands over my face, to avoid being cut. When I look up, the glass barrier is gone and there's clear passage leading out to the balcony.

"That will have tripped the alarm," the woman informs me, speaking for the first time in a low voice. "We have to hurry."

She steps over the jagged glass and out onto the balcony. There, she tosses one end of her rope over the side and clips the other to the banister. I watch, worried about what she's got planned. We must be four stories up.

She hands me what looks like a rock-climbing harness, and instructs me to slip it around my waist. Then she clicks me into the rope. "Climb over the balcony," she instructs. "And on my word, jump."

I have little alternative. I do as she says, my toes curling against the safety of the balcony as I brace and try to psych myself up for the impending rappel.

My rescuer pauses for a moment, as if listening for something, then pulls the sword belt off her waist and wraps it around mine. "I thought you might like it back," she explains after I give her a confused look. Her voice reveals a smile I can't see under her mask. "I've been keeping it safe for you while you've been gone."

I look down at the sword, pull it halfway out of its scabbard. The blade flashes under the artificial light, almost giving off an otherworldly glow. Did this belong to Mariah? I caress the hilt and something inside me flashes with uneasy recognition. Have I worn these blades before? Somewhere? Sometime? In some other life? I remember the photo in Dawn's living room, and I shiver.

"Uh, thanks," I say, not quite sure what else to do.

The figure's eyes crinkle from under her hood, and I can't tell if she's smiling or holding back tears. "I love you, Mariah, my sister," she says. "Whatever happens, always remember that."

I open my mouth to speak, but the words die in my throat as a sudden pounding comes at the bedroom door. They've found us.

"I jammed the door signal," the woman tells me. "But it won't take them long to break through. You have to jump now."

I glance over the railing at the ground far beneath my feet. Unsure, afraid. "What about you?" I ask.

"Don't worry about me. Just jump, Mariah. I'll keep you safe. But you must go."

Desperation in her voice compels me to obey. I take a deep breath, send up a small prayer, close my eyes, then step off the balcony. A moment later, I open my eyes to find myself rappeling down the side of the mansion, my feet hitting the outer wall for a moment then shooting out again as my rescuer lets out the rope. I grip the cord tightly, my fingers burning, threatening to lose their grip.

Without warning, the rope suddenly goes slack. I tumble out of control, the ground flying up at my face at high speed. I reach out—a desperate, stupid attempt to cushion my fall—and land on my hand. My wrist gives way with a sickening crunch.

For a moment, I feel nothing. Then a sharp pain shoots through me and I'm forced to bite down on my lower lip to keep from screaming in agony. I grab at my wrist, pressing it against my stomach. It throbs in protest.

I look up to the balcony far above me, wondering what happened to the rope. The men must have broken through the door. They've likely got my rescuer and are in the process of dragging her away.

Her head appears for a brief moment. "Run, Mariah!" she screams down at me.

I don't wait for a second invitation.

EIGHT

I sprint across the lawn as fast as my legs can carry me, cradling my swollen wrist against my body, pain shooting through me at every step. I don't know where to go, what to do; I just know I have to keep moving. Because whoever got my rescuer is sure to come after me next.

I run down the streets, trying to remember the route to Luna Park. If I can only get there, find Moongazer Station, I could try to journey back to Earth on my own. But is that even the best plan? After all, Duske knows how to find me there. He knows where I live. Where I work. What's to stop him from coming to my world and killing me?

If Earth even is my world.

Find Dawn.

An inner voice, powerful and demanding, thrusts the solution to the forefront of my brain. I try to shake it away; after all, Dawn doesn't even like me. He thinks I'm his ex-girlfriend who betrayed him. But the thought persists. At the very least he can lead me to the

Eclipsers. To Glenda. Maybe she'll be able to tell me what the hell is going on and how I can get home.

I sprint around a corner and realize I've somehow found the outskirts of Luna Park. I pass the Park Terrace restaurant were Duske and I ate, the corner Starbucks, the bulletin boards advertising Moongazing. As I run, the neighborhood deteriorates. Finally, I come to Moongazer Station, in all its gaudy glory. I stop, panting hard. My wrist has now swollen to the size of a softball.

I give a longing glance at Moongazer Station, at a possible trip back to Earth, but then firm my resolve and instead locate the manhole cover Dawn showed me my first day on Terra: the "rabbit hole" leading to the Dark Side. I scramble to my knees and attempt to pry off the cover one-handed. It's not an easy task, but finally I manage to wrench it free, revealing the rickety metal ladder disappearing into the darkness. I crawl down the hole, pulling the cover over my head and beginning a one-handed descent. Rung after rung; I wince at every step, straining to see.

Finally, after what seems an eternity, I reach the bottom, jump down onto the metal floor. I blink a few times, my eyes adjusting to the darkness and dim track lighting, then suck in a deep breath. I'm safe. Well, sort of. Okay, probably not that safe at all. But the immediate threat is gone. I can stop running. Catch my breath. Figure out what to do next.

If only my rescuer had made it out, too. But, in a way, it seemed almost as if she expected to be caught. The way she looked at me. The fact she'd given me the sword. It was as if she knew it was a kamikaze mission.

And yet, she willingly sacrificed herself to get me out. Sacrificed her own life to save mine. Why? Because she thinks I'm Mariah?

I search my brain for some kind of memory, some dim recollection of another life. One where I'm a big-time rebel leader working hard to save her people from an oppressive government regime. It's no use. No matter how hard I try, I still feel like me—Skye Brown, video game designer from Manhattan. There's nothing inside me that remotely resembles any Mariah.

The Eclipsers are going to be so disappointed.

I trudge down the underground road, heading in the direction of the Dark Side city where I assume I'll be able to find Dawn. I'm exhausted, and searing pain burns my arm at every step. My kingdom for one of those hover bikes. The road is empty, silent save for the background whirring of the ventilation fans. I walk on.

Finally, after what seems like three forevers, I notice a twinkling light ahead. Relief floods me as I recognize the gates to the Dark Side. I made it. I approach the gate, pressing my thumb against the sensor, praying it will work.

The doors creak open, welcoming me like giant metal arms. I'm too exhausted to ponder the implications of the gate recognizing my thumbprint. I have to find Dawn.

I wander down the twisty antlike passageways until I step out into the town square. The place is bustling, as it was the first time, but a hush falls over the people as they recognize me. A moment later, I find myself engulfed by the crowd.

"Mariah! Are you okay?" asks a thin, middle-aged woman with missing front teeth and a second pair of lips.

"What did they do to you?" demands a salt-and-pepper-bearded man with three breasts.

"What happened to your wrist?" a young boy with one leg asks, pointing to my swollen arm.

I weakly hold up my good hand. "Please," I croak. "I need Dawn. Is he here?"

The crowd parts and Dawn approaches. His arms are crossed over his chest and his eyes pierce me. He stares me down, his full mouth set in a frown. He doesn't look happy to see me. At least, not as relieved as I am to see him.

"Dawn!" I cry, grateful to lay eyes on a familiar face. "Thank God I found you."

He stops in front of me, staring down with obvious disapproval. Then he pushes me away from the others. "So, you've decided to slum it again. Or have you been sent to spy on us for your new friend?"

"What? No! I—" My face falls as I realize he thinks I've sided with Duske again. Not that I blame him. In a way I did. At first, anyway. But, to my defense, I didn't know.

"Don't you think you've done enough, Mariah?" Dawn demands. "Can't you leave us well enough alone?"

"Please," I beg weakly. "They're . . . they're trying to kill me."

"I'd kill you myself if I didn't think death was too kind a punishment for a traitor like you. You—" He stops short, his eyes falling on the sword strapped to my waist. "How did you get that?" he demands.

I glance down at the weapon. "The woman who rescued me. She helped me escape Duske's house. She saved my life."

"Where is she now?"

I was afraid he'd ask that. "I don't know. They caught her . . ." I trail off, hanging my head. "I'm afraid she sacrificed herself for me."

"She's an idiot. You're not worth it."

Anger burns in my gut at his repeated condemnation. "Look," I say, incensed. I came all this way to find him. A million painful steps. How dare he treat me this way? "You can't blame me for crimes I don't even remember committing!"

He shakes his head wearily but doesn't answer.

"Dawn, she's hurt!" cries the bearded man. "You must heal her."

"Yes, Dawn. Mariah's hurt!"

The crowd takes up the cry for healing. Dawn releases a long sigh, then gently picks up my wrist in his large hands, lifting it to get a better view. I can't avoid a cry of agony as burning pain shoots up my arm. He runs a light cool finger across my wrist, closing his eyes.

"It's broken," he remarks without emotion. "Pretty badly, too, by the feel of it."

"It really hurts," I admit, a tear escaping the corner of my eye and dripping down my cheek. I hate crying, but the pain, along with the emotional stress and uncertainty, is too much.

Dawn pauses a moment, then seems to come to a decision. "Fine. Come inside. Let's see what I can do for you."

He lowers my wrist tenderly, as if wary of causing me any more pain. I meekly follow him through the crowd, out of the town square, and into the tunnel that leads to his little cave house. Once we're inside, he shuts the door behind us and motions for me to sit down on the futon. I sink down into the cushion, grateful to finally be off my feet.

"They were going to kill me," I repeat, half to myself and half to Dawn. He nods slowly and takes my arm and places it across his thigh. A small tingle tickles my stomach as I feel his heat against my bare wrist. His trousers are soft, cottonlike. His touch is careful. Gentle.

"Close your eyes," he instructs in a low voice. "And imagine something pleasant."

I do as he says, too weary to ask why. A moment later I feel his soft fingers trip up my arm, wispy and slow, trailing a warmth that relaxes and soothes. I try to do as he says, to think of something pleasant. For some reason all I can come up with is a fantasy of him taking me into his arms, carrying me into his bed, caressing my entire body as he's now caressing my wrist. Fingers first, then with lips, tongue.

A slash of pain jerks through me. My eyes fly open. Dawn has his own eyes closed as he grips my arm in his hands. I stare down at my wrist and watch with horrified fascination as the bone—the one that just a second ago must have been at a weird angle—slides back into place. The swelling is visibily retreating. My arm still hurts, yet at the same time I feel a strange, overwhelming peace washing over me, almost as if I've been drugged.

A moment later Dawn opens his eyes. He looks at me, his expression one of amused disapproval. "You cheated," he accuses. "You peeked."

I can feel my face heat. "That was amazing," I say. I lift my arm off his lap, flexing my fingers. My wrist still feels a bit stiff, but the bones have somehow knitted together, mended in a way that should have taken six weeks and a cast. "How did you do that?"

Dawn shrugs. "It's a long story. One you used to know." He rises to his feet. "While I was inside you . . ." He trails off, his face coloring a bit at his unintended implication. "Er, when I was working on you . . . I was able to locate the tracking nano they implanted in your bloodstream. That's how the government found you before, I guess. I believe I was able to disable it, but I'm going to activate the house scrambler as well. Just in case."

"House scrambler?"

"Electronic interference. Makes it tougher for the government to locate people. Tomorrow I'll take you to the Eclipsers and they'll likely be able to ensure that your nanotracker is deactivated for good."

"Thank you," I say, feeling awkwardly vulnerable. "I had no idea I was being tracked. When I went off with Duske, he tricked me. Said he knew I was from Earth. That he'd get me more asthma medication. I didn't mean to—I mean, I had no idea . . ." I sigh. "Basically I'm a big blind idiot stumbling around this world. I don't know where I am, who to trust."

Dawn waves a hand. "It's okay. I didn't mean to sound so harsh out there. I know you've lost your memories. It's just frustrating, you know?" He rakes a hand through his hair. "I look at you and I don't know whether to kiss you or kill you." He pauses for a moment, then shakes his head. "Anyway. Are you hungry?"

he asks. "I don't have much. Rations were cut again this week, surprise, surprise. But I have a few tins of beans. Some bread. Tea."

"I don't want to eat all your food," I hedge. But my stomach chooses that moment to betray my intended martyrdom with a loud growl. Dawn chuckles, a soft sweet sound that makes my stomach twist again. Not from hunger this time.

"It's okay," he says, reaching down to ruffle my hair. His fingers, scraping lightly against my scalp, send a tingly feeling down to my toes. What is it about this guy that makes me want him so? He's beautiful, yes. But there's something more. Some kind of deep connection I can't begin to explain. Could I really have suppressed memories of a past relationship buried somewhere deep inside my subconscious? It seems impossible. Yet, how else can I explain the deep longing inside me every time I catch a glimpse of his face?

Dawn heads over to the kitchenette, opening cabinets and pulling out drawers. "I have enough to spare. I just didn't want you to be expecting some kind of gourmet adventure. We Dark Siders don't exactly feast like they do in Luna Park." He sets a kettle onto an electric stove. "Then again, I'm pretty famous for my stone soup around these parts."

"Stone soup," I repeat with a giggle. "Sounds delish. I'd love a bowl."

"Then you, my dear, shall have one. Sit tight. Brother Dawn Grey, Dark Sider chef extraordinaire, is prepared to work his magic." He makes an exaggerated flourish and manages to drop the mixing bowl he's holding. It goes crashing to the floor. "Uh, yeah," he says, reaching down for it. "I meant for that to happen. You may think I'm a bumbling idiot, but really that was a vital part of my very complex and elaborate recipe."

I laugh, clapping my hands like a good audience member. "Of course it was, oh chef extraordinaire." I grin. "I must say, I'm extremely impressed so far, and am waiting with bated breath to see what kinds of wonders you will perform next."

"Likely cutting my finger," Dawn chuckles. "But sometimes I like to mix things up with a burning-my-hand-on-the-stove number. I'm tricky like that."

I lean back into the couch, watching him as he bustles about the small kitchen, pulling out tins and pans, opening packets and adding water. He walks over to the bookshelf and pulls the lone book from the top shelf. I realize it's not a real book at all, but a hollowed-out replica containing a secret compartment. He reaches in and pulls out a small sack, holding it up with a shy smile. "Black market herbs," he says, his voice rich with pride. "We just might have a feast yet."

"Awesome." I curl my feet up and under me, feeling warm and cozy for the first time since I got back to Terra. It seems hard to believe that less than an hour before I'd been running for my life. Under Dawn's protection, I feel completely safe.

Dawn wanders back to the stove, and a few minutes later a rich, spicy aroma permeates the cave house. "Smells delicious," I remark. Dawn tosses me a smile, then walks over to hand me a crude pottery mug containing tea. I take a sip, the sweet beverage warming my insides. "Mmm, thanks," I say, wrapping both hands around the warm cup.

He grins. "Not a problem." He walks back to the kitchen. "Dinner's ready."

"Woot!" I cheer. "Do you need any help?"

"Nah. I'm good." He scoops out ladles of soup into two bowls and brings them over to the coffee table. I dip my spoon into the broth and take a mouthful. My eyes widen at the taste. It's fabulous. Like nothing I've ever eaten. I take another bite as Dawn brings over a small loaf of bread on a plate and sets it before me.

"What is in this soup?" I ask. "It's great."

He beams, the smile bringing a light to his face, making me realize just how beautiful he really is. "Secret recipe," he brags. "It was always your favorite."

My enthusiasm dampens somewhat as reality is shoved back into central focus. I'm not on some first date with a handsome stranger. He believes I am his long-lost girlfriend. *That's* why he's being so sweet to me. Not because he likes me for who I really am.

"Do you really and honestly believe I'm Mariah?" I ask at last, deciding it is time to broach the subject, even if it does destroy the intimacy we're sharing. "I mean, couldn't there be some other explanation as to why I just look like her?" I have no idea what that explanation is, but there has to be one all the same, right?

Dawn swallows his mouthful of bread. "You don't just *look* like her," he corrects. "You sound like her. You smell like her. You walk and talk like her. You *are* her, whether you believe it or not." He takes a sip of tea. "I mean, just because someone has amnesia, it doesn't mean they're suddenly some different person altogether."

"But I don't have amnesia. I remember everything

about my life. Who I am, where I live, what I do. I have family and friends, and memories of birthday parties since I was five years old. If I'm Mariah, where did all that stuff come from?"

He shrugs. "A memory serum, most likely."

Oh. They have those here? I cringe, my mind flashing back to the dream I had a few nights before. The one where I was running through a tunnel, pursued by uniformed men. I didn't know where I was or who I was or what I was doing there. Then they caught me, pinned me down, injected me with some kind of concoction. Could that have been . . . ?

No. I shake my head. I refuse to believe it. There's no way everything I know and love has somehow been implanted into my brain. My memories are real. My family. My friends. I absolutely refuse to believe they've sprung from some kind of total-recall cocktail.

"Tell me about your life on Earth," Dawn suggests, bringing me back to the conversation.

"Okay," I agree. "Well, I'm twenty-four years old and I live in the city of Manhattan. Best city on Earth, really. It's got everything you could ever want." I take a sip of tea. "I'm a video game designer by trade. I'm developing this really amazing virtual world we call RealLife. I think it's going to revolutionize video games as we know them." I shrug. "Well, who knows, but I'm pretty proud of it. My boyfriend, Craig, says that I . . ."

I stop as I catch Dawn's face. Hmm, maybe I shouldn't have mentioned Craig. Now the poor guy's going to think that not only did his precious Mariah betray him by going to Earth in the first place, but once there she hooked up with some random guy and has been having a grand old time banging away while he's been sitting around pining for her.

But what am I supposed to say? I've already told him I'm not Mariah.

"Sorry," I mutter, just because he looks so hurt.

He swallows hard. "It's okay. I need to hear it straight. Even if some of it isn't pleasant," he says. "What about your memories? Do you remember growing up on Earth?"

"Well, sure. I grew up in Boston, Massachusetts—that's about two hundred miles from New York. I have a mother and father, of course, though they've got the old Winnebago and are always off wandering through one national park or another these days. Oh, and I have a brother, too. But he and his wife are out in Colorado." I trail off, my brain going fuzzy at the edges. Why does my life story suddenly somehow seem so clichéd and stereotypical?

"Tell me a memory you have," Dawn suggests. "A real one. I want to hear about you and your experiences, not just a listing of profession and family tree."

"Right. Sure. Well, there was one time . . ." I stop. What story was I about to relate? I try to think of something funny, but I keep drawing a blank. I know we went cross-country as a family when I was seven, but I can't remember any of our specific adventures. I know I moved to Manhattan to go to NYU six years ago, but I can't seem to recall a good "one time I got so drunk that I . . ." story to tell. I remember everything about my life on Earth, yet suddenly it's all feeling like some foggy dream.

"Sorry," I say, shaking my head. "My brain's totally dead tonight. Too much stress most likely," I rationalize, pushing the frightening alternate possibility to the back of my brain. After all, having trouble recalling some cute family anecdotes doesn't necessarily mean my whole life was syringe-injected to prevent me from remembering that I'm truly a revolutionary leader who bailed on redeeming a postapocalyptic world.

Dawn reaches over to stroke my head, probably jumping to the same conclusion I'm trying to avoid. He wants nothing more than to believe my memories were indeed implanted. Fabricated. So, how do I convince him it's just not true?

Especially when I'm not quite sure of that myself.

"My life's not made up," I insist, knowing my argument sounds weak and unsubstantiated.

"Don't worry," Dawn says. "We'll get this whole mess figured out soon enough. Tomorrow we'll go visit the Eclipsers. I'll take you there this time—no more leaving you alone. They have doctors on staff. Maybe they can tell you what's going on in your head."

He lowers his hand to my cheek, caressing it with light, feathery fingers. I close my eyes, relaxing under his gentle touch, breathing in his musky scent, wondering if I should pull away, resist the tender advance. It feels so good. So right. And yet, I still have a boyfriend on Earth. Would this be considered cheating? Of course it would. Yet for some reason I can't seem to summon an appropriately guilty feeling. Maybe it's because right now life on Earth seems so distant and foggy, while this moment on Terra is richly detailed and real. The heat Dawn's touch stirs deep inside me is powerful, seductive, and impossible to resist.

I swallow back my hesitation and allow myself to submit to his touch, folding myself into him, hyperaware of his flushed skin against my own. He does not disappoint, wrapping his arm around me so I can cuddle my head in the nook between his shoulder and chest. He strokes my shoulder with a gentle, slow touch.

"Tell me about Mariah," I suggest, after a few moments of comforting silence. "Maybe it'll jog some memory or something." Now that I'm feeling warm and safe, I'm able to broach the topic without an overwhelming suffocating fear pounding through my brain.

Dawn's fingers pause for a moment, then continue their caress, weaving gentle threads of warmth through my entire body. It takes everything inside me not to literally purr.

"Mariah was passionate. Determined. Extremely intelligent. She rallied the Dark Siders effortlessly. She had an uncanny power to convince anyone to do anything, with just a quick smile or wink in their direction," he says. "Hell, she had me wrapped around her little finger."

"But you're angry with her now," I say, opening my eyes to study his expression. His face clouds and I can almost see the hurt wash over him.

"Yes, because you—sorry, she," he corrects. "It's so hard to look at you and say 'she.' " He shakes his head. "Because she—Mariah—betrayed us all. She who started the Eclipsers and the campaign for a better life for Dark Siders sold us all out to the Senate and abandoned us for a better life on Earth. The very night that should have been our ultimate victory became instead our worst nightmare. All thanks to her."

"I don't understand. What exactly happened?"

"I told you how Mariah started getting addicted to the 'Gazers the more she traveled back and forth from Earth. It happened slowly. I noticed small things at first. A few white lies as to where she'd been. I soon realized that she was out of control, running away to Earth every chance she could get. And the revolution—all the plans we had started putting into place—began to suffer from her absence."

"What did the other Eclipsers think?"

"They didn't know. Stupid me, I covered for her. I didn't want her to lose all she'd worked so hard to get. I told them she was sick. And she was, in a sense. So the Eclipsers pushed on without her, moving ahead with preparations for our Moongazing seminar sabotage. The idea was to incapacitate the guards and change the program—sending Mariah on stage to inform the gathered Indys of all the atrocities the Senate was performing right under their very noses." Dawn sighs. "But Mariah never made it to the seminar. That afternoon she made the jump to Earth and left us all with useless best-laid plans."

"Why couldn't someone else just get on stage and give the same spiel?"

"There was no one else. It had to be her," Dawn says. "After all, she was born of royal blood. Destined to become one of the Circle of Eight. Hearing the message from her would convince the Indys of its legitimacy much more than if one of us random Dark Side shmoes spouted off wild conspiracy theories."

"That makes sense, I guess," I say. "She's obviously a valuable commodity to both sides. I suppose that's why the Eclipsers want her back so badly."

Dawn nods. "The Eclipsers refused to believe that

Mariah 'Gazed of her own free will. They insisted she must have been tricked or forced to go by the Circle. And of course, because I was hiding the signs of her addiction, my explanation of what really happened fell on deaf ears."

"But how can you be sure? Maybe she was kidnapped or something."

"No," Dawn says firmly. "She went of her own accord. The morning before she disappeared, she came to my house. She told me she'd found happiness on Earth and begged me to come with her. She wanted me to go to Earth and start a new life." Dawn scowls. "I asked her how she was going to pay for this pilgrimage. Moongazing's not cheap, and she'd already used up most of her family's trust fund to start programs to aid the Dark Siders. She just smiled at me—this sick, sad smile—and said it was all taken care of. At the time I didn't know what she meant." He squeezes his hands into fists. "But that night, when the government soldiers swept in at the seminar and stopped us in our tracks, I realized the truth. There was only one way they could have been so prepared for us. Mariah sold them the information in exchange for her trip to Earth."

"Wow, that's horrible," I say, trying to imagine how such a betrayal must have stung. No wonder he's so bitter about his ex.

"Many good men and women died that night. And it set our rebellion back miles. Not to mention morale. We'd been working almost a year to set that night up. And it was over in one fell swoop because our great and glorious leader decided to betray us."

Something still didn't make sense. "But if Mariah did all this, why the hell do the Eclipsers want her back?"

"They don't believe it was her. Because I'd been hiding the signs of her addiction, they didn't believe me when I insisted on it. We got into a huge fight. I've tried to avoid them ever since. I wanted nothing to do with their insane quest to bring you back. It'd be better for everyone if you just rotted on Earth."

I wince, realizing he's gone back to using "you" to refer to Mariah.

"So, you see how it is," Dawn says. "How I sit here, with you mere inches away. And yet you're not here at all. I want to blame you for your crimes, yet I realize you don't remember committing them." He stares off into space, his eyes unfocused, uneasy, pained. "Is there any Mariah still inside, deep down? Or have the 'Gazers completely gutted your brain? Are you really here of your own accord? Or are you some sort of spy, sent by Duske to figure out what we're up to and betray us all over again?"

I frown. How could he think that of me? "Of course I'm not—"

Dawn waves a weary hand to silence my protest. "Don't bother," he says. "Even if you were a spy, what difference would it make? Even if I knew without a doubt that you had been sent here to destroy me, it wouldn't matter. To have you here, sitting by my side in my living room . . . I'm powerless to turn you away."

He hangs his head, staring at his hands. "I still love you. A part of me wants to believe you didn't have control over what you did. You were sick. If only I'd been able to help you when I first realized it. In many ways, this is all my fault."

He looks so lost and lonely; my heart wrenches in empathy. I reach over and thread my fingers through his, hoping he'll find some small comfort in my touch, since at this moment it's all I can give.

He looks down at my hand, strokes my thumb with his own. He closes his eyes and leans back, head against the sofa. "Do you know how many nights I've lain awake, too tormented by dreams of you to dare close my eyes and sleep? Wondering if I made the right decision by refusing to join you on Earth? We could have been rich, happy—maybe we would even have had children. But instead I gave that all up for an endless fight that we can never hope to win."

His regret sucks the breath from my lungs and I struggle to swallow and protest. "You don't really believe that," I argue. "You know, deep in your heart, that what you did was the only real choice. You chose the unselfish path. You refused to run away. To me, that seems noble, brave, good."

"Does it?" Dawn asks, his voice scarcely louder than a whisper. He looks over, instantly capturing my eyes with his own. They glow blue. "God, Mariah, it feels like I've waited an eternity to hear those words from your lips."

I lower my eyelids, the hopefulness radiating from his stare too much for me to take in. I don't know this man. I don't remember him at all. But his desperate words, his earnest eyes, his soft touch are able to capture me all the same. The power in his look is indescribable, melting my resistances, my willpower, my soul all in one foul blow.

The softness that brushes my lips is so light that at first it barely registers. Then there's added pressure. My eyes flutter open in surprise. Dawn presses his mouth against mine, lips caressing lips, eyes closed, face enraptured.

I close my eyes again, wondering what I should do. This is nothing like the angry kiss he stole in the alleyway. That kiss was one of violent passion, domination, control—hate, even. This kiss is different. A caress, a fearful tenderness, it's almost as if pressing too hard will cause me to vanish into thin air. My stomach twists as electrified sprites dance over every membrane, tickling me and sparking a fire low in my belly. He feels so good. Smells so sweet. His lips are tender. Worshipful, almost.

No, this is not a kiss of desire; this is a kiss of someone in love.

But not someone in love with me.

Sick and disgusted, I jerk away, pushing past him to rise to my feet. My knees buckle and I'm forced to take a moment to steady myself before taking another step away from the seductive scene. When I've found some semblance of my center, I turn to face him, looking down to get his reaction to my rejection. Guilt stabs my heart as I catch the pain in his eyes.

He doesn't move. He doesn't protest. He doesn't even question why. He just stares up at me, devastated.

And it's my fault.

But it's for the best.

"Dawn . . ." I start, trailing off, not even sure how to begin. I mean, how do I get him to understand? Deep inside, with every fiber in my body, I want nothing more than to leap back on that futon couch and throw myself at him with wild abandon. To kiss him senseless, claim his mouth as mine, and never let go. But it's wrong, wrong, wrong, wrong, wrong.

"Dawn," I start again, swallowing back the lump the size of a basketball that's formed in my throat. "I'm so sorry, but this isn't right. You know it's not, deep down. After all, you don't want me. You want Mariah. And even if in some crazy way I was once her, I'm not right now. I'm Skye Brown and we . . . well, we barely know each other."

Even as the words spill from my lips, I know that I'm protesting too much. After all, even though I barely know anything about Dawn, the connection between us is undeniable. There's a bond so strong it feels dangerous. Which is why, I remind myself, it's best to stay aloof. At least until we figure out what's going on.

Because if I'm not Mariah—which, of course, I know I'm not—that means someone else is. And if I let myself succumb to Dawn's advances, fall for him and allow myself to care, then the real Mariah could someday come back to reclaim Dawn as her own. And then where will that leave me, the one who freely gave away her heart and soul to a man who loved her only because he thought she was someone else?

I shake my head. It's better to resist.

"You're right," Dawn agrees at last, a slight quivering of his lower lip giving away his unhappiness. "Of course you're right." He rises from the couch, stiff and slow, and heads to a small cabinet at the far end of the living room. He pulls it open by its handle and grabs a pillow and blanket from a shelf. He presents them to me. "It's late," he says. "Let's call it a night. Go ahead and take my bed. I'm fine out here on the couch."

I take the pillow and blanket from him. "Don't be silly," I protest. "I can sleep on the couch. I don't want to take your bed."

"I want you to have it," Dawn says, in a voice that leaves no room for argument.

"Okay, thanks," I say, giving in. I gather up the bedding and head into the adjoining room. Like the rest of the apartment, it's a small cave—and there's no room for anything but the full-sized mattress on the ground. I wrap the blanket around me and lay my head on the slightly musty-smelling pillow. Once still, I can hear Dawn in the next room, still shuffling around.

An ache of emptiness fills my stomach and a small fear twists up my spine. If only I could call out to him. Invite him into the bed. Not for some tawdry sexual encounter. No, at the moment I just want to curl up in his strong arms and let him cuddle me to sleep.

I force my mind away from his imagined warmth. It isn't fair to lead him on. To make him hope for a future that we cannot share. I have to be strong for the both of us. And tomorrow, we'll figure things out. Somehow.

I close my eyes and slow my breathing, begging for sleep to take me quickly. The goddess of slumber ignores my pleas and so I lie awake, in the dark cave bedroom, and content myself to just listen. Listen to Dawn collapse on the futon, listen to him toss and turn. Listen to his breathing slow until he finally falls into a restless sleep. Listen to him cry out, as if in pain, over a nightmare from which he can't awake.

And through it all, I lie still, resisting the temptation to crawl out of bed and rouse him from his nocturnal terror. To comfort him and tell him everything will be okay. That he's just having a dream.

"Mariah!" he cries out, anguished and uncensored in sleep. "Oh God, please Mariah!"

I sigh and roll over, pulling the covers over my head, feeling helpless and sad and oh so alone.

NINE

As the name implies, there's no sunlight down here in the Dark Side to draw me gradually into wakefulness. Instead, a nudge at my arm, a presence over my bed, snaps me awake. I open my eyes and find Dawn standing above me, dressed in a black jacket with a high collar, a tight black T-shirt cutting across his chest, and a pair of low-slung black pants hugging his lean hips. He looks fresh and awake, as if he's been up for hours. Maybe he has.

"I'm sorry to wake you," he apologizes, "but the Eclipsers are asking for you. There's a major event scheduled for tonight that they've been organizing, and they're hoping to get the day's business squared away first, so they can finish up the party plans."

"What . . . time is it?" I ask. Besides the artificial light streaming in from the living room, there's no indication. It could be midnight. It could be high noon. Or somewhere in between.

Dawn glances at the watch on his wrist. "Five o'clock," he says.

"It's . . . early." Unless time in Terra does not work the same way it does on Earth.

"Actually, it's late. Five in the evening."

I sit up in bed, shocked. "I slept all day?" I ask, rubbing the sleep from my eyes.

"You slept two days. Nearly twenty hours. But you looked so peaceful, lying there. I didn't want to wake you until I absolutely had to."

I can't believe I've been out for so long. Though, I guess it's not surprising. After all, it's not like I was getting much shut-eye back on Earth for the last few months. My body must have just collapsed. Thank goodness it picked a place where I was safe. At least, I think it's safe here.

"Did they come looking for me?" I ask. "Duske and his men, I mean."

Dawn shakes his head. "We haven't seen signs of them. I'm sure they'll be here soon, though. Which is why we need to get you together with the Eclipsers so we can discuss our strategy. Then we can get you settled back into your old house. No one will find you there."

"I have a house?" I ask, surprised. Alternate reality real estate. Obviously Mariah was more efficient at saving up that old down payment than I've been. I wonder what it looks like. Is it a simple cave like Dawn's place? Or something completely different? Will stepping inside jog any revealing memories of another life? Or will it seem, as everything else in this world, completely foreign to me?

"Of course you have a house." A smile plays at the

corner of Dawn's lips. "Did you think you were home-less? Or that you lived with me, perhaps?"

"I . . . well, I guess I just never thought about it."

"You have a very pretty apartment, well hidden in an old, abandoned building, deep underground in Stratum Three. It's small, of course. But you've done an excellent job making it homey and cozy."

"Well, I can't wait to see it." I think, anyway. Or maybe not. I mean, homey house or no, the last thing I want is to be left alone in some abandoned apartment building deep underground in a postapocalyptic reality. Unless Dawn would stay with me. I wonder if he would. Would that be weird of me to ask?

I shake my head. Time for those questions later. First I must meet with the Eclipsers, who will finally be able to provide some answers as to what the hell is going on here. I hope, anyway. Then again, they may be too busy trying to mess with my brain like everyone else, trying to get me to remember this supposed life I led as Mariah. Dawn even mentioned doctors. Ugh. I'm *so* not going to let some stranger in a white coat who claims to be an MD mess with my brain, not at the risk of me losing my real identity and being tricked into thinking I'm the person they wish I was.

She's utterly convinced she's from Earth.

I angrily push Duske's words to the back of my brain and firm my resolve. I'll go to the Eclipsers' meeting, hear what they have to say, ask my questions, then petition to be sent back home to Earth once and for all. Keep a low profile for a few weeks, until Duske and his men have given up looking for me, then go on with my real life and put this nightmare behind me. Renew my relationship with Craig, launch my video game—hell, I might even go try to visit my parents out at whatever national park they're currently trekking around in.

One thing's for sure, this whole adventure has really made me see how great my life is back on Earth. It's so easy to fall into a pattern of unhappiness. To become bored and disenchanted and wish for more than you've been given. But now, having been taken away from everything I've known and loved and thrust into a nightmare from which I can't awaken, I am starting to realize how much I love my little life in New York. Wandering around Central Park, hand in hand with Craig on warm Saturday afternoons. Sipping wine with friends at that tiny Moroccan bar on Seventieth and Columbus. Dancing the night away at Luna down in the East Village. Even curling up under my aunt's homemade quilt in my cozy little studio on a cold winter's night. They're simple pleasures and joys I've taken for granted as I've gotten bogged down with work and stress. I need to start appreciating these things. Be happy for the good things that I've got.

But first I have to figure out a way home.

What will the Eclipsers say when I ask to go? They'll be disappointed, I'm sure. But they'll understand, right? I'll simply explain that no matter how much they wish I was Mariah, I'm not, and that they're just going to have to continue fighting their revolution without me. I mean, what can they really expect from me anyway? Charity only goes so far. And this isn't throwing a couple of quarters in a jar to help save polar bears from global warming. They're asking me to undergo a complete identity transplant and lead a revolution that I don't know anything about. Quite a lot to ask of a girl, no?

Dawn shows me the bathroom and explains how to turn on the shower. There's only cold, rusty water drizzling from the showerhead, but really, that's not a hell of a lot different from what I'm used to in Manhattan. I wash my hair quickly, thankful they at least have sweet-smelling shampoos and soaps. From the black market, Dawn explained when he handed them to me moments before. He evidently went out and purchased some essential supplies while I slept, saying he wanted me to at least have a few comforts to wake up to. The fact that he did that, obviously at great expense, makes the soaps smell even sweeter and the cold shower almost pleasant. He really is a great guy. So sweet and thoughtful. Mariah's a fool to have left him.

After bathing, I wrap myself in a threadbare towel, suddenly realizing I don't have any clean clothes to change into. My one outfit is soiled and caked with blood, reeking of sweat from my narrow escape. I'm so not interested in putting that back on.

"Dawn?" I call out, peeking out from behind the closed door. "Um, do you have anything I could wear?"

"One second." He appears in the doorway, a folded pile of clothes in his hands. He averts his eyes from my toweled body as he hands them to me. The consummate gentleman. "I borrowed an outfit from one of my neighbors. She's about your size."

"Thanks. I really appreciate that." The guy thought of everything, didn't he? This really *is* an alternate reality.

I close the bathroom door and slide the beige jumpsuit up one leg, then the other. It's a bit scratchy and more than a bit ugly, but beggars can't be choosers, right? I wonder what clothes Mariah keeps in her closet. Do we share the same fashion sense? Would she mind me wearing her clothes if we do? After all, we'll be the same size.

"Okay, ready," I say, appearing from the bathroom. I've tied my still-wet hair back in a messy ponytail and, of course, am wearing no makeup, but I feel fresh and clean and well rested. I slide on my boots and, on a whim, grab the sword belt and strap it around my waist, feeling more than a bit self-conscious about wearing a weapon. Especially one I have no idea how to use. But then I catch a glimpse of myself in a mirror. The jumpsuit actually fits. And there's a certain primitive style to it, I realize now—raw and powerful.

I can feel eyes on me and I whirl around, catching Dawn giving me a once-over. "You clean up well," he says, a small smile playing at his lips. I can feel my face heat at the compliment.

We walk out of the house and into the cave corridor, Dawn locking the front door with his thumb. It takes me a moment, as we head toward the town square, to adjust my eyes to the dim lighting. I think I would go insane down here long term. It's so depressing without the sun. My body lets out an involuntary shiver, cold. Dawn reaches over and rubs my back a few times, a much appreciated attempt at a quick warm-up.

Dawn locates his hover bike behind a Dumpster, hands me a helmet, then gestures for me to climb aboard. I do, no longer uncomfortable with the idea of being forced to wrap my arms around his waist. In fact, I'm looking forward to it.

Dawn revs the engine and the bike lifts off the ground. We float slowly through the Dark Side, residents coming out of their caves to wave to us, their faces alight and hopeful as they watch us fly by. Mariah must have been something else to garner this kind of unabashed worship. What happened to make her betray them all in the end? Was she really that addicted?

We pass through the town gates and then pick up speed as we enter the underground aqueduct tunnels. The ride is as exhilarating as it was the first time around—fast, furious, the wind whipping across my face. I scarcely notice the cold as I hug Dawn tight against me, melting into the ride, giving myself over to the sensations of motion and speed, the curve of Dawn's arched back, and my breasts comfortably squashed against it.

We zoom down the tunnels, the underground world unfolding in seemingly endless twists and turns. We pass through several other towns identical to the one Dawn lives in. Bleak, brown, tattered. My enjoyment of the thrilling ride is sucked away at the faces of the scrawny mutant children and browbeaten adults wandering the streets, without enthusiasm, without hope. My heart aches for them and their situation. How could the government let this underground ghetto exist while they thrive and frolick in a gaudy, opulent playground above? No wonder the revolutionaries are simmering with hatred.

"Why are they all mutated?" I ask as we leave the third area's gates. "I mean, what happened to make them that way?"

"There's radiation deep in the rocks that many Dark Siders are forced to mine," he replies. "It's amazing they can reproduce at all."

"Forced to mine?"

"The government needs crystals embedded in the rocks to run their supercomputers. So they keep the

Dark Siders down here, work them as slaves to satisfy the needs of the high-tech, luxury-rich world above," he explains.

The bike's motor and the wind blend into a roar as we pick up speed, drowning out any chance of further conversation. I settle back against Dawn, feeling an overwhelming sadness for the plight of these people. I couldn't imagine a life like they lead: stuck deep underground, forced to work a job that will poison not only your own body, but that of your future offspring. How could the government be so cruel? And how can the people aboveground tolerate it knowing their comfort comes at the expense of others'? But then I remember the Holocaust back on Earth. Are the Indys aware of what's going on beneath the surface of their world? They can't be. There's no way they could consciously so selfish, could there?

After about a half hour of travel time and a ride across a colorless and dismal underground landscape, we arrive at a large iron gate looming in front of us with menacing spiked bars. Dawn lowers his bike to the ground and dismounts, walking over to the gate, pressing his thumb against the sensor.

"Dawn Grey. REJECTED," a robotic voice pronounces solemnly. Dawn scowls and kicks the gate with his boot.

"Goddamn it," he grumbles. "The Eclipsers must have revoked my pass when I told them all to go to hell. When they first told me they were working to pull you out." He motions to the sensor. "Try your thumb."

I stare at him. There's no way my thumb will work here. Is there?

I get off the bike and walk over to the gate, fear making my heart pound. This is a test, I realize. A major test to see who I really am. I may look like Mariah Quinn, but do we share fingerprints? DNA?

I press my thumb against the sensor, sucking in a breath, not sure which outcome to pray for. Do I want the gate to open? Or do I want to prove I'm not who they think I am?

I don't have a choice. "Mariah Quinn," the robotic voice chirps, sounding a lot friendlier this time around. "Welcome back." The gates creak open, revealing a decrepit, windowless stone tower embedded into the cliff and stretching up into the darkness.

"Still convinced you're not Mariah?" Dawn asks, eyebrow raised in question. I turn away, too freaked out to answer. For a moment I can't breathe, instinctively grasping for my inhaler. Of course I don't have it with me, so I run through my breathing exercises instead. Could it be true? Am I really Mariah? Or maybe we've got some kind of alternate-reality-twins scenario going on here. She and I are different people but share the same fingerprints. Or DNA. Or whatever those thumb sensor things register. That could happen, right?

Keep rationalizing, Skye. Maybe at some point you'll talk yourself into believing.

I shake my head. No use to dwell on such things now. Better to just get to the Eclipsers and hope they can shed some light on this whole mess.

Dawn leads his bike through the gate and releases its kickstand. The gate swings shut behind us, coming together with a metallic clang that causes me to nearly jump out of my skin. I hurry to follow Dawn into the building.

The entrance was once made of glass-paned double

doors, but the glass has long been smashed into oblivion and swept away. I'm careful as I step through to dodge the jagged shards still clinging to the frame. No need to accidentally cut myself on top of everything else. Who knows what kind of first aid they've got down here?

Through the doors is a small vacant lobby painted a dismal olive color that only succeeds in sucking out most of the already sickly orange light coming from several table lamps scattered throughout. Cobwebs cling to every crevice, and the tables and chairs are covered in thick dust. It looks as if no one's entered this place in years.

I glance down at my boots. They're going to get filthy tramping around here. But wait . . . they're not dirty at all. They're still as shiny as when I first pulled them onto my feet. I glance behind me for my dusty footprints, but there's no sign I just walked through the lobby whatsoever.

What the hell? I look to Dawn, head cocked in confusion.

He grins. "Optical illusion," he explains. "The floor's actually made out of a thin film screen. We project a dusty floor image onto it to make it look like the place has been abandoned. Really, we sweep every other day."

"Amazing." I crouch down to touch the floor. Sure enough, I can drag my finger through the dust and not get a speck of dirt on my hand. "You guys thought of everything."

"Actually, you did. It was your idea," Dawn informs me. "Smart, too. We can't be too careful these days." He heads over to the antique-looking elevators at the far side of the lobby and presses a black button. "The last thing we need is for the government to start snooping around our headquarters. In fact, only a few people know this place exists."

The elevator doors open with a loud groan, sparking a question of its last safety inspection. But I keep my mouth shut and follow Dawn inside. Who knows, maybe this is another trick to keep the bad guys away. The door slides shut and I watch the mechanical dial counting up the floor numbers, fighting the urge to grab Dawn's hand. Not out of some misplaced romantic gesture, mind you, but simply because this whole scenario has me jumping out of my skin.

The elevator bings when it reaches the top floor, and the doors slide open. We're greeted by a much cleaner scene: a red-carpeted hallway stretching off into the darkness, dimly lit by small ceiling lamps every few feet. The whole place reminds me of that Tower of Terror ride at Disney World, and I jump off the elevator before it can send me spiraling down thirteen stories.

Dawn smiles and grabs my hand in his, squeezing it. "Don't worry," he assures me. "We're almost there."

"Great," I mutter, not willing to admit how much better I feel with his hand in mine. I grip him tightly as we walk down the nondescript hallway, passing door after door. Finally, we stop at one of them. To me, it's undistinguishable from the other dozen doors we've passed, but Dawn seems to know where he's going. He drops my hand and gestures to the tiny sensor I hadn't noticed by the handle. I press my thumb against it, grimacing as the robotic voice cuts through the silent hallway, addressing me once again as Mariah. Just what I need in this spooky place: a reminder that I may very well be the resident ghost.

The door slides open and we step over the threshold, into what appears to be an old vacant tenement apartment. There's tacky floral wallpaper, faded and peeling from the walls, cheap ceramic frogs and unicorns on the shelves, and cracked red vinyl couches and armchairs.

"What is this place?" I ask, glancing around the room. "I thought we were going to some secret headquarters." This can't be where the Eclipsers meet, can it? I mean, it's so . . . so tacky.

"Well, you're certainly as impatient as Mariah, I have to say." Dawn chuckles. He walks across the room and points to a three-foot-high wooden bear statue standing like a sentinel in the corner. "Do you recognize Melvin at least?"

"Melvin?" I repeat, staring at the bear. "Well, back on Earth I have a stuffed bear I call Melvin. . . ."

Dawn's eyes light up. "Really? That's great. Maybe there is something left inside you," he says excitedly.

I shrug, not wanting to disappoint him. "It's just a stuffed animal. I mean, I wouldn't read too much—"

"You and I went up to the surface once," Dawn says. "We found this old resort by a dried-up lake. One of the crumbly places from back before the war. We wandered around a bit, until we came across an ancient wooden carving of a big brown bear. Obviously a relic of the prewar world."

"But wasn't that a long time ago? How could a wooden statue still remain intact?"

Dawn shrugs. "I don't know. But that's partially what made him so special to us." He looks down at the bear statue. "In any case, I named him Melvin. You loved him so much that the next time I was aboveground I stole a log and smuggled it back down here. Had it de-radiated and did my best to carve you a replica." His eyes shine as he relates the story. "Since then, Melvin here has always been a symbol of our revolution. A de-ified bear, if you will. Our symbol of hope. We know that no matter what happens down here, he's standing in wait up on the surface, withstanding weather, age, and radiation—never doubting that someday man-kind will return to him. He's never given up faith after all these years . . . and so we decided neither should we."

I watch as he relates the story, his fingers tracing over the wooden bear's head. He's so passionate, so happy in this memory of a time shared with his pre-cious Mariah. I suddenly find myself wanting desper-ately to be able to share it with him. I search inside myself, trying to imagine a taller version of the bear, trying to remember a love and affection for him. But, try as I might, I come up blank. Empty.

"I wish I could remember Melvin," I say wistfully.

Dawn walks over to me and takes my hands in his. "But don't you see?" he asks. "You do. You named your stuffed bear on Earth after him. That's too big to just be a coincidence. There must be something there, deep inside your subconscious. On some level you re-member him. Maybe soon you'll remember other things too."

Or maybe not. But I can't bear to crush Dawn's glim-mer of hope, so I keep my mouth shut.

"How did Melvin wind up here?" I ask, twirling around and gesturing to the tacky room. "Doesn't look like much of a place for a god bear to take up residence."

Dawn nods. "I agree completely. But you insisted. Said there would be no better guardian to keep the Eclipsers' secret headquarters safe." He walks back over to Melvin and presses two fingers into the bear's slightly rounded tummy. The back wall slides open, revealing a secret passageway leading off into the darkness.

"Wow. Melvin's a tricky little bear, isn't he?" I say, impressed.

Dawn grins. "He is a wise and all-powerful bear, indeed." He gestures me to follow him down the passageway. "Come on. We're almost there."

We walk down the hall, the wall sliding shut behind us. But for some reason I no longer feel frightened. After all, Melvin's standing guard behind us. What could possibly happen on his watch?

Dawn pushes open a door and we enter what appears to be a small conference room made entirely of metal. Metal chairs, metal table—even the walls are shiny, slick, polished. Several people stand around the table, all dressed in black, high-collared jackets like Dawn's. They look up when we enter, voices trailing off into a hushed silence. They pause for a moment, and then one of them starts to clap. The others join in and soon the room is filled with applause, echoing off the metal floors and ceiling. I hover at the doorway, unsure how to react. Should I bow? Smile? Wave?

I catalog them quickly. Three women, four men, all of varying ages and looks, though a couple have the same glowing blue eyes as Dawn. I wonder if that's some side effect from living underground. Maybe they have better night vision or something.

Before I can analyze further, I'm rushed by the mob, all of them evidently wanting to be first to give Mariah her welcome-home hug. Each seems determined not to have the others get a coherent word in edgewise, all talking over one another until I'm deafened by unintelligible babble.

"Hey, hey!" Dawn cries, his voice breaking through the cacophony. "Give her a second, okay? Back up! Jesus. Don't you all remember the three-foot bubble rule?"

The room falls silent and the Eclipsers (for that's who I assume they are) retreat to their seats around the table, offering me precious breathing room and mumbled apologies. Dawn nods approvingly and steps forward to stand at my side. "That's better," he says, addressing the room's occupants as if they're all small children who need to be reprimanded. "I mean, really! I know you're all excited to see her, but you're as bad as the Dark Siders. Remember, the girl doesn't even remember who *she* is, never mind the rest of you clowns."

"Our sincerest apologies, Sister Mariah," offers an apple-cheeked, middle-aged woman at the far end of the table, nodding her head in apology. Her hair is cropped flush to her skull and she wears large golden hoop earrings. She looks just like a Gypsy. "It's just . . . so good to see you. Here. In the flesh. Amongst your people once again."

"Indeed," adds a twenty-something man with a trimmed black beard. His green eyes glow with enthusiasm as he looks up at me with what can only be described as unabashed adoration. "We weren't sure we'd ever see you again." He throws a self-satisfied smirk in Dawn's direction. "Of course *some* of us had more faith than others."

Dawn holds up his hands in protest. "Fine, fine. Mock me if you must," he says with an amused smile. "But even you have to admit—pulling a 'Gazer back from Earth against her will? That's usually a mission impossible."

"Yes, well, that'll teach you to underestimate the Eclipsers!" cheers a teenage male in the back. He sports large silver piercings in just about every visible orifice (and probably some I can't see.) "We don't let some silly alternate reality get in our way." The others whoop in agreement and a spattering of high fives circle the table.

Their extreme enthusiasm sends a nagging sense of guilt straight to my insides. They're all so happy to see me. So excited to think they've finally gotten their long-lost Mariah back. How am I going to ever convince them that I'm not really her? And what will they think when they finally realize that all their hard work pulling Mariah out of Earth was in vain? At the end of the day, they got the wrong girl. One who can't help them—unless they have a virtual dungeon they need rendered at the last minute. They need a brave, revolutionary leader to step up to the plate and save their world, but somehow got stuck with an incompetent club kid gamer who can't even remember to save her electricity bill by switching off lights when she leaves the apartment.

They're going to be disappointed when they finally face reality.

"Where's Glenda?" I ask, scanning the room but not seeing the serene face of my yoga instructor amongst the motley crew. "I thought she'd be here." At least Glenda's been to Earth. She's met me as Skye. She'll probably be the easiest person to convince of the truth.

The Eclipsers grow silent. A few of them slump into their chairs. I frown. Was it something I said? Then Dawn touches my arm. "You know the woman who freed you from Duske's mansion?" he asks.

I stare at him, dumbfounded, the blood rushing from my face. "That was . . . Glenda?"

Dawn nods.

My mind chooses this moment as a good time to replay the "Glenda Getting Captured" scene in excruciating slow motion. I sink to a vacant chair as I recall the guards dragging her away. She gambled her very life to get me out of that prison, and may have come up snake eyes.

"She was captured," I say, voice hoarse. "Do you think they . . . I mean, do you think she's . . . ?" I trail off, not able to voice my fears.

"We're trying to get some intelligence on her now," explains a middle-aged Asian man at the left side of the table. "We think she might still be alive. After all, she's got a lot of information on the Eclipsers. Things the government would do anything to learn. Killing her would be counterproductive to their ultimate goal."

"At least without torturing her first," mutters the black-bearded man.

"Torture?" I repeat weakly, my heart sinking.

"Do not fret, Mariah," insists the apple-cheeked woman. "Glenda did not go blindly into this. She knew her mission was risky from the start, but she truly believed her life was worth sacrificing to save yours."

Guilt mixed with anger swirls through my gut. I rise from my chair and lean my hands on the table as I stare at the Eclipsers. "But that's so stupid!" I cry, furious. "My life's not worth shit to you guys."

The room goes silent. The Eclipsers stare at me. Then the pierced teen pipes up. "Are you kidding? Your life is worth *everything*," he says. "You're Mariah. You're our only hope." The others murmur their agreement.

Oh God, this has gone way too far. I squeeze my hands into fists and suck in a deep breath. It's time for these people to hear the truth. Face reality. "Look," I say flatly. "I don't care what you think. I'm not Mariah. You have the wrong girl. And even if by some weird stretch of psycho imagination I was once Mariah in another life, I don't remember anything about her or you or the revolution now. I can't help you. I wish I could, but I just can't. I'm not the person you want me to be."

There. I said it. At least I can relieve my guilty conscience and know I've done everything in my power to tell them the truth. Hopefully they'll be able to accept this and no more insane sacrifices will be made on my behalf.

I look around the room, trying to glean whether they're buying my statement. The somber faces sap my resolve. I've disappointed them. Crushed their hopes and dreams of getting their Mariah back. I slump back into my chair, scrubbing my face with my hands, feeling guilty and angry and helpless all at the same time. "God, I wish I *could* help you guys somehow. I really do. I mean, you went through so much to get me here. But I'm useless. Utterly useless."

The silence in the room is thick, thoughts heavy, eyes downcast. Then I feel hands on my shoulders. I look up and see Dawn standing over me, still by my side. His touch imparts to me a small strength.

"Don't look so glum," he says, addressing the room in a clear, confident voice. "Even without her memories, Mariah is still a powerful symbol of the revolution. She can still be much help in reinvigorating our people. We can present her to them tonight. Let them see that the news reports were false—that Mariah Quinn has returned to us and is still fighting by our side. Right now, that's all we need." He looks down at me. "Surely you can help us with that."

"I . . . I guess so," I say, trying not to sound too reluctant. It's not that I don't want to help; just seeing the desperate faces of the starving mutant children made me realize that. But for how long will they need me to fill this Symbol of the Revolution role? As much as I feel for their cause, the reality is I need to get back to Earth. To my real life. And to *RealLife*. We're launching so soon! And I have so many bugs to work out. . . .

I shake my head. Let's be realistic. It's not some video game project that's stopping me here. It's just that I'm so not qualified to be Mariah. I mean, seriously, how can I lead a revolution? My biggest challenge to date has been to find a boyfriend who doesn't still live with his mother. I'm so underqualified for this heroine/save-the-world stuff it's not even funny. Still, they did so much to get me here. I feel I should do *something* before going back to Earth. *Something* to further their cause in some small way. To help those poor people who lived like slave ants to an overbearing, selfish queen.

I realize they're waiting for me to speak. "Look," I say. "If you need help, well, I'll try to do what I can. But I gotta be straight with you. I need to get back to Earth as soon as possible. I've got a lot on my plate these days." I decide not to go into detail about what exactly are the contents of said plate, on the suspicion that they may think it's less important than the salvation of their world. "But let me know what I can do."

The room erupts in murmurs as the Eclipsers debate amongst themselves. Finally, the apple-cheeked woman turns to me, nodding her head. "Very well," she says. "We will respect your wishes. After all, we would never force someone to stay and fight with us if their heart and mind lie elsewhere."

"Thank you," I say, surprised that they've agreed to give up without an argument. I expected them to be more like Duske, I guess. Forcing me to stay against my will.

The woman continues. "I don't know if Dawn's told you, but there's a large gathering of Dark Siders tonight. A celebration, if you will—though there is little before now to actually cheer about. Would you be willing to make an appearance? You could simply stand onstage, let the people see you in the flesh." She rises from her seat. "They will likely be so heartened to see you have returned that they will scarcely notice you have nothing to say." She turns to the other Eclipsers. "Perhaps Mariah's presence this very night will be enough to invigorate the cause and motivate the people back into action. At the very least they will realize that she did not betray our cause, as the government caused many to believe."

I glance at Dawn, but he says nothing.

The Eclipsers all nod their agreement, appearing pretty excited about the plan. I smile, happy that I'm going to be able to help. I may not be a Grade-A revolutionary leader, but I certainly can stand in front of a crowd and wave or something. And maybe that really will push their fight forward. Then I'll be able to go back to Earth knowing I've made a difference.

Satisfied, I glance again at Dawn. My face falls as I realize he's not sharing everyone's enthusiasm. In fact, his face remains tight, his expression frosty. My enthusiasm wanes as I realize I've disappointed him. But what can I do? He's asking for way too much. And as much as I feel bad for him and his situation, I can't live my life playing the part of his amnesiac girlfriend. In the end, it'll be better if he's able to just let go, to forget Mariah and all the pain she caused him and move on with his life. And me being around would only serve to remind him on a daily basis of all he's lost—my presence bursting open the scabs time and time again, and his wound will never heal.

And besides, at the end of the day, no matter how sweet he is, how devoted he seems, he doesn't even want me. He doesn't want Skye Brown, the person I am. He's simply searching for Mariah's soul when he looks deep into my eyes. That's not fair to me. I deserve someone who loves me for who I am, not who he wishes I were.

"Then it's settled," the woman says. "And now, I guess, since you don't remember us, Mariah, some introductions are in order." She pats herself on the chest. "I'm Ruth," she says. "I'm the geographer. You need to get somewhere in Terra, you need a Rabbit Hole, call me and I'll get you where you need to go."

"And I'm Kayce," the bearded man beside her pipes in. "Techno-geek of the group. You need a gadget, I'm your man."

"You can call me Hiro," says the young Asian man in the back of the room. "I'm the weapons specialist. You want to relearn how to swing that sword on your belt, you come to me."

The others introduce themselves and their roles. Each has a different area of expertise or skill set. Together they seem to form a pretty dynamic group. I can see why they've had some successes, even though they are completely outnumbered by their oppressors.

"So, what was Mariah, then?" I ask. I'm still not able to use the first person when talking about my alter ego, even though they would probably prefer it.

"The inspiration," says Ruth with a small smile. "And the planner. You chose our fights and decided which objectives we would pursue when and which were best left for another day."

"One of those objectives was Moongazing," I conclude.

Kayce nods. "You were never a fan of any government programs, but after Senator Duske introduced Moongazing, you decided to make it your ultimate crusade. You insisted that if Earth was such a great place, then everyone had the right to go, not only the rich."

"What happens when one migrates to Earth?" I ask, curiously. "Does everyone lose their memories?" I almost add *like I did*, but chicken out at the last minute.

"Depends," Hiro says. "If you're just going as a tourist, trying it out, you retain all of who you are. Of course, it's strictly forbidden to run around Earth telling everyone you're from another plane of existence. You've probably heard of people who have tried that—they get locked up pretty quick!" He chuckles wryly. "The idea is to blend. So when you finally commit and buy a permanent relocation package, you're allowed to choose from a variety of new professions. Actress, socialite, artist, stockbroker, what have you. The 'Gazer agents then set you up with a new life, based on your specifications."

"But do you remember your old life?" I ask again, not satisfied with his roundabout answer.

Kayce shrugs. "Supposedly. But who knows? No one making the permanent migration ever comes back. We only get scattered reports from the tourists. And since they always enter and leave from the same point— some club, I guess—most never have time to venture outside the neighborhood they're dropped in. So, chances are they'll never run into the 'Gazing lifers, who are likely spread out over Earth."

"This is all theoretical," Ruth pipes in. "We're not sure of all the details. That's why you started 'Gazing to begin with—to figure out how it all works. After all, you said you didn't want to advocate something you'd never tried yourself."

I raise an eyebrow. "This club," I say slowly. "It's not called Luna by any chance, is it?" It's a needle in a haystack with all the thousands of Manhattan clubs, but somehow I know I'm right.

Hiro snaps his fingers. "That's it," he says. "Why? Have you been there?"

I sit back in my metal chair, stunned. Luna, which had once been a hole in the wall, had recently become the most popular club in town. I had blamed the *Village Voice* write-up, but evidently it was just suddenly being patronized by denizens of this alternate universe. In a strange way it all made perfect sense. After all, it *was* the place where I'd recognized the man from my nightmare. And I had blacked out there and woken up on Terra.

"Are the 'Gazers pretty well off when they jump to Earth?" I ask, remembering how the crowd had changed at the club from raver kids to high society practically overnight.

"Oh yes," Hiro says. "You get money. Especially if you're migrating permanently. You see, the government lets you try it out a few times, a few days here or there to see if you like the place. But when you finally commit, you're required to hand over all your Terran possessions to the government."

"And in exchange for giving up all your Terran possessions, you receive a bank account number to be used on Earth," Kayce jumps in. "That's your start-up capital. After all, Terrans are essentially homeless, illegal aliens when they first arrive. But the government supposedly takes pretty good care of you, and you're certainly not forced out starving on the streets."

"So when you first get there, you're just wandering around, undocumented?" I ask.

"Well, yes, though actually that's a person's first quest, from what we can tell," says Ruth.

"Quest?" I scrunch my eyebrows. "What do you mean, 'quest'?"

Hiro shrugs. "Um, like a mission, I guess? From

what we understand, Terrans are given a list of tasks to accomplish when they first reach Earth. They're rewarded for accomplishing these tasks with things like driver's licenses, Social Security cards, and money."

I snort. "It sounds like a game."

"Well, it is, sort of, right?" Kayce says. "The game of life." He laughs. "I think the government is just trying to make it interesting so 'Gazers will want to stay forever. After all, if they came back, the government would have to return all their money. I doubt they're very interested in doing that."

"They don't have to worry," pipes up the pierced boy who earlier introduced himself as Taryn. "No one ever comes back. Except you. And we had to pull you out by force."

"True," agrees Hiro. He looks a bit resigned. "Anyway, that's about it. The Indys are evacuating Terra on a daily basis. The government is taking over all their assets—houses, land, the works. Officials claim the people are migrating to a better world—"

"But if that's true, how come none of them 'Gaze?" finishes Kayce. "That's the question."

"And that's part of what Mariah was trying to find out," I said.

"Yes. But if you ever did learn the reason, you never told any of us," Ruth admits. "And shortly after that, you were taken from us."

"What a horrible night," Hiro says solemnly. "The government kidnaps you and decimates our attempts to sabotage their seminar, all in one blow."

"Such an odd coincidence," Dawn mutters under his breath so only I can hear.

"But now we've brought you back!" Ruth crows. "An unquantifiable success for our team. We can only pray that your return—even if it's only temporary—will bring some hope back to the cause."

"Hell, I feel some of mine returning already!" cries Taryn, crossing the room and slapping me on the back. "I can't wait for tonight. I believe you're still you, even if you don't think so!"

I force a smile to my lips, hoping they'll buy the half-hearted expression. How did I get myself into this?

I shake my head. *Don't be selfish, Skye.* It's just one night. One event. And it's for a good cause, too. I'll do my part, help them out with a little inspiration, then head back to Earth tomorrow. Back to normality. I can put this whole thing behind me for good.

So how come I'm suddenly not so sure?

TEN

A few hours later I find myself standing behind a thick red curtain strung across some sort of large stage that's been carved out of solid rock. I can hear the crowd gathering on the other side, a building roar of excited murmurs, shouts and laughter rising above the pounding techno music that blasts from large speakers strategically placed around the cave.

"They sound like they're having a good time," I remark to Ruth, who is in the process of attaching a wireless microphone to the lapel of my jacket. Earlier, I was fitted with a new outfit: a sweeping black duster jacket, like the rest of the Eclipsers wear, tight black pants, knee-high boots. I now look the part. Hopefully I can talk the talk.

Ruth nods. "Indeed. The Dark Siders work hard all day, slaving away in the mines and factories. When they clock out, they're in desperate need of stress relief. Actually, it was you who came up with the idea of holding weekly gatherings. To dance and drink and let off steam. By doing this, you believed, it would cut down on the in-fighting and add to the community spirit of the different Dark Sider enclaves."

"And has it worked?" I guess it's not so odd to think of me, former club-kid girl extraordinaire with the DJ boyfriend, coming up with the idea to hold weekly dance parties. Maybe Mariah and I have more in common than I thought.

"Definitely. We've seen a marked decrease in violence since we started holding the raves. People work off their anger and frustration on the dance floor. And they get to know their neighbors better. It's made us into a more cohesive group, rather than a bunch of independent slave pods. And the more we can align, the more power we have to fight against oppression."

"We even have our own alcohol," Kayce says, stepping up with two drinks in his hand. He presents one to me. Clouds of purple steam rise from the glass, as if it's been dusted with dry ice. I take a tentative sip, immediately recoiling at the potency. I think I've just swallowed fire. Kayce laughs. "Yeah, strong stuff," he says. "Total black market, of course. The government has their own watered-down gin they send down with the rations. Just enough to lull you to sleep, not get you rip-roaring drunk like this will. This," he says, taking a swig from his own glass, "will totally kick your ass."

I raise my glass in a salute. "Here's to getting my ass kicked," I toast, then tip the glass backward and swallow the reminder. It scorches my throat and heats my insides. But it's worth it. After all, in a few moments I have to face the throng, pretend I'm their valiant leader, back from an alternate reality prison. A little liquid courage can't hurt.

"I wish you would have gotten a chance to talk to some of the Dark Siders while you were here," Ruth says, taking my glass from me and setting it on a nearby tray. "They're really amazing people. They have so little, and yet they refuse to curl up and die. They have a passion that's truly impressive. And you are solely responsible for it all."

"I wish I could have stayed longer," I say, honestly more than a bit regretful. There's so much here I'd like to learn. It's too bad I couldn't travel back and forth between worlds at will. Go back to Earth, finish my game, then come back here for a time, help them reinvigorate their cause. It would be nice to meet the people. The ones in town were so sweet. So welcoming.

"Okay, we're going to make the final preparations," Ruth says. "We'll come get you in a minute." She turns on her heel and walks over to another part of the stage, Kayce in tow.

"Are you ready?" Dawn asks, coming up behind me and placing his hands on my shoulders. His touch sends a now familiar tingle through me, but I try to ignore it. Getting all turned on is not going to help me face the masses. Or face leaving Terra for Earth tomorrow.

"As ready as I'll ever be," I say, turning to him. I look into his beautiful glowing eyes. "Though I have no idea what I'm supposed to say. Did you write me a speech or something?"

Dawn smiles down at me and takes my hands in his. "You don't have to say a word," he says. "Just having you standing there onstage will be enough. The people will see that Mariah has returned. That she is leading the Eclipsers again. They will find hope and courage just realizing that."

I laugh self-consciously. It's still blowing my mind that people would see little old me as a symbol of hope. "Okay, if you're sure . . ."

Dawn squeezes my hands. "I want to thank you for doing this," he says. "I can't imagine what it's been like for you. Thrown headfirst into a raging war and being told you're the leader of the losing side. It's got to be a lot to take in. And yet, you've agreed to help us. You can't begin to know what that means to the Eclipsers." He pauses, then adds, "What it means to me."

I can feel my face heat at his compliment. "Yeah, well, I mean, it's not really a big deal . . ." I reply.

He catches my eyes in his, and my knees almost buckle at the intensity of his gaze. But he holds me up. "It *is* a big deal," he says softly. "It's a huge deal. So accept my thank-you and don't argue."

I laugh nervously. "Okay, okay," I say, admitting defeat. "You're welcome. I'm glad I can help in some small way." Suddenly, I'm embarrassed that all I've been thinking of is my trip home. These people need me. Even though I don't quite understand why or how, I'm doing a great service by being here. I'm helping Dawn. And that's what matters. Thoughts of returning to my real life can be set aside for a bit. Tonight is about the oppressed people of Terra, the Dark Siders. And whatever little thing I can do to help their cause, I should be prepared to do.

"We're ready for you now," Ruth says. She reaches over and straightens my microphone. "Are you going to be okay?"

"Yes," I say, glancing back at Dawn. "I think I am."

The music fades and I can hear the MC silencing the crowd. He's a pro, and a moment later the chatter and murmuring fades to an almost eerie silence. "It's good to see everyone out and about tonight," he says, his voice echoing through the cavern. "I know with the recent production increase mandates you've been working long, hard hours. And with the cut in rations, it's not been on very much food."

A few boos erupt, the crowd evidently not big fans of hard work with ration cutting.

"But tonight is a special night. And we have a special surprise for all of you."

"Tickets to Earth?" shouts one heckler, prompting a smattering of laughter and appreciative applause.

"Better," says the MC, a smile in his voice. "Tonight we have a very important guest here to see you."

"Is it the Circle of Eight?" another heckler calls out. "And have they agreed to let us tar and feather them?" More laughter.

The MC shakes his head. "Even better," he says, then pauses dramatically. A hush falls over the crowd. It's as if this entire room of thousands is holding its breath at once. "Tonight only. Making her glorious return to Terra after months on Earth. I give you the one, the only—"

"Get to the center of the stage," Ruth urges, pushing me forward. The curtain begins to draw back. I take a hesitant step, all of a sudden not one bit ready to meet my public.

"Mariah Quinn!" the MC bellows as the curtain sweeps open. A spotlight shines down on me, blinding me where I stand. The crowd goes silent. I can feel thousands of eyes staring at me in shocked disbelief as

I make my way to the front of the stage. Not sure what to do, I give the crowd a little Miss America–type wave. Cheesy, but I can't think of anything else on the fly.

Then it happens. One by one every member of the audience, every Dark Sider in the crowd, gets down on his or her knees. They raise their hands over their heads and open their mouths, one single word leaving their lips, over and over again. Pulsing, throbbing, electrifying.

Mar-i-ah. Mar-i-ah. Mar-i-ah.

The chant starts low, but grows in volume and intensity.

Mar-i-ah. Mar-i-ah. Mar-i-ah.

The sound washes over me. My name. I mean, *her* name, rolling off their tongues in an all-powerful caress.

Mar-i-ah. Mar-i-ah. Mar-i-ah.

I shiver, chills wracking my body with the power their chant invokes. I certainly wasn't prepared for this kind of worship. What could Mariah have possibly done to inspire such loyalty? Could her plans and actions actually have made this much of a difference in these people's lives? I wonder if she enjoyed this: playing the role of goddess. Everywhere she went, people worshipped her. Did she get off on it? Or was she a reluctant leader?

And again, what happened in the end? She left them high and dry? Abandoned them for a happier, richer life on Earth? Betrayed their eternal devotion—not to mention Dawn's love—'to look into the moon'?

No wonder Dawn hates her so much. She's beginning to strike a sour note with me as well. Not that in a way I'm not doing the same kind of thing, returning to Earth after this night and all. But the difference is, this isn't my fight. I didn't start something I couldn't finish like she did.

Not that rationalizing eases the guilt all that much as I look down at the people on their knees before me.

I open my mouth to speak, not at all sure what I should say, if anything. Still, I feel the need to at least send a few encouraging thoughts their way. After all, it's not every day I get bowed down to and chanted at.

"People of Terra," I begin, my voice quavering. "It has been a long time. I know you've been through some terrible ordeals while I've been away. And I know the government's asked you to believe some horrible things about my departure. But I stand here before you tonight, dedicated to our cause and asking you to renew your faith as well. I understand how easy it can be to settle into your daily existence. To give up and figure it's not worth fighting the good fight. But we all know, deep in our hearts, it *is* worth it. Every bead of sweat, every drop of blood, every salty tear shed—it all brings us one step closer to our ultimate goal. To our . . . freedom!"

The crowd leaps to its feet as one, cheering and clapping and whooping. I've got to admit, I'm pretty impressed myself. I have no idea where that speech came from. But I'm glad it touched them somehow. I steal a glance at Ruth, who's standing at the side of the stage. She's beaming and clapping. A sense of pride swells inside me. I've not let them down.

But suddenly the cheers are replaced by screams of terror. I look back at the audience and see armed men in silver-plated body armor bursting through the auditorium doors, throwing smoke bombs into the crowd, assaulting the Dark Siders where they stand.

"Stay where you are!" a voice from a megaphone commands. "You are all under arrest for violation of the Terra Code 1-55435-4. Unauthorized political gatherings are not permitted under the law."

Panic ensues, the blinded crowd trying unsuccessfully to dissipate before being knocked down by the gas fumes. It's chaos—running, trampling, screaming, begging. I watch the scene in horror from the stage, my hands fingering my sword belt, wondering if drawing a weapon I don't know how to use will do any good. I'm so lost in the riot before me that at first I don't feel the hand at my arm, frantically trying to pull me offstage. Then something registers and I whirl around, ready to meet friend or foe head-on.

I realize it's Dawn who's grabbed me, his face ashen and his eyes wide.

"They're looking for *you*," he says, his terror clear. "We have to get out of here. Now!" He thrusts a gas mask–like contraption at me and yanks another over his own face.

I don't need a second invitation; I pull the mask over my head.

Dawn leaps off the stage and I follow. My boot heel snaps as it hits the concrete floor and I'm forced to kick off my footwear and leave it behind. We weave into the panicked mob, pushing and shoving our way through the crush, heading for the exit. There's an overwhelming smell of sweat and fear, and the smoke from the bombs makes it nearly impossible to see where we're going. Someone steps on my bare foot, causing me to stumble, falling into the mob and onto the ground. For a moment I fear I'll be trampled to death, but Dawn grabs my hand and yanks me to my feet just in time. Then, without releasing his hold, he drags me down the side of the stage and into the orchestra pit.

We come to a small door cut into the stage, maybe once used as a discreet exit for musicians and their conductor. Tonight, it's a lifesaving portal. Dawn presses his thumb against a sensor and it swings open. We have to duck to make it through the small entrance. As soon as we're on the other side, Dawn pulls the door shut and the LCD lights turn red, letting us know it's been locked.

"Come on," Dawn says. "We can get out this way."

"What about the others?" I ask, looking back at the door.

"There's nothing we can do. It's more important to get you out."

"But we can't just leave them!"

"Mariah—I mean . . . Skye," Dawn cries. "What are you going to do if you go back out there? Take on the entire regiment yourself? You're good with that sword, but not that good."

He's right, of course, though it breaks my heart to think of the Dark Siders out there, being brutally punished for their devotion to me—er, Mariah.

"What if I gave myself up?" I asked. "I mean, if they're looking for me."

Dawn shakes his head furiously. "No. That won't help. And you'll be doing your people a disservice. They need you. They need to believe in you."

I give up. After all, it's not like I want to go turn myself in and face torture and death at the hands of crazed totalitarian government officials. And Dawn's right; there's nothing I can do at this moment to save those people out there. Better to live and fight another day.

"Besides," Dawn adds, "they'll be fine. We get gassed by soldiers on a regular basis these days. It's not pleasant, but they won't suffer any permanent damage."

Knowing this makes me feel a bit better as I follow Dawn down the dark passageway, past dusty trombones and tubas and stage props. At the end of the room there's a door. Dawn presses his ear to it before activating the thumb sensor.

"I can't tell for sure if anyone's out there," he says. "We'll just have to risk it."

He pushes open the door and looks from side to side. Then he motions for me. I step out into the hallway.

"We need to get to my bike," he says. "It's parked outside."

We rush down the corridor, the background of screams sound-tracking our journey. The smell of smoke and fear hangs heavy in the air. We turn a corner and stop short as we see our exit is blocked. Two burly guards, dressed in silver uniforms and wearing swords, are standing in front of the door. They look up and see us, and motion to one another.

"Shit," Dawn mutters. "We're going to have to fight."

He's on them before they can pull out their communication devices and report. With strength and speed I've never seen in a man, Dawn grabs the two of them by their necks and effortlessly lifts them a foot off the ground. They claw and kick and choke, but can't break free from his grasp of steel. His eyes are wild as he bashes their heads into one another, skulls colliding with a sickening crack. He releases them, their bodies crumpling to the ground. They're not getting up. Maybe ever.

I stare in disbelief at sweet, gentle Dawn, who has suddenly transformed into the Incredible Hulk right before my eyes. My thoughts fly back to the fight we had in the alleyway over the knife. He must not have been even trying.

"How did you . . . ?" I start to ask, amazed at his superpowers. But I can't finish my question. Someone grabs me from behind, yanking me by my hair. I whirl, drawing my sword on instinct as I turn and thrusting out my arm. The blade slices through my attacker's middle as if he were made of butter, meeting resistance only at his vertebrae, before completing its journey to the other side. The man's face freezes in a death gaze as his top half slides off his bottom and onto the floor. Blood spurts out like a waterfall, soaking me.

I sway, dizzy and light-headed, my eyes blurred with panic and fear. But I have no time to be sick or afraid. No time to hesitate. A second guard rises behind him, brandishing his own sword. I raise my weapon, hoping and praying I can either channel Mariah or pick up some sword skills on the fly.

"They've jammed the door," Dawn calls out to me, his voice panicked. "Try to fend him off while I decode it."

My katana flashes under the artificial light, almost as if it's shining with an inner glow. My opponent raises his own sword, smiling maniacally. He charges forward, swinging his blade in sweeping slashes—upper left to lower right, upper right to lower left. I stand still, my blade shimmering in the silence, judging his distance, then parrying just at the moment his sword's parallel to mine. The blades clash, and we strain against one another until his slides free. I leap back just in time to avoid his second swing, a calculated slash designed to slice me in half. My heart pounds in my chest as I steady my hands and prepare for round two.

He charges again, and I surprise myself with another easy block. Something deep inside me, emerging from some hidden recess in my brain, seems to be giving my hands effective instruction. Have my sword-fighting skills come from a few too many rounds of *Mortal Kombat* in my youth? Or am I really finding some inner Mariah?

I shake my head. Time to ponder the *why* later. Right now I have a sword fight to win. I check my opponent. Up close, I realize he's a bit overweight and drowning in sweat. His initial attacks have worn him out. Time to make my move.

I parry his weak attempt at a blow, then whirl and stab my sword forward, catching him off balance and off guard. He bellows in agony as the blade slips between his ribs, pinning him to the pillar. Blood soaks his silver uniform.

This time I can't bear it. My stomach heaves and I bend over to be sick. I can feel Dawn behind me, pulling me away. "The door's open. We have to go now!" he cries, yanking my sword out of my victim. It makes a disturbing sound as it's pulled free—a sound I can confidently say I've never heard before. Dawn tosses the blood-soaked weapon to me and I can feel my stomach lurch again. So much blood. So much death. All at my own hands.

But better them than me.

Dawn opens the door and we run down the corridor, jump on his hover bike, and zoom off down the black tunnels as fast as the vehicle can take us. We're really flying. I hold on for dear life, my heart slamming against my rib cage, my whole body shaking. The wind whips through my hair, through my jacket, freezing me to the bone.

We ride for what seems like hours. I can't help but keep turning around, paranoid that we're still being followed by sword-wielding maniacs. Unwanted visions of the invasion still parade through my mind. Both sides are locked in an endless war over a girl who isn't even remotely sure she's who they think she is.

But *am* I Mariah? Am I really? The thought nags and tears at me, unwilling to be ignored. Skye never picked up a sword in her life. I just fought like the bride in *Kill Bill*. How is that possible? I'd love to say I just got lucky, but I know that's not the case. I knew what I was doing. Somehow, some way, I was completely in control of my actions. How is that possible?

An uneasy chill shivers through me. It's not from the bike ride this time. Who am I? It should be an easy question. So, how come I'm starting to doubt the most obvious answer?

Dawn finally slows the bike and it settles back to the ground. He jumps off, then helps me do the same. My muscles are aching, my knees shake, my face is on fire. I look around, assessing my surroundings. We seem to be in the center of a Dark Sider community of some sort, but it appears deserted. At first I have the troubling thought that perhaps this is because its inhabitants are all lying unconscious back in the arena, but then I notice the crumbling buildings are covered in cobwebs. Either it's another illusion, like the tower, or this place hasn't been lived in for a while.

Dawn walks up to a metal door of a tall tenement

building and yanks it open. We step into the ruined lobby. There are scuffed, dirty linoleum floors, a crumbling stone concierge desk at the far end. Paintings that depict children romping in the sunshine hang haphazardly from the wall, and a row of elevators stand to the right. It's similar to the lobby of the Eclipsers' secret hideout, but it's even more depressing, if that's possible.

"What's this?" I ask.

Dawn doesn't answer. He simply motions for me to do the thumb thing to call the elevator. A moment later, the door slides silently open. We step inside and Dawn pushes the button for the tenth floor. We shoot upward, the elevator car creaking and shaking from side to side as we rise.

Dawn and I both stare straight ahead, as if mesmerized by the numbers rising to meet our destined floor. The tension between us is thick. We don't touch, but at the same time, I can feel him just inches away. As I breathe in, his scent fills my nostrils—musky, dark, intense. I squeeze my hands into fists, trying to resist the overwhelming urge to give in to the near-escape adrenaline thrumming through my veins and throw myself into his arms.

The doors slide silently open, revealing a decrepit hallway with peeling wallpaper, pulled-up carpet, and trash strewn everywhere. Graffiti promises the apocalypse is near. Um, hasn't it already come and gone?

I follow Dawn down the musty corridor, careful not to step in puddles. Must be plumbing problems here on top of everything else. He certainly picked the most remote building in Terra to hide out in. Which, I guess, is probably best, given the circumstances.

He comes to a door and motions for my magic thumb again. I press it against the sensor, amazed that even here it works as a magical key. The door slides open and we step inside.

I gasp in surprise when I see the cozy apartment that greets me. If I hadn't made the journey myself I wouldn't have believed this well-decorated space was part of the building we just wandered through. There's a plush, cozy couch in one corner, a flat-panel TV hanging on the adjacent wall. A full-service kitchen leads off from the living room, complete with breakfast bar. On the walls are numerous framed photos of people. I take a closer look. Some I recognize as Eclipsers. Others are unfamiliar. But it's the center picture that grabs my attention.

It's of me, cuddled in Dawn's arms, both of us smiling happily into the camera. Dawn's face is so radiant, so unguarded and joyful. It breaks my heart. I glance over at him, standing awkwardly by the door, as if not sure to make himself at home. His fingers twitch by his side. His face is white and his eyes dart everywhere but to me.

Poor Dawn. Poor, poor Dawn.

Something inside me breaks—a thin filament keeping me together, keeping me hanging on to life on Earth and all the decencies that go with it. Blame it on the senseless attack and our narrow escape. Or perhaps it's just some lingering memory deep inside my subconscious.

Whatever. I just have to have him. Here. Now. Mine.

I cross the room in seconds, throwing myself into his arms. Smashing my face against his—seeking, finding his lips, his mouth. I slide my fingers from his cheeks to his hair, digging into the long smooth strands while I wrestle to open his mouth.

He's still for a second, as if in shock; then he returns my kiss, opening to me, allowing me inside, sharing all that he has to give without hesitation, without remorse. He slams me against the wall, pinning my arms above me with one hand. His other restlessly explores, palm flat and dragging up my body, curving around my hip, across my stomach, rounding over my breasts. I moan as his fingers explore each, cupping them, stroking them, as if he's a blind man trying to get a lifetime of images with his hands. All the while his mouth claims mine. I shudder and let out a small squeak. The ache inside me is nearly unbearable. I twist my calf around his thigh, pressing myself into him, desperate to feel him against me, to find relief in flesh. He's rock hard, radiating a pulsating burn between his legs that I can feel even through the rough fabric of his trousers. He wants me. Perhaps as badly as I want him.

He releases my hands and uses both of his to rip apart my shirt, still crusty with dried blood. The tough material tears in his grasp as if it's made of tissue paper. Suddenly I'm open, exposed, my breasts bared, my nipples puckered and standing at attention, not shy in their desire to be touched. He catches one in his hands, then dips his head to suckle it, wrapping his full lips around me and biting down softly. I cry out. It's pain, it's pleasure, all mixed together in a delicious ag-onizing soup of sensations. I try to grind against him, but he pulls away, just far enough to torture me and keep me from finding relief. He slides his other hand behind me, down my back, cupping my buttocks and squeezing lightly. Sweat drips down my forehead as I fight for some control. But he's not giving an inch. I claw at his back, digging my nails into his shoulders so deep I'm afraid I'll draw blood. Would he mind if I did?

He pulls at my pants, lowering them to midthigh. Yanking aside my panties, he slips his hand into me. He skims two fingers between my sex, slowly stroking up and down, up and down, all the while still sucking hard on my breast. It's like being struck by lightning, and my vision's fast going spotty under his touch. But he's not done. Not by a long shot. He reaches down with his other hand and slides two fingers deep inside me, pumping in a slow, torturous rhythm. Unable to take it anymore, I rock against his hand, desperately trying to satisfy my body's demand for release. My skin is flushed and burning. I'm sweating and writhing and panting as he plunges fingers into me again and again with an increasing pace that I struggle to match with my hips.

I don't last long. A moment later a piercing pleasure slams into my brain, releasing endorphins to ignite every inch of my body. My ears burn, my toes tingle, my fingers go numb. I gasp, breathless and barely conscious as I ride out the tidal wave of sensations, the agony exploding into the purest ecstasy. The pain transforming into unadulterated pleasure.

"Dawn," I moan. "Oh, Dawn . . ."

There's no response. I open my eyes, aware of a sudden emptiness, a sudden vacancy. It's then that I realize Dawn has retreated to the other side of the room. What the hell? Here I am, half naked, fully exposed, leaning against the wall, panting, sweating, barely able to form a thought in my head, and he's gone off to read a magazine?

"But, wait . . ." I start, not sure what's going on. Why did he walk away? Fear and confusion shoot through me as I fight to regain my senses and figure out what happened. Did I do something? Say something? "Don't you want to . . . ? I mean . . . ?" I trail off, not sure what to say, not sure what to do.

I can see his hands trembling, belying his nonchalance. He does want me. Wants to continue where he left off. But something's stopping him. What?

"Dawn, talk to me," I beg, my voice croaky and concerned.

"This isn't right," he says at last. "We shouldn't do this. After all, as you've told me a hundred times, you're not Mariah. You're not the girl I love."

An aching emptiness floods me as I pull up my pants and wrap my jacket over my ripped shirt. I feel disgusted at myself. For allowing this to happen. For succumbing to my desire for a man I don't even know. One who's in love with someone else.

I look over at Dawn, at the pain and frustration clear on his face. He squeezes his hands into fists, staring so intensely at the ground I'm half afraid it will burst into flames under his gaze. He's so passionate. So unguarded and desperate in his love for this girl who betrayed him. A part of me suddenly wishes I really was Mariah. To be the recipient of such intense, powerful devotion from this beautiful man. To be loved with all of someone's heart, soul, and mind. I've never had that. My relationships have always been more about sex and fun and hanging out than any kind of deep connection. Shallow. Brief. Meaningless.

Fearless leader of Terra or no, Mariah must be one stupid girl. She had it all. Had Dawn's unwavering attention and yet she let it slide away. And now I'm the one left to pick up the pieces of this broken man's heart. A walking, talking empty ghost of the person he once loved. I don't deserve his devotion. His passion. I've done nothing to earn it. And a cheap fuck against a wall is not going to change that.

"I'm sorry," I say, though I'm not sure exactly why I feel the need to apologize. Am I sorry I kissed him? Sorry I let him act on that kiss? Sorry I'm not the girl he wishes I were?

"It's like making love to a ghost," Dawn mutters, half to himself, not acknowledging my apology. "To a shell of someone I loved."

Great. Just great. That's exactly what I want to hear after opening myself up to a man I'm really starting to like. I'm not good enough. I'm not the one he wants. The encounter between us meant absolutely nothing. Shame wells up inside me and my stomach burns. I feel so dirty, so vile. How could I have accepted his touch, burned under his mouth? Succumbed to a cheap, tawdry act and confused it with more that that? Ugh, ugh, ugh.

"I'm sorry," he says, running a hand through his hair. "I don't mean it like that. I enjoyed . . . well, I mean . . . It's just . . . what are we doing here? There's no way we should be getting involved. You're leaving tomorrow to go back to your life. I don't want to get attached to you just to have you abandon me all over again."

"Right. Of course. I understand," I say stiffly. I sit down on the couch, as far away from him as possible. "I'm sorry. It won't happen again."

We're both silent for a moment, each locked in our own heads, trying to sort out what happened and what can be done about it. Finally, I decide to change the subject. "So, um, where are we?" I ask. "Who lives here?"

Dawn releases a long sigh and I realize I've once again said something wrong. "This is Mariah's apartment," he says. Oh. Duh. Of course.

"Er, yeah. Of course it is. It's, um, nice."

"You should have seen where she used to live."

"Oh right," I say, remembering Duske's story. "She was of some kind of royal blood, right? She must have had a fancy house, huh?"

"Yes. If Mariah had continued on the path she was born to take, she would have been one of the Circle of Eight by now," he says. "And probably married to Senator Duske."

I raise an eyebrow. "She and Duske were together?"

Dawn nods. "I think to this day he still holds a torch for her. That's probably why he allowed her to jump to Earth instead of killing her when he had the chance."

"Interesting." No wonder he'd been staring at me like that back at his house. That Mariah girl really got around.

"In any case, The Circle of Eight consists of four men and four women, and the positions are passed down from generation to generation," Dawn explains. "The idea is that unlike the democracy we had before the war, no appeal for votes or campaign contributions will force the governing official to be swayed in policy. The Circle will always be in power, and therefore there is no threat to them ruling fairly and decisively." He shakes his head. "That's the bullshit they feed us, anyway. In reality, The Circle is probably more corrupt than any democracy ever was. And because you can't vote them out of office, they are able to do anything they please."

"Absolute power corrupts absolutely," I murmer. "So, what made Mariah decide to rebel?"

Dawn is silent for a moment, staring at the blank wall in front of him. "She met me."

"Ah. So it was like a Romeo and Juliet kind of thing? Indy and Dark Sider?" I'm almost amused at the cliché.

Dawn shakes his head. "Not exactly." He fiddles with a ring, pulling it off and on again. "I wasn't always a Dark Sider either."

"So you were an Indy as well?"

"It's a long story."

"I don't think we're going anywhere tonight."

"It's also a big secret. If word got out about who I really am, I would be killed on sight."

I remember the identification card back at his apartment. "So, what? Are you on some ten most wanted list or something? I kind of figured all the Eclipsers were anyway."

"The Eclipsers are a nuisance to the government, yes," Dawn says. "But I'm a walking, talking liability. And the senate doesn't exactly like to leave loose ends like me wandering around."

"What do you mean?" I'm beyond curious.

"Look," Dawn says, turning to me. His blue eyes are earnest and concerned. "What I'm about to tell you can't leave this room. If they find out who I really am, they'll track me down and kill me without a moment's hesitation." He rakes a hand through his hair. "I'm trusting you here. Am I right to do so?"

I nod. "Of course. I'd never betray your secret," I assure him. I lean forward on the couch, eager to hear what he has to say. What secret could be so big?

"The surface of our world, as you know, was made unlivable after warring nations decided to bomb each other into oblivion," Dawn explains. "The types of bombs they used allowed for the decimation of life without destroying the infrastructure. So there are a lot of treasures up there on the surface. Stuff the government would kill to possess."

"I can imagine."

"In any case, my birth wasn't the result of two people making love," Dawn continues. "I was an experiment by the government. Egg, sperm, a boatload of cybernetics—all mixed together in a one big genetic soup. A few semiconductors in the brain, lead/titanium plates under my skin, and the piece de résistance—a palm implant that emits special radioactive nanoparticles, which allow me to heal." He stares down at his hands. "I don't know all the details. Never got to see my own blueprint, you know." He shrugs. "In any case, the idea was to create super humans that were immune to radiation. Beings that were extra strong and able to go up to the surface and labor for long hours, looting old buildings and bringing their treasures back below."

"So you're a . . ." I'm not sure what words I'm looking for.

"Nothing awful." Dawn shakes his head. "I'm just a genetically enhanced human. I'm flesh and blood. I can feel. I can think. I have all the emotions a regular person would have. I'm just . . . more."

I nod, feeling a bit relieved that at least I hadn't just been making out with a robot.

"That's how I healed your arm," Dawn adds. "I was created to be a surface medic. To take care of the others when something went wrong."

"That's a pretty useful skill," I remark, glancing down at my wrist. You could never even tell it'd been broken. "So, what happened? Obviously you're not working on the surface now."

"The experiment was a failure. No matter how hard they tried, they couldn't create a radiation-proof neuro-Terran—or nT, as they call us. Eventually, just like any human, we'd get sick. But did the government decide to stop the program when they learned this? No." He shakes his head, disgust twisting his mouth into a frown. "The treasure retrieval is too valuable to their operations. So they continue to use us. Once we become too sick to work, they dispose of us and create new nT workers to fill our slots. Luckily for them, we're cheap to manufacture."

I stare at him, horrified. "They'd dispose of you? Like, kill you?"

"They call it 'retiring'. But yeah, it's pretty much just murder. Of course, by the time they take someone off the job, they're so sick with radiation poisoning, it's almost better to just die and get it over with."

"How do people stand for that? How can they just sit back and watch it happen?"

Dawn shrugs. "One, the government *tells* people that nTs are robots. That we don't have any life or feelings. That we're just up there doing a necessary job."

"And people believe?"

"Some do. Some don't care either way. They choose to stick their heads in the sand and ignore all the atrocities. The government pacifies Indys anyway—alcohol, drugs, little luxuries, and nowadays, Moongazing. When life is good and you're feeling happy, people tend to ignore what's going on, as long as it's not in their faces. Indys figure it doesn't involve them. They don't know any nTs, so they simply don't care what happens to us. Just like they don't care what happens to the Dark Siders."

I screw up my face in disgust. "I can't believe they'd just look the other way, enjoy their lives, sponsored by the labors of the exploited classes."

"In their defense, some don't know the truth," Dawn amends. "They believe what the government tells them. That the nTs are manufactured worker robots without feelings or family. If you think of it that way, the fact that we're supposedly disposable doesn't seem all that bad. I mean, would you feel empathy for a burned-out toaster oven? No. You'd be happy it was useful while it lasted and quick to replace it once it wore out."

"So that's where Mariah came in," I conclude. "She learned the truth about the nTs and decided she wanted to help."

Dawn nods. "We met accidentally. I had escaped my work crew, broken a tunnel seal, and shot down a Rabbit Hole. Dazed and confused and lost, I wandered into Luna Park. I didn't know where I was or what I was doing. I'd spent my whole life in a work camp. Mariah found me hiding in a ditch. She felt bad for me, I guess, and took me into her home and fed me. Risked her life to save mine, to hide me when my platoon came looking. No matter what, I'll always be grateful to her for that."

"And then you fell in love."

YES! ☐

Sign me up for the **Historical Romance Book Club** and send my TWO FREE BOOKS! If I choose to stay in the club, I will pay only $8.50* each month, a savings of $5.48!

YES! ☐

Sign me up for the **Love Spell Book Club** and send my TWO FREE BOOKS! If I choose to stay in the club, I will pay only $8.50* each month, a savings of $5.48!

NAME: _____

ADDRESS: _____

_____

TELEPHONE: _____

E-MAIL: _____

☐ I WANT TO PAY BY CREDIT CARD.

☐ VISA   ☐ MasterCard.   ☐ DISCOVER

ACCOUNT #: _____

EXPIRATION DATE: _____

SIGNATURE: _____

Send this card along with $2.00 shipping & handling for each club you wish to join, to:

**Romance Book Clubs
1 Mechanic Street
Norwalk, CT 06850-3431**

Or fax (must include credit card information!) to: 610.995.9274.
You can also sign up online at www.dorchesterpub.com.

*Plus $2.00 for shipping. Offer open to residents of the U.S. and Canada only.
Canadian residents please call 1.800.481.9191 for pricing information.

If under 18, a parent or guardian must sign. Terms, prices and conditions subject to change. Subscription subject
to acceptance. Dorchester Publishing reserves the right to reject any order or cancel any subscription.

Dawn smiles, his eyes far away. "We did. She was so passionate. So angry when she learned the truth about what the Circle was actually doing to people. She decided then and there that it wasn't enough to save only me. She wanted to save all of us."

"And so she started the Eclipsers."

"First, she went around trying to garner support amongst her own friends. Other wealthy Indys and Circle members. They mostly just laughed at her. They said she should give up her silly crusade and get back to her training. Take her chosen position in the Circle of Eight and then she'd be free to voice any concerns she had there."

"That does seem like a reasonable idea. I mean, she would have had the power."

"Not really. It is a circle of *eight,* remember. Each member still must accede to the majority. And Mariah realized very quickly that she'd never be able to gain support from within. The senate is too set in its ways. Too greedy. Without the Dark Siders and nT slave labor, the economy would collapse. No one was interested in their extravagant lifestyles being taken from them just to relieve the daily drudgery of a working class they never even met."

"Good point. So then, what did she do?"

"Well, she did manage to drum up some support from a few sympathetic Indys. And so, with their help, she formed the Eclipsers. She set up secret meetings and laid the seeds of our eventual revolution. At first her ideas were small, but as she grew into her new role, she began to implement major initiatives designed to improve day-to-day life for the Dark Siders."

"They must have been thrilled to have her," I remark, remembering the throng chanting her name.

"Oh yes. The would-be senator who lived down in Stratum 3, getting her hands dirty while helping the Dark Siders? No one had seen anything like it. And the people fell in love with her. She was so well-spoken, so strong in her belief that they could really make a difference—she quickly became a symbol of hope for the people. She gave them something to live for."

"It must have been so satisfying. To see them start to dream again."

Dawn nods. "It was great. But it was also really hard. The pressure was a lot for Mariah to handle. The Dark Siders began to see her as some kind of demi-god, and made their demands accordingly. And she was just a girl. No magical powers, no enhanced DNA. By the end of each day she was exhausted—not to mention an outcast amongst her former friends and family. She couldn't return to her home. Her own mother, Senator Estelle, denounced her as a traitor and a threat to the Circle. She swore up and down it didn't bother her, but we all knew she was lying."

"She sounds like an amazing person," I comment quietly. No wonder Dawn's not interested in me. He's got this super ex-girlfriend, able to leap social injustices in a single bound. And here I am, a silly video game designer from Manhattan. I once sponsored a boy from Guatemala for the price of a cup of coffee each day, but that's where my unselfish, charitable works end. I'm nothing compared to the great, illustrious Mariah. Nothing at all.

"She was," Dawn says, staring down at his hands. "Until her betrayal."

"Tell me again what happened with that?"

Dawn shrugs.

"As I told you before, she'd been Moongazing for a while and becoming more and more addicted. Her original intent was to study the program to see if Earth was a viable place for Dark Siders to emigrate to. If it was, she was somehow going to figure out a way to capture some of the Moongazer Stations and start sending people for free. She didn't think it was fair that only the rich could live in paradise."

"And so she started to 'Gaze to check it out."

"And got addicted. What none of us knew at the time—they don't exactly advertise it on the billboards—is that the more times you take 'Gazers and go to Earth, the more your mind must bond with Earth's reality. You start to lose your Terran identity. I started realizing what was going on, but when I tried to stop her, she'd get really, really angry. Just like any junkie, she refused to admit there was a problem."

"That must have torn you up inside. To watch her start to slide away like that." I'd seen the same thing happen to friends back on Earth: Club kids who started out taking a little Ecstasy to dance the night away soon turning into smack-heads who would sell their own mothers for a hit.

"It was. And the worst thing was, when we weren't fighting about her 'Gazing, she'd try to get me to come with her. She told me Earth was a whole new world, a wonderful new existence that she wanted to share with me. She said we wouldn't have to hide anymore, that we could be free to start a new life. A better life without fear."

"But you didn't want to?"

Dawn shakes his head. "Not that I didn't want to start a new life with Mariah. I loved her more than anything.

But I witnessed a marked change in her personality. The 'Gazing trips were affecting her mind." He sighs. "Suddenly our fearless leader, the hope of our people, the leader of our cause had become nothing more than a strung out 'Gazer, talking gibberish and confusing everyone she came in contact with."

"How terrifying. And sad."

"Indeed. And it was getting harder to hide her addiction from the others. I shouldn't have—I realize that now. But at the time I wanted only to protect her. I didn't want her to lose what she'd worked so hard to build. I thought maybe she'd be able to kick it. If I helped her . . ." He trails off. "Sounds stupid in retrospect."

"Not really. We all want to protect the people we love."

"Right. But I didn't realize at the time that protecting Mariah would be at the cost of so many lives." Dawn rakes a hand through his platinum hair. "I never dreamed she'd go so far as to actually betray us to the Senate—her archenemies. I guess I underestimated the extent of the addicion." He shakes his head. "I still remember that night, clear as if it were yesterday. The soldiers rushing in, brandishing weapons, cutting down the Eclipsers where they stood. Watching as all of our great plans were decimated in one fell swoop." He fists his hands. "We had the opportunity to show the world the atrocities he government was inflicting on the Dark Siders. A chance to sway them to our side once and for all. Instead, because of Mariah's betrayal, that night became just one more atrocity and the Indys still have no idea what's really going on in Terra. But I've told you all this before. You don't need to hear it again."

The pain in his voice is tangible. I can't imagine how he must have felt that night as he realized what was happening. To have the person you love more than anything turn on you and destroy everything you've worked for—it must have been devastating.

"We fought back, of course," Dawn adds, unable to let it go. "But we were greatly outnumbered. In fact, it was a massacre. And I just remember thinking over and over again, *Oh Mariah, what have you done to us?*"

"You're *sure* it was Mariah?"

"Think about it. She was a strung-out junkie, wanting to make that last migration to Earth. She had no money—she'd emptied her savings to help fund the revolution long ago. How did she get to Earth? She had to pay somehow."

"Right. I can see where you would think that." Still, to me something wasn't adding up. How could someone be so passionate about a cause one day and then just abandon it and sell out her friends the next? There had to be some missing piece to this puzzle.

"So," Dawn says, "the next time I saw her—you—was in that alleyway on the outskirts of Luna Park. Obviously I was more than a bit confused at that point. I'm sorry about my reaction."

"It's okay. I understand completely, given the circumstances."

Dawn rises from his seat and stalks the length of the room. He takes the photo of him and Mariah off the wall and studies it closely. "It's still not easy," he says, looking back at me for a moment before returning his focus to the portrait. "You look like her. You smell like her. You walk and talk and have all of her mannerisms. But you don't have her inside you. You don't remember me. Our life together. You don't remember all we had—what you threw away without ever telling me why!" His voice breaks on the "why," and he slams his fist into the wall, punching easily through the plaster.

Empathy consumes me as I watch him lean his head against the wall. It's impossible to comprehend what he's feeling. His true love, discarding him like an old habit in exchange for a new one, betraying not only him, but everything they'd fought for. No wonder he'd acted so hateful toward me. I'd hate me too.

I approach him slowly. He's shaking, hands curled into fists. His face is crimson. His eyes narrow, and he's still seething with anger. I'm half afraid that if I touch him he'll hit me, knock me across the room with his super strength. But at the same time, I know he needs me. On some base level, he knows it, too. And so I risk it, coming up behind him and wrapping my arms around his waist, burying my head in his back, squeezing him tight, not saying a word.

At first he's stiff, resists my touch. Refuses to accept my offer of comfort. But then he breaks. His muscles relax under my hold. I can feel his hard swallow, and a moment later he turns to face me. His eyes are rimmed with angry tears.

He reaches up and brushes the back of his hand against my cheek. A shiver flitters through me. "I should kill you," he says. "For what you've done to me. For what you've done to the Dark Siders. And yet, I can't manage to hate you. No matter how hard I try."

His words break my heart. I can't bear it—all this pain, all this hurt. If only there was a way to take it away. To draw it into my body and leave him with nothing but peace. Instead, I stand uselessly. Holding him. Giving him as much comfort as I can.

We stand there for what seems like hours, barely moving, just looking into one another's eyes. The connection between us, the bond, is so strong it makes me want to cry.

"It's late," he says finally. "And you've had a big day, if not a long one. It's best if you get some rest. I'll take the couch."

He breaks away, and emptiness consumes me once again. I want to run across the room and throw myself back into his arms, beg for him to hold me for just five more seconds. Or minutes. Or hours. Or years. Instead, I head reluctantly to the bedroom, not bothering to flip on the light, and collapse on the bed.

I'm so exhausted I assume sleep will take me immediately. But there's too much swirling around in my mind. And it's too hard to hear Dawn breathing in the other room. He's way too far away for my liking. I contemplate my options for a moment, then give in to my desire.

"Dawn?" I call out. My voice sounds plaintive and hesitant.

In half a second, he's in the bedroom. "Do you need something?" he asks, shifting from one foot to the other.

I swallow hard before nodding. "Yes," I say at last. "Would you mind . . . I mean, I'm feeling a little uncomfortable and scared in here by myself. So much has happened. This is all so strange and . . ."

"Anything. Name it."

"Could you come in and sleep next to me?"

I see his silhouette in the doorway; he both enters and retreats at the same time. "I . . ." he starts. "I don't know if . . ."

"Look," I say. "I don't know about the past or anything, or all the things you think I did. But I do know that whoever I am, I need this. I'm not asking for anything. Just . . . I need a friend. I don't want to be alone."

He enters the room, shirtless, dressed only in a pair of flannel pants. His chest is as powerful as I'd imagined, all sharp planes of muscle, taut and toned. A few harsh scars mar the otherwise perfect flesh, but they only serve to make him more fascinating. He crawls into bed behind me, wrapping his arms around my body and spooning me close. He nestles his face in my hair and I can feel his hot breath gently tickling my earlobes. I snuggle closer so that our two bodies touch as much as possible, feeling warm, safe, protected. There's a part of me that wants nothing more than to flip around, kiss him full on the mouth. Find out what it's like to make love to this beautiful man. But I know this is not the time for that.

Right now, this is enough.

ELEVEN

I wake up, still wrapped in Dawn's arms. For a moment I don't move; I just lie there, enjoying his warm body snuggled against mine. It's so strange. I barely know this man, yet I already have such a deep connection to him. I should be feeling overwhelmingly guilty, lying here in another man's embrace. But right now, my Earth relationship seems so distant. Almost . . . unreal. As if it were a dream I once had.

It's going to be hard—torturous—to go back to Earth, I realize. To leave Dawn and all he's beginning to mean to me. But in the long run, what choice do I have? We each have our own separate lives and destinies. For a brief moment the stars aligned and we shared something special, but that's where it has to end. An alternate reality one-night stand, I guess. And now, as morning breaks, it's time to say good-bye.

I shift in his arms, rolling over so we're face-to-face. He opens his eyes, mere inches from mine. A beautiful, sleepy blue, they sparkle like crystal from under his long sooty eyelashes. He smiles a shy smile and reaches up to brush a lock of hair from my face. My heart breaks at the simple gesture. How am I going to say good-bye to him?

"Good morning," he whispers, kissing me lightly on the nose.

"Good morning," I say. I wish I could wake up this way every day for the rest of my life. But that's impossible. I know it. He knows it. And we both need to stop pretending and face it.

After a few more minutes.

We lie there together, legs and arms intertwined, stroking each other softly, neither person very interested in moving away. I can feel his morning arousal through his cotton pants, but he makes no move beyond an innocent caress. Which is probably for the best, no matter what naughty ideas my libido has been whispering. It'll only make things harder in the end.

At last, he grins sheepishly and sits up, running a hand through the long strands of his tousled hair. "Would you like some breakfast?" he asks. "I could go stand in line to see if they're doling out egg-synths this morning. It's a long shot, but you never know."

I shake my head. "No, it's okay. I'm not hungry." I'm actually starving, but I can't bear the thought of making him go wait in line. Or even get out of bed.

"It's probably for the best anyway. That fight last night—when I was bashing those guards' heads together. I'm afraid one of them might have realized what I really am."

My cozy thoughts fade as I remember all that had happened the night before. "What will they do if they figure it out?" I ask.

"Work to kill me, probably," Dawns says with a shrug.

I sit up, horrified, worried. "No! They can't! That's . . . that's . . ." I trail off, not knowing what to say. How to appropriately express my horror at the idea.

What difference does it make? a voice jeers in my head. *Dead or alive, you'll never see the guy again.*

I feel a pang in my heart and I want to cry. I need to get back to Earth. I have to. But how can I leave Dawn behind? And I already know he won't come with me. If he wouldn't leave for Mariah, there's no way.

Dawn looks at me, a thoughtful expression on his face, and then he rises from the bed. "Bathroom," he says. "Then we get dressed and head over to HQ to assess the damage."

"But what about . . ." Did he forget that I was supposed to go back to Earth this morning? Great. That's going to make this whole thing even tougher.

Dawn stops at the doorway, shoulders slumped, frozen in place, obviously remembering. "You still want to go back," he realizes aloud.

"Well, I mean, um, yeah," I say, stumbling over the words. It's hard to talk when everything inside me is begging that I reconsider. But no, it's impossible. I have a life on Earth and I need to go back. I have responsibilities, commitments, family, friends. I can't just abandon them, can I? Isn't that what Mariah did going the other way? Wasn't that what she once said was so wrong?

Is what you have on Earth really so special? the voice pipes in again. *Don't you think you could do a lot more good here?*

"Fine," Dawn says, leaning against the door frame. "I'll drive you to Moongazer Station instead. Let you get on with your life. Sorry to have kept you here so long." But he doesn't sound sorry. He sounds angry.

"Thanks," I say, trying to shake the ache that's settled into my bones. "I'd . . . appreciate that."

Dawn shrugs and stalks out of the room. A moment later, I hear the bathroom door slam shut. I curl into the fetal position on the bed, wracked with guilt. How can I do this? Just leave Dawn? Leave the Dark Siders. Go back to my life and never return. Never even hear how their fight ended, if they eventually won equality or were resubjected by the government.

I try to remind myself of all that I'll be going back to: my game—my professional pride and joy—finally being released to the public. Craig—poor guy, I've been so vacant of late. And yet, he's stayed by my side through it all. When this is over, we can resume our relationship where we left off. Spend time with one another. Grow closer. Maybe even look into buying that co-op in Brooklyn. Get married. Have children. Buy the Bugaboo stroller and wheel it around the park with the other urban mommies and daddies.

It's what I've wanted and dreamed of all my life. Why does it suddenly seem empty and meaningless?

My troubling thoughts are interrupted as Dawn returns, standing silhouetted in the doorway. "Well?" he asks, his voice cold. "Let's get a move on. I have a lot to do today after I drop you off."

I crawl out of bed, the cold air biting at my bare legs as I abandon the blanket. Dawn steps aside as I walk out of the bedroom, but I can't help catching a glimmer of hurt in his eyes as I pass. It makes me ache inside, to recognize the pain he can't quite completely mask. Obviously deep inside he's been hoping, praying, that somehow, some way, I'll magically transform into the woman he loves. The woman who is perfectly capable of leading a revolution.

But, I remind myself, even the illustrious Mariah left in the end. She traded all her suffering for a better life on a different world. And now, through me, Dawn has to relive her betrayal, her exodus to Earth, all over again. Not that it's fair, really, to compare the two scenarios. Not totally. She left her world. I want to return to mine. But for some reason, that doesn't make me feel any less guilty.

"Before you go," Dawn says slowly. "May I show you a few things?"

"Of course," I say—probably a bit too quickly, too eagerly, suddenly desperate to spend a few more minutes with him. But life on Earth has waited this long; it can wait a few hours longer.

"Okay. Go shower and get ready." He sounds more cheerful already. "We'll go on the way to Moongazer Station."

I shower and change, finding a closet stuffed full of Mariah's various outfits. I choose something simple: a plain pair of black pants, corset top, trench coat. No need for frilly skirts and platform boots today, no matter how cute they are. After all, I doubt I can take them with me back to Earth.

We head out of the apartment, across the water-soaked hallway, down the creaky elevator, and through the dismal lobby to where Dawn parked his hover bike. We get on the bike and zoom through the tunnels. I want to ask where we're going, but I don't feel much like shouting over the roar of the bike.

We stop at a small building, its metal facade built into the rock. Once inside, I recognize immediately that it must be some kind of one-room schoolhouse. A couple dozen Terran children of various ages sit cross-legged on the floor in front of a teacher who is reading from a tattered old-looking book. The children are dressed in rags and some of them wear soiled bandages wrapped around their arms or heads. All are terribly mutated. Extra fingers. Third eyes. Humped backs. They're hideous in appearance, yet the light shining on their faces as their teacher reads makes them somehow more beautiful than a playground full of Gap Kids models.

"The government doesn't allow the Dark Siders to go to school," Dawn explains. "They figure a little education can be dangerous, so they banned it. Kids are supposed to go to work in the mines as soon as they're old enough to carry rocks. But Mariah felt everyone should learn to read and write. She said the more knowledge we could acquire, the less helpless we would be."

"That makes sense," I say, taken aback by the sight of a child with an extra arm trying to write on a clay slate.

"So we rotate them in and out. One week mining, the next learning. That way there always appear to be children in the mines if the government comes down to check up on us," Dawn says. "The problem, of course, is getting teachers. That's one of the reasons Mariah was so desperate to bring more Indys to our side. Sister Anne here is one such instructor. She's retired from her headmistress job in Luna Park and risks her life daily to come down here to teach. If the government knew of her behavior, she'd be punished for sure."

I look at the teacher with newfound respect. "So, some of the Indys do help?"

"A few. Not enough. Not by a long shot. Most Indys are too blinded by whatever the government dangles in front of them. They spend their lives enjoying the restaurants and alcohols and shops. And now there's 'Gazing. Why help the people in your own world when you can hop over to a better one?"

Once again I feel that pang of guilt stab at my gut. Here I am, judging the Indys, when really, aren't I just as bad? Wanting to go back to Earth, refusing to help these poor people, these destitute children whom I could easily teach to read and write if I wanted? When I'm back, will I be able to forget their faces? Or am I in for a lifetime of guilt, knowing I turned my back on them in their moment of need?

Bet you wished you chose the blue pill, Neo.

This wasn't fair. At least Neo was given a choice. He wanted to know. I never asked to be dragged into Terra. To learn the truth of its world. I would have been totally content living out my days in the Matrix, innocent and unaware of it all.

But now that I've seen, what can I do?

The teacher looks up from her book. Her face brightens as she sees us at the back of the room. "Mariah," she cries. "Oh my goodness, children, look here! It's Sister Mariah!"

The kids break into applause and I can feel my face heat at the oh-so-undeserved praise. Here I am, standing, wishing I'd never met them, and they're gazing up at me like I'm their savior.

I give a weak wave. What else can I do? I'm not cruel

or selfish enough to disappoint a room full of poverty-stricken, mutant children.

"Mariah used to come here and read," Dawn whispers. "Even with her busy schedule, she always made time to do it, at least once a week. And she brought the best stories with her. Stolen from the Indy libraries above."

I nod, suddenly realizing what I should do. I take a step forward. "Well, guys," I say. "I didn't bring a book today, but if you like, I can tell you a little story."

The kids cheer. Sister Anne smiles gratefully, standing up so that I can take her seat. I walk to the front of the room and sit down, facing the kids, letting their radiating joy beam onto me like sunshine as they wait with bated breath.

I smile back at them. "Once upon a time . . ."

I tell three stories—each taken from adventures I created for my video game—my rapt audience begging for more each time I finish. Finally Sister Anne laughingly waves them down, saying that obviously Mariah has more important things to do and they need to let me get on with my day. I reluctantly agree; I'd have stayed for another hour or two if she hadn't intervened. I've never had such a captive audience.

I rise from my seat, wave good-bye to the children then head to the back of the room where Dawn stands waiting, a small smile on his face. One of the children, a blond pigtailed pixie, runs over and throws her arms around my legs, squeezing me with a tiny fierceness.

"I knew you'd return, Sister Mariah," she murmurs, refusing to let go. "I just knew it."

Her words are almost too much. I shoot a look at Dawn, feeling the tears well in my eyes. He smiles at me, looking a tiny bit smug. So, this was his plan when he said he had to "show me something"? His clever way to convince me to stay?

He certainly is making it harder.

"What's your name?" I ask the little girl.

"Crystal," she says, then sticks a dirty thumb in her mouth.

"Well, Crystal, you study hard in school and someday you can grow up to be an Eclipser, too," I tell her.

She grins from ear to ear and prances back to her classmates. "I'm gonna be an Eclipser," she brags. "Sister Mariah told me so."

We say our good-byes and exit the schoolhouse. I give one more longing glance as we board the hover bike. Those children, their faces so full of hope. What lives are they destined to lead?

"Can I show you one more thing before we go?" Dawn asks.

"Sure," I say, giving in easily. The last thing I want to do right now is leave.

Our second destination turns out to be a secret underground greenhouse. The workers take the time to show me how they carefully cultivate plants and give them the artificial sunlight they need to survive underground. The greenhouses, like the schoolhouse, are illegal. The government doesn't allow Dark Siders to grow their own food—they're supposed to only eat rations grown on government-sanctioned farms. But rations are always being cut, the gardeners explain, and the old and sick Dark Siders are often cut out completely. The government doesn't seem to have a problem with starving their slave labor force once they've become superfluous.

"So Mariah decided it would be good if we created our own food to supplement rations. We stole the technology from the government-sanctioned places—after all, Dark Siders usually make up most of the labor—and started our own," Dawn tells me. "Maybe someday we'll be able to completely feed ourselves and not be dependent on them for food. That'll be a major step toward our independence."

"I'll bet," I say, walking up and down the rows of plants. "I can't believe you can grow all this stuff underground."

"They're specially bred plants that don't need as much light for photosynthesis."

"Next thing you're going to tell me is you have a whole hidden underground farm. With cows and horses."

Dawn beams. "Now that you mention it . . ." He reaches for my hand. I hesitate a moment, then slide my fingers into his. "Come with me."

We get back on the bike and zoom down another tunnel, this time going deeper underground. Finally, we come to what appears to be a dead end, the passageway blocked by crumbling rubble, as if there was a cave-in long ago. Dawn parks his bike and motions for me to follow as he weaves through the boulder field. I keep up, wondering what on earth—make that Terra—he's going to do when he arrives at the dead end.

"Where are you going?" I ask.

"You'll see."

He stops right in front of the massive wall of rubble. Then he turns around, winks at me, and . . . steps right through! The rocks shimmer a moment, and suddenly I'm alone on the wrong side of the wall.

"Another optical illusion?" I ask, wondering if he can hear me on the other side.

He pops his head back through. The effect is more than a bit disconcerting. "Something like that," he says. "Gotta hide our most valuable treasures any way we can."

I take a deep breath, put out my hands, and take a step toward what looks like solid rock. Sure enough, my hand slides through easily and I manage to step to the other side with no effort at all.

"Huh," I say, looking back. On this side, it appears as if there's no barricade whatsoever. I can even see Dawn's bike, parked down the road. "You guys really have thought of everything."

"Well, Mariah believed if you have secrets as important as we have, we'd better do a damn good job hiding them," Dawn says. He steps up to a massive steel door set into the wall, complete with a high-tech-looking combination lock.

"No thumb sensor?" I ask, raising an eyebrow.

"No," Dawn says. "Only a handful of people know the combination to this safe, and we change it all the time so that no one can give it away, even under torture." He turns the safe combination lock a few times and the door squeaks open. "Here we go." He bows. "After you, m'lady."

I step through the door and gasp as I realize what's

on the other side: a series of metal cages, cut into the caves. Each contains animals. Cow, goats, chickens. It's a regular Old McDonald's farm.

"Nice," I say, wandering from cage to cage. "I haven't seen an animal since I got to this place. Duske told me they were practically extinct." I reach my hand between the bars to pat a docile pinto horse on the nose. "Hey, baby," I coo. "Sorry I don't have any carrots."

I can feel Dawn's presence as he comes up behind me. "This was Mariah's pride and joy," he says. "Far beyond any of the petty tricks we'd play on the government. This is our real future here. Our own little Noah's Ark."

"Where did you get them?"

"We stole embryos from the government labs and grew them. They're clones. One male and one female of each species."

"But Duske said the animals are impotent. That they can't breed."

"Funny, that," Dawn says, pointing to a tiny snow-white lamb in one pen. "We haven't had that problem. I think perhaps that's just another one of the government's lies. Another way to control us."

I crouch to my knees to pet the lamb's soft wool coat. "So, you're breeding them?"

"Yup. We have six cows, fourteen sheep, and twenty-two goats. It's not enough milk by far, but it does help with orphan babies who don't have a wet nurse. And we're widening the facilities in hopes to someday accommodate all of our children. Our ultimate goal is to someday have enough animals to use them for daily necessities—leather, food, that kind of thing."

"It's funny," I say, getting up off my knees. "When you

first said stuff like 'rebellion' and 'revolution', all I could think of was Star Wars or something. You know, guns and battles and . . . well, lightsabers and stuff."

"Maybe someday," Dawn says with a small smile. "But we're not ready yet. We've been stockpiling weapons, training soldiers, and creating complex computer defense barriers for Strata 2 and 3. But we can't let on to any of this before we're fully operational. The Circle would simply send in their army and stamp us out—like they did the day Mariah disappeared. They set us back pretty far. But we're still going. If we keep working as we have been, in a couple years perhaps we'll be ready for the real action."

He says the last bit with such intensity that I suddenly feel sad to think I won't actually be here to see that day come. I bet the battle will be spectacular, with the dedicated, downtrodden Dark Siders rising up to finally take back their world.

"In the meantime," Dawn continues, "we're also putting effort into bettering the day-to-day lives of the Dark Siders. By introducing education, growing our own food and raising animals, we can create a more habitable world that's less dependent on this government. Healthy, happy, educated Dark Siders will be much better equipped when the final showdown does come."

"You really have it all figured out," I say with admiration.

Dawn nods. "But none of this would have ever happened without Mariah."

"She must have been an amazing person."

"She was," he agrees. "It's easy for me to forget that sometimes. I've been so angry . . . But she really did do wonderful things for the people here. Set this whole revolution in motion. It's just a shame it had to end as it did."

Our discussion is interrupted by two Dark Siders dressed in belted tunics and loose cotton pants. They enter the room, carrying a large crate, and set it down in the corner. They both nod to us and then exit again.

"New shipment," Dawn says excitedly. "I wonder what they were able to steal this time."

I look over at the cage, straining to see through the slats. I catch a tuft of grayish hair and hear a distinctive whimper. "That sounds like . . ."

A mournful howl echoes through the room.

"A dog!" I cry, running over to the cage. Dawn is right behind me. I get down on my knees and peer inside. Sure enough, a sweet-faced, blue-eyed Australian Shepherd looks up at us, tongue lolling from his mouth.

"Wow," Dawn exclaims. "I've never seen one of these before."

I look up at him, surprised. "You've never seen a dog?" I ask, trying to keep the incredulity out of my voice.

He blushes. "Well, in movies, sure. But never in real life. I figured they were wiped out during the war. Extinct."

I can't believe Dawn's lived his whole life without the joy of a fuzzy nose nuzzling at his face, the friendly wag of a tail to greet him as he arrives home from work, a cuddle under the blankets after the dog manages to wheedle his way onto the bed. What a sad life, to live without the love of a dog.

Definitely time to change that.

"Let him out of his cage!" I instruct, trying to hide my anticipatory smile.

Dawn hesitates. "Well, I'm not sure that's such a good idea," he says. "We don't really know what this animal is capable of . . . and . . ."

"Trust me."

He shrugs and complies, lifting the latch and freeing the Aussie. I stick two fingers in my mouth and whistle. The dog pads over, jumping up to put his forepaws on my shoulders, and starts licking my face with wild abandon. Poor thing. He's been totally starved of attention.

"What is he doing?" Dawn asks, incredulously, staring at us.

I laugh. "Kissing me!" I gently set the dog back on the ground and glance around the room. I locate a small piece of rope lying in one corner. "Watch this." I grab the rope and hurl it down the corridor. The dog runs after it, grabbing it in his mouth and bringing it back to me. He drops it by my feet. For a dog that's been stuck in a government lab, his fetching instincts are evidently still very much intact.

"That's incredible!" Dawn says. "How did he know to do that?"

I shrug. "He's a dog. That's what dogs do."

Dawn grabs the rope and gives it a throw. The dog scampers after it, retrieving. But instead of dropping it at Dawn's feet, he tosses the rope up in the air, letting it hit the ground, then grabbing it again for another toss.

"He wants to play tug-of-war," I explain.

Dawn grabs the rope's other end and pulls. The dog gets into a fighting position, teeth bared, defending his rope. Dawn drops the rope immediately, taking a leap back in surprise. "Er, I think I'm pissing him off."

I laugh. "No, no! He's playing! That's just play-growling. Trust me."

Dawn hesitantly grabs the end of the rope again. "I'm holding you responsible if he bites off my hand or something," he warns.

"He won't, I promise."

A fierce tug-of-war ensues, the opponents seemingly evenly matched. Finally Dawn manages to wrench the rope away and throws it down the corridor. The dog bolts after it.

Dawn turns to me, his eyes shining. "I think I'm in love," he says with a laugh. "This is better than I imagined."

"What is his name?"

Dawn glances at the cage. "Um, they call him C-1-045-3."

I wrinkle my nose. "That won't do. We should name him." I crouch down to scratch the pup's ear. He drops the rope and leans his head against my hand, tail wagging happily. "Hmmm," I ponder.

"How about Noah?" Dawn suggests.

"Noah?"

"Yeah. Noah was in charge of the ark, right? Our Noah can watch over our underground one."

I smile. "Perfect. Noah it is." I ruffle the dog's head. "Hey, Noah, boy. You're a good boy, aren't you? Yes, you are! I wish I had a widdle tweet to give you."

Dawn laughs. "You talk to it like you're speaking to a child."

"A lot of people on Earth these days treat their dogs like children," I defend, feeling my face heat. "They let them sleep in their beds, even."

"I bet Noah here would be a great bedfellow. Keep you warm at night."

"Totally."

"Want the rope?" Dawn asks the dog, grabbing it off the ground and waving it in the air. Noah's eyes light up and he bounds forward. I watch Dawn watch Noah retrieve, my heart warming. There's nothing like a boy and his dog.

We play with Noah for a while longer, alternating between fetch, tug-of-war, and wrestling. The dog is a complete goof, and soon we're dying of laughter.

"I hope we can find Noah here a girlfriend," Dawn says at last. "It'd be great if all Dark Siders could someday have a dog to play with."

I nod. "That would be awesome. Talk about a morale booster."

"So," Dawn says, straightening up, his smile fading. "I guess that's the end of the tour. I should take you back to Moongazer Station. Unless," he adds hopefully, "after this tour you've changed your mind about leaving us."

My heart tears at his words. Of course that's what this was all about. He hoped by showing me his world he'd make me want to stay. To help with all the ongoing projects that Mariah started. To see that they were doing great work. Work that couldn't continue without my help.

"Look, Dawn," I say, my heart breaking to have to say these words to him. "I think you're doing amazing things here. I really do. I'm impressed beyond belief. But that doesn't change things for me. I still have to go home. I still have to return to my own life. I just can't abandon my world, the same way you can't abandon yours. I mean, what if I asked you to come back with me to Earth? Would you do it?"

He scowls. "That's not a fair question. You know I'm needed here."

"Well, I'm needed there. I know you don't think the cause is as noble. Hell, I'd be the first to tell you that. But it's still my role. My life. My existence. My destiny. And I need to fulfill that."

"But it's not your world and your destiny. You just think it is because of the drugs."

I shake my head. He really, truly thinks I'm still Mariah. "Dawn, as much as you want to believe that, it's just not true. I'm not sure what happened to your girl-friend. But I know that I'm not her." I pause, then add in a choked voice, "As much as I'd sometimes like to be."

His face falls. He crouches down to pet Noah, seeking comfort from the animal just as Earth people have been doing for generations. Noah licks his face, perhaps in an attempt to cheer him. But the kiss does nothing to lighten the atmosphere this time. My stomach aches as I watch the scene, wishing there were some other way, some method to split myself to live two existences. But even as I wish it, I know it's no use. And the sooner I rip off the Band-Aid and resolve myself to just go home, the less difficult it will be for everyone.

Dawn nuzzles his face up to Noah's and my heart lurches. I can't believe I'll never see him again. "Dawn—," I start. But he waves a hand to interrupt.

"Save it," he says, rising to his feet. "I'll take you to Moongazer Station. Sorry to have wasted your time."

I cringe at the pain in his voice. The bitter hurt. "No, no," I protest. "It wasn't a waste of time. I'm so thankful you showed me all you did. I'm so impressed by your work. But don't you see? It proves that you don't really need me. Mariah's just a figurehead. You've done all this on your own, and you can keep it going as long as you want."

"Right. We'll be fine without you. Whatever eases your conscience at the end of the day," Dawn grumbles. He ushers a reluctant Noah back to his pen. "Come on. Let's go."

"Bye, Noah-boy!" I cry, looking back at the Aussie. The dog whimpers in response, looking as abandoned and lost as Dawn.

Dawn slows his bike next to a ladder that leads up to Stratum 1. Time for me to emerge from my rabbit hole and head back to Earth. Alice, no longer in Wonderland. I jump off the bike and shake myself off, then look over at Dawn. He stands still, one foot on the ground, one on the gas pedal of his hover bike, as if more than ready to take off into the night.

Even under the dim track lighting, I can see his face is cold, stone, ashen. He either is glad to see me go or he's hiding his sadness well. I'm not sure I'm doing quite as good a job. The lump in my throat, the quiver in my jaw, both make it hard to throw on a brave smile.

What's wrong with me? I'm getting what I want. The chance to return to Earth. To be back with my family, my friends, even Craig. But I feel only emptiness gnawing as I stare at Dawn. Why do I have the overwhelming urge to throw myself into his arms and beg him to let me stay?

"Well, I guess this is it," he says. "Have a nice trip."

I drop my head, feeling the tears coming. I can't let him see how his blasé statement crushes me. "Thanks,"

I say. The word seems so empty, so useless to profess the gratitude I feel toward him. For needlessly risking his life to save mine. For holding me close last night, even though the thought of me as someone else probably broke his heart.

He pauses for a second, as if considering something, then reaches into his pocket and pulls out a wad of paper that appears to be some sort of currency. He thrusts it in my direction. "Here," he says. "Pay with these. If you use your thumb, the government will know you've gone. It'll make it easier for them to find you if they want to."

I accept the bills gratefully. "Thanks," I say. "I really appreciate that."

Dawn shoves his foot onto the pedal and revs his bike without responding. My heart breaks as I realize this is good-bye. Forever good-bye.

"Dawn . . ." I try to grab his shoulder, but he jerks away, hand up to stop me.

"Enough," he says. "You've made your decision. Just go." He yanks the bike's handlebars and starts down the road, leaving only billowing smoke in his wake. He doesn't turn around once. I stand under the rabbit hole, watching the bike's lights fade into the darkness until there's nothing left but a black hole.

I sigh. I slip the wad of bills in my pocket. Then I start to climb.

A few minutes later I emerge on Stratum 1, down the street from Moongazer Station. The gaudy neon lights are buzzing, still on their (evidently very sturdy) last legs. Wind from a nearby fan whips up debris and I hurry to enter the building, creeped out by the desolation.

Inside, the place is packed with young Indys eagerly sucking on their 'Gazer inhalers and getting ready to vacation on Earth. I now realize that some are going for a short visit, a quick lark to another land. Others are here for permanent migration, weeping as they say good-bye to loved ones, begging them to join them on Earth as soon as they possibly can.

The old Asian proprietor I met during my first few minutes here greets me with a low bow. He's still wearing the same old-fashioned suit. It seems so long ago, and at the same time as if I never left. "You come back," the proprietor says. "I wonder if you would. You gone long time on that last trip. I figure you must like it in there." He chuckles, low and guttural. "I figure you return. Want to go back in."

Go back in. His stilted English and bad choice of phrase freak me out a bit. "I'm ready to return to Earth," I correct, pulling the cash from my pocket.

"One way or round-trip?" he asks, walking over to the computerized cash register.

"One . . ." I stop, something making me reconsider. I hand him my wad of bills. "Is this enough for a round-trip?"

He counts it. "Yes," he says. "Exactly enough. One-way cost lot more. Also, you need official migration permission papers from Circle."

I remember now how the Eclipsers said a permanent migration to Earth cost an Indy's life savings—something I certainly didn't have at my disposal. Did Dawn know I'd be forced to buy a round-trip ticket? Of course he must have. Sneaky bastard didn't warn me.

"I guess I'll take a round-trip," I say with a shrug, resigning myself to figuring out the whole thing once I get back to Earth. Maybe I can hide out somewhere and just never take that return 'Gazer bus back, whenever and however it comes.

The proprietor nods, giving me a once-over. "You need new necklace," he pronounces, walking over to the cabinet and pulling out one of the many. He drapes it over my neck. "And here is your 'Gazer," he says, handing me the inhaler.

I stuff the inhaler in my pocket. "Um, what's the necklace for again?" I start to ask, but he's already turned away to help another guest.

"You push the button here," a blonde elfish girl next to me says, reaching over to flip the necklace's moon charm around. "It'll indicate you're ready to return to Terra."

"Ah cool. Thanks," I tell her. So that's how the tourists get back. Interesting.

"Of course, the return's only good for one week," she informs me. "And they'll totally charge you huge late fees if you stay overtime. Best to get out with an hour or so to spare, just to be safe."

"Okay," I say, not that I really expect to ever activate the thing. I'm going back to Earth, and this time I'm staying there for good. No matter what I have to do.

She looks at me oddly. "Aren't you Sister Mariah?" she asks.

"No," I say quickly, before she starts alerting the others. "But sometimes people say I look like her."

Luckily, the girl seems to buy this. She wanders back over to where her friends are hanging out and plops down on the couch next to them.

"Remember," the oldest-looking one in her group, a

guy, is saying to the others. "Once you're there, you're supposed to pretend that you're, like, from Earth. It's called role-playing. You don't go just to be your same old boring self. When you're on Earth you're like a rock star or an actor or something."

"What's it like on Earth?" asks a pig-tailed girl. "Is it really as cool as they say?"

"Cooler," the guy affirms. "In fact, it's like one big, never-ending party. Lots of food, lots of booze, and lots of . . ." He trails off as he eyes the younger members of his group. "Lots of dancing," he finishes, though I'm pretty sure that's not what he's really looking forward to. "Well, you'll see for yourselves."

"Let's do it!" cries a redheaded boy in the back. "Let's look into the moon!" He says the last bit exactly like the guy in the commercial, and the other group members titter.

Their leader nods and pulls out his inhaler. He raises it up as if he's toasting someone's health. "To the moon!" he cheers, putting the inhaler to his mouth and taking a chuff.

The others follow suit. "To the moon!" they chorus.

I realize I'm just standing there, watching them, totally stalling on my own trip to the moon. As if I don't really want to go back. Stupid. I take a deep puff from my inhaler and head down the hallway and toward the 'Gazing boths. I remember my first time walking through this corridor. How lost and confused I had been. I had no idea where I was. Or even who I was. Has it gotten any clearer?

I square my shoulders as I approach room 12. Clarity doesn't matter at this point. I'm through with Oz.

I'm clicking my ruby-red heels three times and returning home.

So why do I suddenly feel more like the Cowardly Lion than the heroic Dorothy? And I wonder just who is the Wizard behind the curtain.

TWELVE

I woke up in my bedroom, not screaming from a nightmare, no cold sweat soaking through my clothes, no anxious boyfriend by my side. Just a dark room with a glowing clock illuminating the hour of 9:00 p.m. At least the Moongaze had dropped me off safe and sound in my own abode. How it was able to pinpoint where I lived and send me there, I had no idea, but I didn't want to know. I was just glad to be home.

Though, the whole thing did make me wonder: How did it work for real Terrans? Were they allocated an apartment or a house before they 'Gazed? That seemed unlikely, especially for the ones who were just visiting. Maybe they got assigned hotel rooms to wake up in. Or was there an arrival platform somewhere? A Grand Central 'Gazing Station perhaps? But then, why would I wake up here and not there? Were all Terrans dumped in NYC for that matter? Or were they spread out around the country? Or the world, even. I guess it wouldn't be a bad thing to end up in the Big Apple.

Here they wouldn't have to worry about not fitting in, as no one knows their neighbors anyway. And what were a few extra bodies in a city of eight million? The cash the government gave them on arrival probably really came in handy. Did they get identification documents as well? A black market immigration operation just for Terrans? And once they had their docs, did they go get jobs? Were there Terrans living and breathing and working among us? I wondered if any of them worked at Chix0r.

I shook my head. It didn't matter. I was back and supposed to be concentrating on my real life from here on out. The Moongazing Terrans would have to take care of themselves. Their reality was fading, even now.

I slipped out of bed and padded around my small apartment, taking in all my treasures that I'd left behind. I picked up my stuffed bear Melvin and hugged him against my body, triggering a memory of buying him on a trip to Tahoe last year. But for some reason now that trip seemed distant. Almost . . . generic. I could remember going, but I couldn't recall any of the details of what happened. No quirky anecdote to share.

I glanced over at the posters hanging on my wall. *Star Wars, The Matrix, Blade Runner.* My eyes caught on the last one, squinting in confusion. *Blade Runner*? But the movie was *Phaze Runner*. I'd seen it a thousand times. There was no way I'd confuse the title. Did I buy the wrong poster? Some Japanese import or something? But no. The last time I was in my bedroom it was definitely *Phaze Runner*. I'd bet my life on it.

What was going on here?

Unnerved, I dropped Melvin back on the bed and

headed to my bookcase, pulling a book out at random. I knew I'd read the fantasy epic in my hands a hundred times. I could see my ink-stained fingerprints at the page edges, the folded corners where I'd left off for the night. But while I had an overall impression regarding what the book was about, it wasn't in any greater detail than what was written on the back cover.

I set the book down, a panicky feeling fluttering through my insides. Everything in my room, all my precious possessions tied up with memories and meaning suddenly seemed fake and altered, flat, one-dimensional, almost an obscene parody of a character I was supposed to be playing. I was in a cliché apartment of a twenty-something video-game-designer geek. I had the sci-fi posters, the fantasy epics, the killer computer. It could have been a movie set.

I grabbed my photo album, plopping into a butterfly chair and flipping through to find pictures of my parents and quell the fear bubbling to my throat. I took a deep breath and forced myself to focus on the people in the pictures. Smiling. Waving. But were these shiny, happy people really Mom and Dad, or just some random folks that came with the album?

I felt sick. I threw the book across the room and jumped from the chair to make a dash for the bathroom. My stomach heaved and I barely made it to the toilet in time. I threw up violently. Hacking. Coughing up something I didn't remember eating. Then I sank to my knees and leaned my head against the porcelain seat, sobbing my eyes out.

What was I doing? Why was I freaking out like this? I knew going back to reality might take a little adjustment, but I had no idea it'd be this hard for my brain to accept. Was I losing my mind? I should be dancing around my apartment, overjoyed to be back, instead of doubting all the things I'd trusted throughout my life.

This was my stuff. My reality. My life. It was Terra that I didn't remember. Terra that I should mistrust. So how come memories of Terra suddenly seemed so solid and real and those of Earth so fake?

A vision of Dawn, of his beautiful glowing eyes, his comforting smile, his warm embrace, flooded my memories. If only he were here. If only he had come back with me and could comfort me in my terror, tell me everything was going to be all right. But Dawn was gone from my life forever. That was my choice, and now I had to live with it. I had another man here on Earth who loved me very much and would be over-joyed to have me back. My real boyfriend, Craig. A popular techno DJ at a Lower East Side club.

The club-kid gamer and her DJ boyfriend. My life really did seem a cliché.

Desperate, I rummaged through my pocket and took a whiff of my inhaler. After all, the medication suppos-edly helped bond the body with the new reality of Earth. The more I puffed, the more real Earth would seem. Maybe that's what I needed. I took a second dose, breathing in deeply, just in case.

A few minutes later, the medication kicked in. My breathing slowed and my heart stopped racing. The panic receded to the back of my brain and I rose to my feet to, once again, take stock of my surroundings. My reality.

I stepped into my bedroom. I was home. Everything was as it should be. I was just having a panic attack from the transition. But I was okay now. All that I owned was here and familiar. My teddy bear, my family photos, my well-worn books, my computer. They were all suddenly teeming with resonance. Feeling better, I crawled into bed and stuck my feet deep under the quilt my aunt had made me. Snuggled into my pillow and closed my eyes.

Everything was going to be okay. I was safe. I was home. I was me again.

So why did it take sucking down a drug to make me feel that way?

I slept for nearly twenty-four hours. When I woke, I was still feeling out of sorts—itchy and uncomfortable in my own skin. I sucked down more asthma medication. It was the only thing keeping me from going completely insane. I lay in bed for hours, staring up at the ceiling, wondering if I'd made a huge mistake. I should be happy to be home, but all I could think about was Dawn. His hurt, pained eyes, his cracking voice as he said good-bye. Sure, I wanted my old life back, but being so distant from him—knowing I'd never see him again—it was tearing me apart.

I slept. I woke. I ate a few random things I had in my cabinets. Then I slept again. It wasn't till my third day back that I finally forced myself out of bed. My answering machine was blinking madly, filled with messages from work and Craig. I was going to be even more behind on my game than I ever thought possible, but for some reason I couldn't bring myself to care. It was just a video game, right? Nothing that would bring on the salvation of our world.

But while work could wait, I realized I couldn't reasonably put off Craig any longer. His messages had grown more frequent, more worried. He'd even come to my door at one point, but I couldn't bear to drag myself over to let him in. I felt sick and weak and drugged, and I missed Dawn with every fiber of my being.

But I had to put him behind me and regain some semblance of control over my life. My *real* life. So I decided to face reality and head down to Luna to find Craig. I'd apologize for all I'd put him through, and assure him that from here on out he would have a normal girlfriend who didn't disappear for days on end. Hopefully he'd accept my apology. Hopefully I'd fall back in love with him and forget Dawn's haunted face.

I threw on some clothes—skinny jeans, slouchy boots, a long black belted sweater—and walked out of my apartment. As I locked my door behind me, I noticed a discarded bag of moldy vegetarian food sitting outside my place. My heart sank as I remembered I'd invited Craig to come over right before I'd gotten pulled back to Terra. Poor guy. Here he'd been waiting for me and I was off in some alternate universe, throwing myself at another guy. How long did he stand out here knocking before giving up and going home? I really had to find him and make good.

I headed down the elevator and into my lobby. "Good evening, Skye," the doorman said as I stepped out.

But I didn't have a doorman. And wasn't this building a walk-up last time I was here? When did we get elevators?

God, what was happening to me?

The night was warm, and a full moon shone down on the streets of Manhattan. The sky was so bright, in fact, you could even manage to make out a star or two.

Unusual, in the city. Hurried people hustled up and down the sidewalks, anxious to get to the next restaurant, the next bar, the next place to see and be seen. All were living empty existences—just like the Indys back on Terra. I reached into my purse and handed a bum on the sidewalk a ten-dollar bill.

I headed down into the subway, ready for a ridiculous wait. To my surprise, the train came immediately, pulling up just as I stepped onto the platform. What luck! And it wasn't even packed like the normal can of sardines. Unheard of for a Saturday night. The other people seemed surprised, too. At least I wasn't the only one who noticed the change.

I emerged just south of Alphabet City and headed down Houston to Luna. As usual, the club was packed and the line wrapped halfway around the block. I found myself staring at the club-goers more closely this time, wondering which ones were Terrans and which were regular Earthers. All I could tell was that the 80s look had caught on big-time. Nearly everyone sported legwarmers, long sweaters and leggings. What sheep! I caught a few teen girls pointing at me and whispering. Probably Terrans, recognizing Mariah. Super.

I headed to the front of the line, where Bruno was attending the door. "Hey, baby!" he said, wrapping me in a huge hug. "Where have you been all my life?"

"You wouldn't believe me if I told you, Bruno," I said, forcing a casual laugh. "But I'm back now. For good."

"Well, I'm glad to hear it," he said. "Craig's been going nuts without you, and the crowd's starting to pick up on bad mixes and skipping records. You guys have a fight or something?"

"It's a long story. But I'm here to make it up to him."

Bruno nodded approvingly and unclipped the velvet rope. "Enjoy the make-up sex," he said with a toothy grin. "That's the best part."

I laughed, waved off his suggestion, and stepped inside. The thought of sex was too much for me to even consider at this point. Not with me hanging on to reality by a thread.

You just would rather have sex with Dawn, that inner voice jeered. I shoved it to the back of my brain. That might have been true, but it wasn't a thought I was prepared to deal with at the moment. What brief closeness I had with Dawn, that was over forever. It was time to leave the dream behind and bond with reality. Get closer to Craig. Renew our relationship. Find happiness with the man I was with. Not the man I had left behind.

I pushed my way through the club and soon found myself in the center of the room, lights flashing, bass pounding, people dancing. I knew I should head straight to the DJ booth, find Craig, and work it all out, but I realized I wasn't quite ready to face him just yet. I'd dance a bit first, I decided. Then I'd go talk to him when he was on a break. After all, I always felt better after dancing, after letting thunderous jungle beats flow through me, losing myself in the rhythm.

And so I danced. Became one with the others on the dance floor, swaying my hips, swinging my arms, nodding my head, trying to find my true self somewhere in the music. Trying to seek out even a moment of peace and thoughtlessness.

It used to work wonders back in the day; on the dance floor I could shut off my mind and allow the music to take me to a higher plane of existence. Tonight, my mind wasn't surrendering that easy. Instead of retreating to a high mountain of unconscious-bliss, it chose to stay firmly on the ground, rehashing images of Terra. The Dark Siders. Dawn.

I stopped short as a vision slammed through my consciousness: Dawn's tortured eyes, as clear as if they were blinking right in front of me. I smelled his fear. Felt his horror. Heard him call my name—Skye, not Mariah. He was begging for my help.

It was as if the wind had been knocked out of me. Was this some kind of premonition? Was something wrong on Terra? Had the government done something? Were people being hurt? Was it because of my leaving?

I shook my head. I had to give it a rest. I was back on Earth. I had to forget Terra. It wasn't my world. It wasn't my fight. I had my own shit to deal with. An angry boyfriend, a ton of unfinished work—the last thing I needed to be worrying about was Terra.

But something inside me wouldn't allow me to let it go. I couldn't dry-swallow the blue pill now that I'd partaken of the red. Now that I knew about Terra, I'd never be able to forget. Those people—how they suffered. My mind flashed back to the little mutant schoolgirl, Crystal, who'd wrapped her scrawny arms around my legs and thanked me. How could I have left her behind? And for what? I looked around the room. For this empty shell of a life I led? Clubbing, video-gaming, shallow relationships with people who didn't mean anything. I was just as bad as the Indys on Terra.

"Sister Mariah!" A girl's voice cut through the loud music. I turned, surprised to be addressed that way. Two teenage girls, dressed in matching short skirts and thigh-high stockings, stood behind me. At first glance, they could be club kids. But I realized they must be Indy teens out for a night of 'Gazing.

"Now you've done it," the second girl said, kicking her friend. "We're supposed to be staying in character, remember? What if she tells on us?"

"Please. It's Sister Mariah. She's not going to tell on us. Are you? She looked up at me beseechingly.

"No. I won't tell," I say. "But maybe you two should run along—"

"Wow," interrupted the first girl, her eyes glistening under the flashing lights. "I had no idea you'd be here. All the news feeds said you'd been kidnapped by the Dark Siders."

"Yeah, the government has been doing everything to try to find you, Mariah!" said the second girl, who sported long brown braids. "There's, like, a huge reward and everything."

"There is?" Not surprising, I guess.

"And, of course, those weirdo Dark Siders are so getting punished for stealing you away," added the first girl, tossing her long blond ponytail over her shoulder.

"Which is so totally stupid," complained the second girl. "I mean, if the Dark Siders all die, who's going to mine the tellurium? And then how are people going to 'Gaze?"

"Puh-leeze. They've gotta have some kind of other plan in mind. They're, like, the Circle of Eight, right? Anyway, I'd simply die if I couldn't 'Gaze anymore!" lamented girl number one. "I mean, what else is there for fun these days?" She gestured to the club. "It's so awesome here, don't you agree, Mariah? I'm super psyched you made it back."

"Yeah," agreed her friend. "Are you here for good? I

want to move here, but my parents say I have to wait till I'm eighteen. They're so old-fashioned."

I held up my hands to slow them down. "Wait a second," I said. "Did you say the Dark Siders are dying?"

The girls nodded in sync. "Yeah," says girl number two. "And they totally deserve it, too, for what they did to you. I heard from my friend that they've started pumping in this slow-acting poison gas through the ventilation fans down on Stratum 2." She shook her head. "Which is totally short-sighted, in my opinion. I mean, what, do they want to kill off the Dark Siders and then have the Indys start to mine or something? As if!"

"They wouldn't make Indys mine!" girl number one retorted, rolling her eyes. "They'll just, like, get some of the nTs to do it. If you ask me, that should have been done a long time ago. NTs would produce so much more than those lazy mutant freaks."

"Wait, wait, hang on a second," I cried, my heart pounding. I imagined the little mutant children gasping for breath in their one-room schoolhouse, the brittle-boned senior citizens collapsing in the market square. Dawn, alone, lying in bed, choking on his last breath. "Why would they poison the Dark Siders?"

"They think the Dark Siders kidnapped you, of course," said girl number two, as if I were the slow kid. "Which is ridiculous, 'cause obviously you're here!" She grinned. "Will you party with us tonight, Mariah? Our friends will be so impressed when we tell them we hung with a legend like yourself."

"Sorry. I've . . . I've got to go," I stammered. "Um, are there . . . Moongazing booths around here somewhere?" Or was I supposed to use the necklace? I should have asked more questions . . .

"Yeah, up in the VIP lounge," said girl number one. "Well, they don't look like the booths back in Terra, though. They're just chairs. Sit in a chair and activate your necklace. You'll be back in no time."

"But do you have to go now?" whined girl number two. "Can't you hang with us first?"

"Yeah, hang with us!" begs girl number one. "Supposedly Paris Hilton is going to show up tonight. And she might dance on tables. How cool would that be?"

"I think it's Paris *Milton*," I muttered, but suddenly I wasn't so sure.

"Sorry, girls," I said, backing away. "It was great to meet you." I turned and made a dash for the VIP section. The chairs? Of course. That's exactly where I was sitting when I was transported to Terra the first time. I ran through the club, pushing past sweaty bodies, ignoring the protests of the jostled dancers. No time for apologies; I had to get to the lounge.

My body stopped short as it slammed into something solid. I looked up, realizing that I'd just smacked into the very person I'd first wanted to find but now sought to avoid. Craig looked down at me in a mixture of surprise and annoyance. He grabbed me by the shoulders, his eyes piercing.

"Where the hell have you been?" he demanded.

I didn't have time for explanations. For excuses. He wouldn't understand anyway. He wouldn't believe. I suddenly realized that, Mariah or no, Terra had become a huge part of me. And he couldn't share that. There was no use wasting any more time on this superficial relationship built out of attraction and convenience.

"Long story," I muttered. "Let me go."

"I'm on my break. I have time for a long story. Let's go to the back room and you can tell me."

"I'm sorry," I said, and I was, in a way. "But I don't have time right now."

He didn't let go of me. "Why?" he demanded. I looked down at his hand gripping my arm. How come I'd never noticed he had one of those weird moon tattoos? "Got a hot date?" he asked. He was bluffing, of course, not having any idea how close he was to the truth. "You know, usually it's custom to break up with someone you don't want to see anymore, instead of just disappearing off the face of the Earth, leaving them standing at your door with a bag of vegetarian takeout."

I cringed a little, feeling his disappointment, his anger. He didn't deserve the treatment he'd gotten from me. He'd been a decent boyfriend for a lot of years. Just because I didn't share the connection with him that I did with Dawn didn't mean I should hurt him.

But this was an emergency. I couldn't waste any more time. If what the girls said was true, then Dark Siders were dying and it was all because of me. I had to get back there and figure out a plan to stop the government from killing them. And I needed all the time I could get.

I reached up, kissed Craig on the cheek, and said good-bye forever. I felt terrible, especially after catching a glimpse of his hurt face, but I saw no alternative. My life here was trivial and unimportant, and I was wasting valuable time. I had to help the people who needed me.

"I'm sorry," I said one more time, really meaning it.

Then I pushed past him and raced up to the VIP room before he could stop me, and plopped down in a chair. Out of the corner of my eye I saw that he was running after me, taking the steps two at a time. I had to act fast. I grabbed for the necklace, fumbling with it for a moment before my fingers located the tiny button.

I pressed down hard, closed my eyes, and readied myself to go back to hell.

A hell that was feeling more and more like my real home.

THIRTEEN

I open my eyes and find myself in a now-familiar, swirling Technicolor Moongazing booth. I let out a sigh of relief. It worked. I'm back.

I take off the Moongazing glasses and step outside the booth and into the hallway, feeling a bit freaked out at what I've just done: left my home, willingly, and perhaps, a nagging thought at the back of my brain reminds me, for good this time.

I shake my head. I can regret this all later. Right now I have to find the Eclipsers and get an update of what's going on and how I can help. I have to find Dawn.

I dash down the hallway and burst out into the lobby of Moongazer Station. It's completely empty now, making me wonder what time it is on Terra.

"Short trip," the proprietor notes coolly from behind the counter, looking me up and down with his spectacle-covered eyes. Does this guy ever take a break? A day off?

I shrug. "Long enough," I reply, suddenly realizing how oddly good it feels to be back. The weird, displaced vertigo I'd been suffering on Earth has totally disappeared, and I'm almost getting this strange home-sweet-home vibe. I feel like . . . me again. Which doesn't make any sense, I realize, but there you go.

I grab the phone off the counter and dial Dawn's number, praying that he has his cell phone on him.

"Hello?" he answers a moment later, his voice low and sleepy sounding.

I let out the breath I hadn't realized I'd been holding. "Oh my God, Dawn," I cry, relief and happiness flooding through me just from hearing him answer. "I'm so glad you're there."

"Mariah?"

I pause, consider, then force myself to correct him. "It's . . . it's Skye."

"Um, right. Sorry," he stammers, sounding a bit out of breath. I remember the Indy girls' tales of the poison. My heart quickens. Is Dawn down there, literally asphyxiating as we speak? "Where are you?" he asks, finding his questions. "I thought—aren't you on Earth? How can you be calling me?"

Oh yeah, I guess an explanation is in order. But perhaps not with the nosy proprietor eavesdropping while pretending to sweep the floor. "It's a long story. I can't explain now. But I'm at Moongazer Station. Can you come get me?"

"I'll be there in five minutes. They've latched the rabbit holes from above, so you'll have to come down to me. I'll meet you at the bottom of the ladder. But be careful, Skye. The government's looking for you. And they'll pretty much stop at nothing to get you back."

"I know," I say. "Please hurry."

I head outside and down the street till I find the rabbit hole. It's the one Dawn and I climbed down on my first trip to Terra. That day seems a lifetime ago, and my heart thuds in anticipation of seeing him again. I've missed him, I realize. Even in this short time of being apart, I've missed him dreadfully.

I climb down, replacing the manhole cover above, realizing this could very well be a one-way trip. As I head down into the darkness, the air becomes thicker and sickly sweet. My lungs struggle to take it in, and panic swells. But I force myself to practice my breathing exercises. As long as I stay calm, there's plenty of air. At least for now.

I step off the ladder and onto the road. The air is still and quiet. A moment later, Dawn pulls up on his bike, parking it and jumping off, throwing his arms around me and squeezing me so tightly it's even more difficult to breathe. "Oh, Skye," he cries, burying his face in my hair. "Oh, sweetie, I thought I'd never see you again."

I nestle my head against his chest, feeling his rapid heartbeat against my ear. He feels so good. So solid, warm. I breathe him in, his musky scent tickling my every extremity. He's so beautiful, so wonderful. So passionate and loving. How could I have ever thought to leave him, to abandon him for my shallow existence on Earth?

Never again, a voice inside me whispers. *You belong with him. And you should do everything in your power to stay by his side.*

Dawn pulls out of the hug, cupping my face in his hands, looking down at me with loving, desperate eyes. "Why did you come back?" he asks, his voice fraught with concern. "I mean, don't get me wrong, I'm happy to see you. But it's not safe here. The government— they've . . ." He trails off, gesturing weakly to the fans. "We'll be dead in a week if they have their way."

"I heard," I say, standing on my tiptoes to kiss him lightly on the mouth. His lips tremble as they meet mine. "That's why I came back. You need me."

He sighs. "I'd rather you were safe," he says, pointing at his bike. "Get on, we'll go to headquarters. Everyone's already gathered. We're trying to work out a plan."

We arrive at the Eclipser headquarters and go through all the bells and whistles to obtain admittance. Inside, all the usual suspects are gathered. Their faces are drawn with worry and stress, and it doesn't appear that they've eaten or slept for days. The air inside is even thicker and staler, and it's very difficult to breathe.

They look up when we enter, concern etched on each face.

"Sister Mariah," Ruth greets me, rising from the table to walk over. Her movements are slow, probably to conserve air. "We thought you left. That you went back to Earth."

I accept her weak hug. "I did. But then I heard what the Circle had done. All because of me. I couldn't just stay on Earth and let you guys suffer for my sake."

Kayce frowns. "But at least there you would have been safe. I don't think you realize how dangerous your situation here is. They'll wait until we're half dead and too weak to fight back, then charge in here full force, leaving no stone unturned until they locate you." He sighs. "On Earth, at least they wouldn't have found you."

"Then what? You'd all be dead. What good is it for me to be safe for the revolution if the revolution has been reduced to a pile of bodies at the bottom of a pit? That's stupid." I realize I'm being harsh, but what else can I do? They've got to see reason here.

"They're bluffing," suggests Hiro. "They wouldn't really kill us all. They need us for mining."

"Maybe they're planning to use nTs to do that," I say quietly, remembering the Indy teen's theory. Dawn cringes. In fact, they all do. I guess none of them really wants to admit this could be one act of mass genocide, taking care of a troublesome population once and for all.

"No," Kayce says finally. "I refuse to believe it. This will all blow over. We just have to stay strong. In the meantime, we need to get you out of here."

Dawn nods. "Yes, Skye. We need you to go back to Earth."

I stare at him, mouth open. "*You* want me to go back?" I can't believe what I'm hearing.

He shrugs. "I'm not a fan of you Moongazing, but it's better than leaving you here like a sitting duck. They'll find you and kill you if you stay." He shoots me a pointed look. "And I'm not going to stand around and let that happen."

The room erupts in murmurs as the Eclipsers discuss the situation. I grab Dawn's hand and drag him to the back of the room. "Are you crazy?" I hiss. "You really want me to hide out on Earth while you guys suffer here?"

"Yes," he says simply.

"But you think 'Gazing is dangerous. Addictive."

"Potential addiction is better than immediate poisoning."

MARIANNE MANCUSI

"But I can't leave you guys."

He grabs my hands in his and squeezes. "I appreciate your loyalty," he says. "But there's another thing to consider. If we're weak and they charge in, if we're found harboring you, maybe they really will kill us all. If you're not here when they raid, maybe they'll figure they made a mistake. They'll stop the siege, hand out antidotes . . ." He's really clutching at straws to protect me.

In the center of the room, Ruth raps her gavel against the table. "We'll take an hour recess," she announces. "And then make our decision."

The Eclipsers file out of the room one by one, slowly and deliberately, so as not to use up excess air. Soon Dawn and I are the only ones left. I climb up on the table and plop myself down.

"Skye, it's the only way you'll be safe," Dawn says, joining me. He reaches over and threads his fingers through mine. "And I can't bear to lose you again."

"But you will lose me. I'll be on Earth. I want to be here. With you."

Dawn pauses for a moment. "You *will* be with me."

I turn to look at him, uncomprehending. "What? What do you mean?"

"I'm going to go with you."

"To Earth? You're going to 'Gaze?" I cry, disbelieving. "I don't understand."

"It's simple. As I said before, I won't lose you again. You offered me a choice the last time: go with you or stay to help the Eclipsers. I stayed. I thought I was doing the right thing by doing so. But maybe I was just afraid. Maybe I should have trusted you. What would life be like now if we'd just gone? Said good-bye to it all. We'd be happy on Earth. Wandering the parks, playing with the dogs, cooking fabulous meals, and sipping real wine . . ."

"You can't mean that."

"Why not?" he asks, jumping off the table, raking a hand through his hair. "I'm sick of living like this! Like a rat in a cage, worried every day that one of us will be killed. And for what? Have we really made a difference?" He shrugs. "I don't know. Seems to me the Dark Siders are worse off than they ever were. At least before we had simple things like air to breathe and food to eat. Now, because of our rebellion, their very existence is in jeopardy. It would have been better for everyone if I'd just gone to Earth and stayed there."

"No!" I cry, sliding off the table. I grab him by the shoulder and pull him around to face me. "You're so wrong. The reason the government is so up in arms is because we're succeeding. They're scared by our victories. They're threatened by our success. We've accomplished so much. We've given the people new hope. A reason to live. The Eclipsers have worked hard, scraping their fingers to the bone for every small victory. And I'm not about to give up now. Fuck Earth. I'm a Terran. An Eclipser. And I'll never run away from my destiny, no matter what they try to do to me."

I pause for breath, but get none as Dawn's mouth clamps down on mine. His lips are crushing and his tongue invades my mouth, taking, imbibing, devouring, as if he's starving and has finally come across life-saving nourishment. My entire body ignites, taking his inner fire through some sort of osmosis, my passion and his intertwining like strands of DNA. His hands dig through my hair and I wrap my arms around his waist, pulling him close, so close—I'd crawl inside him if I could.

"I love you," he says against my mouth, breathless and husky. "Oh God, how I love you."

My heart soars at his words; his tone leaves no question that he means them. "I love you, too," I whisper back. "And I'm glad you understand."

He pulls back so that he can meet my eyes. His expression is flushed but serious. "Of course," he says. "You're right. I was a coward and selfish to suggest we run away to Earth. I just wanted to protect you—to have you. But you're right. It's better to fight back. It's what Mariah would have wanted." He smiles down at me. "I wish I had your strength. Your courage. I wish I wasn't afraid to die."

I shrug. "Don't think I'm not afraid to die," I tell him. "I just can't be afraid to live."

Dawn presses his lips against mine again, kissing me as if there's no tomorrow. And perhaps there won't be, if the poison keeps coming. If the food doesn't arrive.

"Um, sorry. Did you two need more time?"

We break apart from our embrace and my face burns as I realize Ruth and Kayce have reentered the room. I can see Ruth holding back a smile. Dawn grins sheepishly.

"I think we're good," he says.

Ruth widens the door and the other Eclipsers file in.

"So, it's time to take a vote," she says, after everyone's settled. "Should Mariah go back to Earth?"

"There's no need for a vote," I interject. "I've already made my decision."

"She's not going," Dawn adds. "No one is. We're going to fight back."

FOURTEEN

"Fight back?" Hiro echoes skeptically. "And how do you propose we do that? What can we possibly do to defend ourselves against this kind of siege?"

"Well, first off, how is the poison being piped in?" I ask.

"Up on Stratum One, there's a top-security bunker that serves as both a physical plant and a high-tech headquarters," Kayce explains. "It's a huge sprawling complex that houses almost every project the government's got its mitts in; the controls for everything from traffic lights to Moongazing are all inside. I'm positive this is where they'd run the fan operations."

"So we could go in and somehow stop the poison flow?" I ask. "Reroute the air or something? Do we have that kind of technological expertise?"

"Sure," Kayce says. "It's be no problem at all if we had access to their systems. Just hack in, re-code the ventilation program. Maybe even throw in a little computer virus to prevent them from taking back control once we do it."

"So, that's what we'll do then," I say, proud of my plan.

"If it were that easy, we would have already done it," Ruth interjects.

"As Kayce said, it's a top-security place. We've already tried to hack into their computers to get the thumbprint needed to unlock such doors, but you need a thumb of the highest security clearance imaginable to gain admittance to this place. And those thumb codes aren't listed on regular government files."

"What about the people who work there?"

"They never leave," Hiro explains. "They're nTs. They're grown to work in the building and spend their entire lives inside—eating, working, sleeping. You go in, but you don't ever come out."

"Talk about job security," I mutter. "Okay, so basically what you're saying is we need to create a copy of one of the high government official's thumbs."

"Yes." Ruth nods. "But that's something we'll never be able to—"

"I'm on it."

Dawn cocks his head, looking at me with suspicion. "What do you mean?" he demands.

"Easy. Duske wants me back, right? He has the thumb we need. I simply go pay him a visit, tell him I was kidnapped by you guys the entire time and finally managed to escape. Now I want to go home. Once I get him to start trusting me, I'll get his thumbprint."

"No way. It's too dangerous," Dawn says. "You . . . alone in that . . . house?" He shakes his head. "I won't allow it."

"I won't be alone," I argue. "You have Thom working on the inside. Probably a whole slew of others, too. They can help if I get into a jam. And once I have the thumbprint, I'll have security clearance to walk right out the front door."

Dawn frowns. "And what if he doesn't believe you? What if he decides to kill you on sight?"

I think for a moment. "Duske used to date Mariah. He was supposed to marry her at one point. And he's definitely attracted to her. You should have seen the way he was staring at me with those beady eyes of his when I was in his house. Not to mention, the horny little bastard's the type to screw anything in a skirt. I bet he wouldn't mind getting a little action from Mariah. Especially if she's all willing and ready to go."

"That's not a bad idea," Ruth says thoughtfully. "We all know the most powerful men on Terra can be reduced to putty with the right smile. And Sister Mariah is definitely many men's right woman."

"I don't like it," Dawn interrupts. "Him, putting his hands on you. I can't—"

"Dawn, it's the only way," I say, laying a hand on his arm. His muscles are hard, tensed. "I'm the only one who can do this. And what alternative do we have— stay down here until we're weak from hunger and dying of slow poison? If I'm going to die, I want to die in an attempt to save our people."

And I mean it, too, I realize, as the words spill from my mouth. I've lost my chance to go back to Earth. To be safe and sound with the man I love. But for some reason I don't feel the least bit of regret. I don't know how, I don't know why, but I do know, like it or not, this is now my fight. And I plan to give it my all.

As I'm standing here now, my old life, the one on Earth, seems nothing more than a very long dream, a halfhearted excuse of an existence where I never accomplished anything meaningful. Who cares about a video game, about fame and fortune and all the rest? It's all empty and useless when standing beside the opportunity to save a world. Today I'm alive as I've never been. I have a reason to live. To fight. I have a cause and a people who need me. And I alone have the power to help them.

I gotta say, in a weird way, I love playing Mariah.

"She's right," Ruth says in an effort to stop Dawn's continued protest. "It's a good plan. The best chance we've got right now. And Mariah's the only one who can really carry it out."

"We'll put a tracker on her," suggests Kayce. "So we'll know where she is at all times. If she gets in trouble, she can just hit the panic button and we can figure out a way to storm the house."

"And Brother Thom's a great swordsman," Hiro adds. "I trained him myself. He can always break cover and help her, if need be. It's not like there'll be much point of cover if we all die."

Dawn slumps his shoulders. He can't argue with everyone. "Fine," he says. "I can see you're not going to be dissuaded. I don't like it, but I understand why you think it has to be done." He throws me a sad smile. "You're very brave, sweetie. I'll give you that."

"I have to be," I say simply, getting a warm tickle from his term of endearment. "There's no other choice."

"I still think you're crazy," Dawn says as we walk through the door and into my apartment. He heads over to the couch and sits down, scrubbing his face with his hands. "It's so dangerous. What if Duske isn't fooled? What if he kills you?" He looks up at me, his eyes hollow and shadowed. "I can't bear the idea of something bad happening to you."

"I know," I say, taking a seat beside him. I wrap my arms around him and cuddle my head to his shoulder. He body feels warm and taut against mine. Solid, strong. Only the smallest tremble gives away his fear. "I'm scared, too, believe me. But it's a good plan. It can work. And once we get the high-security clearance thumb mold made, we can not only stop the poison, but maybe we can figure out some other government tricks. Imagine what secrets are being held in that building."

"You're right, I know," Dawn relents. He turns his head to kiss me on the forehead. "It is a good plan. And you're extremely brave to volunteer." He shakes his head. "Enough talk now. I have one night with you and I don't plan to waste it by worrying about the future."

He rises to his feet and leans down to scoop me up as if I'm a baby. I start to laugh, but he silences me with a kiss and makes his way to my bedroom, cradling me in his arms. He lays me gently on the bed and then crawls on top of me, parting my thighs with his knee and finding my mouth. His lips brush against mine. Soft. Reverent. And I realize something's changed between us. Some barrier that prevented us from becoming close has now melted away. Perhaps it's due to me giving up my life on Earth, giving up all the baggage I've been carrying around and accepting my role on Terra. Whatever the reason, there's no longer anything standing in our way. Tonight we will experience each other fully, accept the bond between us, and finally join as one.

I can't wait.

Dawn's hands reach up to stroke my hair, my face. He caresses my cheeks softly with the back of his palm, then lowers his mouth to my neck, kissing a path of heat. I arch my neck as his mouth nibbles my sensitive skin. "You smell so sweet," he murmurs. "So . . ." His words trail off. He must realize there's no need to speak. His touch is a thousand words, telling me everything he feels.

"Make love to me, Dawn," I say, unable to hold back. After all, this may be our only chance. Our last night to admit and express the feelings that have grown between us. Tomorrow I go into the lion's den. Tonight I want to be loved by the lamb.

"I will," he mouths against my skin. He looks up for a moment, catching my eyes in his own glowing blue ones. "I most definitely will."

He goes back to work, pulling up my shirt, revealing my bare stomach. He trails kisses along my belly as his hands reach up to cradle my breasts. He grazes the tips with his thumb, coaxing them into his power. I squirm under his touch, multiple sensations torpedoing through my insides. His kisses lower and my stomach burns. I claw at the sheets, struggling to retain control.

He reaches down to remove my pants, then pulls aside my lacy panties, exposing me to his mouth. His tongue begins to explore, velvet softness against my sensitive flesh. I arch my back and squeeze my eyes shut as he delves in for a deeper exploration, tasting, sucking, lapping. All the while his fingers toy with my breasts. So gentle, so sweet, yet so powerful and wild.

It's all too much and it takes no time at all for a tidal wave of ecstasy to wash over me. I cry out as I allow the sensations to consume me, surrendering the charade of control. There's no need for it. I trust him, I realize, to take the steering wheel. To bring me where I've never been before. I know he'll keep me safe. And whether I'll return unscathed or changed forever, it doesn't matter.

He lifts his head, smiling a shy smile, looking pleased to have brought me so effortlessly to such heights. And this time there's no regret lingering in his eyes. No hesitation. He trusts me, too. He loves me. And suddenly I want to give him as much as he's already given me. More, if I'm able.

I sit up in bed and motion for him to flip over on his back. He blushes but obeys. I crawl on top of him, straddling him with my thighs, unbuckling his utility belt, pulling it through the loops of his pants, then tossing it aside. I help him out of his jacket and pull his shirt over his head, exposing his strong, muscular chest. I run my fingers over the six-pack abs, exploring each muscle individually. He jerks as my fingers trail lower, his face taut and pale as he searches for control.

I smile. *Nice try. But you won't keep that up for long. Not if I have anything to say about it.*

I go down on my knees at the side of the bed, unbuttoning and unzipping his pants, pulling them down, releasing him from his cloth restraints. I smile up at him. He's hard. Ready. Clearly wanting me as badly as I want him. I take his swollen cock in my hands and run my fingers down its length. He winces a bit, so I pause.

"Sorry," he apologizes, his face reddening. "It's . . . been a while. I hope I can—"

I shake my head, then press a finger to my lips. There's no need to talk. No need for excuses.

He chuckles and reaches down to stroke my hair. "Okay, okay," he relents. I nod approvingly, then go back to work, bringing his shaft to my mouth, while still stroking his length with my hands, guiding him in and out, in and out. He groans and digs his hands deeper into my hair, his nails biting at my scalp. But I don't stop. He begins to thrust, matching my rhythm with his hips, rocking against my mouth. I can feel his whole body tremble as I engulf him over and over.

"Enough!" he cries suddenly, jerking himself away. He rakes a hand through his tousled hair, his face flushed and sweat dripping from his forehead. "God, woman! Are you trying to render me completely useless?"

"May-be," I say with a small grin. "Perhaps I like you as putty in my hands."

"I see," he says. "But now it's your turn." He hooks his hands under my arms and yanks me to my feet. He rises, too, spinning me around, kissing me once, then pushing me backward so I fall onto the bed. The gentleness is gone. Now his face is a mask of desire, of raw want that refuses to be gentled. He kicks off his pants and nudges my legs apart, running his hands down my inner thighs, then settles between them, his cock a divining rod easily finding my slick wet core and hovering just above it, teasing my swollen mound. I bite down on my lower lip hard enough to draw blood. It's all I can do not to tilt my pelvis upward, to swallow him inside me, take him as my own. But I wait. Breathless and ready, I wait. The next move is clearly his. And I'm not about to spoil his fun.

He pauses for a moment, his face a mask of concentration, then thrusts forward, sheathing his full length in me. I cry out, no longer able to hold back. The wash of pleasure at our joining, the divine moment when we first become one flesh—it's almost too much to take. He feels so good, as if his body were built to enter only mine. At that moment, I want to keep him inside me forever.

He leans forward and kisses me hard on the mouth, crushing me with almost primal passion. He slips out of me, then in, then out again. His thrusts—slow at first—gradually increase in velocity. I find his rhythm and make it my own, our stomachs slapping against one another, sweaty and slick, as our bodies move in a dance as old as time. Through it all, he kisses me, his tongue intertwining with mine. Worshiping my mouth. Making me really feel like the goddess all the people of Terra think I am.

He stops for a moment, capturing my face in his hands, sliding his callused palms up my cheeks, finding my eyes with his own. His gaze makes my breath hitch in my throat. He smiles at me. A completely unguarded, vulnerable smile. His face is so beautiful I want to cry and laugh all at the same time. Instead, I smile back, hoping he sees the expression for what it is: an offering of everything that I am. I want to give him all of it.

He lowers his hands to my hips, locking me against him. I wrap my legs around his back, clenching my inner muscles tight around him. He shudders for a moment, then finds his rhythm again, his strokes gaining momentum; harder, faster, deeper. The pressure builds as we grind against one another. Soon, almost too soon, the crescendo rises within me again. The heat scorches from his body bucking against mine. I'm over the edge, out of control, surrendering to him and the burning, bone-melting heat. I cry out as the sensations consume me too hard and too fast to catalog individually. At that moment, there is no Earth. No Terra. No Mariah. There's only two people, destined to have been brought together like this, to be consumed by a holy, unquenchable fire.

He gasps, joining me in ecstasy, finding his own release, biting down on my shoulder as he succumbs to the pleasure and spills himself deep inside me. His body convulses before collapsing atop me, heavy and solid, his breath coming in uneven gasps, his heart beating erratically against my sweat-soaked breasts.

"That was . . . ," he murmers against my shoulder. He lifts his head. Finds me. Captures me with an earnest gaze that makes me want to weep. "That was . . ."

I reach up to kiss him on the nose, feeling warm and safe and desired and oh so happy. I can't remember a time on Earth when I felt this way—as if I'd just shared a divine, spiritual experience. An encounter destined to change my life forever. How could I ever just have sex again, knowing now all that it can be with the right person? All it can be with him.

"That *was*," I agree, giving him a shy smile of my own. "And it will be again if you want it to."

"Oh, I want. I most definitely want." He laughs. We kiss again, our mouths explaining what neither of us can find the words to say.

FIFTEEN

I lift my hand to grab the brass knocker affixed to the mammoth door in front of me. My knees are knocking together so hard I'm half convinced they'll buck out from under me, giving way completely and reducing me to a quivering pile of nerves on Duske's front steps. That wouldn't be the ideal way to make my entrance, to say the least.

More than a small part of me wants to play the coward, to turn and flee and never look back. Hit Moongazer Palace running, return to Earth, and live out my life in peace, never giving any of this nightmare another thought.

But then I remember Dawn's face. The love shining from his glowing eyes this morning as he kissed me good-bye and sent me on my impossible mission. The pride in his voice as he praised my courage and told me that, Mariah or Skye, now I really would be the savior of the people. The one they would sing about for generations to come.

How could I possibly deny my new destiny?

I draw in a breath, trying to quell my nervous energy as I wrap my hands around the knocker and rap it against the door three times. *Here goes nothing.*

I wait for a moment, and then the door swings inward. The butler, Thom, secret operative of the Eclipsers, greets me from the foyer with a nearly imperceptible nod. At least I'm not entirely alone, even though I know he won't break his cover unless the situation gets dire.

"Sister Mariah," he cries, keeping in character. "We have been looking everywhere for you. Let me tell the master you are here. Please step inside."

Thom moves to allow me entrance. Swallowing hard, I cross the threshold and the door swings silently shut behind me. I'm now at the point of no return. Inside the belly of the beast. Let's hope he's hungry.

Thom leaves me, heads up the sweeping staircase, and disappears down a hallway. I shuffle from foot to foot, my heart pounding with fear. Was I crazy to think this plan would work? What will Duske do when he sees me? What if he decides I'm worth more dead than alive? Will he simply kill me on sight, never giving me a chance to accomplish my mission?

"Well, well, well." A booming voice above interrupts my racing thoughts. I look up. Duske's standing at the top of the stairs, dressed in an old-fashioned black suit. His hair is slicked back and his face is cold and unreadable. "It appears the prodigal sister has returned."

Time to earn that Academy Award.

"Brother Duske!" I cry, rushing up the stairs. Before he can react, I throw my arms around him, squeezing him in the most enthusiastic hug I can muster. I press my whole body against him, hoping to spark some heat in his cold, unyielding frame. "Thank God you're here!"

The government official lets me hold him for a moment, then steps back out of the embrace. He looks me over, eyebrow raised in skepticism.

"You seem . . . happy to see me," he observes.

"Of course!" I say, practically bouncing with enthusiasm. "You're the first friendly face I've laid eyes on in days. You have no idea what I've been through. This gang of rebels—I think they're called Eclipsers or something—kidnapped me from your house and dragged me underground. It was horrible."

"Kidnapped, huh?" Duske repeats slowly. "And here I was sure you'd left of your own free will."

"Are you kidding me?" I give him a disgusted look. "Leave all this? Abandon my chance to get back to Earth where I belong? Do you know where they took me? Some horrible underground ghetto with these crazy mutant freaks. They kept insisting I was that girl named Mariah, their rebel leader or whatever. And they wanted to use me somehow to unite the people against the government." I shake my head, as if reliving the horror. "Of course, I'm, like, 'Dudes, I'm so not Mariah. I'm Skye, and I'm from Earth and I need to get back.' But did they believe me? No! They locked me up and only took me out when they wanted to show me off like some kind of animal." I allow my voice to crack. "Oh God, Duske, I thought I was going to die down there. It was horrible. Thank God I finally escaped and got back here." I throw my arms around him again, sobbing into his shoulder.

Duske stands still for a moment, then awkwardly pats me on the back a few times. I try to gauge his reaction. Does he believe me? Even a little? I step back from the embrace and study his face. It's hard to tell.

"An interesting story," he says slowly.

"Interesting?" I screw up my face in disgust. "Horrible is more like. All I want to do is get back to Earth. To my real life. Please. You've got to help me."

"How did you escape?" he asks, ignoring my request.

"There's something going on down there," I explain, glad Dawn and I had role-played this encounter last night so I knew exactly what to say. "Some kind of weird thing in the air. And so they're all weak and stuff. I saw my opportunity, and when they were transporting me, I acted. I killed two guards and went up one of the hatches. You can go look, if you don't believe me. Their bodies are still there, right under the rabbit hole by Moongazer Station."

This was a small insurance the Eclipsers had arranged to make my story more believable. The bodies in question were two asthmatic Dark Siders who had succumbed to the poisoned air a day before. Hiro and Kayce had worked on the two already dead bodies and laid them by the exit to provide legitimacy to my tale.

Duske claps his hands, and two silver-suited soldiers appear at the bottom of the stairs. "Go down to Luna Park," he says. "Go down the rabbit hole by Moongazer Station. See if there are bodies there."

The guards bow low, then exit the building to carry out their orders. Duske turns back to me. "I'm sorry not to take your story at face value," he says. "But these days we cannot be too careful." He claps his hands again and two more guards show up. He gestures to me and instructs them to pat me down. Luckily, we'd envisioned this kind of scenario and so I'd come without weapons.

"Right. I understand," I say as the guards search me. "So, soon you'll believe me and we can move on. Did I miss your Moongazing seminar? I'll still do it if you want. I'll do whatever it takes. I just want to get back to Earth—like you promised." I'm crying now. Easy to fake tears when I'm this terrified. "I'm so sick of this creepy place. All I want to do is go home. To see my family. My friends."

Duske's face softens. He reaches out to stroke my hair. "Shh," he says. "Don't cry. It'll be okay. The nightmare is over. You're safe with me."

I breathe a sigh of relief. He's buying it. He's actually buying it.

"So, can I go to my room?" I ask. "I'm dying for a bath. And then maybe we could go to dinner tonight? I loved that place you took me originally. What was it called again? The Park Terrace? Those ravioli are divine."

Duske scratches his chin, studying me with his piercing eyes. "All in due time," he says. "But first we must take a little trip." He turns to walk down the hall, beckoning me to follow.

I cock my head. A trip? What kind of trip? Does he believe me or not?

"Come along," he says and I realize I have no choice but to follow him.

We walk down the hall until we come to an elevator. He presses his thumb to call it, and a moment later the doors slide open. We step inside and Duske uses his thumb to select a bottom floor. The doors close and the elevator shoots downward. We travel for what feels like a long time. I wonder how deep we're going. My heart pounds in my chest, so hard and fast I worry it'll burst. I steal a glance at Duske, trying to read his expression. He simply stares at the descending numbers flickering above the doors, his face inscrutable. Finally, the elevator shudders to a stop and the doors slide open.

We step out into a long corridor, highly guarded by thumb-sensored doors, seemingly every few feet. This place is more secure than Fort Knox. But Duske's thumb works magic on every lock. Wow, I *so* have to get a copy of it, no matter what it takes. I consider jumping him now—after all, we are alone—but then reconsider. At present I have no means to get his thumbprint. I must wait for Thom to slip me supplies.

"Where are we going?" I ask, praying this is not some trick—some one-way trip to a high-security prison he plans to throw me in.

"Bunker Twelve," Duske says, stopping in front of a small golf-cart-looking vehicle. "Get in."

I obey, joining him in the cart as he activates the hover controls. Soon we're floating down the corridor at low speed, and about ten minutes later we come to another door. This one's flanked by human guards in addition to thumb-sensor locks.

Duske steps out of the cart, nods to the guards, and waves an identification card at them. They step aside, pressing their thumbs against matching sensors, and Duske does the same with his own. The locks click simultaneously and the door swings open.

We step into a long, featureless hallway, illuminated by dim fluorescent lighting lining the ceiling. I follow Duske down a hall, trying to memorize each twist and turn. The place is like a maze. An industrial catacomb. There are a million doors dotting the myriad hallways.

Finally, we come to a door at the end of one corridor. Duske presses his thumb against the sensor and the door slides open. We step inside, into some sort of prison, though it certainly wouldn't meet Geneva Convention standards. The smell of decay and rot permeates the air, and I have to resist a nearly overwhelming urge to block my nose with my hand. The floor is strewn with debris, and behind each iron-barred cell there's a prisoner, dressed in rags and lying on the ground, covered in her own filth. There are no beds, no toilets, not a single creature comfort to be seen.

But I can't go off on him. I can't sneer and rage and assault him and his government's character. "Where the hell are we?" I demand. "I thought we were going to Moongaze. I really need to get back to Earth, you know."

"All in good time, my dear," Duske says, patting my arm. Then he turns to one of the cells and gestures. "Do you recognize this prisoner?" he asks.

I peer in, unable to stop the gasp escaping my lips as my eyes fall on the woman inside. Glenda. She's barely recognizable as my former yoga teacher back on Earth. Her always lithe frame is now skeletal, her face gaunt, and her eyes blackened. She's shivering in her thin slip dress, and her arms and legs are riddled with pus-filled sores.

Horror slams through my body, and I struggle to keep my composure. So, they didn't kill her. She's been here this whole time. Starved, probably tortured—all for rescuing me. My stomach heaves and

I struggle not to be sick. I turn away, unable to look at her bruised face.

Oh, Glenda, I'm so sorry. I'm so sorry you had to suffer like this for me.

"That's . . . Glenda," I say, calling upon every molecule of strength inside me to keep up the charade. Every fiber of my body yearns to turn around and attack my host. To kill him for what he's done to this poor woman who only wants to better the world. But I know I can't act now. There are guards milling about, armed with heavy artillery. I have to wait. Bide my time. Play selfish Skye from Earth for a little longer. "That's my yoga instructor back on Earth. What the hell is she doing on Terra?" I ask, turning to Duske, mostly to avoid looking at the disappointment radiating from Glenda's hollow eyes. If only I could send her a signal. Somehow relay to her that I'm only acting. That her sacrifice was not in vain.

Duske shakes his head. "This woman only pretended to be from Earth to lure you into the Dark Siders' trap. She's actually one of the head Eclipsers. She was the one who broke in and attempted to kidnap you that day you left us."

"Really? That was her?" I turn back to throw her my most disgusted look. "So, it's her fault I'm still stuck in Terra? That I was dragged underground to that hell and forced to live with those disgusting mutants?"

Glenda whimpers from inside her cell.

Duske nods. "It is," he says. "All her fault." He reaches down, pulling up the hem of his trousers, and produces a knife banded to his ankle. He unsheathes the blade, stands back up, and holds it out to me. "Obviously, she needs to pay for her crimes—for what she did to you." He smiles. "Go ahead. Take this knife and kill her."

I stare at him and then the knife, horrified beyond belief. Oh God, this is like what always happens in the movies; the hero's supposed to prove his loyalty to the villain by killing someone from his own side.

But I can't be that hero! There's no way I can take a knife and slice up an innocent woman—one who risked everything just to save me from my own death. There's just no way! But if I don't, then Duske will doubt my story. He'll likely turn the knife on me instead. If I don't kill Glenda, I'll die. And everyone else will, too. The Dark Siders, the Eclipsers, Dawn.

Oh God, what am I going to do?

I try to swallow, but my throat's too dry. I try to think, try to remember back to the day the Eclipsers told me that Glenda had been captured trying to rescue me. I remember them telling me that to her, the cause was more important than life. Did she still feel that way? Would she want me to kill her if it meant saving the others? How close was she to death already? Would I only be putting her out of her misery?

"Go on," Duske goads smugly. He's obviously enjoying my indecision. "We don't have all day, you know. I mean, you do want to get back to Earth, right?"

I stare at Glenda, cowering in the corner, hands over her head, not so brave anymore. My mind races with indecision. She's weak. It'd take one blow. She'll probably die anyway. She'd want me to do it. I have to do it. The cause is more important than one life. How many times have the Eclipsers told me that?

I grab the knife from Duske, step into the cell, raise the blade. I stand above Glenda's quivering skeletal body, drawing in a breath, garnering every ounce of resolve within me. If only I had Mariah's strength. She'd be able to do this. She'd be able to act decisively if it meant furthering the cause.

"Do it!" Duske commands. "Now!"

But I can't. I just can't. I drop the blade. It clatters uselessly to the stone floor.

"No," I croak, resigning myself to the fact that I've likely signed the death sentence for all of the Dark Siders and myself. But what else can I do? I just don't have it in me to kill a defenseless human being. "I'm sorry. I know you guys have different rules on Terra, but on Earth we don't go around killing helpless women for no reason. Even if she's a criminal, it's murder. And I'm not a murderer."

Duske reaches down and scoops up the blade. He shoves it back into its sheath. "Very well," he says. "Let's head back to the house. We're finished here."

I stare at him, not understanding. "B-but . . ." I stammer. "I thought . . ."

Duske shrugs. "It was a test," he says. "If you were really working for the Eclipsers, you would have killed her to keep up your act. That's how they work. Sacrifice one person to save all the others. To them, their silly cause is more important than individual life."

Realization hits me with the force of a ten-ton truck. I made the right decision. My weakness actually proved my character. Of course! He was testing me to see if I acted like Mariah. And she would have done it. By refusing, I've effectively proved myself to be Skye.

"So you . . . believe me," I say, praying it's not too good to be true.

"In my position, I'd be a fool to believe anyone," Duske replies. "For all I know—"

A burst of static interrupts him. He reaches down and pulls out his comm device. "Yes, what is it?" he asks impatiently.

"We found the bodies, sir," says the voice on the other end. "Just where you said they'd be."

"Did you test them?"

"Yes. They appear to have beaten to death with a bat that we found discarded a few feet away. Fingerprints on the bat appear to belong to one Mariah Quinn. There are also a few blood splatters on the body that also appear to belong to her."

Phew. And here I thought Kayce and Hiro were crazy when they insisted on me giving a blood sample before I left.

"Very good," Duske says into the device. He switches it off, shoves it in his back pocket, and turns to me with a thoughtful expression on his face. "You're either telling the truth," he says, "or you're really, really clever." He shrugs. "I guess in the end it makes no difference."

"I'm telling the truth. I swear to God," I say. "Please, just let me go back to Earth. I can't take this anymore."

Duske frowns. "Let's not get ahead of ourselves, Sister," he says. "Even if I do believe you, which I'm not saying I necessarily do, nothing else has changed. I still need you to speak about Earth at one of my seminars. Only then can I allow you to return."

"Oh yeah," I say. "And you're still going to give me a million dollars, right?" I try not to grimace as I ask the question. Is it possible to believe someone would actually be so shallow? To be more concerned with her burgeoning bank account and free trip back to Earth than the plight of the poor woman languishing in this cell? The plight of the people down in Stratum 2?

Of course it's possible, I realize, feeling a bit sick to my stomach at the thought. In fact, it's not only possible, but exactly how I had been acting only days before. Imagine what Dawn must have thought of me, those first days in Terra. For him to have to stand by and witness the only woman who had the power to save his people prattle on about a meaningless video game and a shallow, pointless life on another plane of existence. Refusing to step up to the plate, face her destiny, and do something meaningful with the life she'd been given. It must have been completely unbearable. No wonder he'd been so hesitant to let me into his life. Into his heart. I must have come off as the most selfish bitch in the universe.

Well, no more. From now on I'm promising to live my life for a higher purpose. Even if that purpose ends up hastening my ultimate demise. Whether I was born Mariah or Skye, right now people are depending on me. I'm holding thousands of lives in my hands. And I can't turn my back. No matter what the danger to my personal self.

But Duske can't know this. He has to see Skye—greedy, one-track-minded Skye.

" 'Cause, like, a million dollars would totally rock," I add. "I can buy this apartment I've been eyeing and stop paying my bloodsucking landlord." I flash Duske my most guileless grin. "How awesome would that be?"

Duske smiles and pats me on the back—as if I'm some silly child he can patronize. Perfect. I've got him completely buying this act. "Truly awesome," he returns. "And of *course* you will get your money. As soon as you take part in the presentation."

We walk out of the cell. I try to block out Glenda's whimpers. I wish I could do something to help her. But at least she's alive. I only wish there was some way to relay a message to her: *Just hold on a little longer and we'll get you out.*

We head back to the main house. As we're walking down a hallway, we come across Thom, heading in the other direction. He's looking down at a list in his hands and slams into me, as if he hadn't been looking where he was going. I fall backward, as planned, and he reaches down to pull me to my feet.

"Watch where you're going," I grumble.

"I am so sorry, Sister," Thom says, brushing me off.

"Yes, yes. Be more careful, Brother Thom," Duske interrupts. But not before Thom manages to press a small object into my hand. He continues on and I slip the object into my pocket. It's what I need to complete my mission. A razor.

At first I'd been horrified when they told me the plan. Me, cut off a guy's thumb? But them they'd said I only needed the print. That was gruesome, but more manageable. I didn't want to think of anyone—even Duske—running around with a bloody stump.

"Are you taking me to my room?" I ask. "The one I was supposed to stay in that first day?"

Duske nods. "Of course. Then you'll have a chance to bathe and change."

"Thank God for that." I scowl down at my outfit. "This thing stinks to high heaven."

"And if you like, I can make a reservation at the Park Terrace for this evening," Duske continues. "Of course, it's last minute and they are usually at capacity, but I'm sure I could pull a few strings."

"Sounds like a plan." I throw him a grin. "Thank you so much for taking me back. I owe you more than I can possibly say."

"It's my pleasure. I'm just sorry you had to spend time with those barbarians down below," Duske says, his voice getting a sudden soothing, seductive tone. "Now, if you'll follow me, I'll show you to your room."

I draw in a breath and finger the razor in my pocket. God, I hope this works. It has to. There's no plan B.

We arrive at my room a few moments later. It's just as I left it. All perfect and princesslike with its canopy bed and big-screen TV. I can't believe this is just a spare bedroom to someone like Duske while the people down below live like rats. Maybe he does deserve whole digits cut off his hand.

I force thoughts of injustice from my head and concentrate on my mission, sending up a prayer to whatever Terran gods are listening that that this will actually work. It seemed so perfect while discussing it down in the safety of Eclipser headquarters. Now it seems impossible. Crazy, even. How the hell am I going to pull this off?

I step inside the room, my heart pounding in my chest. Duske hovers at the door. I frown. I need to get him inside and in private if this plan is going to work.

"So, um, is this it?" I ask, swaying my body slightly from side to side. "Are you going to go off into that big house of yours and leave me all alone now?" The forwardness feels out of character, but I pray Duske lives up to his sleazy leanings and gives in to his lust.

Duske raises an eyebrow, interest and confusion

washing over his face. He's not sure where I'm going with this line of questioning, but he's not shutting me out, either. That's a start. "Well, I figured you'd want a shower," he says hesitantly. "To freshen up before dinner."

I shrug and wander over to the bed, slowly brushing the pastel-colored comforter with my hand. "Yeah, I suppose I'd like to get clean—eventually," I say, throwing him a glance past lowered eyelids. I bat my lashes once, hoping it's not overkill. But the hungry look on Duske's face makes me realize that I've hit my mark. He's wanted Mariah back for a long time, and now he's thinking he may finally have his chance.

It won't play out exactly as he hopes.

"Is there . . . something you require?" he asks, stepping into the room. *Yes.* He's taken the bait. Now it's time to move in for the kill. Here goes nothing.

"Require?" I repeat, cocking my head to one side. I catch his eyes with my own wide, innocent ones. "I'm not sure about that. But there is something that I . . . want." The words sound so cheesy coming from my lips. Will he buy them? I suck in a breath, waiting for his reaction.

Duske steps forward, positioning himself so he's only inches away from me. *Oh yeah, baby. Come to Mama.* I let out my breath, not sure why I'd been so worried. Of course he'd go for my ploy. He thinks he has *me* brainwashed. He thinks he has the upper hand in this situation. Why not take advantage of sweet little lost me?

"Yes, my lady?" he asks gallantly. "What is it that you want? Be it half my kingdom," he jokes, bowing low. I can't help feeling mocked. "You shall have it."

Yuck. He's so cheesy I'm suddenly in dire need of

crackers. But I smile. "Forget the kingdom," I say saucily. "I just want you."

"Good," he says with a toothy grin. He reaches up to trail a hand down my cheek. "Because I didn't really mean it about the kingdom."

Of course you didn't, buster. But I have a few jokes of my own up my sleeve. You're going to love them.

Time for phase two.

I stand on my tiptoes to press my lips against his. His mouth is cold and clammy. Disgusting. He responds to my advance, however, flicking his tongue at my lips. It's like being kissed by a snake, and I have to resist the urge to jerk away and ruin everything. I remind myself that this slimy kiss is for all the people of the Dark Side.

I part my lips, allowing his slithering tongue entrance. He groans and presses his body against me, pawing my breasts. So much for foreplay with this guy, I guess. At least he's going for it. I love that at the end of the day, evil government leader or no, he's still a man and thus a slave to his penis.

His squeezes my breast as if he's a quarterback grabbing a football, and I realize it's time to make my move before I end up throwing up all over him in disgust. I lower myself to my knees and slowly begin to unzip his pants. He moans in delight.

"Wait," I say. "We'd better close the door."

He agrees, shuffling over and slamming it shut. He presses his thumb against the sensor to lock it up from the inside. "There," he says. "Now no one can disturb us."

"Excellent," I say, though not for the reason he assumes. I smile coyly and beckon him back to me. He complies, of course, eager for his impending blow job.

Which, he doesn't yet realize, is really going to blow, big time.

I pull his pants down to his ankles, leaving him fully exposed. Then I rise to my feet and kiss him again, pressing my body against his. He nibbles like a mouse at my lips. I draw in a breath, tensing my body for action.

As he leans forward to deepen the kiss, I bring up my knee and slam it as hard as I can into his groin. He doubles over in a convoluted mixture of shock and pain. I follow with an uppercut to his jaw and his head flails backward. He trips over his pulled-down pants and crashes to the floor. I slam my heel into his stomach, and he bellows in rage. Luckily, as he so proudly told me during my first visit here, the walls are soundproof.

I grab a vase off the dresser, ready to slam it over his head and render him unconscious. He's too quick, rolling to one side to avoid the blow. He grabs my ankle and pulls it out from under me, knocking me onto my ass. Before I can scramble to my feet, he's whipped out his knife. My element of surprise is gone. He's ready now. It'll be a fair fight from here on out. I hope the preliminary injuries slow him a bit; otherwise I'm outmatched.

"I knew this had to be a trick," he growls, waving the knife at me. "I'm going to gut you, bitch," he says. "And crucify your body for every Dark Sider to witness before I kill them all."

I jump to my feet, assuming a battle stance, hands in front of my face. "Go ahead," I challenge. "Kill me if you can."

Luckily, he appears more interested in personal revenge than calling for backup. He's sure he can best me; after all, he has the weapon. I wait for him to charge, which he does, bellowing in rage, then round-house kick with my back leg, making contact with his hand. The knife he holds slices the side of my foot, but the impact causes it to go flying. Now he's unarmed.

At first I think he'll dive for the weapon, but instead he comes after me—throws his entire weight into it. I lose my balance and crash to the floor. He pins me there, clamping my neck between his hands and squeezing down on my carotid. I can't breathe. I grab his wrists, desperately trying to pull his hands away, but I'm not strong enough, especially with my breath cut off. My vision starts to grow spotty; I'm going to pass out. I struggle to stay focused, to remain in control—to black out will be to sign my death warrant.

It's then that I remember Thom's gift. I drop my hands, grab the razor from my pocket, and use it. I manage to slice Duske's abdomen just above his ex-posed, still semierect penis. He bellows in surprised pain, staggering backward and thankfully letting go of my neck. I pull my knees out from under him and kick my feet forward, slamming them into his chest and knocking him backward. I leap forward, on top of him now, straddling him, my razor inches from his face.

"Don't fucking move," I tell him. "Or I will stab this blade right into your eye."

"Killing me will do no good," he growls, but he drops his hands to his side.

"I'm not going to kill you," I say. "I'm going to take your thumbprints."

His eyes widen as he realizes the meaning of my words. I grab his thumb and take a deep breath. I remind myself that, gruesome as this is, the bastard will live and the skin will heal. He likely deserves much worse.

I swallow hard and line up the blade. Then, I slice. Blood covers the razor, pooling, making it difficult to make my cut. I have to be accurate, the Eclipsers warned, or the function will be cancelled. Duske's writhing body increases the difficulty.

"Stop squirming," I command. "Or I'll kill you and take this anyway."

He stops his movements, his face white. I take the opportunity, before he changes his mind, and I slice fast, hard. A moment later I have the invaluable flap of skin separated from his body. I take the other thumbprint too, rendering him unable to leave the locked room. Then I crawl off him. He sits up, looking dizzy, trying to stop the bleeding by pressing his bloody thumbs into his shirt.

"It'll heal," I say. "You're lucky I'm so merciful."

"You won't get away with this, bitch," he says.

"You keep saying that," I note. "But I don't really see how you're going to stop me." I scramble to my feet, grabbing his knife off the floor. "I'm leaving now," I inform him. "Perhaps at some point you'll be rescued. Though it's a shame this house is so big and no one knows where you are. It may take them a while to find you."

Duske spits at me. I shake my head.

"Such manners." I *tsk* at him. "And here you're supposed to be the politician." I press his bloody skin against the door sensor. It beeps and the door slides open. I throw Duske a grin. "Thank you so much for loaning me your keys," I say as I exit the room. "I'll be sure to put them to good use."

SIXTEEN

A few hours later, back down on Stratum 2, at the Eclipsers' underground headquarters, I triumphantly present my souvenirs to the rebels. I'm the big hero, as you can imagine. But no one's more excited than Dawn. I get the feeling that it's nothing to do with Duske's thumb.

He scoops me up in his strong arms and twirls me around as if I'm a rag doll, then sets me down and plants an enthusiastic kiss on my lips. "Oh, Skye, you're back," he mumbles, nuzzling his cheek against mine, as if no one else is in the room. "I didn't breathe the whole time you were gone."

"Trying to conserve air?" I joke, though secretly I'm delighted by his response. "That's very noble of you, Brother Dawn."

He laughs and ruffles my hair. "Silly girl," he scolds. "You know what I mean."

I do. And it warms me inside to realize how much he cares for me. We're a team now, fighting for a cause bigger than us. It's an exhilarating feeling to know you have a truly dedicated partner in crime who loves you. How did I ever want to go through life alone?

"I still can't believe I pulled it off," I comment as we join the rest of the Eclipsers at the conference room table. I'd handed off the thumb to one of the Dark Sider technicians who was now working to upload the print data into the computer and craft a less bloody simulation.

"But you did. And now we can fight back. Get the clean air flowing again," Ruth says, her voice bursting with pride.

"We'll show the Circle they can't mess with the Eclipsers," chimes in Hiro. Everyone applauds.

"So, what's the next step?" I ask, after the cheering fades. "Once the simulation is done?"

"Long ago, one of our spies managed to steal blue-prints of the bunker," Ruth says, pulling a set of prints from a metal tube and rolling them out on the table. "We've had them on file forever, with no way to make use of them." She looks up at me. "But thanks to you, that's all changed."

I study the prints. The place is huge, bigger than I'd imagined. Full of twisty passageways, seemingly without rhyme or reason. Ruth points out the physical plant, where the mechanisms needed to restore the fans are located. "That's where you need to go," she says.

"Got it," Dawn says after a few moments of study. "I'll head out tonight as soon as the technicians are finished with the key."

I look at him in surprise. "You're going?" I ask, suddenly realizing I'd never thought about who would actually do the rest of the dirty work.

He nods. "It only makes sense. I'm an nT, just like the guards inside. I'm the only one with the strength to overpower them, if need be. Plus, I have the skill to reprogram the ventilation system and recode it. I'll put in a bypass to any government controls, throw in a pesky virus to really mess up their works." He smiles at me. "Thanks to you, the Dark Side will no longer ever have to be dependent on the government for air."

"B-but . . ." I stammer. "But I don't want you to—"

"Risk my life for the cause like you did?" Dawn finishes my sentence with a pointed look. "It's my turn, dear. And I'm the only one who can do it. Sorry, but there's no other way."

"Well, then, I'm going with you," I determine. No way am I letting him risk his life alone.

"No." He shakes his head. "It's too risky."

"Tough luck. I'm not letting you out of my sight again, Dawn Grey," I say. "And besides, I can be useful. You need someone as a lookout while you do your reprogramming thing."

Dawn scrubs his face with his hands. "You've been in enough danger already—"

"And look at me! I'm completely unscathed. Don't be pigheaded. You know we have a better chance doing this together."

"She's right, Brother," Ruth interrupts. "And you should know better than to let your personal attachments interfere with the cause."

"Besides, with her sword skills, she'll be very useful

to have," adds Hiro. "After all, back in her school days she was a legendary. No one could touch her."

Dawn releases a sigh and holds up his hands in defeat. "Fine, fine," he says. "I can see I'm not going to win. As usual." He turns to me. "It's not that I don't admire your bravery, you understand," he says. "I just can't bear the thought of anything happening to you."

I lean over to kiss him on the cheek. "I'll be with you," I remind him. "You can keep me safe."

He smiles and kisses me softly on the mouth. "That's true. And I promise to protect every little hair on your head."

"I'll hold you to that."

Ruth clears her throat. We jerk apart, red-faced. I giggle. They must think we're like a couple of schoolkids, silly in love. Not that they'd be way off base.

"Brother Thom was able to obtain a couple of uniforms," Kayce adds. "Like what the nT workers wear inside. So as long as you keep a low profile, you should be able to fit in."

A knock sounds on the door and a technician steps inside. He presents the thumb simulation to us. "All done," he says proudly. "You're now in possession of the most powerful key in all of Terra."

"Great," I say, grabbing the simulation and affixing it to my thumb. "Let's go save the world."

I swallow hard as the bunker door slides shut behind us, sealing us in with a loud, echoing clang. We're in. I grab for Dawn's hand, needing to draw from his strength, to hold on to something steady and solid and unwavering for at least a moment before we begin our quest.

But I realize even Dawn is shaking.

It'd been easy to enter the place. Almost too easy, in fact. The token guards at the back entrance were a cinch to sneak up on and neutralize with the injections Kayce had cooked up. Once they were rendered unconscious, we dragged them behind a nearby trash bin and then used the thumb simulation to activate the lock. Security seemed almost . . . lax—especially for a building of this importance. But I guess when you only have a few thumbs in the whole world keyed to enter, you don't need an army to guard the door. And I'm not about to look a gift horse in the mouth.

Dawn points to security cameras slowly panning back and forth every few yards down the long hallway. Thank God we have uniforms. I've also drawn a rough rendition of the blueprints on my palm. Last thing we need is to get caught whipping out a map.

I study my hand for a moment, then point down the hallway. "This way," I whisper to Dawn. "We'll take our third left."

Dawn nods and follows me down the hall. We walk slowly, our faces turned downward, to minimize risk of recognition by whoever's monitoring the cameras. Of course, according to Ruth, everyone in here is an nT, born and raised on the inside. They've never seen a news feed and thus would never be able to recognize Terra's most notorious rebel and her boyfriend. But in my opinion, you can never be too careful.

We turn left, into an identical featureless hallway stretching off into apparent infinity. A few uniformed workers pass us, nodding a slight greeting and mumbling "Brother, Sister," as they walk by. I exhale a sigh of relief. Our costumes and demeanor are evidently passable to the drones.

"These are newer models—much less . . . human than I," Dawn whispers. "I'd heard this was happening. The government's replaced the reasoning center in their brains with a superior work ethic. They can't think for themselves. They only have time for their work."

"Like ants serving a queen," I murmur, though I realize late that Dawn probably won't get that reference. "How very sad. Though, I guess they aren't thinking enough to feel sadness. Maybe they're completely content. But still . . ."

Dawn speaks up, clearly unnerved. "So, these are what the government wants to replace the Dark Siders with, I suppose. It makes sense, I guess. They'll produce more and never demand fair treatment. They'll never fight back, never rebel. They're dream employees, in many ways."

"But to massacre people and replace them with drones?" I say, shaking my head. "It's just not right. We can't let that happen."

"We won't," Dawn says, stealing a glance at me. "Together we can beat them. I know it."

I throw him a small smile, hoping he's right. It just all seems so big, so elaborate. How can a ragged band of rebels stop a government as cruel and powerful as this?

I shake my head. No time to think of the big picture. Not now. Win the battle before considering the war. If we pull this off, it'll be a major coup—a victory for the Dark Siders and a way for them to regain some independence. We must stay focused, accomplish our mission, and arrive home safe. Then we can worry about the rest.

We trudge farther down the passageway, following my hand maps, making various twists and turns until we finally come to the room for which we've been searching. The place is filled with high-tech machinery, and monitors everywhere are blinking with red, green, and yellow lights. I'm glad Dawn's here with me; I wouldn't even know where to begin.

"Go for it, stud," I whisper, poking him in the side. "Work your magic."

Dawn nods, keeping his head down, so as to not alert the drones inside the room. Luckily, as the others had, they barely acknowledge our presence as we head to the back of the room. Dawn locates an unattended computer and takes a seat in front of it. His face is tense, anxious, as his fingers swiftly dance across the keyboard. His brow furrows.

"What's wrong?" I whisper.

He shakes his head. "Nothing. It's just a little more complicated than I thought it would be." He types a few more command lines. I scan the room. We haven't been noticed yet. That's good. Though, odd, really. Eerie. I mean, I know there's a skeleton crew on because it's nighttime, and I know that the crew is made up of nearly mindless bioworkers, but still. There's just something strange about two people being able to waltz into a high-security government facility and mess with whatever we want with little interruption.

"Hurry," I hiss at Dawn as he slips a small flash drive into a terminal. A sudden chill seeps through me. What if they know we're here? What if they're watching us as we speak, lulling us into a false sense of security before they pounce? I glance up at one of the cameras that silently scan the room. Who is on the other side of the lens watching, waiting?

"Okay, okay, I've almost got it. There!" Dawn hits enter and the screen flashes twice. He looks up at me with a grin. "The air should be not only rerouted through a cleansing filter, but completely under Eclipser control. I programmed in new authorization codes and rerouted the control center to one of the megacomputers back at headquarters. I also inserted a virus into their server that should make it extremely difficult to wrest control back from us."

"Great," I say, pride welling inside me. "So then, mission accomplished. Let's get the hell out of here."

Dawn nods. "Sounds like a good idea to me."

We head out of the room, the drones going about their work, barely registering our intrusion. I glance back at them one more time, pity stirring in my heart. I'm so glad Dawn escaped before they did that to him.

We wander through the low-ceilinged passageways, guided by my hand map. The building is so big and twisty it's hard to tell if we're going the right way. Soon, I realize in dismay, the map doesn't line up at all.

"Which way?" Dawn asks as we stop at an intersection.

"Uh . . ." I scan one direction, then the other. "I hate to say this, but . . ." I throw him an apologetic look. "I think we might be lost."

"Great." He rakes a hand through his hair in frustration. "That's just what we need."

"Well, let's keep going. Maybe something will start

to look familiar again," I suggest, not seeing any other options.

We continue on, taking random lefts and rights in a seemingly endless maze of tunnels. My heart pounds in my chest. What if we never get out? What if they find us wandering here? At least we accomplished our mission, I try to remind myself. We may die, but others will live.

It's not as comforting a thought as I'd like.

"What's this?" Dawn asks suddenly, stopping in front of a door. I come up behind him to see what's got his attention. It's a set of metal double doors with a single word sign affixed.

Moongazing.

"This must be where they developed the astrophysics program to send people to Earth," I exclaim, scarcely able to draw breath. An insatiable curiosity overwhelms me. Maybe I can finally find out some answers. About the program. And more importantly, about me and who I really am. "We should check it out," I say, trying to keep my voice nonchalant.

Dawn narrows his eyes. "That's not on the agenda," he reminds me. "We're supposed to be in and out."

"I know, but . . ." I trail off, not knowing exactly how to explain.

Luckily, Dawn seems to recognize my need. He reaches over and squeezes my hand. "You want to know whether or not you're really Mariah," he concludes.

I nod. "It's important to me."

"Okay," he agrees. "We'll check it out. But just for a minute. Then we've got to get out of here before we end up setting off some alarm."

I run the thumb simulator over the sensor and the doors swing open. I suck in a breath as we step inside, nervous beyond belief. I want to know. But at the same time, I'm scared to find out the truth. What if it's something I'm not ready to hear?

I steal a glance at Dawn. Beautiful, wonderful Dawn. He loves me, I tell myself. And he will love me no matter who I really am, right? Skye or Mariah. He cares for me. I have to trust in that.

Somewhat reassured, I look around. Confidence fades as I recognize what we've stepped into. The room is like a football-field-sized warehouse, with row upon row of computers. Black boxes with blinking red and yellow lights are stacked one on top of the other from floor to ceiling, with only narrow passageways allowing access between them. Wires rope the floor and metal-beamed ceiling, all leading to the back side of the room. A few nTs wander the aisles, checking the computers. They ignore us, as the rest have, thank God.

I throw a confused look at Dawn, wondering what all this machinery, all this major computer power amassed in one room could possibly be for. I mean, I know what the computers are. I'm a game designer and would recognize a room full of servers anywhere. This is definitely a central command center for some kind of massive network. Do they use it for Moongazing somehow?

We need more information. We walk toward the back of the room, stepping over wires in our path and avoiding the nTs. We come across a door labeled OPERATIONS. Dawn glances over at me. I nod and open the door with the thumb simulation. We step inside.

The room we enter reminds me of NASA's Ground Control. NTs man rows of terminals, all facing a wall-sized computer screen with a satellite map of . . .

I scrunch my eyes. Is that Manhattan?

"Wow," I whisper. "That's . . . that's . . ."

"Earth?" Dawn concludes.

"Well, it's a map of one city on Earth. New York. Where I'm from."

As if on cue, one of the nTs chooses that moment to type a command into her terminal, and the screen zooms in. I can now see people bustling up and down a busy Midtown street, as clearly as if I were watching a movie or a live video feed, or just simply looking out a window.

"They must be monitoring Earth or something," I reason, trying to make sense of it all. "Keeping an eye on the Terrans who 'Gaze."

"Yeah," Dawn says, sounding doubtful. He sits down at one of the computer terminals and starts typing in commands. "Look," he says, "Other feeds."

I peer over his shoulder, fascinated. "You're right," I exclaim. "This one's the Upper West Side where I live. Lincoln Center. See, I sometimes go sit by that fountain and read." I look at the next screen over. "And that's the East Village," I say, pointing to it. "Outside Club Luna. That's where the 'Gazers all hang out." I scratch my head. "I wonder if they just sit here and watch all the places 'Gazers visit. To make sure they're safe or something."

But even as I say this, doubts niggle at my brain. Something's not quite adding up here. How could the government monitor an alternate reality from Terra? How could they place cameras on the streets and somehow send the live signal back to headquarters? My interdimensional physics training is spotty—okay; well, nonexistent—but this doesn't make sense. And even if they could monitor everyone, why would they bother? Why would they care what their citizens are doing on Earth?

And, most troubling, what are all these servers for?

"Skye, check this out," Dawn says, typing a few commands on the keyboard. He pulls up a 3-D architecture program that's currently busy rendering a skyscraper. I stare at the screen, horrified confusion swirling through me. "That's my new job site," I say, gulping. "We're supposed to move offices there after the game is finished."

Dawn looks at me. "They're building it *here*," he says slowly. "Skye, I think I understand what's going on now. You might want to sit down."

His words might as well be a truck barreling me over at a hundred miles an hour. I sink into a chair, crazy thoughts pinging all over my brain. It can't be, can it? No. This is impossible. But . . . the massive servers. The map rooms and rendering programs . . .

I dive for a computer and latch on to a keyboard, typing commands as fast as my fingers can handle. The network is surprisingly simple to navigate, nearly identical to my game back on Earth. I open directories, scan folders, read files. A dawning horror consumes me at each turn as I recognize people, places, objects. It's all here. Everything to do about the Earth I know.

I find a folder listed *PATCH CONTENTS* and click open the READ ME file.

Notes to Earth Patch 11.09.02.

· *Major subway upgrade. System Users will no longer have to wait twenty minutes for a train.*
· *Doorman NUCs added to several apartment buildings.*
· *New celebrity NUCs added to Luna locale.*
· *Several cultural and historical name inaccuracies fixed.*
· *Fashion update: We've introduced a 1980s retro wardrobe players can choose from, including legwarmers, horizontal striped tops, and leggings.*
· *New goals added: In order to keep visiting Terrans involved, they will be approached and offered a variety of new objectives when they interact with NUCs. Each objective will reward the User in a new way.*

"What are you reading?" Dawn asks, coming over behind me. "What's an NUC?"

"Non-user character," I guess, my voice choked by horror. This all seems to be falling into place. "An NPC is a video game term for a computer-generated character. They look like regular players, but they're actually just computer programs, designed to assist or distract players from their goals. I think an NUC is something very similar. . . ."

"So, why would there be those on Earth?" Dawn asks.

That's is the sixty-four-thousand dollar question. I stare at the screen, trying to make sense of it all. Trying to come up with some logical explanation besides the very obvious one right in front of me.

I think back to my last trip to Earth. The doorman, the express subway, the change in club clothes, the whispers that Paris Hilton was hanging out at Luna. My stomach churns. My vision grows spotty. I want to be sick.

It can't be. This has to be some kind of sick joke. Some kind of mistake. I'm reading it all wrong. I'm drawing conclusions that shouldn't be made. This is impossible. Absolutely impossible.

And yet . . .

"What if Earth isn't another world after all?" I ask slowly. "What if 'Gazing is really just a game?"

Dawn sits down beside me, face solemn, stroking my back with a gentle hand. He's already figured it out, I realize. He knows it's true.

"Oh God, it's all here," I say, choking out the words past the huge lump in my throat. "Maps, people, objects, quests. All the tools game designers need to create a virtual reality. Terrans aren't being transported to another world at all. They're just being uploaded into some fucking video game!"

Desperate to be wrong, I open another folder. One labeled NUCs. Inside are three-dimensional renderings of people, and data. Some characters I know. Bruno, the burly bouncer from Luna. Suzy. My boss, Madeline.

And Craig. My own boyfriend.

" 'Computer-generated nonuser characters shall enhance the world, provide a more realistic atmosphere to the game, and offer quests to eligible players,' " I read quietly. " 'They can be identified by moon tattoos on their hands or necks.' " I think back to Suzy. To Craig. To the tattoos they sported. I thought it was a new trend. Stupid, stupid me.

I lean back in my chair, trying to absorb it all, to take

it all in. My mind feels like it's going to explode. It has been hard enough coming to terms with the fact that maybe I'm actually someone I don't know, that I could be Mariah from Terra and not Skye from Earth. It's quite another to realize that not only am I definitely not from Earth, but Earth doesn't exist, except in a room of computer servers and the imaginations of some very creative programmers.

No wonder Earth is so much like Terra. Terrans re-created it. That's why we have the same pop culture references, the same Starbucks on the corner, the same fashion sense, the same language. Not because of some ridiculous parallel universe theory. But because everything on Earth was literally created by Terran game designers. They've simply taken a snapshot of their pre-war past and expanded on it. Made it cooler, better, nicer. Added some sunshine. Some moonbeams. And there you have it: a pleasing diversion for bored Indys.

Just like my own game—*RealLife*—that I'd created for people on Earth. From the start, I've imagined people playing my game, using it as an escape from their day-to-day lives, allowing them to transform into someone they aren't for a few hours. To escape from the stresses and annoyances of real life.

And what have I been doing really? Creating a game for people to get away from a game. How fucking ironic.

"Are you okay, Skye?" Dawn asks, peering at me with worried eyes.

"Skye?" I repeat bitterly. "Skye? I'm not Skye. Skye's just a made-up persona by a video game designer. Earth doesn't exist, so obviously I'm from here. You were right. You were all right all along, Dawn. I'm Mariah. Obviously I'm Mariah."

Dawn pulls me into a hug, squeezing me tight. I try to relax in his arms, but my body is trembling too hard. I bury my face in his shoulder and sob. It's all too much to take. I can barely breathe.

My whole life has been a lie. My every memory—obviously implanted, just as Dawn warned. My parents, my boyfriend, my very world? Not only will I never see them again, but in reality I've never seen them at all. They don't really exist.

Oh God, I can't take this.

"I'm so sorry, sweetie," Dawn murmurs. "This must be so hard for you."

I pull away from his hug. Angry. Hurt. Confused. Alone. *This must be hard?* Please. *Hard* doesn't even begin to explain the pain, the anguish, the horror at what I've just seen. How can I deal with this? How can I just accept the fact that my whole reality exists solely on a fucking computer server?

"So, what does this mean for the Eclipsers?" I demand, my voice harsh. "I mean, the fact that Earth's a computer program instead of another world? Will that help or hurt their cause? What does this mean?"

Dawn looks at me helplessly. "I don't know," he says. "I hadn't thought about it, really. I'm more worried about you."

His words bring a small comfort. I remind myself that I am not facing this horror alone. I've had a great shock, sure, but at the same time, I'd already long ago given up my world in exchange for a life here. I belong on Terra. With the Eclipsers, with the Dark Siders—with Dawn, who loves me completely, no matter what. So, as horrifying as it is to realize my whole past has been a lie, at least I can be assured that my future is true.

"It does prove a point, I suppose," Dawn adds. "Now we know for sure that the government is just trying to steal the Indys' money and land."

"We need to find a way to let the Indys know," I say, pulling out my camera and taking a few snapshots of the room—trying to focus, to push down the panic growing inside me. "For proof," I explain.

Dawn looks at me. "Are you okay?" he asks again. "You don't have to be strong here. You've just been through a horrible shock. It's okay to be upset."

I swallow hard, loving him so much at that moment I can barely stand it. "I know," I manage to say without choking. "I'll deal with it later. Right now, we have to focus on our mission."

I finish taking photos and we step outside the room. My legs feel like lead, making it nearly impossible to walk. My brain won't calm down, reeling at top speed. I'd like nothing more than to find a quiet room and just sit down and process it all in my head, alone. But analysis will have to wait until we're safe.

We head back through the server room, my chest hurting as I see the whirring machines, knowing my whole life is stored somewhere on those hard drives. Everything that means anything to me could simply be deleted at a moment's notice. A simple patch to fix a bug could wipe out my whole existence.

No. I'm a real person, I try to reassure myself. Most of my memories may be fake, but I'm real. I'm Mariah. A revolutionary leader. A savior to the downtrodden. The woman Dawn loves. That's something. I have a life and people who need me. I've got to hold on to that.

We go back out into the hallway to continue our search for the exit. We come to a dead end with a locked door that I open with the simulator, praying it's a way out. Instead, it opens into a room filled with large file cabinet like things against the walls. Curious, I walk over to one, peering at its label.

Rupert Smith
11-01-2107

I pull open the drawer, to see what kind of files they might have on old Rupert. To my surprise, the drawer actually contains Rupert himself. Or what's left of him, anyway. His corpse lies white and stiff on a cold metal slab. I put two and two together and realize what this whole room must be.

"A morgue," I exclaim. "Dawn, come look at this."

Dawn walks over to my side, peering down at poor Rupert, a former middle-aged Indy by the look of it. His corpse is swollen, naked, drained of blood, and pasty white, a pair of Moongazing glasses over his eyes. I reach down, slowly pulling the dark glasses off his face, wondering why he's wearing them and nothing else. But what's behind the shades makes me stumble backward in shock. Dawn catches me, propping me up, looking as horrified as I feel.

And here I'd thought it couldn't get any worse.

"Oh my God!" I murmur, desperate but unable to look away. The sockets where Rupert's eyes should have been are now hollow, blackened pits; charred remnants of his former peepers. "How strange." I hurriedly replace the sunglasses. "It's almost as if he gazed into the sun too long. But that's crazy. You guys don't even have sunshine. So, what could have burned out his eyes?"

"Maybe the moon."

I whirl around, eyes wide. Will this day ever stop surprising me? "Moongazing," I whisper in shocked realization. "Do you think? I mean, could it really . . ." I gesture helplessly to the corpse.

Dawn shrugs. "Seems entirely possible. If Earth really is just a computer-generated game, then that obviously means you're not really traveling to another world when they lock you in one of their rooms. You're stuck twenty-four-seven in a video game simulation. And the visuals are intense, right? So intense you believe they're real. What if, after wearing these glasses long-term, they end up literally burning up your eyes?"

"And kill you, evidently, as well," I add, shoving Rupert's corpse back into the cabinet and slamming the drawer. I lean against the wall, sucking in a breath. "I guess that's not something they'd put in the brochure."

Dawn grimaces. "All along you're thinking you've just traveled to a whole other plane of existence, a brave new world that you and your fellow Indys are populating. You're ready to start a new life," he says. "But in reality, you're stuck in a box, lost in a drug-induced hallucination until your brain crumbles and your eyes are literally burnt out of your head."

"And the government pockets all your assets," I say. "This would solve the population problem to boot. It's brilliant in a way. Sick, but brilliant."

I stare at the rows upon rows of boxes, each labeled with a name and date. All these people went willingly to their deaths, lambs to the slaughter, with no one the wiser. Rupert's friends, his family, his coworkers—they all assume he's now living a perfect life on a better world. No one has any idea of his real new digs: a nine-by-three drawer in a government fridge.

I pull out the drawer again and take a photo of the body. Then I go to the next drawer, slide out the dead Indy there, and take another. I repeat this over and over, taking photos of corpse after corpse. Each looks exactly the same—naked, bloated, blackened pits for eyes. My stomach churns with nausea, begging me to stop, but I ignore it. This is too important to be queasy.

"The dates of death," Dawn observes, scanning the drawers, "are all recent. These are all labeled from the last week." He walks to the other side of the room. "These are a bit older. It looks like these people died a few months ago."

I cross the room to join him, yanking open a drawer of one of the less recently deceased. I take a photo. The body still has the telltale blackened eyes, but it looks yellowed, shrunken.

"Why do they keep them?" I wonder aloud. "Why not just bury them or something?"

"Who knows? Maybe they don't want them found. Or maybe they're experimenting on them, trying to discover why they die prematurely. Or perhaps they even harvest their organs. I mean, if it's only their minds and eyes that go, they die with healthy livers and kidneys and hearts, right? Perfect for the fat-cat government officials to use to prolong their own miserable lives."

I shiver at the thought. "That's disgusting."

I head to the back of the room to another set of drawers. Just a few more pictures and I'll have enough evidence to rally the Indys and get them to force the government to shut down the Moongazing program for good. It won't save these poor people, of course, but at least it will prevent others from dying the same horrible way.

"I wonder how long it takes for someone to die," Dawn says, pulling out another drawer. "It must be a while. After all, you were inside for a few months before the Eclipsers pulled you out."

"Thank God they did," I say, scanning the drawers. I've shot a lot of male bodies. I'd like a woman this time. "Or I'd have ended up—" The words die in my throat as my eyes focus on a name on one of the drawers. My camera falls out of my hands and crashes onto the floor. "Dawn," I cry, my voice scratchy and hoarse. "I think you'd better get over here."

I stare at the name, hoping, begging, praying that I'm somehow reading it wrong. But no. It's there, clear as day. The name I never expected in a million years to read on a drawer in a morgue:

Mariah Quinn.

SEVENTEEN

"What is it?" Dawn asks, instantly appearing at my side. My throat's closed up. I can't speak. I point a shaky finger at the drawer. Dawn stares, his mouth gaping, then turns to me, an uncomprehending look on his face.

"What the hell . . . ?" he whispers. "How can that . . . how can that be?"

I shake my head. I have no idea. I really thought nothing could top the shock of learning that Earth was just a virtual reality video game. But if Earth is a game, then by all rights I have to be Mariah. And if I'm Mariah, I'm obviously not a corpse. Which leads us to the sixty-four-thousand-dollar question. Who's in the drawer?

"Maybe it's empty," Dawn reasons, not sounding all that convinced. "Maybe they're . . . saving it for you, hoping to kill you and then put you there."

I swallow hard. "Right," I agree. "That must be it. The drawer's probably empty."

We fall silent, staring at the drawer, neither one ready to test the theory.

"Should . . . should I open it?" I ask at last. "I mean, so we have proof that there's no one inside?" I really would rather not, but how can I just walk away not knowing? I've come this far. I have to know the truth, no matter what it turns out to be.

"I don't know," Dawn says, sounding at a loss. He reaches down and grabs the camera on the floor, fingering the lens. I stare at the drawer, my heart thudding painfully in my chest. What to do, what to do, what to do?

I take a deep breath and yank it open.

The drawer isn't empty. There's a corpse lying on the slab. The body of a girl. A naked girl with glasses who looks exactly like me.

I stumble backward, then fall to my knees, unable to catch my breath. I double over and throw up, sickly yellow bile spewing from my lips and pooling onto the stone floor. Dawn's soon next to me, holding my hair back from my face and rubbing a hand over my back. He's saying something, something soothing, but the blood pounding in my ears makes it impossible to hear what's coming from his lips. I take a deep breath and pull myself to my feet, vision blurry with unshed tears. I shiver, my body suddenly freezing cold. I realize I'm likely going into shock and I try to break free from the darkness, pull myself together. Losing it now could end very badly.

"Wow, it's not every day you get to see your own dead body," I mutter, going for gallows humor. Or 'Gazing humor, I guess, as the case might be.

Dawn grabs and pulls me into a fierce, smothering

hug, squeezing me tightly against him. I realize he's shaking, too, as terrified and confused as me but trying to be strong for the both of us. I bury my face in his chest, sobbing.

"I don't understand," I blubber. "I'm not dead. How can my body be in this morgue?"

"I don't know," Dawn answers helplessly. "I just don't know."

"It's definitely me, though, right? It's definitely Mariah?" I can't bear to take another look.

Dawns shifts in my arms for a second glance. "Yes," he says after a pause. "It is definitely Mariah. And it appears she's got the burned-out eyeball thing like the rest of them." He takes a few pictures of the corpse. "I'm going to upload these photos and send them back to headquarters," he says, pressing a few buttons on the camera. "They have to see this. *Now.*"

I nod, barely listening, my whole world spun off its axis. "So, if that's Mariah, then . . . who am I?"

"You, my dear," pipes in a voice from across the room, "are not exactly a 'who' at all."

Dawn and I whirl around. At the entrance to the morgue stands Duske, flanked by six heavily armed guards. He's dressed in a severe black suit, and his thumbs are swathed in white cotton bandages.

Without giving reason a second thought, I rip my sword from its sheath and charge forward, blinded by rage and madness. My vision is red, my heart pounds in my chest. This man must die. Die for what he did to the people. Die for what he did to Mariah. Die for whatever the hell he's done to me. Whoever I am.

The guards step in front of him, pulling out their own swords and effectively protecting their master. I stop my advance, sword still held high in the air, glowering at the man who is responsible for so many torn lives. Duske grins and gestures for the guards to withdraw. He pulls out his own sword. "This is excellent," he says. "I've wanted to see you fight ever since I created you. After all, you were programmed with the top martial arts training."

I squint at him. "Programmed me? What the hell is that supposed that mean?"

Duske shakes his head. "Fight first," he commands. "If you best me, I will tell you everything."

"If I best you, you will be dead and thus unable to speak."

"No, no, my dear," Duske says laughingly. "My guards will not let me die. Don't be stupid. We'll simply spar until there is a clear champion. But we must agree not to shed any blood. I will not kill you if you agree not to kill me."

"From what I saw in the drawer over there, it appears I'm already dead. And why should I believe even for a second that you won't just have me killed later?" I glare at him, not wanting to play games anymore. I should have killed him back at the house. Not doing so was a big mistake.

Duske shrugs. "Because you know I am a man of honor?" he suggests. Then he laughs. "No, I guess that could not be it. How about because you need to know the truth? You're desperate for answers and you know I'm the only one who can give them to you. If you're going to die anyway, wouldn't you prefer to die knowing the truth?"

He's got me there. There's no way I can even pretend the truth does not concern me. After seeing my own face dead in a drawer, realizing the world I thought I was from is just a virtual dream, it's now vitally important I find out who I really am.

I raise my sword again, the blade flashing under the artificial florescent ceiling lights. "All right," I say. "Let's do this." Maybe he'll be weak. After all, how does one grasp a sword with cut thumbs? But then I remember Dawn healing my wrist. He probably just went to an nT medic and had the skin grown back in minutes.

"Skye . . ." Dawn interrupts my racing thoughts. "You don't have to do this."

"Actually, I think I do," I reply, feeling an inner power swell inside me. It's a growing strength and retreating fear. This is a fight for the truth. And I have to win.

Duske brandishes his blade and steps forward. I launch into an attack, swinging my sword expertly in one hand. I don't remember learning to fight, but somehow something inside me knows how to do it— as if I were born with the knowledge.

You weren't born at all, an inner voice nags. I push it aside.

Our swords clash, the blades singing high-pitched squeals. I slide my sword downward, freeing the blade, then swing upward. Duske catches it again easily. He's good, I realize. Maybe too good.

Back and forth we flurry, blades coming together, separating, then meeting once again. Sweat drips down my forehead, between my breasts, as I dance around him, looking for a sign of weakness. But he seems to effortlessly predict my every move. I'm not sure he's even trying that hard. He certainly doesn't seem winded.

Thinking I see an opening, I lunge. He parries with a

twist of the wrist, tossing me a self-satisfied grin. He's toying with me, I realize. If I want to win I can't do it this way. I have to try something he won't expect. Something that's not "all fair in love and swordplay." It's then that I remember my character Allora's finishing move in my *RealLife* video game. The one my boss Madeline criticized and told me I needed to fix. *Chivalry is based on a code*, she had lectured. Everything is based on rules. But she's just an NPC, a computer-generated character.

Whoever I am, I'm done playing by the rules. Time to make my own destiny.

I drop to my knees, swing my blade, and slash at his ankles. He screams in pain as the sword makes contact with his Achilles tendon. He stumbles backward, bellowing in rage. I leap to my feet and point my blade at his now unprotected throat.

"You bitch," he snaps. "You weren't supposed to hurt me."

"You'll live," I snarl back. "Unless I decide to kill you." I press the blade against his throat, just enough to draw a tiny droplet of blood. One step forward and I can drive the weapon straight through and no number of guards can save his life. But, I realize, then I'd never find out the truth. And the guards will simply kill me and then Dawn after their master is dead. If I am going to have a chance to get out of this, I need to stay alive.

Reluctantly, I lower the sword. The guards step forward and disarm me, then tie my hands behind my back. They do the same to Dawn, roughly shuffling us both to one wall.

Duske reaches down and wraps a strip of cloth torn from his suit over his wound, still grumbling. It's immediately soaked in blood. That's got to really hurt. I can't believe he's still conscious. One of the guards kneels before him and takes the ankle in his hands, closing his eyes, just as Dawn did to my wrist. Must be a Healer. How convenient to have one on staff.

A few moments later, the bleeding's stopped and Duske's able to walk. He saunters over to me, positioning himself so he's inches from my face. "You should have killed me when you had the chance," he says with a bitter laugh.

"Yes, yes," I reply, trying to sound nonchalant, while inside everything is trembling with fear. "But I didn't. So how about you keep up your end of the bargain? Tell me everything."

Duske grins. "Gladly. In fact, I'm looking forward to it. Ask away."

I swallow hard, get up my nerve. Ignore my pounding heart. "Is . . . Earth just a game?" I manage to spit out.

Duske frowns. "It's not *just* a game. It's the most miraculous creation in the history of the world. It's a new form of reality. A virtual escape, if you will, for all that plagues the Terran people. An amazing recreation of Terra the century before the war."

"Some escape," I mutter, glancing over at the drawers of bodies.

"Well, yes, we're still working out the kinks. Right now it's too expensive to run on a long-term basis. Do you think we want to be stuck intravenously feeding players for their entire Terran life spans? Or worrying about disposing of their bodily fluids? Also, we've found that after a few weeks, the Terran mind starts to decay from the fully immersive experience. So it's far better to pull the 'Gazers from their misery before their organs rot and their bodies are rendered unusable."

"But you've promised these people a new life on Earth! Instead, you kill them."

"But don't you see? They *do* get a whole life. We speed up the game. Twenty Earth years can pass within a day of Terran time if we want. When someone commits to a full emigration we put their life on fast forward. By the time their mind starts to decay, they've already experienced an entirely full life. They're old. They're *ready* to die." He smiles, obviously proud. "And in return, here on Terra, we solve the overpopulation problem and help fund government programs. Besides, all of our subjects are perfectly willing to go."

"But if they knew how they'd end up . . ."

Duske shrugs. "What's the difference, because they never will. They'll die peacefully, thinking they've lived out an entire life in paradise. What could be better than that?"

"What about Mariah?" Dawn interrupts.

"Ah, Mariah," Dawn says. "Beautiful, sweet Mariah." He wanders over to the back of the room and looks adoringly down at the naked body lying on the slab. "We started noticing her poking around Earth about six months ago. She tried to give a false identity, but there's not much our *daemons*—the program's security subroutines—don't pick up on. Not to mention it's nearly impossible for a celebrated rebel like her to keep a low profile. We were amused by her interest, and so we let her take a peek around, knowing she would never find anything wrong. Not on the surface."

"And then she got addicted?" Dawn asks.

"Sure." Duske shrugs. "If you want to call it that. The

more she jumped back and forth, the more taxing it became on her brain. With all the 'Gaze she was inhaling, her life on Earth started seeming more real to her than her life on Terra." He smirks. "So that's when we decided to make our move—make it look like the infamous Mariah Quinn, would-be savior of the Dark Siders, turned traitor."

"Make it look like?" Dawn repeats. "You mean she didn't actually . . . ?"

Duske stares at him, then starts to laugh. "Didn't actually betray you?" he asks. "You really think she did?" He shakes his head in mirth. "You two may have slept together, but you obviously didn't know the girl very well at all. She was as loyal as they come. I mean, sure, she became a brainless, desperate drug addict, but still she refused to betray the Eclipsers up until the very end. And believe me, we tried a great deal to make her spill."

"So then, how did you know about our plans to sabotage the seminar?" Dawn demands. "You know things that only she could have told you."

Duske smiles. "Once we realized that no amount of convincing was going to get her to talk, we simply allowed her to go 'Gazing in a specially doctored booth. While she was inside, we ran a brain scan and stripped her mind of all short-term memories. After running a quick analysis through a supercomputer, we got all the details we needed to thwart your pathetic plan. And Mariah never had any idea."

Dawn is silent for a moment, probably trying to digest this startling revelation. The girl he's been thinking a villain all this time is actually an innocent victim. He must feel so guilty for judging her. But how could he have known that in this instance two plus two did not equal four?

"But she still left us," he says at last, grasping at straws. "She still abandoned her people for a better life on Earth."

"Please." Duske snorts. "She didn't go anywhere. She was too sick. Her brain wouldn't have survived another trip. We didn't waste the resources. Once we had the information we needed, we cloned her and killed her and sent in Skye here to start 'Gazing in her place."

"So then . . . who am I?" I interject. My head is spinning. "Where do I come from and why do I look exactly like Mariah?" Even as I ask, I'm not sure I want to hear the truth.

"You're the spare."

"The spare?" I think I'm going to be sick again.

"Sure. A clone. Similar to the nTs. We took a sample of Mariah's genetic code and grew a new version. Then we implanted false memories of Earth into her brain, mostly stolen from our non-user character designs. The idea was to send the new Mariah to Earth in place of the real one so people would see her. We could relay back clips of your new life if we wanted, prove that Mariah had really migrated there. And if we needed you for something, we could bring you back. Hell, you never do know when a spare revolutionary leader turned traitor might come in handy." He laughs.

I stare at him, unable to even breathe. "You mean . . . ?"

He smiles. "Yes, Skye. You are that clone. You have the same genetic makeup as Mariah. Same fingerprints, same DNA. But your brain is filled with a false life on Earth that we created especially for you. You are not now, nor were you ever Mariah. In fact, you are not, nor were you ever a real person at all."

My face crumbles, tears robbing me of my vision. So, I'm not Mariah. I'm not the girl Dawn is in love with. I'm just a clone. A nonuser character. A fantasy. My whole life, every memory, is a lie.

"In reality, Skye, you've only been alive for about three months," Duske says.

"But how come . . ." I'm grasping at the falling straws. "How come I remember sometimes? I mean, fleeting images, feelings. In Terra I feel like I have déjà vu all the time."

Duske nods grimly. "Our experiment wasn't a hundred percent successful. For some reason you seem to retain a few memories of Mariah. We're still not quite sure why. You even tried to escape us once. Do you remember? Before we implanted those memories in you? Then you were a shell of a person, with no past, present, or future, and yet you took off, almost escaped into the underground. It could have been a disaster had my men not captured you in time."

The dream of my running through the underground flashes into my mind. I remember being frightened, absolutely terrified, not remembering who I was. I'd had no idea that was because at that moment I wasn't anyone to remember.

"Aw, she looks as if she's going to cry," Duske remarks to his guards. They snicker. He turns back to me. "You pathetic bitch," he spits. "You really thought you could be like *her,* didn't you? You thought you could simply waltz into Terra and did take over Mariah's legacy. Pathetic." He sneers. "Please. You're not fit to lick her boots. You're not even a real person. You're just an empty shell that I can fill with whatever I see fit." He motions to the guards. "Take them to their cell," he commands.

EIGHTEEN

We're thrown into a bare cell on the other side of the building, similar in style to the one that caged Glenda, though *style* may be the wrong word. The cell is filthy, the walls stained fecal brown, the floors are damp and reeking of piss. A rickety cot in the corner is the only furnishing, clothed with thin gray sheets and a ratty yellow blanket.

"Sorry about the room," Duske says as the guards lock us in, not really sounding all that broken up about it. "It's the best we can do on such short notice. Next time, do warn us when you'll be dropping by." He pauses. "Oh, wait," he adds, as if something just occurred to him. "There won't be a next time. So sorry." He peers between the bars. "Better say your good-byes now, dearies. In a couple of hours, Skye here will be going under another little memory transplant."

"Memory transplant?" I repeat, not liking the sound of that.

"Oh yes," Duske says. "It's a two-part procedure, actually. Part one will get rid of all the memories you currently have in your head. It's like one big magnet, erasing your brain like a disk. And then, after that happens, my doctors will perform the second part. They'll inject you with a little memory cocktail we've whipped up, give you a brand-new identity. We're going to turn you into a Mariah who has spent time on Earth as herself. She remembers all of her past revolutionary activities but has now found peace and happiness in her new world. She has returned for one night only, to speak at my Moongazing seminar and let all the Indys know just how wonderful Earth really is."

"That's crazy!" I cry. "I'd never—"

"You'd never what?" Duske asks, his face darkening. "Lie for me? As far as you know you'll be telling the truth, my dear. When the doctors are through with you, you won't have any recollection of this conversation. Or *any* conversations, really, besides the made-up ones we'll inject into your head. Sorry to break it to you, sweetie, but remember you're just a clone to do with what we like. With just a small dose of serum injected into your cerebral cortex, we can transform you into anyone at all." He pats the bars of the cell. "So, it was nice knowing you, *Skye*," he says. "I look forward to meeting the new you very shortly. Maybe I'll even throw in a crush on me this time. So we can finish what you started."

He turns and exits the room, flanked by his guards. The metal doors clank shut, leaving Dawn and me alone in filth and darkness. I consider screaming and yelling, and even begging for freedom, but I know there's no use, so instead I resignedly wander over to the cot and slump down on the grimy mattress. It creaks under my weight, but I scarcely notice, I'm so wrapped up in my terrified thoughts.

Dawn joins me, his face ashen. He kneels in front of me, taking my hands in his. He brings them to his lips, pressing my knuckles against his soft mouth, capturing my eyes with his. We sit there for a long while, thoughts whirling madly inside our heads, but nothing seemingly worth saying out loud.

"I can't bear this," Dawn finally says in a choked voice, breaking the silence. He drops my hands and rises to his feet, pacing the cell like a wild tiger, caged. "To lose you again. It's just—"

I sigh, feeling very old, even though I now know I'm a mere babe of three months. "What are you talking about?" I snarl. "Didn't you hear a word Duske said? You're not losing me again. I'm not Mariah. Your precious Mariah is lying in a drawer."

"I meant lose you again like when you went back to Earth. As Skye," Dawn corrects.

I screw up my face in frustration. "But don't you get it? I'm not Skye either! I'm no one! I'm just some fucking clone that, at the end of the day, doesn't really even exist. You were right when you said being with me is like being with a shell. That's all I am."

Dawn turns to me, eyes wild, face haunted. "Skye, don't say that," he says. "Don't buy into their game. You're a person. Just like me or anyone else. You're real. Special."

"Special? Please. I'm nothing more than a puppet designed to promote government propaganda. Everything about me, everything in my head is all made up." I squeeze my hands into fists, angry tears blurring my vision and pity wracking me. "Admit it, Dawn. You never loved me. You only wanted me because you thought deep down I was really your ex-girlfriend. But I'm not. And I never was."

"You're wrong," Dawn exclaims, dropping back to his knees in front of me. "You're so, so wrong. Sure, my early affections for you may have been sparked because I thought you were Mariah. But I've known for a while now that you aren't."

"Yeah, right."

"I'm serious," he says. "Mariah was a wonderful person, and at one time I loved her more than life itself. In a way, I probably always will hold a special spot for her in my heart." He rakes a hand through his hair. "You can't imagine what it means to me to find out that she didn't really betray us. That, even weakened by addiction, she stayed strong and never sold us out. Never took the easy road. What a woman she was!"

"Yes, yes, the great and wonderful Mariah," I mutter, trying to keep the bitterness at bay. His lauding is not exactly making me feel any better.

"It's funny," he says, stroking his chin thoughtfully. "I figured that finding out the truth would finally allow me to finally put my anger aside. But the weird thing is, it's already long gone." He smiles. "And that's got a lot to do with you."

I cock my head. "What did I do?"

"You were just . . . you. Passionate. Self-sacrificing. Patient. Kind. You helped even pigheaded, stuck-in-the-past me realize that it really is possible to learn to love again. To completely fall head over heels for someone who is completely different than Mariah— but equally as special."

"But how can you love me?" I ask, choking on my words. "I'm not even a person. I'm not real."

"Are you kidding me?" Dawn asks, incredulous. "In the short time you've been here, you've done so much. And not for your own gain. When given the chance to go home, you decided to stay. You risked your life by seducing Duske to get his thumbprint. Then you risked it again by coming here with me. You did this all to save a people you didn't even know. To redeem a world that isn't even yours. And you weren't after fame and glory from your heroics. You helped because you couldn't bear to see people suffer. You've done more in the few months you've been alive than most people do in their entire lives. I'm in awe of you. And I'm in love with you."

Tears fall from my eyes as I listen to his words. Can it be true? Can at some point his feelings have really shifted from mourning Mariah to loving me?

"Before you came I'd given up hope. I'd quit the Eclipsers and resigned myself to living an empty life," Dawn continues. "You changed all that. Now, when I look at you, I get this crazy feeling inside. A feeling that we could take over the world or something." He searches my face with an earnest, open expression. "Mariah means nothing to me anymore. I love you, Skye."

It's all I can bear. I throw myself into his arms, burying my head into his shoulder, sobbing. "I love you, too," I cry. "So much more than anything, ever. You say I'm noble, but the truth is, one of the main reasons I came back was for you."

Dawn pulls out of our embrace, then leans forward

to press his lips against mine. I kiss him, knowing that this may be the last time I recognize his lips. He lays me down on the cot, crawling on top of me, and kissing me over and over again.

We make love slowly, tolerating the horrible conditions out of a desperate need to be close. Every caress—every touch—is a knife through my heart as I realize it may be the last. I desperately try to burn memories of each touch into my brain. Memories that can't be erased, no matter how strong the magnet. The trail of kisses against the hollow of my throat. The tender fingers tracing my inner thigh. How is it possible I could forget all of this? Forget him? I'd easier forget my very self.

Oh God, this isn't fair.

We fall asleep in each other's arms, but it's not a restful slumber. I keep waking up, panicked and worried about falling back into dreamland and losing my last moments of reality. I want to remember this night forever: the warmth of Dawn's arms wrapped securely around me, his body spooning mine. His heartbeat, his musky scent, his sweet breath exhaling in my ear—priceless sensations that should embed in my brain as everlasting memories, not be robbed from my consciousness to further a government plot.

But there's nothing we can do. And soon, way too soon, the prison door clangs open. Jarred awake, we leap from bed, realizing the time is here. The point of no return is upon us too soon. Two guards enter the cell. Dawn steps in front of me, fists raised. He's not letting me go without a fight.

But the guards aren't interested. They club him several times until he stumbles, then collapses to the floor. "No!" he cries, pain and fear choking his voice. "Don't take her! Don't you fucking bastards take her from me!"

The guards laugh. One of them kicks Dawn in the stomach. He bellows in rage, helpless and emasculated on the filthy floor. The guard with the club approaches me, waving it in my face with a smirk. "You going to come along quietly, Sister?" he asks. "Or would you like to be 'managed' as well?"

"Fuck off," I growl, kicking him in the groin. If I'm going to go down, it's going to be fighting. After all, in a few minutes, I won't remember the pain anyway. But these guys will.

The guard doubles over, stumbling backward. The club goes skidding across the floor. I make a dive for it, my one hope, my one chance, but the second guard reaches it before I do. He picks it up and strikes me hard enough to make me see stars. I collapse. He laughs and motions to the first guard to help him pick me up. One takes my shoulders and the other my feet, and they carry me outside the cell and onto a gurney. They must have expected they'd have to beat me. Or maybe they would have even if I hadn't resisted.

I look back at Dawn, who's still lying on the floor. There's blood on his face. Tears flood my eyes. This will be the last time I ever see him. Or at least the last time I recognize his face.

"Skye," Dawn calls out in a hoarse voice. "I love you. No matter what happens, never forget that I love you!"

"I love you, too, Dawn," I tell him, forcing the words from my throat. They seem so useless. Though, at least for him, he'll be able to remember.

Is it better to have loved and forgotten, than to have never loved at all?

"What a sweet good-bye," sneers the guard. "Too bad in a few minutes you won't know this guy from Duske."

Furious, I spit on him. The guard just laughs, not even bothering to wipe the loogie off his cheek. If only I had my sword, I'd chop him into a thousand pieces. A thousand and ten pieces, so even his mother wouldn't recognize him. And I'd do it slowly, too. So he'd feel every cut. So he'd know what it's like to lose something he cares about.

But I'm weaponless, powerless, and so I lie helpless on the gurney as the guards wheel me down the hall and into a sterile, all-white room—a sharp contrast to the disgustingly filthy cell. From the stethoscopes and hammers and blood-pressure cuffs hanging on the wall, I gather this is some kind of doctor's office. But I know I'm not just here for a checkup. The guards drag me up onto the bed and bind my arms and legs in four-point restraints, then exit the room.

A few moments later, a man in a white coat enters the room. He's about fifty, slender of build, with graying blond hair and a stethoscope around his neck. He pulls a chart from the wall and peers down at it before speaking.

"So, you're here for a memory transplant," he says, hanging the clipboard back on the wall.

"No. I'm here to see your balls cut off," I spit out.

He raises an eyebrow. "I see." He reaches into a drawer and pulls out a plastic cap with electrodes and wires. "As fun as that sounds, I think today we'll stick to the transplant, if you don't mind."

"You'll never get away with this," I tell him, though I'm not sure what the hell will stop him. "You can erase my memory a thousand times. But I'll find you, some-day, somehow. I'll track you to the ends of the earth—er, Terra—and make you pay for what you've done."

"Do whatever you feel is necessary," he says mildly. I squeeze my hands into fists, furious that I can't get any reaction from him.

He places the cap over my head and flips a switch on a large metal machine next to my bedside. A whirring noise starts. "Here we go," he says. "Don't worry. This won't hurt a bit."

But he's lying. A moment later, icy cold shards stab through my scalp. The machine's whirring grows louder and louder, its only competition: my screams of agony. I can feel tiny fingers invading my brain, rob-bing my thoughts, sucking out my memories. Oh God, it's really happening.

I desperately try to cling to one simple image: Dawn's face. I etch it firmly in my consciousness. If everything else goes, at least maybe I can somehow hold that. Somehow, some way. Grab the memory of his love and not let go, no matter what the pressure.

But it's like trying to hold on to grains of sand. Even-tually, like everything else, he slips from my grasp.

NINETEEN

I open my eyes. I'm in a small white room, strapped to some kind of bed in four point restraints. There are instruments everywhere, as if this is some kind of doctor's office or something.

But how did I get here? And where is here? And while we're asking the questions . . . who am I, anyway?

I have no idea.

TWENTY

I lie, tied to a chair, trying to think, trying to process, to remember, for what seems like hours. It's no use. I can't recall my name, never mind who I am or why I'd possibly be lying here, strapped to a bed. All I know is that I'm terrified and my empty brain races a mile a minute, trying to make sense of it all.

A middle-aged man in a white lab coat enters the room, flanked by two uniformed guards. He lifts a plastic cap from my head and pulls out a lighted instrument from his pocket to peer into my eyes.

"Who are you?" he asks in a conversational tone.

"I was hoping you'd be able to tell me that," I reply.

I notice the guards tossing each other self-satisfied glances. Evidently my answer pleases them, though I don't have the faintest idea why it would. The doctor says nothing, continuing with his examination, listening to my heartbeat with his stethoscope and then following up with a check on my blood pressure. I know all the tests he's doing. I get what each of them is designed to do. I understand words, can interpret body language. So, how come I can't remember who the hell I am or what I'm doing here?

"She's good to go back," the doctor announces to the guards. "She'll have to rest a couple of hours before we perform stage two of the operation. Go ahead and inform your boss that the procedure was successful."

I cock my head in confusion over his words. Stage two of the operation? I'm supposed to undergo some kind of surgery? More surgery? I glance down at my body, searching for marks of some previous procedure. But there's no evidence I was ever touched.

"What's going on here?" I demand, my voice quaking.

The doctor waves a dismissive hand. "Don't worry," he says, walking over to the sink to clean some instruments. "You'll understand everything after phase two." He turns to the guards. "Well, what are you waiting for?" he demands. "Take her back to her cell."

"They haven't removed the man yet," one of the guards says.

"What does it matter?" the doctor says. "She won't know him."

Appearing satisfied, the guards step up to my sides and unlatch my restraints. They help me to my feet. I'm weak, but I can walk. I wonder for a moment if I should fight them, try to get away. But where would I go? Best maybe to bide my time and figure out what's going on before I make any rash moves.

I regret this decision a moment later when they drag me into a small holding cell, near empty save a small cot in one corner. I wrinkle my nose. The place is filthy. Disgusting. The stench is nearly overwhelming. I shud-

der. Am I a prisoner here? And if so, who are my cap-
tors and what do they want from me?

The guards shove me into the cell and lock the door
behind me. It's then that I realize I'm not alone. There's
a man in here, probably the one they were referring to,
squatting in a corner of the cage, his head buried in his
hands. When the cell door slams shut, he leaps to his
feet, his face white and questioning. His eyes fall on
me and I gasp at their beauty. They're so blue they almost glow. And the way he's staring at me . . . as if he
knows me. As if he's had a lifetime with me. I search my
empty brain for recognition, but none comes. I have
no idea who this man is. If he's a stranger or soul mate.

"Skye!" the man cries as he rushes over, throwing his
arms around me. Alarmed by his sudden embrace, I
jump back, but he grabs on, clamping down on my
shoulders with strong hands. Reflexively, I knee him in
the groin. He stumbles backward, hunching over,
hands over his privates. His squints up at me, his expression a mix of physical agony and mental anguish.
Suddenly I feel bad that I hurt him. Though, in my defense, he shouldn't have just jumped me like that.

"Nice to see you again, too, Skye," he says, retreating
to the cot. He slumps down and it groans under his
weight. "Déjà vu all over again, I guess."

"What is that supposed to mean?" I demand, keeping my back to the cell door. "And who are you? And
who—" I start to ask about my own identity, but think
twice before the words escape my lips. I might not
want to let on how vulnerable I am right now. He may
try to take advantage. Make up some story to get me on
his side before he rapes and murders me.

The man stares at me for a minute, with horror I've

never seen before on a face. (At least that I can remember.) Then he buries his face in his hands and lets out a wailing cry. "God!" he says. "I can't do this again. I just can't. Oh God."

I shift from left hip to right, not sure what to do, what to say. The poor guy looks completely devastated and I have no idea why.

"Look, man," I try, "I'm sorry I kneed you and all. But I'm a bit lost, you see. Not sure where I am or what I'm doing here. First I wake up in four-point restraints. Then I'm dragged into this disgusting cell. Then you jump all over me and . . ." I shrug. "I assumed the worst, I guess."

The man draws in a deep breath. "Right. I'm sorry, too. I didn't mean to scare you. I was just happy to see you alive. I forgot for a moment that you wouldn't remember me." He scrubs his face with his hands, then rises from the couch, hand outstretched. "Hello, I'm Dawn Grey, your fellow prisoner here in the Terran government jail."

I stick out my hand hesitantly. He takes it and pumps it twice. His grip is strong, firm, but there's a bit of a tremble just beneath the surface.

I decide to go for it. Who knows, maybe he can help me. We *are* both stuck in the same cell. "Do you . . . do you know who I am, by chance?" I ask, crossing my fingers he'll be able to at least answer that.

"Yes. Of course," he says. "You're Skye Brown."

Okay, we have a name. I run it through my brain to check for resonance. Nothing. But at least I have something to call myself now. "And why are we here, locked up?" I question. "Did we commit some sort of crime?" Could I be a bad guy? That seems so unlikely, yet why else would I be behind bars?

"If you call fighting for freedom a crime," Dawn says cryptically.

"God, I wish I could remember." I groan, plopping down on the cot and rubbing my temples.

"It's probably not worth trying too hard," Dawn says, sitting down beside me. "They're only going to fill your brain with new memories in a few hours. I doubt you'll remember any of this conversation."

I look up. "New memories? What about my old ones?"

"They erased them."

I raise my eyebrows. "Erased my memories? You mean, like, on purpose?" I stare at him, even more baffled than before. "Why would anyone want to do that?"

Dawn shrugs. "Because they need you to convince a bunch of innocent people to spend a great deal of money on something that will kill them."

I don't understand half of what he's talking about. But I do know one thing. "Look, I may not know who I am, but I do know there's no way I'd do something that would end up with people being killed."

"Not now. But you will tomorrow. Because when they implant new memories in you, you'll suddenly believe that Moongazing's the ticket to happiness. And you won't remember anything about the dangers."

I slump my shoulders, defeated and scared. I have no idea what he's talking about, but none of it sounds good. Oh God, if only I could remember something!

I feel a warm breath on my cheek and turn my head to face Dawn. He slowly reaches out and cups my chin in his hand, finding my eyes. It's as if he's searching somehow, desperately attempting to locate my lost self deep inside. I stare back at him, trying as hard as I can to remember his face. His earnest, soulful eyes. How could I forget someone as beautiful as him? How could I forget my own self?

"Don't worry, Skye," he whispers, gently brushing the lone tear that's dripped down my cheek. "I won't let them hurt you. I can't stop them from implanting new memories in you, but I do promise that somehow, some way, I'll save you in the end." He pauses, his eyes cloudy. "You won't remember me when I do. In fact, you'll probably think I'm some crazy person set on kidnapping you. But it doesn't matter."

He drops my gaze and stares down at his lap. "And then . . . and then I'll just start over," he says, more to himself than me. "I'll make you love me again. Somehow. Some way. If it takes the rest of my life, I'll never give up. They can erase your memory a hundred times. I won't stop making you love me all over again." He rises from his seat and begins to pace the cell. "I once gave up on Mariah. I let her go. Let her pursue her own death. I won't make that mistake again." He stands above me, then drops to his knees, grabbing my hands in his and squeezing them tightly. "I'll protect you, Skye, no matter what. I'll never let go."

I can feel tears cascading down my cheeks like so much rain. The passion and meaning in his words are overwhelming, almost too much to bear. He loves me. Truly. Madly. Deeply. Have I been deserving of such an epic love? Did I once feel the same about him? And if so, how could I have forgotten? How could such powerful, life-changing love have slipped through the cracks of my consciousness and flowed uselessly down a drain?

I throw myself into Dawn's arms, unable to resist the offered comfort. I start to sob into his shoulder, out of frustration, out of fear, out of anger at all that has been stolen from my mind without my permission. Through it all, Dawn holds me tight, stroking my back with both hands, kissing me softly on the side of my neck.

"I love you, Skye Brown," he murmurs. "And somehow, someday, you will love me again, too. I promise."

And the scary thing is, I realize as I cuddle closer into his arms, I think I already do.

TWENTY-ONE

I cry for a long time, but eventually, the tears dry up and the sobs start to trail off. Dawn pulls me onto the cot and we cuddle close to one another. He feels so good, arms wrapped around me protectively, and I snuggle in closer. I may not remember him, but I believe with everything left inside me that he's someone I can trust. After a while, my eyelids grow heavy and sleep overtakes my mind.

When I awake, I find Dawn leaning over me, watching me with intense eyes.

"What?" I ask, self-consciously sitting up in bed, wondering what he could be staring at.

His face reddens. "Sorry," he says. "I just . . . I just didn't want to miss a single memory of you lying here next to me."

I smile shyly. "You're sweet."

"Maybe sometimes," he says, grinning shyly. "But only to you."

I cuddle back into his outstretched arms again, seeking that loving warmth he's only too ready to offer. He smoothes my hair and kisses me softly on top of my head. And even though we're in a disgusting prison cell, a small part of me wants this moment to last forever.

It doesn't, however. Only minutes later the door bursts open and the two guards step into the prison. We jump to our feet and Dawn grips me tightly.

"Time for phase two," one of the guards announces. "Let's go."

"No. We want to see Duske first," Dawn says, keeping a firm grip on me.

The guards laugh. "Yeah? Well, Brother Bill and I would like to see Sleazy Sheena down at the strip club. But right now, it looks like none of us are gonna get our wishes." He holds up his club. "Want another taste of this? Come on, big boy. Have at me."

Dawn swallows hard, then turns to me. "I'm sorry," he whispers. "There's nothing I can do now. But I promise I will come for you. Try to hold on to that thought. That, and the fact that I love you. More than I can ever explain."

I can feel the tears spring to my eyes again, and I throw myself into his arms for a final hug. I feel like I've only known him a few hours and yet the bond between us is unbearable to break. But the guards aren't in the mood to wait for our hug to come to its natural conclusion. They yank me backward by the collar, wrenching me from Dawn's grasp. Our fingers lock for one moment and our eyes meet, a thousand truths passing between us in just one glance. Then I'm pulled out of the cell, kicking and screaming. Try as I might, I can't fight them. They're too strong.

They drag me down the hallway and back into the operating room where I woke up hours before without my memories. The man with the white coat is there. He nods to the guards after they strap me on the bed. "Thank you," he says. "You may leave now. I'd like to begin the procedure."

The guards hesitate by the door. "We were ordered to stay," one informs the doc. "In case she causes trouble."

The doctor snorts. "This lamb?" he asks disdainfully. "I think I can handle one little girl. Besides, when she wakes up, she's going to think we're best friends."

"Like hell," I growl, but no one pays attention.

The guards grunt, then head toward the exit. Maybe they figure they can go catch that strip show after all. The doctor closes the door behind them. Then he heads back to my bedside, his casual expression fading into one that's much more serious.

"Don't worry," he says in a low voice that I have to strain to hear. "I'm an Eclipser. I'm on your side here."

"You have a funny way of showing it," I hiss back. "Erasing my memories and all. And who are the Eclipsers, anyway?"

He shakes his head. "Listen to me. I had to make it appear that you had lost all your memories so they would believe the procedure was a success. But I didn't erase them. Not really. They've simply been flash-frozen in your brain. Everything you knew before the operation is still intact—it's just inaccessible at the moment. But now I'm going to flash-bake you, reactive your cerebral cortex. You'll be yourself in just a few more minutes."

I stare at him, eyes wide, hoping, praying, begging that what he says is actually true. "So, I'll get all my memories back?" I ask, crossing my fingers for an affirmative.

"It'll be as if you never lost them," the doctor says with a nod as he places a gel cap, threaded with wires, over my head. "But you can't let anyone know you've got them back. You'll have to act like I injected the new memories just as they ordered me to. Once the procedure is complete, you have to start playing the part of Mariah. A Mariah who's been living on Earth and loves it there." He plugs a cord leading from the cap into a tall, thin red metallic machine by my bedside. "You'll understand this better once you get your memories back."

"I hope so," I say. "Because at the moment I really don't have any clue as to what you're talking about."

"Don't worry. You will," the doctor says, patting me on the shoulder. "Very soon."

He flips a switch on the metallic machine and the cap begins to heat. I can feel lighting bolts pierce my skull and burrow into my brain. I open my mouth to scream. . . .

Memories slam back into my brain and I suddenly remember everything.

"Dawn!" I cry out.

The doctor rushes to my bedside and clamps a hand over my mouth. "Do you want to get us both killed?" he hisses. "Remember what I told you! You have to pretend you're Mariah."

"Sorry," I mutter. But Mariah loved Dawn, too.

"Listen," the doctor says in a hurried voice. "The Eclipsers are mobilizing. They're planning to sabotage the Moongazing seminar, just like they tried to do the last time. But this time, there's no one to stop them. When you get there, just follow their lead, okay? Pay attention and you'll realize what you need to do." He removes his hand from my mouth. "So, Mariah," he calls out in a loud cheerful voice. "Are you excited about speaking at the Moongazing seminar tomorrow?"

"Oh yes," I say. "I can't wait to tell everyone about Earth. How wrong I was to lead a revolution against the government when really they've found us the loveliest alternate world to inhabit."

"Uh, let's not overkill," the doctor whispers.

"Mariah, darling!" Duske calls out, choosing that moment to swagger through the door. "It's so good to have you back."

"It's good to be back, Brother Duske," I say, watching as he removes my restraints. "Though, of course, I miss my home. When do you think I'll be able to return?"

"All in good time, my dear, all in good time," he says. Out of the corner of my eye I catch him giving the doctor a thumbs-up. He's buying my act. "But first, remember, I need you to speak at my seminar tonight. To tell the Indys all about the wonderful new world you have discovered."

"Of course," I say, sitting up in bed and shaking out my wrists and ankles. "I look forward to sharing all I've learned. Who wouldn't love Earth? I don't know why more of the population hasn't already gone."

"Indeed, my dear," Duske says. He gives a smirk that I'd like nothing more than to smack off his face. "Indeed."

We leave the surgery center and Duske escorts me back to his mansion. I'm set up in my old suite of rooms. I lie down on the bed, staring up at its canopy, wondering how Dawn is faring. I wish there was a way I could get word to him that I have my memories back. The poor guy's languishing in his cell, thinking he's lost me all over again. If only I could tell him that I'm okay. That I remember his love for me. And mine for him.

I look over at the clock. Three hours till the seminar. I wonder what kind of sabotage the Eclipsers have planned. And will it work? Will we be able to prove to the Indys once and for all what a death trap Moongazing really is?

We have to, I realize. Everything is riding on this.

TWENTY-TWO

The Moongazing convention is being held in a large auditorium in the center of Luna Park. From what I can see from my quick peek behind the curtain, the place is packed beyond capacity. I guess the infamous Mariah Quinn as keynote speaker really draws them in. Fine by me. The more people who hear the truth, the better.

In my hands I shuffle the pages of the speech Duske prepared for me. The one I'm not planning to read. I wonder how quickly the government will catch on and realize that I'm condemning them rather than reciting their propaganda. Perhaps it'll be once they hear the word "paradise" replaced with "deadly virtual reality that will burn out your eyes and rot your brain." Or maybe it will be when I replace the words "new life" with "genocide, designed to rob you of your cash and vital organs." How much will I be able to tell them before I'm dragged offstage? And will I be sentenced to death for my crime against the government, or will they attempt a second brain erasure?

A lump forms in my throat. I know I have to do this. So many lives depend on it. But at the same time, I don't want to die. Especially not before I see Dawn again. Not that I'm positive he's still alive himself. Would they have killed him? Did he die thinking I'd forgotten who he was? If only I could have one more minute with him. Throw my arms around him and squeeze him tight and let him know that I remember everything. Every whisper, every caress, every evocation of love.

At least if he's still alive he'll hear of my last act, when word of my speech trickles down through the underground. At least he'll know that I sacrificed my life for the people. I hope he realizes that every word will be dedicated to him.

"It's almost time, my dear," Duske says, coming up behind me and yanking me from my troubled thoughts. "Are you ready for your glorious debut?"

I turn around and toss him a guileless smile. "I'm ready," I say brightly. "So very ready."

"Good," he says. "I will go out and introduce you. Warm up the crowd a bit. When I call your name, you step out onto the stage and then read the speech that I gave you." He pats me on the shoulder. "We'll have the slides you took of Earth up on a large screen behind you. Feel free to reference those as you speak."

"Great. I can do that."

Duske smiles, then leans forward and kisses me lightly on the cheek. It takes all my willpower not to swipe at the moisture left behind on my skin. Instead, I force myself to return the gesture. "I'm glad we're working together now, Brother Duske," I say softly, looking up through my lashes.

He grins like the fool that he is and ruffles my hair. God, didn't he learn his lesson the first time? "My dear," he says, "I do believe this could be the start of a beautiful friendship."

Oh, so do I, Duske. So do I.

He steps out to center stage and gestures for the stagehand to get the show on the road. The curtains silently slide apart and a spotlight is cast down on the government leader. From backstage left, I can now see out into the crowd. It's standing room only and everyone's going wild, cheering, screaming. It makes me sick. I hope they have brains enough to listen to what I have to say.

"Thank you, thank you!" Duske says, leaning into a microphone. A whiny feedback hisses for a moment, then dies away. "But I'm not the one you should be applauding. For tonight, as you know, we have a very special guest. She just arrived from Earth, where she has spent the last few months living a brand-new life. A life aboveground, out in the sunshine. A life full of new friends and new relationships. Untold riches and the companionship of animals. In short, our guest is much like the legendary Eve of the Bible—and she has been to Earth and found a real-life Garden of Eden."

The crowd erupts into more cheers. They're loving this. If only they had any idea of the truth, where their friends and family really ended up after visiting this so-called Garden of Eden.

"People of Terra," Duske shouts, then pauses dramatically. "I give you . . . Mariah Quinn!"

And here I thought they were loud before. Now the

crowd goes truly crazy. Their applause and screams are deafening. Unnerved, my heart being a mile a minute, I step out onto the stage. My knees are wobbling, my hands are shaking. I suck in a breath and join Duske by the podium. He makes a grand show of bowing low to me when presenting the microphone. Then he steps to the side of the stage, leaving me in the spotlight.

I glance behind me and, sure enough, just as Duske said, my photos of Earth are projected onto the wall. Currently there's a shot of Central Park's Great Lawn on a sunny afternoon. People are lounging on blankets, sampling picnic goodies. Two softball teams compete on the field. A man stands frozen in motion, tossing a Frisbee to his girlfriend. I have to admit, it does look a lot like paradise. And then I remember that none of it is real.

So, now what? I glance around, looking for some sign, some hint that the Eclipsers are in the house and ready for action. The doctor told me there was a plan in place; I just wish I were clued in on what exactly it entailed.

The spotlight shines down on me. The crowd stirs, restless. Duske frowns from his position at the side of the stage. I realize I'd better get this show on the road or people will start getting suspicious.

"This is a picture of what they call Central Park," I explain, pointing to the photo behind me. "As you can see, it's an aboveground park right in the middle of the city. New Yorkers like to come here on their days off, to read and eat and play ball . . . or just hang out. They have a zoo and exhibits and lakes, and in the summers they perform Shakespeare in an outdoor theater."

The crowd oohs and aahs, clapping politely. I click to the next slide, feeling more confident. At least I know what I'm talking about. And when the Eclipsers decide to make their presence known, I'll be ready for them.

Suddenly, the applause dies midclap, a dead silence falling over the room. What the . . . ? I glance behind me at the slide presentation, wondering what on earth has shut them up. It's then that I realize it's not something on Earth at all.

Projected on the wall is one of the photos we took in the morgue: a naked, bloated Indy lying on a slab. So, this is what the Eclipsers have planned. They must have hacked into the slideshow somehow.

"No!"

I whirl around to see Duske charging at the slide projector, face enraged. But before he can reach me, he's tackled by two of the onstage guards—evidently Eclipser plants—and sent flying to the floor. They club him, then clamp handcuffs over his wrists and drag him offstage. I watch, shocked, stunned, not sure what to do next. I glance around the room wildly, wondering if any other guards will suddenly burst through to interrupt the presentation. It's then that I catch sight of Hiro, standing at one of the exit doors in the crowd. At the next is Kayce. At the next, Tayrn. All three nod to me, prompting me to go on. I realize the Eclipsers are not only *in* the house, they've got complete ownership of it.

Time to get this show on the road.

"But I'm here to tell you not to be fooled by such luxurious lies," I say into the microphone to my horrified audience. Their panicked murmurs die away and they listen with rapt faces. "Moongazing is not a journey to a new world. It's not a one-way ticket to paradise. In fact, Earth doesn't really even exist. Well, not anymore." I click the remote and the slide switches to a view of the computer control center. "This is where they create Earth. It's a virtual reality simulation. A *game,* if you will, based on the past of what Terra looked like before the war tore it apart." I click the slide again, to another computer room shot. "That's why you need the drugs. They trick your brain into believing this video game—this *illusion*—is reality."

My audience is silent, their faces pale and shocked. I've got their complete attention now, that's for sure. Time to move in for the kill. "Problem is, your bodies aren't able to handle this simulation," I explain, clicking the slide again. We're now back at the morgue. "A few weeks or months after you go on your so-called pilgrimage, your mind begins to decay. Your eyes burn out of your head. You'll die. And the government will dump your body into this morgue and likely harvest your vital organs."

"But . . . why would they do this?" cries a teenage boy in the front row. "Why would the Circle sponsor a program that kills its citizens?"

"Easy," I reply, clicking the slideshow to reveal yet another burned-out body in a drawer. "You on Terra have an overpopulation problem, and the Circle of Eight's figured out a method of genocide that no one will object to. Not to mention it's a great moneymaker."

"What about you?" demands an older woman a few rows back. "You went. And you didn't die."

I swallow hard, but as I flip the slide, I find my answer: Mariah's corpse flashes on the screen. The crowd gasps. I stare at them, still too unnerved to look at my own dead body.

"This is what happened to the real Mariah," I say. "She became addicted to Moongazing and it led to her own death. You think I'm Mariah, but you're wrong. I'm simply an nT, produced by the government to trick people into thinking she is still around and enjoying life on Earth." I glance at the Eclipsers, still guarding the doors. "But thanks to a few brave rebels who did not give up, I know what side I'm really on."

The crowd erupts in murmurs, the Indys anxiously discussing all that has just been revealed to them. Satisfied that I've done my part, I walk offstage and locate the Eclipsers who are holding Duske captive.

"By the way, I have my memories back," I inform him as I approach. I resist the urge to make "nyah-nyah" noises.

"So I see," he says, not looking very happy. "Not that they were ever *your* memories to begin with. But how lovely that you're able to take ownership of them all the same."

Furious, I slap his face as hard as I can, my hand making a loud noise as it connects with his cheek. "That's for trying to turn me into someone I'm not," I spit at him.

He narrows his eyes. "Please. You were never anyone to begin with."

"That may be true," I agree. "But I *am* someone *now.* Someone important. And you know what? I like that person. I wouldn't trade who I've become for any alternate reality in the world."

"Neither would I," says a voice behind me.

I whirl around, my eyes widening and my mouth dropping open in shocked joy. "Dawn!" I cry, running to him—Duske forgotten—and throwing myself into his arms. He twirls me around, squeezing me tight. "You're here! You're okay!" I bury my face in his shoulder, wanting to cry and laugh, sing and scream, all at the same time. "I thought maybe you were . . ." I trail off, unable to finish.

"I told you I'd find you again," Dawn reminds me, setting me back on the floor. "Though, maybe you don't remember."

"I remember everything. Every last little thing," I tell him. "And I'll remember it all forever. I promise."

"I know you will, Skye Brown," Dawn says, leaning down to kiss me on the mouth. "Because I plan to remind you every day for the rest of your life."

EPILOGUE

Three mornings later I wake up in Dawn's arms back at my house. Our house. We've decided there's no reason to keep separate residences anymore. After all, we don't want to spend any time apart from one another. In fact, we've even talked about getting married. How crazy is that? And yet, at the same time, it seems very right.

Dawn sits up in bed, glancing at his watch. "We should get moving. We have a big meeting with the Eclipsers in an hour," he reminds me.

I yawn, stretching my hands above my head. "Let them wait a few minutes. I'm too comfortable to move."

He kisses me softly on the forehead and lies back. "Me too."

"Besides, I know what they're going to say," I groan. "That we need a new plan. Something to follow our glorious victory."

"Yup. An Eclipser's work is never done."

"I don't know," I say, snuggling against him. "Maybe a few more minutes of resting on our laurels wouldn't be such a crime. After all, we did destroy the government's number-one moneymaking program and united the Indys against them."

"I wouldn't go as far as that," Dawn says. "The Indys rebelled against Moongazing, not the Circle of Eight. They'll only be outraged for so long, and then they'll settle back into their everyday existences. The remaining senators will find something else to lull them into their typical trancelike existence. A new drug. A new alcohol. A new soap opera on the telescreen. They'll give away hover cars. Whatever."

I nod. "I know you're right. But it makes me so mad. Why won't they change? After they saw what the government did . . ."

"Because they're comfortable. Content," Dawn says. "And the Circle's spin-doctors are all-powerful. Look how Senator Estelle, Mariah's mother, vilified Duske and blamed the Moongazing fiasco wholly on him. And Mariah's death. As if the whole damn program was his brainchild and nothing to do with a vast government conspiracy. As if he could have done it alone. But now all the senators have to do is stage Duske's execution, dismantle the 'Gazing booths, and they're the big heroes." He shrugs. "Why would Indys rebel against a government who just saved their lives?"

I sigh. "So then, I guess we just have to keep fighting? To show them that Moongazing was just the tip of the iceberg."

"Yes. And we will," Dawn says resolutely. "And so will the Eclipsers. And the Dark Siders. And I think this time we've managed to sway quite a few Indys to our side as well. And more will come every day. Slowly but surely, we'll win this war. Someday we'll be a free people again."

"And you and I will be together. No matter what," I say. Right now, that's what matters most.

"Too true," he agrees. "And together, I truly believe we'll be a force to be reckoned with."

"Definitely—we'll do great things, you and I. And we won't rest until every Dark Sider and every nT is free."

There's a woof and then we're joined on the bed by Noah. The dog wags his tail, his mouth open in a lazy pant. He pushes himself between us and curls up in our arms. Laughing, we both reach over to pet him, running fingers through his soft fur.

"I think Noah is pretty happy we moved him from the animal shelter here to your house," Dawn notes.

"Yup." I grin. "Lots more begging opportunities up here with us suckers."

"And lots more doggie cuddles."

"You know," I say. "That should be our next mission. Find old Noah here a mate. Maybe we can start a whole new breed of companion animals. I think the Dark Siders would like that."

"Definitely. What do you think, Noah, old boy?" Dawn asks, scratching the pup behind his ear. "You want a girlfriend?"

Woof! Noah barks in affirmation, wagging his tail eagerly. He jumps on me and laps one cheek. Dawn leans over, presenting me with a far less sloppy kiss on the other. I giggle and return kisses to both of the boys.

With this kind of paradise, who needs the moon?

WIRED

LIZ MAVERICK

Seconds aren't like pennies. They can't be saved in a jar and spent later. Pluck a second out of time or slip an extra one in, the consequences will change your life forever.

L. Roxanne Zaborovsky discovers that fate is comprised of an infinite number of wires, filaments that can be manipulated, and she's not the one at the controls. From the roguishly charming Mason Merrick—a shadow from her increasingly tenebrous past—to the dangerously seductive Leonardo Kaysar, she's barely holding on. This isn't a game, and the pennies are rolling all over the floor. Roxy just has to figure out which are the ones worth picking up.

ISBN 10: 0-505-52724-3
ISBN 13: 978-0-505-52724-0 $6.99 US/$8.99 CAN